The House of Mystery

ELLIE McEWAN MYSTERIES

Book 1: An Aura of Mystery
Book 2: The Colour of Mystery
Book 3: The House of Mystery

THE HOUSE OF MYSTERY

JOY ELLIS

JOFFE BOOKS

Joffe Books, London
www.joffebooks.com

First published in Great Britain in 2026

This book is a work of fiction. Names, characters, businesses, organisations, places and events are either the product of the author's imagination or are used fictitiously. Any resemblance to actual persons, living or dead, events or locales is entirely coincidental. The spelling used is British English except where fidelity to the author's rendering of accent or dialect supersedes this. The right of Joy Ellis to be identified as author of this work has been asserted in accordance with the Copyright, Designs and Patents Act 1988.

Cover art by Nick Castle

ISBN: 978-1-80573-498-7

This dedication is to my amazing publisher, and a great friend, Jasper Joffe.

As we enter 2026, I realise that this will be a whole decade together! Ten incredible years that have seen the birth of thirty-eight books and two novellas. I am SO glad that you found me when you did, as I was about to give up on any thoughts of being published. Fate, it would seem had other ideas. Now it's time for a thank you, and no matter what I say, it won't be enough, so, thank you Jasper, for believing in me. And that is especially true of the Ellie McEwan mysteries, as I know you took a risk in publishing a very different genre to my usual police procedural novels, and that meant such a lot to me. To see them in print after so many years gathering dust in the attic, was just magical! So, in the words of the Golden Girls, "Thank you for being a Friend!"

Joy x

CHAPTER ONE

Surrey, England 2004

Ellie McEwan woke at four thirty that morning with a distinct feeling of apprehension. It was nothing that she could identify, just a nagging anxiety that something was wrong. It was the second time this had happened in a week, and it worried her.

Digger, her little cocker spaniel, lifted his head and stared at her, clearly unimpressed by having to wake so early, and on a weekend too.

'It's all right, dumpling,' she said softly, stroking his ears. 'You snuggle back down. I'm going to make a hot drink. It might help me to think straight, and hopefully doze off again.'

Digger did a little circle in the duvet cover, and when he was quite certain that he'd found the comfiest spot, flopped down with a sigh, and promptly went back to sleep.

'Lucky little sod,' muttered Ellie, wishing she could do the same.

Ten minutes later, she returned with a mug of tea, and sliding into the small space generously left by Digger, propped herself up on three soft fluffy pillows.

She missed the closeness of her partner, Dr Alice Cross, formerly a doctor at University College Hospital. Alice was staying in her London mews cottage for a couple of days as she was giving a series of lectures on brain chemicals that were released during head trauma. It was her specialist field, particularly a condition called the Azimah Syndrome, which was how they had met. Alice had been called down to the Royal Surrey Hospital to try to help a patient who had suffered a severe head trauma in a car crash. That patient had been Ellie McEwan.

Ellie absent-mindedly touched the long, scoop-shaped scar that ran in a line across her forehead. The crash seemed light years away now, even though it was only five years since she had been cut out of her wrecked car on the A3. Such a lot had happened in that time that it was hard to make sense of it all. Her whole life had changed in the blink of an eye, and whereas it had originally appeared that it was all but over, with nothing to look forward to but pain and suffering, something bordering on the miraculous had happened, and Ellie was projected into a very different life indeed.

She sipped her tea and gave thanks, as she did every day, for her amazing good fortune. She had been lifted from a frenetic life as the hard-working owner of a flower shop, trying to keep her business afloat in pretty dire financial times, to becoming the co-owner of a thriving healing centre situated in a beautiful old manor house in ten acres of ground on the outskirts of Ripley. She had gone from a disastrous relationship that had ended in hurtful rejection, to a loving one that, even though considerable compromise was needed on both sides, as two precious vocations had to be allowed for, was becoming stronger and closer all the time.

What Ellie *had* lost during that traumatic time was her dearest old friend, Carole Cavendish-Meyer. However, her passing had presented Ellie, and her other dear friend, Professor Michael Seale, with not only a very unexpected fortune, but a means to help others. The Cavendish-Meyer Healing Centre offered diagnoses, treatments and therapies for all manner of health conditions, both medical and psychological, and its reputation was growing with every passing day. One of her greatest happinesses had been that some of their therapists had been able to help her own brother, Phil, who suffered from a number of terrible phobias. Although his life would never be totally free of them, it had been considerably improved, and he was now her staunchest ally.

Ellie shifted a little, flexing an aching leg — another casualty of the accident — but as always, she pushed the discomfort aside when she considered how badly things could have turned out. Okay, the leg was full of metal pins and plates, but she could now walk with barely a limp, and if she treated it with consideration, it served her well.

She sat in the dim light of her bedside lamp, and frowned. So why was she so anxious? The business was thriving. She would never have any money worries, thanks to Carole. She and Alice were solid. Michael, albeit much older than her, was going from strength to strength. Their loyal staff, and all the various practitioners that came and went, taking full advantage of the facilities the C-M Centre offered them, seemed to be more than happy. Even her own special gift, her almost unique talent, something that she would never have had without the accident, seemed to be getting more powerful and more refined with each passing month.

Ellie possessed auric sight. She had the ability to see the energy fields of colour that surround every living thing. Not only that, she had learned to identify exactly what they meant. She could read people, simply by looking at the colours that glowed around them in an aura. This talent was shared by Michael, but in a slightly different form. Ellie could diagnose problems within the body and mind by reading people's depleted auras and various colours; Michael could heal the damaged auras by infusing healthy colours back into them like blessed sunshine falling on a failing plant.

So why this nagging feeling that something was terribly wrong? Ellie finished her tea, placed the mug on the bedside cabinet, and shuffled down in the bed. Digger grunted, displeased at losing a few inches of duvet, but she held her ground, and she soon felt his warmth permeating her side. In moments he was snoring softly, but Ellie remained awake. Awake and worried. Maybe it was time to talk to Michael.

Ellie finally slipped into a shallow and troubled sleep, waking an hour later unrefreshed and even more uneasy than before. As she pushed back the duvet and wearily got up, she decided that, yes, it really was time to talk to Michael.

Ellie lived in Snug Cottage in Compton. It had been Carole and her partner Vera's dream home, and was another wonderful gift bequeathed to Ellie in their joint will. Vera had predeceased Carole by a few years, and Ellie, who had adored the lovely older woman, missed her badly. Despite its name, Snug Cottage was a picturesque old lodge house set in a beautiful garden surrounded by an old red brick wall with an arch that led through to a three-acre grassed meadow and orchard. As Ellie was now the guardian of Carole's four remaining spaniels, the orchard was a godsend.

Her thick dressing gown fastened tightly around her and wellington boots on her feet, she shivered her way through the back door to let her furry charges out for a wee. Apart from Digger, who was a little cocker, the other three, Benji, Tug and Badger, were English Springer spaniels. When she had first met Carole and Vera, there had been six of them, but Monty had died of a broken heart when his beloved Vera passed away, and Orlando went into a similar decline when Carole died.

Ellie loved them all without exception. She was extremely lucky that the elderly man, known simply as Scrubbs, and his wife, Mrs S, who looked after house and garden, were also happy to act as dog sitters on the occasions when Ellie was held up at work. Her nearest neighbour, Marie Littlewood and her son Daniel, came every day to exercise them in the orchard, and Ellie herself often arranged her work appointments to allow her to slip away and spend an hour with them during the day, so the dogs were rarely alone for long.

Job done, she shepherded them back inside and went upstairs for a shower. She would go in early, and buttonhole Michael before they both pitched into the day's work. She wasn't too sure what she could tell him, but she knew that Michael would take her seriously, no matter what. Their lives were not as simple or straightforward as those of most people, and past experience had taught them never to ignore even the slightest or most insubstantial foreboding.

Ellie stepped into the shower, and despite the hot water, shivered. The word 'foreboding' had suddenly entered her mind. Yes, that was it. It wasn't just a vague uneasiness that she felt, but dread. A dreadful sense of déjà vu came over her and she prayed that this wasn't the beginning of another adventure into the unknown, putting herself and those she loved in danger.

* * *

Callum Church tossed around in sheets damp with sweat. Another nightmare was tearing his sleep to shreds. It was hardly surprising, but he wished fervently that they would stop. It was over four and half years since he had been sent to Rwanda with Médecins Sans Frontières, and he had hoped that by now, back in relatively safe and leafy Surrey, they would have receded in his memory, yet still they came back to haunt his nights.

He dragged himself from his dishevelled bed, and took several deep breaths before making his way to the shower. As he padded across the landing, he heard his dad downstairs and the sound of a kettle coming to the boil. He smiled to himself. Good old Dad, he didn't need to get up this early, but he insisted on making sure Callum had a proper breakfast before he headed off to work at the C-M Healing Centre. Callum was a nurse, and a first-class medic. His job at the centre was a far cry from the war zones he was used to, but he loved it. One of the best things, apart from working with the incredible Ellie McEwan and Professor Michael Seale, was that he was learning how to use some special talents of his own. His mum and dad called him 'fey' and blamed it on his Irish ancestry, but even though he'd never quite understood what they meant by it, he had to admit that he was hypersensitive to atmosphere, and often saw things that others didn't. Like the dog.

Callum stepped into the shower cubicle and stood, his face turned up to the cascade of hot water, which fell over him like a waterfall. He saw the dog again in his mind's eye. A big brown-and-white spaniel, a friendly fellow with one snowy white ear. He knew it was Orlando. Ellie had told him about Vera and Carole and their dogs, so he knew too that Orlando was dead. Oddly, that didn't bother him at all. From childhood onwards, he'd known he was different to others, and now that odd phenomenon, the 'seeing things' which seemed perfectly natural to him, was getting stronger. Last year he had been unlucky enough to have what he called a 'brush with evil' which had all but killed him. Without Ellie and Michael, and strange as it might sound, Carole and Vera, he knew that he would be in the spirit world himself, and his passing would not have been peaceful. They had collectively saved his life, and probably, his soul. He didn't dwell on what had happened, because thankfully he remembered very little of it — practically nothing in fact — but he knew that from then on, some kind of awareness in him had escalated.

As he dried himself, he decided that if it were not for the nightmares — remnants of a very different place and time — his life would be pretty well perfect. He'd even met a really nice young woman who attended one of the yoga classes at the centre, whom he was planning to ask out to dinner some time in the coming week, if she was free. They had spoken a few times over the last month, and he knew that she was a primary schoolteacher who lived in a tiny cottage in Great Bookham, only ten minutes away from where his parents lived in West Horsley, but that was about it. She wore no ring, nor, in the course of their several short conversations, had she mentioned a significant other, so he hoped she was single. Oh well, he'd find out today, when he planned to catch her as soon as her classes finished. He had no idea what he was going to say to her, he just hoped he wouldn't make a mess of it.

After a breakfast of bacon, scrambled eggs, tomatoes and toast, Callum set off for work. He had recently bought a small second-hand car, mainly for use in the winter months, as he felt bad about continually borrowing his dad's motor rather than take his own motorbike. He enjoyed biking to the C-M Centre, but not when it was below zero! Now, as he drove to work in his bright red Ford Escort, he considered the fact that he seemed to be seeing both the dog and the two old ladies rather more often than usual. A tiny shiver of apprehension traced its way down his spine. He hoped it wasn't some kind of presentiment of things to come. He knew that both Vera and Carole had sworn that if Ellie were ever in trouble, she had only to ask them for help and they would be there for her. Ellie had a precious gift, something to be protected at all costs, and there had been several occurrences in the past of that help coming from beyond the grave.

The things he saw were not the stuff of horror movies. They weren't monsters with flesh falling from their bones, nor wailing white cadavers draped in mouldy shrouds. Callum either saw people exactly as they were — well, as they had been — perfectly normal people, or as misty patches of colour that moved and swirled, as if they were caught up in a gentle breeze that set them dancing slowly to unheard music. He saw Vera as an older lady emanating kindness and wisdom. She was always dressed in a jacket of deep purple with a lavender-coloured blouse. Pinned to the lapel of the jacket was a brooch in an intricate Celtic design of silver and coloured enamel. Sometimes she was silent, and when she did speak, her voice was cultured and gentle. Her spirit — because Callum knew exactly what it was — always arrived accompanied by the scent of lilacs. There was very often a dog with her, but not Orlando — he had been Carole's dog, this one was bigger. Ellie had told him it was called Monty, and had been the oldest dog in their well-loved pack. Vera's colour, if she didn't assume her human form but remained as a swirling mist, was a delicate amethyst. He saw her more often than he did Carole, whose colour was Aegean blue, that of a sunlit Greek sea. Carole tended to manifest as a hazy mist, and spoke to him in more commanding tones than gentle Vera.

Remembering the two ladies, Callum smiled to himself as he drove along the straight, tree-lined road to Ripley.

Ellie had described Carole Cavendish-Meyer as a force of nature. A sometimes irascible, less than patient harridan of a woman, who didn't suffer fools gladly — in fact she didn't suffer fools at all! But she had a heart of gold. Carole had taken Ellie in after her accident, and had nurtured her back to life and health. It was she who had first recognised Ellie's wonderful gift, and had taught her how to use it. And after her death came the legacy that had made the healing centre possible.

As he pulled off the main road and onto the lane that led to the centre, he wondered why it was Carole's dog, Orlando, that he saw so often. Michael had told him that sometimes a spirit form found certain living souls more receptive to their appearance, and formed an affinity with that person. It made a kind of sense, he supposed, and there was no denying that he liked the spaniel with the snowy ear. It made him smile. The dog had a happy face, with a wide, open-mouthed doggy grin. He just wished that its appearance wasn't so often the precursor to some happening, often something scary.

Callum indicated and turned into the wide drive that ran down to the lovely old manor that housed the C-M clinic. He was always amazed at how it had grown, even in the comparatively brief time he had been with them. All the additions had been sensitively designed, and older parts of the house had been restored for practical use while retaining their original character. There was even a pool complex for hydrotherapy, and the old manor house itself, still with its classical façade, was used to accommodate all manner of treatments, including complementary and allopathic therapies. Like Ellie and Michael, his favourite place was the old Orangery, a vast conservatory with a domed glass roof that housed a spectacular collection of plants and indoor trees, along with a stone pool containing some brilliantly coloured Koi carp swimming beneath a carpet of waterlilies.

As he drove past the impressive frontage, heading for the staff car park, he was startled to see two women sitting on a stone bench close to the Orangery doors. They were familiar figures, one in purple, and the other wearing an old Barbour jacket that had seen better days. Lying quietly at their feet were two brown-and-white Springer spaniels.

Callum drew in a breath. Vera raised a hand in greeting, and then in the blink of an eye, the stone bench was empty. All that was left to mark their presence was a misty haze of amethyst and blue.

He parked in his usual spot, turned off the engine and sat staring out of the windscreen, his earlier bright mood having dissipated like morning mist. Now he was truly anxious. Vera and Carole clearly wanted him to know that they were around, and invariably that meant trouble.

He closed his eyes and exhaled. 'Oh no, not again,' he whispered. 'Please, not again.'

After a while he gathered himself. He didn't want any of the other staff arriving for work to witness him behaving like a big girl's blouse, and of course, he told himself, he could be overreacting. Probably was. After all, he did catch glimpses of his spirit friends every so often, especially if something was worrying him, so perhaps they were just there to support him after another night of bad dreams and flashbacks. Yes, he'd go with that for now.

He got out and locked his car. This could be a big day for him, especially if that pretty girl with the long blonde hair and very attractive smile said yes to his dinner invitation.

* * *

A few miles away, a young woman was standing on the bank of the River Wey staring into the water. She wasn't sure how long she had been there, but her hands were frozen and when she turned to leave, her legs were so stiff she could hardly move.

One question went around and around in her head. How could life have become so difficult, so demanding, and so totally without hope of a better future? Her reflection in the dark water became distorted as a small flock of ducks landed on the river and sent ripples flowing towards her. It reminded her of that horrible Munch painting called *The Scream*, and it summed up her mood perfectly.

Beth Saunders considered her options, and realised they were few. Three at most. She could stick it out and pray for some kind of miracle. She could pack a bag and disappear. Or she could come back here. When there was no traffic on the river, no people around, only the ducks, she could wade in, and disappear for good. In fact, why wait? Beth shivered and took a step forward. Sad to say, the third option seemed like the best.

'You all right, lass? You could catch your death standing there!'

She jumped, and choked back a bitter laugh. Catch your death. If only it were that easy. She turned to see an old man, with an even older dog, standing watching her.

'I . . . I . . .' She threw him a weary smile. 'Sorry, I was miles away.'

He chortled. 'I could see that. But if I were you, lass, I'd get off home or wherever you were going. It's not far off freezing this morning, and young things like you never wear enough clothes. Look at you! Not even got a proper coat on! Go on, get yourself somewhere warm.'

Beth gathered herself, muttered vaguely that yes, he was right, and walked slowly back the way she had come. It seemed that option three would have to wait for another day.

* * *

Lennie Cookson watched the young woman walk dispiritedly down the tow-path with an overwhelming sense of relief. He had arrived just in time to defuse a very bad moment. As soon as he saw her standing there, he had pictured her being carried along downstream like Ophelia, a helpless tangle of flimsy clothes and trails of auburn hair, a white hand reaching up, and then disappearing into the dark, cold water. Old Lennie often saw these pictures, indeed he saw a lot of things, but most of all, he saw despair. He felt it like a physical pain, and visualised it as a thick brown fog wafting from these people and threatening to envelop him too. Dozer, his old rescue dog, felt it, he knew, which was probably why he and his canine friend were so close.

Lenny waited until the girl had reached the path leading away from the river walk, and followed her. Having saved her life, he now felt responsible for her. He needed to know where she was going. He hoped it wasn't far. Neither he nor Dozer were exactly athletic anymore, in fact it was going to be a close call as to who reached the Pearly Gates first. Maybe they'd hobble through together. It was a comforting thought.

He was mighty glad when the girl slowed to a stop outside a small terrace house in a quiet road not too far from the river. She took a deep breath, and fumbled in her bag for a key. After a moment's hesitation, she walked up the path and let herself in.

Lennie heaved a sigh. This must be her home then. From now on, he'd keep a watch on it, and on the pretty young woman with the long auburn hair. She didn't realise it, but she had just acquired a guardian angel.

CHAPTER TWO

Detective Chief Inspector Bob Foreman closed his office door, lumbered over to his desk and flopped down onto his chair. It creaked loudly, but held his weight. The early morning meeting with the superintendent had not exactly gone according to plan. Bob had known for some time that he had a choice to make, but he'd gone from one case to the next and had never found the time to think it over properly. Now it appeared to be crunch time. Did he stay, or did he go?

A few months ago he had been told that he was eligible for retirement. He had done his time and was approaching sixty, so he would be entitled to a full pension. He could apply to stay on, of course, and considering his record, his application would almost certainly be accepted. Now, it seemed as if his answer was needed as a matter of urgency. Changes were underway in the force, and unseen bureaucrats were rewriting the rule books. If he wanted to work on, he needed to get the paperwork in fast, or his colleagues would be passing round the hat for his farewell present.

It had to be now, didn't it? Just when they were in the first week of a new enquiry. Bob swore softly. Just when it was imperative that he give his whole being into gathering up the threads of a new investigation. At this stage he wanted as few interruptions or diversions as possible, and now he had been presented with a life-changing decision to make. Naturally, he'd talked it over with Rosie, his wife, but it had been as a possibility, an idle 'what if' scenario, and the pros and cons they'd come up with had never amounted to a clear-cut yes or no. On one occasion, when his daughter Frankie was on a break from uni, he'd even organised a round table with the whole family, which had given rise to a number of ridiculous suggestions as to what he might do with all the spare time, and had ended in hoots of laughter.

Bob scratched at his iron-grey hair, and realised that he hadn't a clue as to what to tell the super. He had less than a week, and if that request to stay on was not logged by close of play on the coming Monday, DCI Bob Foreman would become an ex-detective (retired).

He found the prospect quite frightening. The Surrey Constabulary had been his whole life for so many years that it had become part of him. It was who he was. What would he be, if it all ended? He had a horrible feeling that the loss would be unbearable. Part of him would die. Of course, he looked forward to spending more time with his lovely Rosie, they could have some wonderful holidays while he was still fit enough to enjoy them. But . . . what about the rest of the time? How would he fill his days, having spent decades working in a highly charged and stressful environment? He was no gardener, that was for sure, neither was he good with his hands, so he wasn't likely to be found in the garage tinkering with an old car, or building wooden bird boxes. He solved murders, for heaven's sake! He tracked down evil and damaged criminals. Where do you go from there? Crossword puzzles? Joining the local bowls club? His heart sank. But there was Rosie to consider. How much longer should he put her through the long nights alone while he sat in a murder room or roamed the dark streets hunting down villains? How many more times would she have to cook a dinner that went uneaten? Hardly fair, was it?

He closed his eyes and gritted his teeth. This time he couldn't put it on the back burner and hope it'd go away. This time he had to face up to reality.

'Sir?' DI Jonathon Leatham stuck his head around the door. 'We've got a witness coming in who might have seen young Oliver Cruise on the evening he disappeared.' He cleared his throat. 'Sorry to be a pain, boss, but the team are waiting for daily orders?'

With a sigh of relief, Bob roughly pushed his chair back, smiled at Jon and stood up. The team were his priority right now. There'd be plenty of time for all this other stuff later.

* * *

Just as Callum was leaving one of the treatment rooms after conducting a clinical assessment of one of Ellie McEwan's new patients, he saw a familiar figure hurrying towards him. It was Lucy, the young woman he had planned to ask out.

'I'm really sorry to bother you when you are working, Callum, but—' Lucy Reynolds looked embarrassed — 'would you have a couple of minutes? My yoga class isn't due to start for another half an hour and I hoped I might catch you.'

'Sure, no sweat. I've finished here and I've nothing pressing for a while.' He smiled warmly at her, then wrinkled his brow. 'Are you all right? You look worried.'

'I guess I am.' She sighed. 'Look, please, do say if you think what I'm going to ask is out of order.'

Callum was intrigued, and a little concerned. 'Why don't we go to the café? We can have a coffee and talk there.'

She agreed, and as he had hoped, there was an empty table, a little away from the main seating area. He bought them coffee and they sat down.

Lucy looked at him earnestly. 'I think I told you I'm a teacher? Young ones mainly, Key Stage 1, children aged five to seven years.'

Callum nodded. 'Yes, a primary school near Effingham, isn't it?'

Lucy smiled. 'You've got a good memory, Callum, I only mentioned it in passing.' She glanced around. 'I came here to try to get back into yoga. I let it slip because work got too demanding, but it helped to relax me, and I soon realised that I really needed to make time for it.'

'Good move,' agreed Callum. 'It does help with so much, and your teacher, Will Ryan, is amazing. I wish I was that together!'

'He is a brilliant and patient teacher,' said Lucy. 'It's the best yoga class I've ever attended, and this place too, it's so unusual, isn't it?' She glanced around. 'I mean, it's so beautiful, the perfect setting for relaxing and healing.'

Callum wondered where this was going, but didn't push her.

'It's because of all the different things that are catered for here . . .' Lucy struggled to find the right words. 'Like, well, stuff a lot of people might make fun of. Things like the two owners seeing auras and being able to read them and see illnesses and then heal them. Honestly, it could be considered a bit — oh, you know what I'm trying to say.'

'Freaky? Weird? Ridiculous? Yes, I know what people think about it, but anyone who has actually met Ellie McEwan knows that she's for real. She's saved lives, Lucy, simply by seeing badly damaged auras and getting urgent treatment for the people concerned.'

She looked at him curiously. 'Can you see auras, Callum?'

'No, I can't. As far as I know it's only the Professor and Ellie who can do that. Is there someone you're concerned about? Someone you think might benefit from an aura reading?'

'Not exactly,' Lucy said, and drew in a breath. 'Have you ever heard of Indigo children?'

Callum nodded. 'Oddly, I was asking about them the other day. I heard someone mention them on the radio, and asked our resident psychotherapist, Sean Peters, about them, and he referred me to another of our counsellors, Jason Adamson. It's a bit of a contentious subject, isn't it?'

Lucy looked rather sad. 'Yes, it certainly is. Some people believe they are children with genuine psychic abilities, who are both empathic and strong willed, while others say that it's a term invented by parents who cannot face the stigma attached to the terms ADHD or autism. Or simple bad behaviour.'

'That's more or less what Jason told me. I've been meaning to do some research into it, but I haven't got around to it yet.' He looked at Lucy. 'Don't tell me you think one of your kids is an Indigo child?'

She hesitated for a moment. 'Er, no, not exactly . . . well, I don't think so, but . . .' Then the floodgates opened. 'Oh, Callum! I have this little boy in my class who's different to any child I've ever met. I'm out of my depth! I daren't go to a professional about him, and the parents don't want to know. They are struggling enough as it is, quietly destroying each other because of their other child who suffers from a genetic disorder and needs constant care.'

Callum grimaced. 'Ouch! That's tough on any relationship, though some get stronger, even if others fall apart.'

Lucy sighed. 'Oh, this family are the latter, in a big way. It might sound a bit harsh, but my main concern is for Harry, my pupil.'

'Is he being neglected? You know, not fed properly, comes to school in dirty clothes and unbrushed teeth?'

'No, no, nothing like that,' said Lucy emphatically. 'He's always clean and tidy, he's actually a fastidious little boy. He looks well-nourished too. No, it's just like I said, he's very different to the other children. He has a . . . I don't even know what to call it. My headteacher seems to think it's a phase he's going through, she puts it down to attention-seeking because his parents put so much time and energy into caring for his little brother. But I'm certain it isn't that, and I think everyone is ignoring the fact that Harry really is different.' She met his gaze. 'That's why I'm talking to you, Callum. I told you that as a teacher I can't involve a professional without the parents' permission, but I badly need another opinion. If I can arrange it, would you come to the school and observe him, maybe have a word with him? We can think of an excuse, and because you are a nurse, there will be no problem, I'm sure.'

This certainly wasn't the kind of date Callum had planned, but seeing the anxiety on her beautiful face, he said that if it was all right with the school, of course he'd go. 'Though I'm not sure my opinion will count for much. I'm not a paediatric nurse or a specialist.'

Lucy looked relieved. 'If I can just get another opinion, in case I'm imagining things, or I've got it all out of proportion. It's really worrying me. Oh, Callum, thank you!' She reached across the table and touched his hand. 'I really appreciate this.'

'You haven't told me what it is that worries you about Harry,' said Callum. 'What makes him so different?'

Lucy went quiet. 'I think you need to see Harry for yourself. I don't want to influence you.' She looked at him directly. 'I overheard one of the staff here talking to Miss McEwan about you, and the work you used to do before you came to the centre. They were really impressed with the way you dealt with one of the clients here, so I decided to come to you for help. Was I stepping out of line?'

Callum shook his head. 'Of course not, and I promise to be honest. I'll tell it how I see it.' He drained his mug. 'I'm on call this weekend, so I have Friday off. How about I call into the school tomorrow, if you can get permission.' He took out his phone. 'Do you have a mobile number?'

After they had sorted out telephone numbers, Lucy said, 'My deputy head has been arranging visits to the classes from all sorts of people — police officers, firefighters, artists and so on. We had an actor come in last week chatting to the kids and answering questions. It's intended for the older children, but the little ones join in too. I thought I'd tell her that you are a friend of mine who was a nurse with Médecins Sans Frontières who is calling in to see me when I finish for the day, and I wondered if you could come back another time and talk to the kids. What do you think?'

'Sure. If your young Harry will be there, why not?'

'Oh, he will. I've got an arrangement with his mother that Harry waits with me until she comes to collect him; she's sometimes late because of the difficulties with her younger child. It's no trouble to me. I like Harry a lot, and as I haven't got anyone to hurry home to, it helps her a bit. I let him do some drawing or colouring.'

Secretly elated that she had no one to get home for, Callum smiled. 'Then shall I get to you at around three?'

'Make it about a quarter to three and I'll meet you in the foyer at the entrance.' She stood up. 'Thank you for the drink, Callum, and for agreeing to help me. I'll see you tomorrow.'

Callum watched her walk away, her long blonde hair swaying gracefully. He recalled the thrill of excitement he had felt when she touched his hand, and felt like dancing. This was a turn-up for the books! What better way to get to know her, hopefully then he could take it a step further. He liked her more each time he saw her, but no way was he going to rush this. He had a very strange feeling about Lucy Reynolds. It was clear to him that they were connected in a way he found difficult to explain. Had he been told that they'd met in a previous life, he would have agreed at once. It was a little like rekindling a friendship from way, way back in the past. And why, out of all the people that she must know — friends, family, fellow teachers, someone at the centre, like Will Ryan for instance — had she chosen him?

Callum went back to work, his mind full of a mysterious little boy called Harry, who might just be an Indigo child.

* * *

'Sorry, but I'm not good at ages, especially children,' apologised the woman. 'Never had any myself, so they are a bit of a mystery to me, and they grow up so fast these days.'

'But you think you saw Oliver Cruise two nights ago? On the tow-path down near Stoke Lock?' asked DI Jonathon Leatham.

'Yes, that's right, just beyond the lock, it's more rural there. It was closer to the weir near Burpham.'

'And you say he was with someone?'

The woman nodded. 'Yes, another boy. He was definitely older and much taller.'

'And what time was this, Mrs Harris?' asked DCI Bob Foreman.

Audrey Harris frowned. 'Must've been a bit after seven thirty because we were home by eight.'

'We?'

'Me and the dog. That's why I was down there. I walk by the river every morning and evening, come rain or shine. She expects it, my little Sandy does, and you owe it to them don't you?'

'You go out on the tow-path alone, Mrs Harris, every night of the year, even in the dark?' asked Jonathon incredulously.

'Of course! I'm not afraid of the dark, and I got a torch! Oh and I've got little Sandy, she'd not let anyone come near me, I can guarantee you that!' She let out a hoarse cackle.

'And what breed might "little Sandy" be, can I ask?' asked Bob, imagining maybe a Corgi, or a Jack Russell — anyway, a terrier of some kind.

'Sandy? Oh, she's a white Swiss Shepherd.'

Jon snorted, earning him a glare from the DCI. 'Not exactly little then. Or sandy-coloured.'

Again that raucous laugh, which was beginning to grate. 'She was the smallest in the litter, her kennel name was Sweet Sanderling Girl. She's as big as a German Shepherd, and white as a ghost.'

Bob was anxious to get this woman off the subject of dogs. They had a boy missing, for heaven's sake, and they were sounding like they were discussing the entries at Crufts! 'What makes you so sure that the boy was Oliver Cruise, Mrs Harris?'

'The clothes, and his hair. I saw the news bulletin about an hour ago, with the photo of that lad, and I knew straightaway it was the boy I saw on the tow-path two nights back. I recognised that red and white baseball jacket immediately, and when I saw that dreadful haircut, I knew exactly who it was. I was a hairdresser, see. I reckon his mum or dad must've cut his hair, and they didn't do him any favours, poor kid.'

'It was dark. How come you saw him so clearly?' Bob asked.

'It was a full moon, wasn't it, and I've already told you I had me torch with me,' she replied impatiently.

'Were they talking? Did you hear what they were saying, Mrs Harris?' asked Jon.

'No, I didn't hear anything, but when I shone my torch on them, the older boy told me to . . .' she wrinkled her brow, 'well, you know. It ended in "off".'

'We get the picture,' said Bob. 'But tell me, did you get the feeling they were friends, or were they arguing?'

Audrey Harris shook her head. 'I couldn't say. When that boy shouted at me, it was all I could do to hang on to little Sandy. She lunged at him. As I said, she's very protective. Then they ran off up the tow-path. They must have branched off somewhere because I never saw them again, not even in the distance. Oh, and the older boy was all in dark clothing — hoodie, joggers and dark shoes or trainers, I'm not sure which.'

Having taken the woman's details, they were preparing to show her out when she said, 'He had a limp.'

'Sorry? Do you mean Oliver?' asked Bob.

'No, the older boy. As they ran away, I remember seeing that he looked odd. He dragged his right leg.'

'Thank you, Mrs Harris,' said Bob, holding the door open for her. 'That could be very useful indeed. Other than that older boy, it seems you might be the last person to see Oliver a— before he disappeared.'

Back in Bob's office, they discussed this possible sighting.

'I think she really did see him, don't you?' said Bob.

'It's a very distinctive jacket that he was wearing, and after having another look at Oliver's photo, she's right about the tragic haircut. Any hairdresser would have a fit seeing that. So, yes, I reckon she did.'

'Then get DS Wendy Brown onto asking Oliver's family and friends if any of his close mates, an older kid, has an injured right leg, or maybe even a congenital defect causing him to limp? We need to find this other boy.'

Jonathon stood up. 'Straight away, guv.' He stopped in the doorway. 'Sir? Is there more to this than we know? I mean, Oliver Cruise is fourteen, and a minor, which is serious, but although his parents disagree, everyone else says he's a bit of a tearaway, so why are the family so certain he hasn't run off to get his own back at them for something?'

'I'm wondering the same thing.' Bob ran a hand through his thick grey hair. 'I'm going to see the parents again this evening. Apparently, someone else is going to be there — I've no idea who, but they want me to speak to them. Come with me, Jon, unless you've got plans for tonight?'

'Of course, sir, I'll be happy to come along. I've nothing on, and I'm curious. I swear there's something odd about this whole thing.'

* * *

Professor Michael Seale was having trouble concentrating. Thankfully, his long-time secretary and assistant, Janet Cooper, had arranged a fairly light patient list for the day, so he had time between appointments to call in to see Ellie. She had left him a message to say that if he had a spare moment, she'd appreciate a chat. He had an idea that something was bothering her which wasn't to do with the day-to-day running of the C-M Centre.

As he made his way through the café, he saw Callum Church in earnest conversation with a rather pretty young woman he hadn't seen before.

As he passed their table, Michael briefly tuned into their auras, and smiled. *Ah-ha, I see.* The lights that surrounded Callum were bright, and Michael noticed little flashes of orange and pink, indicating sexual energy, and that his heart chakra was open and receptive. So young Callum was enamoured of this pretty young woman, was he?

Michael looked closer at her aura, and saw that it was much more complicated, and less brilliant. *Something is worrying you, young lady.* Even so, there was a distinct glimmer of pink and green, so her heart was not exactly closed to the rather attractive, dark-haired, dark-eyed man who sat facing her.

Michael glanced back and saw the woman's hand briefly reach out and touch Callum's. As she did so, Michael saw a sudden flash of silver-white light envelop them both, as if a tiny cloud, composed entirely of frost particles, had burst around them. And then it was gone.

As Michael walked on he realised that he was holding his breath. In all his years, by now amounting to quite a few, he had never seen anything like this. He quickened his pace. Ellie might be wanting to speak to him, but right now, he needed to speak to her, and urgently!

* * *

'Ice! It was like tiny crystals of ice. Honestly, Ellie, that's a first for me!'

Ellie looked at her old friend with both amusement at his excitement, and slight consternation. What he was describing was something she'd never seen, or even heard of.

'I thought it might be a visual disturbance,' Michael went on. 'You know, like those bright jagged lines you get when a migraine is coming on. But it wasn't that, Ellie, it was crystal clear, and everything around them was normal and focused. Oh, if only it were possible to capture a moment in time, and go over it again!'

'Was it like a silver aura around them, Michael?' she asked. 'They are very rare, and a little like white ones, in that they signify abundance and wisdom, and white means spiritual purity. They are both highly evolved and rarely seen.'

He shook his head. 'No, it wasn't like an aura at all. You know when you were a kid, and you had a sherbet sweet, well, it was like that fizz on your tongue, only in visual form. Then it had gone.' He flopped his considerably well-upholstered body into a comfy chair, looking totally bemused.

'I'm a comparative novice in this area,' said Ellie. 'Maybe you should ask a few of your colleagues who work in a similar way? There must be someone who has come across this phenomenon before.'

'You're right. I'll do that as soon as I get back to the office. It's driving me mad!' said Michael. 'And I'm going to be watching Callum like a hawk from now on!'

'It sounds like it's something you'll only see when he's with that young lady you mentioned,' mused Ellie. 'Maybe I should try and find out who she is.'

'I could be wrong, but I've a feeling that lad might be falling in love,' said Michael with a twinkle in his eye. 'Although I was picking up quite a bit of angst in the girl's aura, nothing to do with our Callum, just an underlying concern that's worrying her.'

'It'd be great if Callum could meet someone special,' said Ellie wistfully. 'He hasn't had a girlfriend in all the time he's been with us. He told me that he wasn't ready for a relationship yet, after Rwanda and Bosnia. He said he needed to get his work and home life back on track first, and try to sort himself out emotionally.'

'Well, from the colours in his aura, I'd say he's more than ready for that long overdue relationship,' Michael said.

'Good for him,' Ellie said, then thought of some of the possible downsides. 'As long as she's someone who can accept that Callum is nothing like your average young man. Trying to explain to your new girlfriend that you see dead people could be a bit tricky.'

'Oh dear, I hadn't thought of that,' said Michael. 'That could certainly frighten someone off.'

'Maybe his warm smile and those incredibly dark eyes will outweigh his ability to see "beyond the veil". At least he's sensible. He certainly wouldn't share his unusual talents with a casual girlfriend. He'd keep that close to his chest until he knew an awful lot more about her.'

'Indeed,' Michael said. 'Anyway, moving on from Callum's love life and my strange phenomenon, you said you wanted to talk to me about something, and it sounded serious. What's worrying you, Ellie?'

'Oh, I wish I knew, Michael.' She took a deep breath. 'I have to ask you . . . are you noticing anything — well, out of the ordinary at the moment?'

Michael regarded her curiously. 'As in?'

'In days gone by, I'd be saying portents. Omens.'

'Ah, as in have I been having visitations from our two dear old friends of late?' Michael said softly. 'And the answer is . . . a tenuous maybe. In fact, now I think about it, it's more than likely, but I've been in denial.'

'Which ties in with my growing certainty that something is just not right. So, I think we need to be extra vigilant, don't you?'

'We cannot afford not to be, Ellie, not after that last time. If there is some kind of — how can I put it? — trouble brewing, then we can't ignore it. We'd best be on our guard and remain watchful.'

Ellie glanced around her suite, the place where she interviewed new patients and staff. She had expressly designed it to put people at their ease and relax them, and was grateful for the peace it always instilled in her too. At least here she could think straight. She sat back on the big comfy sofa and looked steadily at Michael. 'Then that's exactly what we'll do. I suggest that we involve Callum Church as well. After all, he was a big part of the last debacle that nearly brought an end to all of us. He is ultra-sensitive, and,' she gave him a smile, 'I get the feeling that our Vera is particularly fond of that young man and finds him easy to contact. Far more easily than contacting me.'

Michael agreed. 'And don't forget Carole's Orlando. Callum sees that dog regularly. It's almost like they have a strange cross-worldly rapport. He was only asking me about him the other day, so I'm guessing that spirit pooch is making his presence felt quite a bit right now.'

'Another reason to keep our eyes wide open. I won't bother him today, but I think his shift rota said he's off tomorrow as he's on call at the weekend, so I suggest we let him have his day off, then bring him in for a chat on Saturday and put him in the picture.

It'll give us time to get our own thoughts in order, and hopefully get a handle on what might be going on.' Ellie frowned. 'Maybe we should also talk to our favourite live-in nursing sister, Maureen Shaw? Okay, she has no special talents, but she is very perceptive and sensible and I'd value her input if we discover that something is . . . awry?'

Michael said that he had been going to suggest Maureen himself. She was very often the voice of reason, and as Ellie had said, she was a good, solid and reliable nurse.

They sat quietly for a moment, then Ellie said, 'Michael. There's one other person that perhaps we should contact.' She left the name unspoken.

'Not yet, Ellie.' Michael was adamant. 'Let's do a little investigating of our own first. He's our last port of call for reasons I'm sure I don't need to go into, and so far all we have is some vague apprehension that something might be wrong. It could be something that is easily dealt with by us, or nothing at all. Let's leave DCI Bob Foreman out of it for now, okay?'

Although she acquiesced at once, something inside her said that soon they themselves would be getting a call from their old friend, the detective chief inspector.

CHAPTER THREE

The rest of the day passed quickly, and as Alice had phoned to say she would not be coming back until Saturday, Ellie thought it might be nice to invite her lovely neighbour and friend, Marie Littlewood, along with her son Daniel and little grandson, Christopher, to supper. It was partly to say thank you for walking the dogs for her, but if she were honest with herself, it was more a case of not wanting to be alone all evening, dwelling on her concerns. The nights were long enough without having to endure that. Ellie loved to cook, and liked nothing better than preparing meals for her friends, so it would be therapeutic for her.

She left work half an hour early with the intention of calling in at the supermarket on the way home, but as she made her way to the car park she saw Michael sitting alone on a stone bench outside the Orangery. Noticing his faraway expression, Ellie went over and sat down next to him.

'It's far too cold to be sitting here, my friend, especially when you have a very comfortable and warm apartment not two hundred yards away.'

'You're right!' Michael patted her hand. 'I'm an old fool, and I'm freezing, but the fact is, Callum told me that he saw Vera and Carole sitting right here as he was driving in to work.' He shivered a bit. 'He said that Vera waved to him, and I thought, well, maybe . . .'

'Maybe you could contact them more easily if you sat in the same place? That maybe they wanted to tell us something?'

'Exactly! But all I'm getting is a possible case of haemorrhoids from sitting on this cold stone!'

'Then I have a better idea. Come home with me. I've got Marie and her little family coming for dinner tonight, so why not join us. You can stay over, and we'll drive into work together tomorrow morning.' Ellie laughed. 'After all, if you want to be close to Carole and Vera, what better place than their own Snug Cottage?'

Michael beamed. 'That's a distinct improvement on this rather foolish and very chilly little experiment. I accept with gratitude! I'll just pop in and grab a few things.'

'Well, don't be long, I've shopping and cooking to do. A toothbrush and some night clothes should suffice, you've already got a change of clothes in my guest room. Off you go then. I'll meet you at the car.'

While she waited for Michael, Ellie wrote a shopping list and put together the evening meal in her head. She wanted to keep it simple so that she could spend time with her friends, and she marvelled that she no longer had to consider a child's meal for Christopher. He was now eight, a very sensible and likeable boy who desired fervently to be 'grown up'. There had been fears for his development and his mental health after a very difficult and traumatic start in life, but remarkably, he seemed to have come through it unscathed.

Shopping forgotten, Ellie was transported back to the year before, when Marie had come to speak with her about the only thing that worried her about Christopher's behaviour — his imaginary friend. Ellie had spoken to the behaviourist at the clinic, and had been able to reassure Marie that it was perfectly normal for a child to have an imaginary friend, even older children had them. It was common among those who had suffered a loss or trauma. Their 'friend' helped them express their emotions, and was a great source of comfort as well as helping to overcome loneliness.

Ellie sighed. If anyone had needed the support of a friend, imaginary or otherwise, it was Christopher. At the age of three, while he played happily in a sand pit in the garden, his four-year-old sister drowned in the paddling pool. As if that were not bad enough, his mother erroneously blamed Daniel. She ran away, taking Christopher with her, leaving Daniel grieving for a dead daughter while the son he adored had been taken from him. He had had a breakdown, from which he took a long time to recover. He and Della were now divorced, and he had moved in with his mother and father, Marie and Dr Marcus Littlewood, who now shared the care of his precious boy with him. Finally, father and son were as close as they had ever been, possibly closer.

The car door opened. 'Look at you! You're miles away. You're not fretting over what might have been, are you?' Michael said.

She turned the key in the ignition. 'No, I was just thinking about how well-balanced young Christopher has turned out to be.'

'Oh yes. Considering how it could have gone for him, and for Daniel and Marie too, it's nothing short of a miracle,' agreed Michael. 'I'm looking forward to seeing Christopher again. The last time I saw him we had a long chat about the best universities to attend.'

'Michael! He's only eight!'

'Oh yes, and very mindful of his future. He has a specific career path already mapped out. Funnily enough, it's your fault, Ellie McEwan.' Michael chuckled.

'My fault?' exclaimed Ellie. 'Whatever do you mean?'

'Ever since you invited Daniel to take him to see the dogs at Snug Cottage, he's been totally in love with them. He is going to be a vet, there's no question about it.'

'Come to think of it, it's actually not that surprising,' Ellie said. 'I've watched his aura when he's around the boys, and I've watched theirs too. He has a real connection with animals, one that few children of his age display.'

'I've seen it too,' said Michael. 'So many lovely colours surround both dogs and child when they are all together. It's refreshing when we see so many damaged and depleted auras in our daily lives. A real breath of spring.'

She smiled. 'I get the feeling that we'll both be tuning in to Christopher and his furry friends tonight.'

'Definitely,' Michael said. 'It'll be a restorative to the spirit.'

They drove in silence for a while. Then Ellie began, 'You said Callum mentioned seeing Vera and Carole.' She paused. 'Did you tell him about our concerns?'

'Oh no. He just mentioned it in passing, but I do think it bothered him. He got called away before he could elaborate, so I guess we'll have to wait until Saturday to talk to him.'

'It sounds as if he's already picking up the same vibes as we are, doesn't it?' Ellie said thoughtfully.

'That's the impression I got, Ellie, which is why you found me freezing my butt off on that stone seat.'

'Which makes me wonder even more about what's going on, Michael.' Ellie felt a wave of anxiety drift over her. 'Last time . . . well, last time we nearly didn't make it, any of us, so . . .'

'Ellie! Ellie! We *did* make it! We were meant to survive, we all were. And if you recall, our dear, dear friend Vera sent us an important message to say that she believed Callum was destined for something very special. She said his life had a purpose, a most important one. That's what that last terrible incident was all about. You and I saving Callum. You know that.'

Ellie forced a smile. 'Yes, I do. I'm being an idiot. It's just that sometimes I think I'm not up to all the responsibility my gift has brought with it. There are times when all I want is to be ordinary. Just Ellie, an average woman living an average life with the people she loves. No gift, and no threats from dark places that most people don't even know exist!' She gripped the steering wheel tightly, her knuckles white. 'Does that sound terribly selfish, Michael? I know I have been given an incredible gift, but sometimes the weight of it . . . I long to be normal.'

'No, you're not being selfish, just human.' Michael laughed softly. 'There would be something wrong with you if you sailed serenely through everything that's been handed you, without the occasional meltdown. It happens to all healers sometimes. All our clients' problems and illnesses just get too much for us. Then someone tells us how we've changed their life for the better, we see a smile where there had only been tears. Maybe it's just a thank you that you know comes from the heart. That's all it takes to put you back on track.' He touched her hand. 'And never underestimate what you've been through, Ellie. You are an amazing young woman, and much stronger than you think.'

They drove on in silence. If Michael noticed the tear that rolled slowly down her cheek, he didn't say.

* * *

Michael watched Ellie very closely that evening. He had made light of her uncharacteristic display of emotion, but in truth, it worried him. It was understandable, he supposed, after everything they'd been through, but he hated to see her so on edge. However, it seemed he needn't have worried. As soon as she got down to preparing their meal, her mood lifted and she was herself again.

The meal took no time to put together, yet it was delicious. Regarding his empty plate with satisfaction, Michael told her so, amid a chorus of agreement.

'Granny's a very good cook too,' announced Christopher, 'though she doesn't make her food look as pretty as this. Daddy is rubbish.' Then, seeing his father's crestfallen expression, he added hastily, 'But he tries very hard, and he does a pretty good omelette.'

'Thanks, son. I love you too,' said Daniel, trying to conceal a grin.

'And I shall try hard to make my chicken casserole look prettier in future,' said Marie Littlewood, rolling her eyes. 'I'll be asking Ellie for tips on how to do it.'

Ellie laughed. 'Even I can't do much with a casserole, and let's face it, it's the taste that counts.' She turned to Christopher. 'And make no mistake about it, your gran's casseroles are the best!'

Looking slightly worried, Christopher asked if they could please change the subject now.

'Tell Ellie and Michael about your project, son. I'm sure they'll be interested.' Daniel threw Michael a surreptitious wink.

Christopher wriggled in his chair and announced, 'I'm going to write a book.'

Even Michael, who was used to the boy's various enthusiasms, wasn't prepared for this. 'A book! Well, well! That's very enterprising, Christopher.'

'What's ent . . . enter prising, Michael?'

'It means you are showing creative initiative,' Michael said, at which Christopher looked even more confused. 'I mean, that's a really cool thing to do.'

Christopher beamed. 'Of course, I can't really write it properly yet, I get mixed up. I know what I want to say, but the words won't come out right. Daddy says the more I write the easier it will be, and I hope he's right, because I don't want to forget what the story is about. It's very important.'

'He gets so frustrated,' said Daniel. 'He's doing brilliantly for his age. He has all these wonderful thoughts and ideas, and he's simply too young to be able to express them properly. It'll come, but patience is not among my lovely son's many attributes.'

'Well, don't give up, young man,' said Michael. 'I might just have a way to help you. Now, I can see Ellie bringing some very pretty ice cream, which has your name on it. We'll talk about your writing afterwards, all right?'

Christopher nodded furiously, his eyes on the approaching dessert.

Ice cream despatched, Ellie and Marie made coffee, while Daniel took the dogs into the garden for a wee. Michael ushered Christopher into the library and sat him down in one of the wing-backed armchairs next to the fire. While the logs crackled and the flames danced brightly, they settled down to a chat about books.

'Do you enjoy reading, Christopher?' asked Michael.

'Oh yes, I've got loads of books. I'm reading the *Chronicles of Narnia* at the moment, and Erik bought me *The Incredible Journey*. I'm really looking forward to that.'

'Erik?' asked Michael.

'Erik's Mum's new friend. He moved in with her not long after she and Dad got divorced. She said I should call him "Dad", but he and I agree that I already have a dad, so he's Erik. He's from somewhere which has a lot of snow, and his parents live on a lake near a forest. He says he'll take me there when I'm a bit older.'

'You like him, do you?'

'Oh yes. He's not a bit like Dad, but he's still nice.'

'He must be nice if he gives you books,' said Michael, settling into the chair on the other side of the hearth. 'So, you want to write a book of your own? Is it about animals? I thought it might be because you want to be a vet.'

'No, it's about three children. They're three special children. Their names are Clover, Zillah and a blind boy called Finn.'

Taken aback, Michael said nothing for a moment or two. He had expected a funny, Famous Five type of adventure, not something involving 'special' children with unusual names. What, he wondered, did Christopher mean by special? And how did he come by those names? 'How did you decide what they were going to be called, Christopher?'

Christopher deliberated for a moment. 'I didn't. That's just who they are.'

'And what is the story about?'

'Good and evil.'

For a moment Michael felt as if he weren't talking to a child at all. Why hadn't the boy said 'goodies and baddies' or heroes and bad guys, villains even? Good and evil, so bluntly stated, seemed almost philosophical.

'Wow! Tell me, Christopher, did you make up this story on your own?'

Christopher looked a little sheepish. 'Not exactly.'

Michael recalled the imaginary friend that Ellie had told him about, and understood.

'Ah, your friend is helping you. That's good. Two heads are always better than one.'

Christopher looked relieved that Michael had simply accepted his 'friend' without further question.

'Well, as I said, I think I can help you,' Michael went on. 'I have a friend of mine who's a counsellor, he helps children with learning and language difficulties. I'm not saying you have any difficulties, no way! But he has a great way of helping you if you struggle to get your thoughts straight. Do you see what I'm saying?'

'Would it help me to write?'

'I think it would. The thing is, you can say what you want to write out loud, can't you? It just gets tricky when you try to figure out how to put it down on paper, right?'

The boy nodded furiously. 'Yes, that's right.'

'Okay, so do you have someone who could help you with some exercises? A grown-up, I mean.'

'Dad would, so would Erik when I'm back with Mum.'

'Perfect! Now, remember. You are very young to be even writing compositions, let alone a book, so don't worry if it takes a bit of time, but it will work. What we are going to do is split up your thoughts, and then get them down on paper with things like spelling, punctuation, and just getting the words in the right order.'

Christopher was starting to look anxious. 'Split up my thoughts? How?'

'It's simple. You think of what you want to say, say it out loud, and then get your dad, or Erik, to write it down for you. Then you study the words, or your thoughts, then you go over them with your dad or Erik and see how a few of them form sentences.' Michael smiled at the frowning boy. 'You can even copy them out in your own writing, and read them over and over so you can see if it comes out as what you or your characters wanted to say. Easy!'

Christopher looked up at Michael and smiled back. 'Can we try it now, Michael?'

'Why not? Go and ask Ellie for a sheet of paper and a pen, and we'll start with a couple of short sentences, so you can see how it works. You can take them away with you and copy them out.'

Christopher ran off, and a few moments later, Michael had a pen in his hand and a sheet of A4 paper on his lap, with a magazine for support.

'What should I say?' asked a small, uncertain voice.

'Think of one of your characters. Maybe one of those children? Now, the reader will want to know all about them, so start by saying something interesting about . . . the girl called Clover maybe?'

There was a long silence, then Christopher began: *'Clover and her mother, Lori, live in a commune. She has never seen her father, and her mother never speaks of him.'* He took a breath, then grinned broadly. 'Is that okay?'

Michael took a moment to respond. Whatever happened to 'Once Upon a Time'? 'Sounds like it's going to be a pretty deep book, Christopher.'

'Deep? How can a book be deep?'

'Intense? Um, serious maybe.' Michael gathered himself. 'I must say, the grammar is *very* good, almost perfect already.' Why, he wondered, should this eight-year-old choose to write about a single parent child who lived in a commune? How did he know what a commune even was? Did something about his parents' break-up run deeper than they had realised?

'Shall I do the next bit?' Christopher said.

Intrigued, Michael told him to go ahead.

'All her life they had moved around, from one camp to another, because bad things happen around them, and when the shadows gather, Clover and her mother move on.'

Michael realised he had been holding his breath. Even the boy's voice had changed. It was deeper, and didn't seem to belong to him. When the shadows gather? Lord love us, what kid ever says that? Not knowing what to say, Michael swallowed, hard.

Christopher was smiling apologetically. 'I goofed, didn't I? I said to my friend that line was a load of poop, but,' he shrugged, 'I was told it had to stay, and that was that.'

Michael assured the lad he hadn't goofed, it was just that he hadn't expected it to be so . . . grown-up. Maybe, he suggested, they should keep these exercises just between them for a while, and not involve anyone else. 'I'll come over a couple of times a week while you're here with your dad, and we'll talk some more about this amazing story. How does that sound? And meantime you can practise writing things out. You can even just copy some sentences from other books after you've read them aloud for practice. Can you do that?'

'Like proper homework? Yes, that sounds good.'

'We'd better go and join the others, or my coffee will have got cold.' Michael shivered. For some reason the fire was no longer warming him.

As he followed Christopher from the room, he had a terrible feeling that Ellie's concerns were about to come to fruition, right here in her home, her precious Snug Cottage. Now he needed to decide how much he should tell her. Maybe he shouldn't tell her at all. Maybe he was being oversensitive.

No, he was overreacting. Kids watched all sorts on TV these days, and who knew what his mum and this Erik watched, what they allowed him to see? Perhaps he should just say that Christopher wasn't quite as well-balanced as they had thought, and the death of his sister and its subsequent fallout had affected him deeply, and it was coming out in the guise of a book? After all, that was perfectly feasible. Not everything that happened around Ellie and himself had to be connected to the supernatural. No, he'd keep it to himself for a while and think it through before he caused Ellie any more anxiety. He decided to talk to his friend Jason Adamson at the clinic before he said anything to anyone.

Michael composed his features into a smile and went back into the kitchen. 'Okay, school's out. So where's that coffee I was promised?'

* * *

Bob Foreman and Jonathon Leatham returned to the car and sat for a while before pulling away. They had just left the Cruise family, and were both feeling unsettled and irritated by their visit.

The lines on Bob's forehead had deepened into folds. They had gone to see Oliver's parents hoping to understand why they were so convinced that their son had been abducted. They had come away even more confused. 'I've seen any number of distraught parents in my time on the force, but that couple are something else. And why do I get the feeling that we've been fed a crock of shit, Jon?'

'Probably because you're right, sir. And we could have done without the kid's creepy schoolteacher telling us that Oliver is a top student, incapable of running away, and therefore has been kidnapped, so we should get our arses into gear and find him. The parents had already made that quite clear when they reported him missing.'

'Along with a long list of the boy's glowing attributes and achievements, while everyone else we've spoken to says he's a right little toe-rag,' added Bob.

'That teacher was really labouring the point, wasn't he?' said Jon thoughtfully. 'It was almost as if he knew something, and was desperately trying to point us in a different direction. It didn't make sense.'

Back at the station, Bob dropped Jon in the car park. 'Get off home, Jon, and I'm sorry I wasted your evening. I honestly believed tonight would help us move forward, not give us more headaches.'

'No worries, sir. If nothing else, it's increased my sense that there's something not right about our missing boy. There's something going on, and I swear it's not a straightforward runaway case, nor an abduction. But if it's neither of those, what is it?'

'Well, we've got every man-jack out there looking for him, plus the media have been asked to assist. There's nothing more we can do. Go and get some sleep, and I'll see you in the morning.'

CHAPTER FOUR

Ellie woke up feeling much more positive than the day before. Maybe her little wobble had been good for her, and as always, Michael's words had made her realise that she should not expect too much of herself. If the care they provided for their clients was to remain at a consistently high level they needed to attend to their own health and well-being, which included enjoying themselves whenever they could. Between them, she and Michael were running a most extraordinary clinic, whose aim — indeed, the creed that they lived by — was to help heal every soul that crossed their threshold. Their treatments varied, depending on the need. Some of the methods they used were deemed unconventional; nevertheless, everyone who attended the clinic left feeling that their problems had been addressed, and that every effort had been made to restore them to well-being.

While Michael showered and dressed, Ellie watched the dogs running around happily in the damp grass of the orchard with a sense of renewed strength. Even if they were destined to face some new battle, somehow they would find the courage to tackle it head on, as they had in the past.

The past. Bad memories started to flood back, but Ellie pushed them away and forced herself to concentrate on the present. Alice was coming home tomorrow, and Ellie had booked a table for them at their favourite local restaurant. She had thought about inviting Michael, but decided that as she hadn't seen Alice for days, the two of them deserved some time to themselves. Things were so much easier now that Alice had her own space at the C-M. The conversion of an old cricket pavilion into a suite where she and her assistants could work and see patients was a huge success, but even so, as Alice was fast becoming the leading light in the ongoing work to understand the brain chemicals involved in the Azimah Syndrome, she was often called away to London, and sometimes to hospitals and universities abroad. Ellie had to feel pleased for her, and proud of what she had achieved, but sometimes she wished they could spend more time together.

Ellie dragged herself back from her reverie, and calling to the boys, ushered them back inside the kitchen and watched them snuggle into their beds. After Carole died, she had done her best to keep to their usual routines. Routines are important to a dog. Theirs consisted of breakfast, then a run in the orchard, a biscuit before Ellie went to work, then switch off until later in the morning when Marie and Daniel came to exercise them. If Scrubbs or Mrs Scrubbs were around, they had the run of the house and garden, and then it was time to welcome Ellie home from work, followed by their dinner, and a final trip out to play. Not a bad life. Most important of all was that they had remained in their old home, and had not been split up. Never for one moment had Ellie resented the time she gave to Carole's dogs. She had always loved them like her own, and now they *were* her own . . . in part. For they would always belong to Carole, and to Vera. Ellie was certain that the dogs sensed that their two old owners were still around and still loved them, just on a different plane.

Having let the dogs back into the kitchen, Ellie went and stood in the orchard again, gazing up at the bare branches of the trees, at the long grass — still too wet for Scrubbs to cut — and across to the summer house, her magical place. The summer house was where she went to find peace and quiet. She had spent hours there with Michael, her patient tutor, learning about auras and colour. Carole had passed over in there, but this hadn't made it feel sad or desolate. If anything, its tranquil atmosphere had intensified. It had been Carole's favourite place to meditate and study her tarot cards, so it was fitting that she should have chosen this of all places to draw her last breath.

It was too late to spend time there this morning — there was breakfast for Michael to prepare — but Ellie determined that come what may, she would go there after work and perform a meditation of her own. The practice calmed and strengthened her, and thinking of the days to come, she thought she might need do a little preparation on herself, just in case.

As she turned to go back to the house, she heard a familiar sound. Vera's wind chimes, shimmering gently through the branches of the apple tree. Ellie took a deep breath and closed her eyes. There was no wind this morning, not even a whisper.

'Okay, Vera,' she whispered, 'I hear you, and, yes, I will prepare myself, I will be ready.'

The melody faded away, and when she turned and looked back, the chimes were perfectly still, faint tendrils of mist, the colour of amethyst, swirling around them.

Ellie swallowed hard, turned and hurried back into Snug Cottage.

* * *

Once they were both at work, Michael barely saw Ellie, other than a brief consultation regarding the coming day's new patients. Nevertheless, on the drive to the clinic, he had noticed that her aura was stronger, and he had detected a new determination in her. He hoped she had been too busy driving to look into *his* aura, which he guessed would reflect the sleepless night he had endured, despite the 'marshmallow' bed in the guest room. Little Christopher and his ideas for a book had robbed him of his precious slumber. At the centre, feeling a little worse for wear, he had downed two strong coffees and gone to seek out Jason Adamson.

He found Jason in the Orangery, sitting in a quiet corner, almost hidden among the plants. He looked up and smiled broadly when he saw Michael approach, apparently perfectly happy to be interrupted. Jason explained that he was struggling with a particularly difficult case study that he was due to present at a symposium in the coming week, and he'd come out here because the atmosphere was more conducive to thought than his office.

'Then I'm sorry to interrupt, but I need to pick that capacious brain of yours.' Michael lowered himself into one of the cane chairs beneath a broad-leafed palm. 'I find myself embroiled in a rather strange situation, and I think it's more your area of expertise than mine.'

'I'm intrigued,' said Jason, setting his paperwork down on a small glass-topped table in front of him. 'Tell me more.'

Michael gave him a summary of the harrowing story of the Littlewood family tragedy, and proceeded to describe Christopher and his apparent recovery.

'He has a wonderfully healthy aura,' added Michael, 'although from time to time some irregularities appear that puzzle me a little. I get the feeling these occur when his imaginary friend is around.'

'So, you're saying that apart from this friend of his, he basically comes over as a confident, well-balanced and generally contented child.'

'Absolutely,' said Michael.

Jason looked thoughtful. 'To your knowledge, has he ever expressed his opinion of what happened between his parents after the death of his sister, or said what he felt about it?'

Michael nodded. 'Not to me, but Ellie says he confided in her, just the once. She said he wasn't upset, he sounded quite matter of fact and adult about it. You know, Jason, it's very strange, but the boy sometimes says things that make you think you're not talking to a child at all.'

'So? What did he say to her?'

'Apparently, he told her that it was very sad, but in the end his parents' separation had been all for the best. He was aware that his mother blamed his father for his sister's death, and he thought this was because she couldn't handle the truth — that it had been her fault, not his. He said he had come to the conclusion that his mum would never be able to admit it, to do so would destroy her. He was just pleased that she had consented to let him spend time with his father again. He loves them both, but he thinks, as he put it, that "adult problems are very complicated, and I just hope I don't get that screwed up when I get to be a grown-up!"'

'And was that the truth? The bit about the mother being responsible?' asked Jason.

'Ellie says Christopher's assessment of the situation is spot on. Apparently, his father had been called back to work. In his absence, his mother had a migraine and took some extremely powerful painkillers, knowing full well that they would probably knock her out and the children would be left unsupervised in the garden. A garden with a paddling pool.'

'And a tragedy occurred.' Jason pulled a face. 'Well, from what you say, it sounds like your Christopher, with the aid of his imaginary friend, has survived this trauma unscathed. What's the problem, then?'

Michael told him that the boy wanted to write a book, but was having trouble getting his thoughts down on paper. He had therefore suggested that Christopher try Jason's self-help exercise to help him. 'I told him he was far too young to worry about things like sentence construction, but he wasn't to be put off. He was adamant that he must write this story before he forgets it.'

Michael took a folded sheet of paper from his pocket. 'I asked him to speak two sentences out loud, and I would write them down, so he'd get an idea of how they looked on paper. This is what he said.' He handed the sheet of paper to Jason.

Jason read them, frowned and read them again. 'Michael, is there a chance I might be able to meet Christopher?'

'I'll have to see. Right now, you and I are the only people who know about it,' Michael said. 'I haven't even told Ellie, I wanted to get your opinion first. Am I being neurotic, Jason? Is it just his past coming out sideways?'

'I'm not sure, not without seeing the lad,' Jason said. 'Two sentences aren't enough to make an assessment. You need to hear more of this story. Frankly, Michael, I'd be concerned about that boy anyway, because if it is the past surfacing, he may need help. Seriously, you know this. Whatever age a person might be, they need professional help if a past trauma starts to affect them. It can be liberating for some and devastating for others. Hell, the boy's only eight! Find a way for me to see him. I really don't want this weighing on me too! It might be nothing, but if it is significant, can we afford to ignore it?'

'Of course not, and not just for his sake, but for his father's sake too. He came very close to the edge when his wife ran off with his son. If anything else were to happen to Christopher, it might push him over the edge.'

'Suppose you suggest a day trip to see the C-M clinic, with the added incentive of beef burgers and fries in the café? Or you could arrange for me to accompany you when you next visit the boy. Just don't leave it too long.' Jason looked at his watch. 'Damn it! Sorry, Michael, but I've got a client in five minutes.' He stood up. 'Do what you can, and keep me in the loop, okay?'

After Jason had left, Michael stayed on for a while, thinking. He wasn't quite sure if he was reassured, or more anxious. He had hoped that his friend would tell him not to worry, that it was to be expected given the boy's history. But he hadn't, had he? He knew Jason well, and his friend was clearly troubled by Michael's story. So now what?

Slowly, he got to his feet. He had no choice. It was time to tell Ellie.

* * *

DCI Bob Foreman sat at his desk and opened his plastic lunch box. It was almost two o'clock, and he'd suddenly realised how hungry he was. He smiled at the sight of the carefully packed sandwich, the foil-wrapped slice of whatever cake Rosie had fancied baking that week, the small handful of seedless grapes, and the obligatory note. *I love you, and I always will, R x.* From the first days of their marriage, Rosie had unfailingly sent him off to work with a packed lunch, lovingly packed, and always with that little message that told him that no matter how bad things were at work, she'd be there to go home to.

As he unwrapped the sandwich, he realised that he was another day closer to the deadline for making that major decision, and he was still at a loss as to what he should do. He had the weekend in which to consider his options, because on Monday he must have his answer on the superintendent's desk. If not, he was history.

He stared at the little handwritten note and had a sudden thought. Maybe it was not his decision to make at all? After all her years as a long-suffering and loyal police wife, perhaps it should be down to Rosie. This did not mean that he would shift the responsibility onto her, not at all. Who knew, somewhere down the line he might resent her for it. The fact was Rosie knew him better than he knew himself. That being the case, he'd find out what she really believed would be best, and he would go with that, one hundred per cent. She had earned this much consideration, for having been so patient with him and his precious job, and for shouldering the task of bringing up three children with a husband considerably older than herself, who was often absent for all the important milestones in the kids' lives.

He ate his lunch feeling almost light-hearted. As soon as he got home that night, they would talk, and all his anguish would disappear. Popping the note into his jacket pocket, he murmured, 'And I love you too, Rosie.'

Ten minutes later, he closed the lid of his lunch box and strode out into the CID room. It was almost empty. Only Jon was there, staring at the whiteboard with its couple of photos and the paltry comments written underneath them.

'Nothing in from the team's enquiries?' asked Bob, looking at the picture of Oliver Cruise.

'Sorry, sir. Zilch at present. No sightings since that one on the River Wey tow-path. Nothing on that older boy either. No one can connect Oliver with a boy with a limp. He certainly doesn't seem to be either at the same school, or run with any of the local kids. He's a bit of a mystery, and I can't help wondering if he isn't the key to Oliver's disappearance.'

Bob felt the same. He lowered himself into a chair with a sigh. 'What have we actually got, Jon? Sod all, I suppose.'

'That's about it, I'm afraid, sir,' said Jon, sinking into a nearby chair. 'One fourteen-year-old boy and contradictory reports as to his behaviour. His peers regard him as a creepy little weirdo, while his parents and his teacher seem to think he's perfection on two legs. Walks out of his home after his tea, taking nothing with him, and apart from that one report from Mrs Audrey Harris, he's never seen again.' Jon glanced up at the wall clock. 'In half an hour I'm going to talk to a man who says he knows Oliver better than most. I'm not pinning too many hopes on him, mind you. He's a rather strange man himself.'

'Strange? In what way?'

'He's reticent to talk to the police, but says that as it's a missing kid, it's his civic duty, and he's willing to meet me. You might have come across him before, sir, name of Sharpy Cousins?'

'Sharpy!' Bob gave a loud guffaw. 'What on earth has he got to do with our missing boy?'

'Ah, you do know him. Before my time, I guess,' said Jon. 'He's doing youth work in a community group helping some kids who are struggling with social skills.'

This prompted more incredulous laughter. Jon looked quite taken aback.

'I've felt Sharpy's collar more times than I've had hot dinners!' Bob said. 'He's a twocker, Jon! Though I have to say I haven't seen him in here for a couple of years now. Are you telling me he's actually doing social work? And how does this tie in with our Oliver?'

Jon grinned. 'Ah, that explains why he wouldn't come to the station. He said he might be able to help us with our enquiries if I met him in town. I've no idea as to his relationship with the boy, but given what you said, it might be better if I go to see him on my own, if you don't mind, sir?'

'For sure! One look at me and he'll run a mile. I've lost count of the number of vehicles he's taken without the owner's consent, and if he has turned over a new leaf he won't want to be seen with the likes of me. At least you are a relatively new face, and forgive me for saying this, but you look far too smart and upmarket to be a copper!'

Jon looked a little sheepish. 'It's all right, sir. I know what the uniforms call me — Gentleman Jon. Still, not all of us want to look like Columbo, do we?'

'I totally agree,' said Bob, smiling. 'I might not have your edge, but my Rosie never lets me out of the house without a clean, well-ironed shirt and a decent suit on.'

'Even if they are all grey,' added Jon. 'Sir.'

Bob glanced down at the mid-grey suit, silver-grey shirt and charcoal-grey tie, and cleared his throat. 'Well, I'm comfortable in grey, and that's that. Anyway, Ellie McEwan, who knows more about colour than anyone, says it's dignified. She says it's solid and stable, the colour of the impartial professional, meaning I'm likely to make fair and balanced judgements. So what better colour for a DCI?'

'Well, I can't argue with Ellie,' said Jon. 'Have you seen her recently?'

'Not for a while. I did see Michael in town a few weeks back, and he said that clinic of theirs is keeping them both busy.'

'Thank heavens that dreadful incident didn't damage their reputation,' said Jon. 'It could have gone one of two ways, couldn't it, sir?'

'We have to take some of the credit there, my friend. For once, the powers that be managed to handle it with remarkable tact.' Bob pointed a thumb at the ceiling. 'Them upstairs soon realised that it was no ordinary case, and that if the truth had come out . . . well, for a start no one would have believed it, and if they had, we'd have become a Mecca for crackpots the world over. The media only ever got the sanitised version, which was perfectly believable. Even so, I suspect that some of the cover-up was intended to play down any connection to that very nasty case we were involved in the year before that. Anyway, it worked, so that's fine with me.' He heaved in a breath, and looked again at the white board. 'Back to the investigation. I don't want to delay your meeting with the infamous Sharpy. Just don't mention my name!'

Jon pulled on his coat. 'Why's he called Sharpy, sir?'

'Because he's not,' said Bob. 'He used to come out with some of the most stupid and ridiculous excuses and alibis I've ever come across. So take what he says with a pinch of salt. Don't get me wrong, mind, he's not a hard-arsed criminal, but he's a bit lacking in common sense and he's not very bright, so be warned.'

* * *

It didn't take Jonathon Leatham long to realise that although Sharpy was rubbish at taking vehicles, he was very good with youngsters. There was something likeable about him, even if he wasn't the best role model in terms of appearance and dress sense. In fact he looked as if he'd fallen out of bed and pulled on whatever clothes were to hand, and had forgotten to comb his hair before leaving home, wherever that was. He couldn't be more different to the neat and stylish Jon Leatham; nonetheless, Jon couldn't help warming to him.

'I s'pose your guvnor's told you all about me dark past,' said Sharpy, stirring the coffee Jon had just bought him with a slightly repentant air. 'Maybe you'd like to tell 'im from me that it's all be'ind me now. I 'aven't touched a motor for two years, three months, and two and a half weeks.'

'That's pretty specific,' said Jon.

'Well, that's how I see it.'

Jon thought about it. He'd heard alcoholics refer to the time they'd been sober in that way, but never a twocker. 'Are you saying it was a compulsion, Sharpy?'

'Got it in one, Detective.' Sharpy nodded sagely. 'Yeah, it were something I had no control over. I just couldn't walk past a tasty-looking motor without taking it for a spin. I never nicked 'em to keep, or burn rubber, I just drove 'em and when I was done I parked 'em up somewhere safe. I bet your boss thought I was thick as shit. He did, didn't 'e? I never had an alibi, I went through police cameras, and the truth was, after I'd done it, I felt pretty bad about it — till the next time.'

'So, how did you kick the habit, Sharpy?'

'Ah, well, that was the thing. I was just thinking I needed help, acting like a first-class prat and ruining my life, when I had this . . . well, something happened, and that was the end of it.'

Jon nodded, assuming Sharpy wouldn't want to share his epiphany with a stranger, especially a copper, but Sharpy look a slurp of his drink and began his story.

'One night I sees this lovely little motor sitting outside a house in Manor Road. Nice area, quiet street.'

'I know where you mean,' said Jon.

'Well, I had a butchers around and there was no one in sight. Then, just as I was about to pop the door, this woman runs out, tears pouring down her face. She was in a terrible state, Detective! She practically cannoned into me. I took me hand off the door and made like I was just walking past, but the state she was in, I had to say something, so I asked her what was the matter, and could I help. She shook her head — honest, one of her tears hit my cheek — and she says, "No, no, thank you. I have to get to the hospital! It's my son! They say he's critical."' Sharpy pulled a face. 'Then she got in the car and was gone, and I thought, *Oh shit, what if I'd taken her car?*' He lapsed into silence, and put a finger to his cheek as if he could still feel that woman's tear on it.

Jon whistled softly. 'Well, that was some wake-up call, wasn't it?' Neither said anything for a minute, then Jon asked, 'Have you had any lunch today, mate?'

'No, I was talking to some kids down at the centre, and we ran over a bit, then I was due to meet you. Doesn't matter, I'll grab something tonight.'

'Why don't I get us both a toastie? I know it's late, but it'll keep us going for a bit.'

Sharpy smiled broadly, showing surprisingly clean, straight teeth. 'Go on, then. Never say no to a toastie, me. Cheese and ham if they do them.'

Jon ordered the sandwiches and more coffee, and returned to the table. 'Okay, so what can you tell me about Oliver Cruise?'

Sharpy bit his lip. 'Bad business him going missing like that. I reckon he's hiding somewhere. I'm pretty sure he hasn't been taken.'

'Can we start at the beginning? How do you know Oliver? Where did you meet him?' asked Jon. 'And do you mind if I just take a few notes?'

'Go ahead. Well, I met him because some wanker of a kid was knocking seven bells out of him. I stepped in and sent the bully boy on his way with a kick up the arse. I took Oliver back to the community centre and cleaned him up. We got talkin' and he came back a few times after that, just for a hot drink and a chat.'

'What's your take on the kid, Sharpy? We've been getting all these conflicting views of him.' Jon paused as a bored young woman appeared with their toasted sandwiches. She plonked them down on the table and Jon returned to questioning Sharpy. 'Before I forget . . . a kid with a limp, older than Oliver. Ever seen him around here?'

'Might 'ave, but I can't be sure, there's a lot of new faces in town these days. More than usual,' he added thoughtfully. 'Now I think about it there was one boy, a teenager, maybe sixteen? Seventeen? I never saw 'im walk far, just a few steps really, but I thought he might have what a cousin of mine had, something called a TB hip. This kid 'ad the same kind of weird, painful way of walking.'

'No chance of finding out what his name is, I suppose?' asked Jon without much hope.

Liberally dousing his toastie with brown sauce, Sharpy said, 'I'll do my best. We've got this woman at the centre who helps out with teas and coffees, and she knows everyone and their granny. If anyone can get me a name, it's her.'

'The thing is, Oliver was seen on the Wey Navigation tow-path with an older boy who had a limp. It's the last sighting we have of him, so it's vital we find that kid.'

'Give me your number, and if I get a name, I'll ring you.'

Jon gave him his card. 'So, tell me more about Oliver.'

'I reckon there's something wrong with him, if truth be told. That's why the other kids pick on him. Then he loses his rag, but he's not as tough as them. He's bright, schoolwork ain't a problem to 'im, 'e could leave most of his schoolmates standing, but . . . I dunno, he just ain't quite right. What do they call it these days? Learning difficulties or something. But that's not him, because he learns stuff dead easy. It's just he's, well, different.'

'I guess that's why his teacher and his parents think he's an ace student, and his peers think he's weird.'

'Bang on, Detective.'

'So what's he hiding from, Sharpy?'

'Best guess, and it's only a guess, mind, is the parents. Anyway, when I find out, you'll be the first to know, DI Leatham.'

'Call me Jon, and I'll be more than grateful for anything you can find out.' Jon took a twenty-pound note from his wallet and offered it to Sharpy.

'Put it away, man! I don't want your money. If I can stop something bad happening to any of these kids, I'll be glad to do so. I don't want paying.'

Jon put the note back. 'I didn't mean to offend you, honestly.'

'I'm not offended.' He gave Jon a narrow gaze. 'I know I look like something the cat dragged in, but I'm not on the breadline. I had big problems as a kid, probably that's why I like helping out at the centre. I left home when I was still young, but unlike some, my parents always made sure I had enough to pay my way.

They've gone now, but they didn't forget me in their will, so save your money for some of the poor buggers around here that really need it.'

Ashamed, Jon told himself not to make assumptions about the people he met. He'd had Sharpy down as little more than a down and out, and he'd been proved wrong, big style.

They finished their food in thoughtful silence. As Jon prepared to leave, Sharpy glanced around and leaned forward. 'Look, I've spent the last couple of years around the town, 'elping out where I can, and I can tell you there's a very strange feeling about the place right now, and it seems to have something to do with the youngsters. Nothing I can put my finger on, but it's definitely there . . . under the surface, like.'

Jon returned his gaze. 'Thank you for the heads up. If you could keep your eyes and ears open, Sharpy, I'd be grateful. You've got my number, ring me any time, and I mean any time, all right?'

Sharpy nodded. 'Thanks for the sarnie, Detective. Next time they're on me.'

CHAPTER FIVE

Callum spent Friday morning at home, wondering if the day would ever end. As the hours dragged on, he tried to keep himself occupied with various jobs for his mother and father, all of which failed to stop his thoughts drifting to Lucy. He kept telling himself their meeting that afternoon wasn't a date. She had asked for his help, that was all. He should simply enjoy her company, and put any plans for a date on hold.

Finally, the long-awaited hour arrived. Lucy met him in the foyer of the school, and, thanking him profusely for his help, hurried him along a maze of corridors to her part of the building.

As they were about to enter the classroom, someone called out to her — a woman, waving to her from the end of the corridor.

'It's my teaching assistant wanting something,' Lucy said. 'Why don't you go in and say hello, I'll just be a couple of minutes.'

When Callum entered the classroom, he was surprised to find two occupants instead of the one boy he had been expecting to see. The boy in question sat at a table with a sketchbook in front of him, working industriously at his drawing. Behind him, looking over his shoulder, was a tall, fair-haired young man in a uniform that Callum didn't recognise. Callum turned to close the door, and when he looked back, the young man was gone.

Callum blinked. No, he wasn't mistaken, there definitely had been someone there . . .

'Hello, I'm Harry. Are you waiting for Miss Reynolds?'

With an effort, Callum pulled himself together. 'Hi, Harry. I'm Callum, I'm a friend of Miss Reynolds's.'

Harry smiled up at him. 'She's nice, isn't she? Are you her boyfriend, then?'

'Oh, well, I, er, no, we're just friends.'

Harry frowned. 'That's a shame. I think you'd suit her rather well.'

He's very well-spoken, thought Callum. This boy would never be raucous.

'You're different,' said Harry.

Callum raised his eyebrows and gave the boy a grin. 'Am I? How do you mean?'

'You know,' said Harry patiently. 'You *know* you're different.'

Before he could reply, Lucy came hurrying in. 'Sorry, guys! Amelie wanted to ask about next week's breakfast club. Getting along okay, are you?'

'Fine, er, Harry's just giving me some tips on choosing girlfriends.'

'Typical!' Lucy said with a laugh, and turned to Harry. 'Amelie said your mum phoned. Apparently, she's been held up for another fifteen minutes, but don't worry, Callum and I will wait with you.'

'I'm not worried,' said Harry. 'I want to finish my drawing.'

Callum glanced at the sketch, and swallowed a gasp. 'What, er . . . what is that, Harry?'

'It's the cockpit of a Lancaster — the flight engineer's controls and instruments,' Harry said, not quite rolling his eyes.

Callum stared at the drawing in disbelief. Indeed, it was perfectly clear. There was the panel of dials, switches, levers, buttons and gauges, rendered in precise detail. Callum flashed a quick glance at Lucy, who gave him an *I told you so* look.

To Callum's untrained eye, this was the work of an engineer. Okay, there was a slightly unprofessional finish to it, but it was very intricate, and Harry was five years old! Callum knew little about World War Two aircraft, but he had no doubt that if he checked it out, those features would be technically correct.

He cleared his throat. 'Wow! That's pretty amazing. What's that lever there, Harry?' He pointed to a lever that protruded from just below the cockpit panel.

'The throttle lever,' said Harry.

'How do you know all this?' Callum asked, struggling to take it all in.

Harry shrugged. 'I just do. I know everything about the Avro Lancaster bomber.' Then a strange look passed over the boy's face, and he said, his voice low, 'I ought to. I flew enough missions, didn't I?'

Callum saw again the tall young man he had seen when he entered, and he realised that the uniform he had been wearing was that of RAF Bomber Command, from World War Two. Callum had watched enough old war films to be able to recognise it. A shiver ran down his spine. The child had spoken in the voice of an adult.

'Miss Reynolds, do you think I could have a drink?' Harry asked, just as any five-year-old boy would do. 'Just in case Mummy is as late as she was yesterday.'

Lucy smiled at him. 'Of course. Let's go down to the kitchen and I'll get drinks for us all. Mummy will know where to find us if we're not here. I'm guessing you'd like a biscuit too?'

As they made their way downstairs, Harry looked up at Callum with a mischievous grin, and whispered, 'She's a pushover when it comes to biscuits. Go for the chocolate ones.'

The ensuing twenty minutes left Callum's head feeling like it had been through a long cycle in a tumble dryer. Ninety per cent of the time, Harry was simply a great little boy — cheeky and funny, and he clearly adored Lucy. As she had said, he was clean and tidy, and in no way withdrawn, but concealed beneath the playful demeanour Callum saw loneliness, melancholy. While Lucy told him about some of the other things Harry was interested in, Callum watched for the figure to reappear.

But the young man in an RAF uniform failed to materialise. Instead, Harry's mother arrived — half an hour late, and more than a little distraught — amid a storm of apologies. The carer hadn't turned up and she'd had to call on a neighbour, and then the car wouldn't start. Like a tornado, she caught little Harry up, whirled him along the corridor and was gone.

'Oh my!' breathed Callum. 'Is she always like that?'

Lucy sighed. 'More often than not.'

'Poor little devil. It makes you wonder about the effect it's having on him, doesn't it? I see what you mean about wanting an outsider's opinion on him.'

'I wish you could have spent more time with him,' Lucy said. 'Come back to my classroom. I have something to show you.'

When they went in, Callum saw that Harry's drawing pad still sat on the table. 'Ah, shame. He didn't take his picture home.'

'He never does. That's what I want to show you. Look.' Lucy went to a cabinet and opened a long, shallow drawer from which she took two sketch books, and a few separate sheets of paper. 'These are Harry's. Most were done while he and I waited for his mother after school.'

Callum flipped through them. Pictures of planes predominated, all from the late thirties to the forties — the war years. He saw Hurricanes, Spitfires, Dakotas, Wellingtons, but mainly Lancasters. Some were simple sketches of the whole plane, some showed parts, like propellers or landing gear, in detail. Some showed the surrounding structures or buildings, such as control towers and hangars. *How . . . ? Why these . . .* Callum gazed at the drawings, his mind flooded with questions he was having trouble sorting out. Eventually, he said, 'Have you shown these to anyone else?'

'The deputy head. I would have liked to show them to his mother, but he said he didn't want her to see them. He got quite upset. He said she wasn't interested anyway, and that she was always telling him off for scribbling instead of going to play outside.'

'What did your deputy head say? I mean these are something else, aren't they? They have a kind of childish quality, but hell, I couldn't do all that in a month of Sundays, and certainly not without something to copy from.'

'Mrs White, the deputy, thinks he has enormous talent, and has the potential to be a great artist, but he's too young to be pushed into anything. The school advocates non-competitive games — you know, activities that encourage teamwork in which there are no winners or losers, so she's rather left him to me.' Lucy pulled a face. 'In her defence, she's never heard him actually talk about those planes.'

'Like when he said he'd flown missions,' Callum said.

'I'm glad you heard that. It was only a few words, but at least you heard something.'

'What other things has he said?' asked Callum urgently.

'Weird stuff. He speaks as if he's a pilot — I mean, in the present tense. Things like . . . *I'm flying back home but the flak is a nightmare tonight. We'll be lucky to see Blighty again.'* She shivered. 'And his voice. It is him, but at the same time it isn't. Do you understand what I'm trying to say?'

Callum understood only too well. 'Do you ever get the feeling he's talking to someone else? Not you, but someone with him?'

She shook her head. 'No, it's more like he's talking to himself. As if he's reliving a memory. I wonder if that's it. It sounds weird, but somehow he's inherited someone else's memory, that of a World War Two fighter pilot. It's the only thing that makes sense to me. How would a child possibly know all this?' She jabbed a finger at the drawing of the instrument panel.

He wouldn't. Callum knew there was a lot more to little Harry than Lucy could even guess at. And who was the airman she couldn't see, but he, Callum, could? He pushed these thoughts aside. It was too early for all that, Lucy would probably freak out. 'I know little about genetic memory, other than that it's a psychological theory that is still being researched.'

'While I've been working with little ones, they've often come out with things that give you goose bumps. It's almost as if some of them are open to things that are way beyond normal perception. They lose it as they get older, but . . . Oh, Callum, I need help with Harry. He *is* different, and I don't know what to do about it.'

'That's what he said about me,' whispered Callum, 'that I'm different. Yes, I'll help you, Lucy. I might not know much myself, but at least I have people around me with a lot more knowledge than I'll ever have. I'll do all I can.'

With a sigh of relief, Lucy turned and gave him a hug. 'Thank you, thank you so much.'

Callum felt as if a firework had just gone off inside him. For a few moments he was unable to speak. When at last he found his voice again, he said, 'Suppose we go and get something to eat somewhere and talk about where we go from here?' He paused. 'In fact, I've got a better idea. Let's drop your car off at your place, and I'll drive us to the C-M Centre. We'll have supper in the new café they've just opened. I can promise you good home-cooked food.'

Lucy smiled. 'I've got a stack of paperwork to do, but as long as we're not too late, I can do it when I get back. It sounds like a great idea, let's go.'

An hour later, they were back at the clinic browsing the new evening menu. Callum quietly told himself that even though it wasn't quite the romantic evening he had envisaged, they were at least spending time together.

'I'll have the scampi, with chips and peas,' said Lucy.

Suddenly hungry, Callum said he would try the chef's home-made pie.

When the waitress had taken their order, Lucy said, 'I'm so relieved that you've seen Harry. Now I know I'm not getting it out of perspective.'

'Far from it,' said Callum. 'I can understand how worried you must have been. He's very fond of you, isn't he?'

'That's another problem, Callum. The poor little kid plays second fiddle to his sick brother all the time, he's starved of genuine love and attention. Please don't think I'm criticising his mother, poor woman, she's at her wits' end trying to cope, but Harry is suffering. I love the little lad, but he is my pupil, and I daren't let him get too attached to me. I'm his teacher, not a surrogate mother.'

'Between a rock and a hard place, as they say,' Callum added. 'Trying to maintain a balance must be a nightmare.'

'You have no idea!' She shook her head. 'It breaks my heart. You saw how she hustled him out of the school, and frankly, I wouldn't be surprised if she had an accident one day because she was too stressed to concentrate properly on her driving.' Lucy looked hopelessly at him. 'I'd never forgive myself if anything were to happen to Harry, but I have absolutely no idea what to do without going against the Teachers' Standards.'

'I'm guessing that's a law regulating professional practice and conduct,' Callum said.

'That, and the Teachers' Code of Conduct. But the part that weighs most heavily on me is where it says I must, quote, "forge positive professional relationships, and work with parents in the best interests of their pupils."'

'Something you'd normally do as a matter of course, but in Harry's case it's not so simple, is it?' Callum said. 'Sounds like it's all about not crossing boundaries. You're trying to be a professional teacher, while also being a caring individual who can see a particular situation more clearly than anyone else involved — including the parents.'

'In their defence, I think they do see it, but they've nothing left to give, which doesn't make them feel good about themselves.'

'And then they get angry, and Harry bears the brunt of it,' said Callum. 'I don't mean physically, but he must feel so rejected.'

'It's almost worse that he's so intelligent and so talented. And I don't care what the school's policy is — in his case, he should be encouraged and praised for things like his artwork. It seems so unfair.'

'I do understand the belief that teamwork and communication is more important than competition, and for some kids I'm sure that relieving them of the pressure of striving to be a winner must be a godsend, but don't you also need to give credit where credit's due?' Callum felt a bit out of his depth. He'd always believed that humans were naturally competitive animals, be it in sport, academic achievement, in one's job, and even in finding a partner. He knew plenty of men who were driven to succeed, but on the other hand he had been part of a team — Médecins Sans Frontières — whose every member played an equally important part.

Their food arrived and they ate in silence for a while, both deep in thought.

'Regarding Harry,' Callum began. 'I think you have two separate issues to deal with. His domestic situation is one, and the fact that he's "special" is another. I'm not in any position to advise you on the first, but on the second, well, that's different. We just need to work out a way for me to talk to him in more depth, and then I can take my observations to one of my colleagues here at the centre. I'd also like to arrange for either Ellie McEwan or Professor Michael Seale to take a look at Harry's aura. How would you feel about that?'

'I'd welcome it.' Lucy dipped a piece of scampi into her tartare sauce. 'At this point, I'd welcome *any* help.'

They continued eating for a while. Then Lucy said, 'To tell you the truth, I've been considering handing in my notice at the school. I'm not boasting, but I'm quite well thought of, and with my qualifications I wouldn't have any trouble finding another job, even as a supply teacher. The thing is, I know that Dawn Davison and her husband Bryan, are considering getting a nanny for Harry, and I thought . . .' She stared at her plate. 'Well, you probably know what I'm thinking.'

'That no one is better qualified to look after him than you.'

'And if they wanted, I could be his private tutor. Naturally, I haven't said anything to Dawn yet, but she has occasionally suggested that a nanny might be the answer. It would take some of the pressure off them.'

'Hmm. That's a big step,' said Callum.

'But one I'm prepared to take,' she said at once. 'For Harry's sake.'

Her words set warning bells ringing in Callum's head. For a moment he wondered if there was more going on here than he was seeing. Could Lucy be obsessed with little Harry? He knew so little about her. What if there was an agenda here that he wasn't aware of? He'd heard about women inveigling themselves into people's homes and then stealing a child. *Oh come on,* he told himself. *This is ridiculous!*

All at once, he smelled flowers. Not just any flowers, but the heady perfume of lilacs. He looked around, but there was no fleeting glimpse of Vera. Instead, he was suffused with a peaceful, mellow sensation, an almost tangible warmth. All his anxiety faded, and he knew that he was being told not to doubt Lucy. There was nothing malign about her, nothing at all.

Thank you, he said silently, and turned again to Lucy. 'What about if we see what we can discover about his very strange abilities before you take such a drastic step? Just a few days. We'll try and get a grip on why Harry is the way he is, and if we fail, or we don't like what we find out, then we can think again. If you agree, we need to come up with a way for me to get to spend time with the boy.' He frowned. 'Which won't be easy, people might misconstrue it. I don't have to tell you how careful schools and parents have to be with their kids these days.'

After some thought, Lucy finally agreed to his suggestion, but she remained adamant about handing in her notice if it came to it.

'In that case,' Callum said, 'I think that if she's agreeable, it would be quite easy for Miss McEwan to get to see Harry. I could come and meet you again, and she could come with me. It doesn't take her long to evaluate an aura, she sees them instantly, like a light coming on. She said that in a healthy person, it takes the form of beautiful colours radiating from the body in pulsating layers, as if they are surrounded by a living rainbow.'

'Amazing. I wish I could see that,' said Lucy.

'Her gift of auric sight came after she sustained a head injury in an accident. She said that if you don't learn to control it, it can literally drive you insane. Thank God, Ellie managed to make it work for her, but others have . . . well, they've been driven to suicide.'

'God. And there was I thinking it was all just pretty lights.'

'Anyway, that's the easy part. How I can get to spend time with him is another question,' Callum said.

Before she could respond, her phone started ringing in her handbag. Seeing who the caller was she apologised and said she'd better answer.

As she turned aside to speak, Callum noticed her phone, and was somewhat surprised that she could afford the latest Nokia on a teacher's wage. Maybe she had well-off parents, or had got it on a decent contract . . . His mind on mobiles, he heard her say, 'Well, of course, Dawn. It's no trouble at all. In fact, if you don't mind my friend Callum coming with us, we could take Harry for a kid's meal before we bring him home? Yes? Perfect. And I hope your appointment with little Jordan goes okay. I'll be thinking of you.'

She ended the call, and looked at Callum with a disbelieving grin. 'The angels must be looking out for us! That was Dawn Davison, and she's in a bit of a state. Her younger son needs some treatment and the specialist wants him at the hospital all day tomorrow. Bryan is working away for a few days and she needs to be with Jordan. I'm going to collect Harry in the morning and take him home with me, then look after him until around seven in the evening. *And* she has no problem with you being with us. Just between us, I think she'd have said yes if I'd told her I was bringing Vlad the Impaler! Please, please, if you have to work tomorrow, try to get away from work early, then we'll have Harry to ourselves.'

Callum didn't hesitate. 'If I explain the circumstances to the Professor and Ellie, I'm certain they'll understand. I'll talk to them as soon as I get in tomorrow, and I'll ring you. That's great, Lucy! If all is well at the C-M, I'll get to your place in the early afternoon, and we can do some fun stuff with Harry. In the meantime, I'll have a chat with Ellie and a couple of the other professionals, so I won't waste a minute of the time we have with that extraordinary boy.' He grinned broadly at her. 'Now, how about pudding?'

* * *

As it so happened, Ellie and Michael were also talking about a child, and they were equally as concerned, even though Christopher's two homes were stable — or so it appeared. Marie and Dr Littlewood's was without question a loving household, and from what Christopher had said, his mother Della was much more settled, and her new partner, Erik, was proving to be a strong but unassuming role model. What worried Ellie and Michael was something less tangible.

Ellie sipped at the espresso coffee that Michael had made for her, and looked around his apartment. The walls were lined with shelves bursting with books on every subject under the sun. The furniture was comfortable, and although not worn or outdated, fitted into the room as if it had been made for it. She was pleased that he was happy living here at the Cavendish-Meyer; the apartment was self-contained, and even had its own walled garden, so he didn't feel that he was 'living over the shop'. It had been designed by the previous owner of the house, a wealthy American businessman, to accommodate guests. Considerably more luxurious than the usual granny flat tacked on as an afterthought, it comprised a large lounge, an open-plan kitchen/breakfast room, a dining room, two spacious bedrooms, both en suite, and even a small conservatory. It suited Michael admirably, and of course, he was always very welcome at Snug Cottage if he should need a break.

Ellie was procrastinating. Michael had asked her a question a few minutes ago, and here she was appraising his living arrangements! She gathered her thoughts. 'Yes, I do think we should arrange for Jason to see Christopher, and I'm sure Daniel would be happy for him to come here, since you and Jason are helping him with his writing. That said, I suggest we keep quiet regarding exactly what his story is about, as well as any reservations we might have about the kind of novel his imaginary friend seems to be demanding that he write.'

Michael met her gaze. 'I completely agree. I'm almost dreading what the little lad is going to come out with next. I ask you, *When the shadows gather.* What on earth is that all about?'

'Whatever it is, when you do find out, make sure you tell me straightaway. I'll have no more tiptoeing around my sensibilities, Michael Seale! One wobble does not turn me into a quivering jelly.'

Michael apologised. 'It won't happen again. Actually, I was wondering if you'd like to be present when Jason comes to talk to him. Christopher knows you better than either of us, so he might like you to be there.'

Ellie considered this, and although she dearly wanted to say yes, she declined. 'I think young Christopher looks up to you as a learned mentor, and perhaps you should keep it as a "man" thing, if you know what I mean. I think he might find it easier to speak if "Auntie" Ellie weren't around, don't you?'

'Possibly,' said Michael. 'You could always join us afterwards, and we could all go to that place the kids and police officers are so fond of. What's it called? Little Chief or something?'

Ellie laughed. 'Little Chef. Kids and coppers aren't the only fans of fast food, Michael. I'm a bit of a foodie myself, as you know, but there are days when all I crave is one of their all-day breakfasts.'

'Philistine,' muttered Michael. 'You're in serious danger of losing your title of Master Chef and be demoted to Little Chef.'

'I'll survive,' she said. 'Seriously, Michael, while you are with him, please do your best to find out about this imaginary friend of his. For some reason it's still bothering me, even though I know they are generally harmless, and sometimes really helpful to stressed kids.'

'I'll do all I can, I promise. Now, I'm not throwing you out, but it's time you returned to your lovely dogs, and I must go and find Jason. He said he's got some early evening appointments tonight, so I'll try and catch him before he leaves. How long is Christopher staying this time?'

'At least another week, so I'd say we should get this arranged as soon as possible.' Ellie drained her cup.

'Absolutely. Jason's very flexible, so I'll see how quickly he can see the boy. Meanwhile, will you check it out with Daniel?' Michael asked.

She stood up. 'As soon as I get home, I'll call in to say hello to Marie. I can mention it while I'm there, and keep it casual. I'll ring you later, okay?'

Michael gave her a hug. 'I'll be here. Oh, and tomorrow we should tackle Callum, don't you think?'

'I agree. I'll get in around eight, and we'll talk to Callum as soon as he arrives, then if all is well, I'll get off home again. Alice will be back later in the morning and I want to be there when she returns.'

'Excellent.' Michael held the door open for her. 'Make sure that you get away as soon as you can so you can have some quality time with Alice. Give her my love, won't you? And, Ellie, try to enjoy at least some time off over the weekend and recharge a bit. I get the feeling that things are building up to a new challenge, and we need to be prepared.'

'That's why I am going to spend some time in the summer house this evening.' She told him about the wind chimes and the misty amethyst glow that had surrounded them. 'Vera is definitely with us, Michael, which I think confirms our suspicions, don't you?'

Michael sighed. 'It certainly does. So, it looks like it's time to gird up our loins once again, my young friend. And I'll most definitely have that early night I was promising myself.'

CHAPTER SIX

By seven thirty on Saturday morning, Ellie was already at work, feeling surprisingly refreshed and ready to take on whatever the day threw at her. Daniel had been delighted that both Michael and his colleague were taking an interest in his son. As for Christopher, he was thrilled at the prospect of seeing the place where Auntie Ellie and Michael worked, even more so when he heard that a burger and chips were on the cards. All was set for either Sunday or Monday morning, depending on Jason, which gave Ellie the rest of Saturday and at least part of Sunday to be with Alice, as long as her workaholic partner didn't want to go into the centre and check how things had gone in her absence.

Ellie had also managed to get over an hour out in the summer house, which she kept heated throughout the winter. At peace after her meditation, she took time to relax and listen to some of Carole's calming music, and that night slept better than she had in weeks.

As eight o'clock approached, she checked her diary for the following week, making sure that she had some slots free every day for any contingencies that might arise. Then she went to find Michael.

Coming out of her room, she saw Callum hurrying towards her.

'Ah, just the person I wanted to see! Morning, Callum. Have you seen Michael yet?'

'No, Miss McEwan, I came straight here. Er . . . I have a big favour to ask.'

Ellie couldn't decide whether he looked excited, or anxious. Both?

'The thing is — well, it's a bit of a long story. Do you have a spare few minutes? I'd like to speak to Michael too, if we can find him.'

Ellie slipped an arm through his. 'As it so happens, we wanted to talk to you, so come on, then, let's go and hunt down the professor.'

They found Michael directing two new patients towards the hydrotherapy department. His eyes lit up when he saw she had Callum in tow. 'Perfect timing! Why don't we go and find a quiet spot in the Orangery.'

Plunging into the tropical shade of the Orangery, Ellie felt her spine tingle. It wasn't fear, she sensed no menace, it was something she couldn't describe. Perhaps there were no words for it. The expression 'something in the air' seemed too banal for what she was feeling, but how else to say that the air itself was charged, almost humming with significance, hidden meaning.

Since neither of her companions seemed to be aware of it, she decided to keep it to herself for the time being.

Among the palms and broad-leafed ferns they found three cane chairs, and settled down to talk. Whatever it was she had been experiencing disappeared, or perhaps evaporated, and Ellie turned to Callum. 'Do you want to go first?'

Callum told them about meeting Lucy, and her 'special' pupil.

As he spoke, she and Michael exchanged glances. Could this be another unusual child? Two at the same time? How likely was that, and what did it mean?

'So I have two favours to ask of you. First, do you think I could leave early tomorrow, so I can spend some time with the lad and get to know him? And do you think you might look at the boy's aura? I know there is something very, very unusual about him, and it'd be easy to start cooking up all sorts of wild theories. Nevertheless, I am absolutely certain that this little child is very important.' He bit his lip, thinking. 'I don't think Harry is aware of that unearthly airman that sometimes appears at his side. As you both know, I've been seeing the souls of the departed since I was a child, but, shit, the way it was watching that boy really gave me the creeps.'

This was a lot more consequential than Christopher and his proposed novel, and prompted Ellie to question him more closely.

'Were the pictures he drew very advanced for his age?'

'Miss McEwan, Harry is *five*, and these drawings could have been made by an engineer! And the pictures of the planes themselves were awesome. They had the odd childlike touch, but that only served to give the impression that two people had drawn it — an artist and a child.'

'I've seen the kind of thing five-year-olds generally produce,' said Ellie. 'Sticklike figures representing a family, or a house, mostly a square front with two windows, a door and a chimney. Often they are little more than scribble. Even gifted children tend to choose these subjects. No matter how much promise they show, they do not produce work like you describe, Callum.'

'I know,' breathed Callum. 'But I stood there and watched him. Believe me, I've never seen anything like that.'

'I think he's channelling,' said Michael. 'In fact, I'm certain of it.'

Ellie had heard Carole speak of channelling, in which someone's body is taken over by a spirit for the purpose of communication, or for imparting wisdom or knowledge. Back in the 1970s and eighties there were hundreds of books in the New Age section of bookstores that were supposedly written by people who'd been channelled, but such stories had since gone out of fashion. Carole hadn't given these stories much credence, but she did believe that information from the spirit world could be transmitted through a medium.

'And you think that little Harry is innocently channelling that spirit airman. Hence all this advanced knowledge about planes,' Ellie said.

'Putting the two phenomena together — the apparition of the airman and Harry's drawings, what else can we deduce?' Michael said.

'But why?'

Michael spread his hands. 'I've no idea. But we need to find out, don't we?'

Before she could answer, Ellie again became conscious of the strangely charged atmosphere, and she shivered involuntarily. 'Of course. Take whatever time you need, Callum, but before you go, I suggest you have a word with Jason Adamson. Tell him what you've told us. He can tell you what to watch out for, and the kind of questions you should ask. Jason spends more time working with children than we do, and is a qualified child psychologist as well as a counsellor. He might not have come across this particular phenomenon before, but he understands the way children think.'

'I will, and will you look at Harry's aura, Miss McEwan?'

'Just tell me where and when, and I'll be there.'

'Our best opportunity will be this afternoon. What if I ring you when we decide where we are going to take Harry, and you can join us. Other than that, it would be after school one day next week. He's always the last to leave, so it wouldn't be a problem.'

Ellie agreed, then she suddenly remembered Alice. No way could she miss her coming home after all those talks in London.

Over the past couple of years they had made a concerted effort to work on their relationship, and endeavoured, whenever possible, not to allow their jobs to take precedence over that. Compromise had not been easy with two demanding careers, and it was clear that with Alice's rising status in the medical world, she now had more demands on her than Ellie. But even that became a double-edged sword, as Ellie hated to waste the decreasing amount of time that she did have with Alice.

'Sorry, Callum. I've just remembered that I have to get away after we've finished here.'

Michael cleared his throat. 'Excuse me, but I can read auras too, you know. I'd be very happy to meet little Harry.'

She smiled at him gratefully. 'Perfect! Thank you, Michael.'

'Now we've settled that, I think we need to tell Callum about our own little dilemma, don't you?' Michael peered at her over the wire frame of his spectacles.

They began by telling him about the warning signs they had observed of late that some new development, possibly misfortunate, seemed to be hovering just below the horizon. They then told him about Christopher.

Callum looked amazed. 'Another little boy showing an aptitude way beyond his years? Wow!'

'He's nothing like Harry,' said Michael, 'but even so, if you'd heard him utter those words, it would have made your blood run cold.'

'Exactly the same as the way Harry's voice changed when he spoke of flying missions. I wonder . . . Have you considered that his imaginary friend could actually be a spirit guide? I know nothing about it, but maybe this book is being channelled through Christopher.'

This was a possibility Ellie hadn't considered, but she wondered if he could be right.

Michael, on the other hand, agreed immediately. 'The moment I heard about your little boy and the airman, I had the same thought. It seems I really do need to spend more time with our young author and his "friend".'

'Hey! What if I tag along too?' exclaimed Callum. 'It seems I'm fairly good at spotting dead airmen. Maybe I can do the same with literary spirits.'

'That's a very good idea!' Michael beamed. 'What say you, Ellie?'

'Absolutely. After all, we can both see auras and spectral lights, but spirits do not appear to us — except for our two lovely old friends and their dogs, that is. So I say yes.' She turned to Callum. 'Christopher is spending part of either Sunday or Monday here with us at the C-M. The intention is for him to meet Jason, so if you are free, you could meet him then.'

Callum nodded furiously. 'I certainly will.' He hesitated. 'I, er . . . You know you said you thought something was about to happen. Well, I've had the same feeling for some time now, and it's making me uneasy. Lately, I've been seeing Orlando practically every day, Vera and Carole too.'

'Well, we can't all be wrong,' said Michael. 'It means we need to be vigilant, and we should share even the slightest concern we might have. Agreed?'

'Agreed. The Three Musketeers against the world,' said Callum.

'Probably not just this one,' added Michael. 'It seems to me that our own world, and that of the spirit, are once again about to become entwined.'

Ellie and Callum received his words in silence. There was no need for further comment.

* * *

That morning, Lennie Cookson woke earlier than usual. As usual, his stiff joints complained, but for once he ignored them. Dozer had shuffled to the bedroom door and was standing with his nose pressed to it, as if he were desperate to go out. However, this didn't fool Lennie, who knew that despite his advanced age, the dog had the bladder of a camel. If it wasn't a call of nature that was causing his old dog to want to escape the room, there was a good chance it could be something less physical.

Lennie pulled on sufficient clothes to keep himself warm and hobbled to the door. Evidently he was needed somewhere, though he wasn't yet sure where. Experience had taught him to follow his instincts, which were telling him to go out in search of whatever had dragged him from his warm bed so early.

Before he knew it, he was approaching the river, and was soon clattering along the tow-path as fast as his arthritic knees allowed. One of the canal boat owners was up and cleaning duck shit off his deck. 'That old mutt of yours got you out early today, Lennie? I'd slip a sleeping draught in its night-time drink and get a lie-in if I was you!'

Lennie waved and smiled, but hurried on. A few minutes later he saw her, standing just as she had the last time he'd seen her, far too close to the river's edge, staring into its murky depths.

Lennie spotted a bench nearby, and gratefully, he and Dozer sat themselves down to watch. If she had noticed them, she gave no sign. Probably she hadn't seen them at all.

Speaking softly so as not to startle her, he said, 'Something is troubling you, girl. Why don't you sit with me for a while and we can have a talk.'

She turned slowly, blinking. She didn't reply, but at least she had stopped staring into the fast-flowing waters.

He patted the seat beside him. One advantage of his advanced age was that he posed no threat to a young woman alone. 'I always think it's easier to talk to a stranger. Old Dozer and me ain't going nowhere . . . and we're good listeners.'

Slowly, like a sleepwalker, she approached the bench and sat down.

'I'm Lennie, and this is my best friend. We're very good at keeping secrets, Dozer and me.'

Speaking in a hoarse whisper, she said, 'I've tried. Heaven knows, I've tried, but I can't put my life back together. It's beyond repair.'

'Very few things are truly beyond repair, my dear, but if they really are, we need to let them go, and find something better. Who knows, you might be able to build a new one from the pieces? What I would suggest is that you don't do it alone. We don't always see things exactly as they are, especially if we are tired and worn down, but someone else might be able to look at it differently, and help you put those broken bits back together. Why don't you tell me what's gone wrong in your life?'

'If I do, you'll think I'm a heartless cow, a wicked, wicked mother.'

'Oh, I doubt that,' said Lennie. 'Now, what's your name?'

'Beth,' she replied. 'Beth Saunders.'

'Well then, Beth, why do you think you're such a terrible person?'

She leaned back slightly and pushed her hands into the pockets of her jacket. At least she was wearing one today.

'I've always loved children. But when we got married, my husband and I decided that we'd have to wait until he had finished his examinations and was fully qualified. Then he'd get better money, and once we'd got some savings I could give up work and be a full-time mum.'

'Nothing too wicked so far,' said Lennie gently.

'Well, when the time was right, it didn't happen, and we had to go through all these tests, and go to special fertility clinics. Finally, six years ago, Izzie was born. She was the most beautiful child I've ever seen — and I'm not saying that because she was mine, she just was. Everyone said so. So I thought, well, if this is what having children is like, I want more, lots of them.' She swallowed. 'But once again, it didn't happen. This time it wasn't so bad, because I already had my wonderful little girl.'

She lapsed into silence. Lennie waited patiently. He knew she would tell him everything in due course. After all, that was why he was here.

Beth stared at the ground. The old dog had not moved, as if it too was listening. 'Last year . . . a year ago it is now, she changed. From the bright happy child I loved so much, she turned into . . .'

Her sigh almost broke Lennie's heart. He thought he'd never heard anything so sad.

'Into . . . I don't know what. She's just not my Izzie anymore. You know what? I'm scared — no, I'm *terrified.* Of my own child.'

* * *

Bob Foreman had gone into work early, and now at just before ten, he was starving. Now he understood why Rosie never let him out of the house until he'd had breakfast, but as it was the weekend, he'd let her sleep on, and had slipped out without waking her. They had talked long into the night and were both exhausted, but he finally had his answer for the superintendent. He looked down at the neatly typed letter on his desk in front of him, and scrawled his signature with a flourish. He put the letter in an envelope and sealed it. There. Job done.

Bob stood up and marched out of his office. 'Back in five!' he called out to DS Wendy Brown, who lifted a hand in acknowledgement.

'I'll tell Jon,' she called. 'Right now he's talking to a snout, but he wants a word with you when he gets back.'

He gave her a thumbs up and made his way to the stairs, hoping that Superintendent Sheffield wouldn't be in today. Happy as he was about his decision, he could do without the third degree that would probably follow.

He knocked on the outer door and went in. Eva, the super's secretary, peered at him over her dark-rimmed glasses.

'Ah, Bob! Sorry, but the boss has been called in to a meeting over at Mount Browne Headquarters this morning. Is it urgent?'

'Not at all.' He beamed at her. 'Can I just leave this with you to give to him?' He laid the envelope on her desk.

She gave him a long look. 'So, is this the long-awaited answer to his question?'

'In all its glory,' said Bob, still smiling.

'And?'

He knew Eva well, and liked her a lot, which was probably why he decided to leave her in suspense. So he laughed. 'That's for me to know, and you to find out, Eva, my love! Ta-ta for now.'

Still laughing, he closed the door on a stream of rather unladylike words.

Back downstairs, he decided that he couldn't go another minute without getting himself some food. A coffee and a chocolate bar wasn't going to cut it this morning — and after the letter containing his monumental decision had been signed and delivered, he felt he had earned himself a bacon sandwich. He could have sent someone out for one, but although cold, it was a bright sunny morning and he thought he'd go out and enjoy the winter sun.

As he went out through the front doors, he saw Jon Leatham approaching him across the car park and called out to him, 'Jon! Got time for a proper coffee, and maybe a bacon butty?'

'Sounds perfect,' said the DI. 'And I've got a bit of info for you from the streets.'

'Anything to do with Sharpy, by any chance?' Bob was still trying to come to terms with how wrong he'd got their serial twocker. But then, as Jon had pointed out, no one could have been expected to know about his inexplicable addiction to nicking cars, nor about his sudden change of heart.

'Sort of,' said Jon. 'He gave me a name, and I've been to have a word with a couple of women who work with the same group of volunteers as Sharpy. One of them, nice lady called Kimberly Clack, tells me that the lad with the limp is from out of the area, and is tight-lipped when it comes to talking about himself. Kimberly is fond of these troubled kids and she made a bit of an effort with him, but every time she thinks she's breaking through the hard exterior, he goes back into his shell and disappears for a while. She did hear another boy call him "Mole".'

'Well, that's something, I suppose,' Bob remarked.

'That, and she said she swears he's from Birmingham. I was thinking of asking Audrey Harris if she could confirm that. After all, she did say that he swore at her, so she might have noticed the accent.'

'Follow it up, Jon. That young man is definitely key to something, although I'm not certain what.'

It was only a short walk to the narrow side street and the café that served the best bacon butties in town. Largely a 'grab-it-and-go', it did have a few tables. Still in celebratory mood, Bob suggested they sit down to eat. He was tempted to tell Jon of his decision, knowing he could trust him not to broadcast the news, but he held back. His superintendent should know of it first. Moreover, the letter contained a proviso: he had requested that no action be taken until he had found Oliver Cruise. That way, he wouldn't be bothered by administrative details. A boy was missing, and it was down to him to find the lad, no matter what his own future might hold.

'I'll ring Audrey Harris the minute I get back in,' said Jon. 'Plus, first thing Monday, I thought I might take Wendy and visit Oliver's school again, now I've heard what Sharpy had to say about him. All I had to go on last time were the opinions of his so-called school friends.'

'Good idea,' said Bob. 'I was going to ask you to do that. I've been thinking about his friends, and I know that most kids have someone they talk to, even the supposed loners. Maybe there's a boy or girl who doesn't want it to be known that they're the "weirdo's" mate?'

'Maybe we can find a teacher who might have an idea. They usually know what's going on with their kids.'

With a sizzle and the mouthwatering aroma of bacon, their sandwiches arrived. Bob took a grateful bite and sighed. 'Good as ever!'

After a couple of mouthfuls, they resumed their conversation. 'Just don't ask that pompous little creep we talked to last time,' Bob said. 'Try and find someone with a bit more understanding.'

Jon nodded. 'When I got home last night I spent an hour with an Ordnance Survey map of Surrey. I enjoy walking, and though there's nothing to beat the North York Moors and the North-East coast, there's plenty of amazing walks right here on our doorstep. Anyway, I had a good look at the area around that tow-path where Oliver was last seen. It starts and stops, and there are places where the path leads away from the river for a bit, and then joins it again further along.'

'Uniform have checked every inch of that path, Jon. It was the first place we sent them to after we'd spoken to Mrs Harris. They found nothing to indicate where those two boys might have gone after they ran away.'

'I know, sir, but I take that path all the time. It's where I walk when I can't get away for a proper hike. Would you mind if I took a look for myself?'

'Not at all. We've got precious little else to go on. It's hard to believe, isn't it? Even with all the media coverage, and those calls from members of the public that have either come to nothing or been hoaxes. Not to mention the Navigation Authority, who have had their people out checking the river itself, it's as if Oliver Cruise has run off that tow-path and into oblivion.'

'With a boy called Mole,' added Jon gloomily. 'Who disappears if you ask him anything about himself. Not exactly much to go on, is it?'

Bob felt his earlier determination start to waver. They needed a break. They needed a proper sighting of the boy, and a recent one too, or they might find themselves hunting for a body instead.

CHAPTER SEVEN

Despite the cold seeping into his bones from the damp seat, old Lennie sat quietly in the early morning sunshine and listened as Beth poured out her story, culminating at the river's edge, and with nowhere else to go.

Finally, when the girl seemed to have run out of words, Lennie asked, 'Does your Izzie's behaviour extend to your husband, or is it just directed at you?'

'At me,' she whispered. 'He sometimes sees flashes of it, but mostly it's me who suffers. And—'

'And it's caused a rift between you,' Lennie finished.

Head bowed and tears streaming down her face, Beth said, 'He thinks I need to see a psychiatrist. He says it's all in my head. He says I'm jealous because they're so close.' She pulled a face. 'As if! I *loved* her! I just can't understand what's happened.' She glanced at him. 'Maybe it *is* me. Maybe I am sick.'

Unseen, Dozer shifted his position, moving closer to Beth's legs, then he leaned against her and looked up adoringly.

'No, it's not you,' said Lennie, indicating the dog. 'Dozer knows. And Dozer is never wrong about people. He understands on a level that we can only touch on the surface. If nothing else comes of this morning, my dear, know that it's not you who's to blame. But you do need help, and so does Izzie. You can't see it now, but she's as much a victim as you.'

He closed his eyes for a moment and felt a hint of warmth from the winter sun. All at once, he sensed that they were not alone on that bench. His eyes still closed, he said, 'Can you smell lilacs?'

Beth raised her head. 'Oh yes, I can. I wonder where it's coming from.'

A sense of peace descended on the two of them.

'Go home, Beth. Look after your little girl. Help is on its way. I can't tell you more than that. But you are not alone anymore, so just hold on a little longer, because Izzie needs you more than you know. Watch, and wait.'

Suddenly, Lennie was terribly weary. He had done enough, and he had to get home. His legs were weak, and he got to his feet with some difficulty. Before he left her, he said, 'If you can weather the coming storm, you and your family will have a good life. Be strong, girl, and when help is offered, you take it.'

The man and the dog limped slowly back the way they had come. He hoped he had helped her to go on, because he had no more left to give.

* * *

Michael joined Callum in Jason Adamson's office. Jason's expression upon learning of another child who was displaying very unusual behaviour was a sight to behold, and Michael had a hard time concealing his amusement. Surprise rapidly morphed into interest when he learned how old Harry was, and of the artwork he produced.

'Sounds like another youngster that needs to be seen, doesn't it? I can give you advice, but without a personal assessment, I can't really say what might work with that particular little boy.' Jason leaned back in his chair. 'So far, you've only heard Harry say one sentence that seemed to be . . . how can I put it, not his own?'

'Yes, that's right,' said Callum. 'He spoke of flying missions in a Lancaster bomber. Oh, and his voice was different. It didn't sound like him at all. My friend Lucy, who teaches him, said he often does this, but only when they are alone together. She finds it really disturbing.'

Jason puffed out his cheeks. 'Well, assuming that he doesn't just have a fantastic imagination and is a brilliant mimic, you need to tread very warily.' He glanced across at Michael. 'I'm not in any way belittling Callum's skill with children, but will you be there this afternoon, Prof?'

Michael assured Jason that he would, as he intended reading the boy's aura. 'But I won't interfere. Callum is building a relationship with Harry, and the more confidence he can instil in the lad, the more likely he is to open up about anything that might bother or frighten him.'

At this point Callum gave Jason a swift overview of Harry's rather loveless home life.

'So sad. Another domestic situation that is mentally unhealthy for a little boy of five,' commented Jason thoughtfully. 'I can see that it's not the parents' fault, *per se*, and that if things were different with the disabled child, it would be a happy home, but as it is, Harry is collateral damage.'

'I swear it's not a form of attention-seeking, Jason,' said Callum. 'He's not a needy boy. Lucy fears that being left out in the cold for too long will make him withdrawn and he won't socialise, and then all manner of difficulties and behavioural issues could arise.'

'She's right to worry,' said Jason. 'Schoolteachers are starting to become very aware of the warning signs, especially with the current focus on ADHD.'

'Well, that's something Harry does *not* suffer from,' stated Callum. 'You only have to watch him drawing. One thing I did notice was how lonely he seemed, but that could have been my imagination, knowing his background. On the surface, he's about as well-balanced as a child can be.'

'In that case I suggest you simply work on building a rapport with him, but watch for any change in his behaviour. Above all, if he has one of those episodes where he speaks as if he's someone else, try to ascertain whether he is aware of what he's doing. Do you understand what I mean?' Both Callum and Michael nodded.

'It wasn't a small child,' Michael said, 'but I once tried to help a woman with what we used to call Multiple Personality Disorder, and which I think is now referred to as DID, or Dissociative Identity Disorder, the presence of two or more distinct identities that take control of a person's behaviour.' The memory of what he had witnessed still gave him a shiver. 'Her condition stemmed from a severe traumatic experience, and it was one of the strangest things I've dealt with. She had two personas, and remarkably, they each had completely different skills and abilities. What I struggled to understand was that the two personas had different medical conditions as well.'

Jason nodded. 'Ah yes, that's quite possible, although not every sufferer experiences that. It happens because the mind and body are interconnected. I've heard of alters — that's the two separate personalities — having different vision, different allergies, and separate medical conditions.'

'The reason I've mentioned her,' Michael said, 'is that she was unaware of having switched between one persona and the other. The onlooker would notice small changes in her that preceded a change, but all she experienced was a slight headache, a few memory gaps, and what she described as not feeling quite in control.'

'I hate to tell you this, Michael, but DID can emerge in childhood, possibly from as early as age five.'

'Ah, I didn't know that,' said Michael. 'I'm sure it's not the case with Harry, but perhaps we should keep it in mind. After all, it's a condition that is often caused by stress.'

'And in the case of children, it starts early due to neglect, abuse, or trauma. Okay, Harry is certainly not being abused, but we can't deny that there is neglect, albeit inadvertent. So, yes, you're right. It could explain this phenomenon that you've described.'

Callum appeared less than convinced, but he agreed to keep an open mind.

'I can only wish you luck,' said Jason. 'And please do let me know how it goes. Although I can't see how this could happen as the parents aren't involved, I'm here for him, and if there's any way I can help, just shout, I'll treat him as an urgent case.'

When they were outside, Callum said, 'If I were looking at this from a physician's point of view, I would agree with Jason, but he didn't see that airman. Maybe I should have mentioned it, but I generally keep the fact that I see spirits to myself, in case I start getting labelled a crackpot.'

'Totally understandable, son,' said Michael with a grin. 'I don't approach strangers with a vivid description of the lights that surround them either. When people outside this clinic get a whiff of the paranormal or the inexplicable, we're immediately called eccentric or even a bunch of full-blown nutters!' He patted Callum's arm. 'But, if Jason's suggestion of early onset DID is worrying you, never fear. I have a secret weapon.'

Callum gave him a puzzled glance.

'The woman I told you about left such an indelible mark on me because of her aura. I'd never seen anything like it. As she went from one persona to another, her aura changed too, as if someone had thrown a light switch. I had always believed that as the aura reflects your innermost being, and that in essence she was one woman, it would have remained at least similar, with a signature colour, like Vera's amazing amethyst, or Carole's Aegean blue. It would vary with mood and emotion, of course, but this lady's aura changed completely. She was to all intents and purposes, another person.'

Callum beamed. 'So what you're telling me is if Harry's aura doesn't fluctuate dramatically when he goes into "airman" mode, it's not DID?' He exhaled. 'That's a relief! Hell, Michael, I'd hate that little chap to have such a serious disorder, and it would devastate Lucy.'

'Oh, I'm with you on this. I don't think he has. I'm still firmly of the opinion that your boy is channelling information about the Second World War from that airman. But we shouldn't dismiss DID completely. We just have to hope that Harry has one of these episodes while I'm there, otherwise we won't know for certain.'

'Well, since he did it with me on a first meeting, and Lucy said it happens regularly, maybe he has no control over it.'

'I've spoken to Ellie, and we agree that you should get over to Lucy's place as soon as you can. There's nothing going on here that someone else can't cover for you. It's always quieter at the weekends. You need as much time as can get with him. Call me when you think it's okay, and I'll join you for a while and check out that aura.'

Callum nodded. 'I'd be really grateful. I'll ring Lucy straightaway.'

After Callum hurried off, Michael made his way back to his apartment. He had been looking forward to meeting this remarkable little boy, now he had a slight feeling of trepidation. What if the boy's aura did change? The thought that he might show indications of a dissociative identity disorder was terrifying. Even worse was the situation at his home, where his parents were already at breaking point with their youngest child. Callum had told him in confidence that Lucy was so concerned about Harry that she was prepared to give up her teaching career to look after him. Yes, it was a wonderfully altruistic idea, but she was young, did she really understand what she would be giving up, and taking on? Michael hoped this young woman would be very, very careful before she made such a major life change.

With a few hours to wait until the call from Callum, Michael decided to look over some of his old patient notes, and in particular those of the woman with Dissociative Identity Disorder. Michael made himself a pot of tea, took down the box file containing his records, and searched for the name Lisa Trent.

Reading it again, he recalled his shock at seeing a fairly muted aura, of a murky blueish green, suddenly erupt into a stream of vivid yellows, reds and oranges. There was no similarity whatsoever between the two; the changing colours reflecting one fairly reticent persona giving way to a second and far more assertive one.

Michael replaced the file back on its shelf with a feeling of disquiet. The presence of two unusual children was bad enough, but what if there were more? He remembered Vera saying that Callum was destined for some special purpose, a very important one. It was significant that having become involved with Lucy and her small pupil, Callum was now showing an interest in Christopher too. If the unease that he and Ellie were both feeling was centred on Callum, it was a distinct possibility that the source of their anxiety lay in these children, with him as the connection.

He sat staring into his rapidly cooling tea, nostalgic for all the deep conversations he used to have with his old friend Carole, which often took place when something was worrying either of them. He had been inordinately fond of the cantankerous old mare, and missed her terribly. If only she were sitting opposite him now, sharing the pot of tea. What would she say to him?

'Okay, old girl,' he said to the empty room, 'help me out here. Are we on the right track by focusing on these children?'

He smiled. He could almost hear her voice: *'For heaven's sake, you old fool! Get a grip! It's staring you in the face!'*

Deep in thought, his gaze fell on a notepad which he used for his shopping lists, and on which he had written *pasta, salt* and *Dijon mustard.* He blinked and focused his eyes. Beneath the household items, scrawled right across the pad in large letters, was the name CHRISTOPHER.

Michael stared at it. Was it his handwriting? It didn't look like it. Could he have written it while his thoughts were on Carole? What was it he had imagined her saying to him? *'It's staring you in the face!'* And so it was: CHRISTOPHER.

He thought back to that last awful time, when they had fought for their lives against the forces of darkness, and Vera had come to them insisting that Callum had to be saved. Her words were that he was 'destined for something very important'. As he thought this, he looked down at the notepad and the name written upon it. He pictured little Christopher looking up at him with round eyes, saying that he *had* to learn how to write, because his story was very important.

Michael understood. 'It's the children, isn't it?' he whispered. 'The children. And Callum.'

He closed his eyes. At last he was at peace. He and Ellie were to be called upon for an important task, one that involved Callum and the children.

'Not quite, Michael. There is something else, something you have forgotten.'

This time the words came from outside of his head. He swung round but no one was there.

'Carole! Vera! Tell me. What have I missed?' He looked again at his notepad. Beneath the boy's name were the words:

The book, Michael. Do not forget
the book.

* * *

Alice returned later that morning, exhausted but full of enthusiasm. Her lectures had been so well received that she had been asked to give a further two talks before her departure.

'Ellie, I can't tell you how wonderful it was to find so many more health professionals now interested in the Azimah Syndrome. And not just psychologists either — GPs, consultants, some really eminent neurologists, physicians, and surgeons, they're all beginning to take it seriously as a genuine condition, and not some crackpot theory. They are treating me with respect at last, and not like some maverick outsider. And it's all because of you, darling, and Michael, and your generosity.' She pulled off her jacket and picked up her case. 'I'll take my things upstairs, and then we'll have a proper chat. I've got so much to tell you, and I want to know everything that's happened while I've been away.'

'I'll put the kettle on,' Ellie said. 'I bet you're gasping for a proper cuppa.'

As she made the tea, Ellie thought she probably shouldn't tell Alice about the signs warning of possible trouble ahead. Alice worried enough about her as it was, and understandably so, since those last terrible events that had almost resulted in the deaths of both herself and Michael. The other side of her remarkable ability to see auras and her gift for healing was a faculty for smelling out evil. This darker gift had on more than one occasion led her into a life-threatening situation, while in one case she had led the police to a murderer. Better wait for a while and see what happened, rather than worry Alice unnecessarily.

Having first said a proper hello to the four excited dogs, Alice flopped down into a chair and gratefully accepted a mug of tea. 'Sweetheart, I'm out on my feet, but it's so good to be back after a full-on four days.'

'But productive, by the sound of it,' said Ellie.

'It went better than any of my previous courses of lectures. It helped that the number of cases of the syndrome have been increasing in the past year, and more and more neurologists are beginning to ask why.' Her eyes lit up. 'And another thing — and this is big, Ellie. We've had an offer from one of the largest medical technology companies to produce high-quality versions of Gordon's AZSEE program! Can you imagine it? Big teaching hospitals, and centres of excellence specialising in neurology could all be running our diagnostic system for understanding how the brain injury affects the patient.'

Alice's research technician, Gordon Lamont, who also had the gift of auric sight, had developed a computer program that produced visual simulations of auras. Later versions of AZSEE enabled the user to 'see' what a person with auric sight was seeing, thereby assisting doctors to assess the severity of a patient's visual disturbances, and to what extent their treatment was working. Alice had wisely advised Gordon to patent his brainchild. Now, it sounded as if the big boys wanted a share.

'Have you told Gordon yet?' Ellie asked.

'I rang him as soon as they put it to me. As you can imagine, he was pretty gobsmacked. Now he's getting his head around it, he's well chuffed. It could make life so much more bearable for sufferers of Azimah. As it is, they are struggling to put into words something they themselves cannot describe, let alone understand.'

'Don't I know it,' murmured Ellie, recalling those early days after regaining consciousness to find the world around her ablaze with lights that often blinded her with their intensity. She felt again the dread that she would have to spend the rest of her life like this, that it would never stop. 'If it weren't for Carole, there's a good chance I wouldn't be here now.' Indeed, many people who had suffered similar head injuries took their own lives, unable to bear the cruel, dazzling, never-diminishing light.

'Just think how amazing it would be if our AZSEE became available world-wide! Oh, Ellie, I wish Azimah Siddiq was still here to see how far we've managed to take her original research.'

'She'd be very proud of you, that's for sure,' said Ellie with a smile. 'As am I. I was talking to Nelli Kuiper while you were away, and she said the drugs trials have made remarkable headway in the last few months, and the success rate is rising.'

'That woman is a force of nature, Ellie!' said Alice, shaking her head. 'I'm so glad I finally listened to you and took on more professional help. To be honest, I had no idea Nelli would actually up sticks and move here from Heidelberg, but I'm mighty glad she did. She covers my back when I'm away, and she's moving the research side on in leaps and bounds. So, along with Gordon and our small admin team, we are cooking with gas!'

It gladdened Ellie to see Alice so enthusiastic. She had Carole to thank for that too. Without her, none of this would have happened, Alice would still be working herself into an early grave putting in long hours at the hospital while trying to carry out her research. With a worn-out car and an overdraft of frightening proportions, still she had fought to carry forward Azimah Siddiq's important work on brain chemicals. Nowadays she had her own clinic, a reliable vehicle and sufficient funds to employ staff of her own. Not only that, but now eminent neurologists were seeking her out to ask her opinion. How good was that!

'Talking about Gordon and AZSEE, I've said I'll meet him tomorrow morning at the clinic to show him all the paperwork on the offer that the big company has made. He needs to be totally in agreement over everything, and as they might want to move fast, I need him to see what they are proposing as soon as possible.' Alice threw her an apologetic smile. 'I hate to screw up the weekend any further, but this is a massive chance to help other sufferers of the syndrome.'

'That's fine,' replied Ellie. 'In fact, that works well, as Marie's grandson is due a trip to the clinic to have a chat with one of our practitioners about how he can improve his writing skills. Monday looks pretty busy, but Sunday is much quieter and Jason is free, so if that suits you, we'll kill two birds with one stone?'

Alice nodded and grinned, 'Perfect. Gosh, this is all so exciting! Things are suddenly forging ahead.'

Ellie watched Alice drink her tea. She was getting a distinct impression that there was something else behind this outpouring of enthusiasm, something she was holding back. She turned her attention to Alice's aura, and saw that it radiated an unusual amount of scarlet that burst into little flares of pulsating orange light.

Alice gave her a narrow look. 'I know what you're up to, Ellie McEwan. You've got that look in your eye that means I'm being "read".'

Ellie grinned. 'Guilty as charged. So tell me, Dr Cross. What's the big secret?'

'Well, okay. I was saving this for later because it's just so amazing, but I might as well tell you now.' Alice's eyes were bright with excitement. 'There's a big symposium on neurology taking place at the end of next week . . . in New York, Ellie. And they've invited me to speak!'

'That's amazing! Where in New York?'

'Mount Sinai Hospital! Can you believe it, darling? Me, addressing an assembly in that prestigious hospital! It's beyond my wildest dreams!'

Ellie decided it might be wise not to look at Alice's aura right now, it might just blind her. Instead, she jumped up and hugged her. 'I'm so pleased for you!'

'I haven't told you the best bit yet. For once, I don't have to leave you behind. They want you to come too! Yours was the first case, Ellie, the one that precipitated the whole Azimah discovery, and they want to meet you.'

Before Alice had even finished speaking, Ellie was overcome with a sensation — no, a force — so strong that she almost collapsed. She knew then that she would not, could not, go to New York.

She hid her face in Alice's hair to conceal her shock at this piece of news, stammering words of praise and amazement. Inside, she was seized with panic. How on earth to tell Alice that she could not leave, not now. To leave Michael, Callum and the clinic — it was unthinkable.

Ellie knew she must consider carefully about how to respond, for fear of saying something she might come to regret. She needed to talk to Michael. Maybe he could think of a way to help her.

When Alice's phone rang, Ellie could have wept with relief, grateful for a few minutes to gather herself. She knew how stressed Alice got when her partner became involved in things she didn't understand, and she certainly wouldn't understand Ellie turning down a trip to the Big Apple because of some vague premonition. She would have to come up with a very convincing reason for why she couldn't come, and soon, before Alice started booking flights and making hotel reservations. Meanwhile, she had to get through the weekend without Alice suspecting that anything was wrong. She just hoped that her acting skills were up to it.

As she cleared away the mugs, she remembered that she had booked a table for dinner that evening. Hopefully, that would be a bit of a distraction.

'Babe?'

Alice had ended her phone conversation and was hovering in the kitchen doorway.

'I hope this doesn't mess up any plans, but that was Nelli Kuiper from the clinic. Would it be a real pain if I popped in this afternoon? She's got a bit of a complicated case and wants to discuss it with me. I feel really bad — I've only just got my foot in the door — and what with meeting Gordon tomorrow…'

Wanting to give a loud hurrah, Ellie shrugged casually. 'Oh, that's no problem. In fact, I might just come with you. I wanted a quick word with Michael anyway I've booked a quiet dinner for just the two of us at the Poacher's Inn, but we don't have to be there till seven, so there's plenty of time.' She glanced down at Benji, who'd just given vent to an urgent *woof.* 'Why don't you get unpacked, and I'll take the boys into the orchard for a run?'

'Good idea. I'll do that, and then I'll join you.'

As soon as she heard Alice's door close, Ellie rang Michael. Receiving no answer, she left him a brief message to say that she and Alice would be at the clinic that afternoon, and she needed to speak to him urgently, in private. Then she gathered the dogs and headed out to the orchard.

As the spaniels raced around, chasing birds and sniffing at interesting smells that needed their immediate attention, Ellie tried to calm herself and think rationally. Her concerns were two-fold, and so pressing that for once, the quiet orchard failed to provide her with the usual solace. First, was her fear of the unknown threat that was hanging over her. Second, how she was to turn down her partner's invitation to accompany her to the biggest and most important occasion in her career.

CHAPTER EIGHT

Callum and Lucy had decided to devote the first part of their day with Harry to have fun. They took him to a small farm park where he could meet the animals and use the playground equipment. They then took him for his first ever lunch in a Pizza Hut.

They were now back at Lucy's. Having had a thoroughly good time, little Harry was exhausted so crashed out while Lucy made coffee, and they discussed how to proceed.

'He's been like any normal little boy all morning,' remarked Callum.

Lucy nodded. 'He usually is, as long as you avoid certain subjects. I'm so glad he had a chance to do some of the things he's been missing out on because his parents are so taken up with the other child. This afternoon, though, we need to bring out the "other" Harry, so you can observe him properly. We daren't waste this opportunity, we might not get another.'

'I know, and don't forget that Michael is going to call by, ostensibly to see me about work. I've got to ring him with a time.'

'How about three thirty to four?' suggested Lucy. 'And if you and he need to talk privately with Harry, I can go and prepare the boy's tea.'

'I'd rather you were there too, Lucy. I'd like you to hear what the Prof says about Harry's aura.'

She smiled at him warmly. 'I was hoping you'd say that.'

'After all, the two of us are together in this weird situation, aren't we? We're a team.'

'Yes, yes we are.' Their eyes met, and neither said anything for a moment or two.

'I'm glad you're here with me,' she said. 'I've never said this to anyone before, but being alone with Harry scares me sometimes — I mean, at those times when his voice changes and he suddenly starts talking like a much older person. If I believed in that kind of thing I'd say he was possessed. It's like there's another person there in the room, and they are speaking through Harry. At times I wonder if I'm going mad.'

Callum remembered the spectral airman. Lucy was closer to the truth than she knew. He was tempted to tell her what he had seen, but it didn't feel right somehow, not yet anyway.

'Well, you're not alone now,' said Callum. 'And we've got a whole team of professionals to call on if we need to. We have a problem with his parents being so preoccupied with his brother, but we'll find ways around it — like today.' He glanced at his watch. 'I should ring Michael and let him know what time he can come.'

'Good idea,' said Lucy. 'I'll go and see if Harry is awake. I've brought a Blue Peter Explorer board game we can play while we wait. It's a bit old for Harry, but since it needs two teams, he and I can play you. I chose that particular game because it involves travel, so we might be able to bring up the subject of planes.'

'Excellent,' said Callum. Jason had encouraged him to find out if Harry was aware of the spectral airman. If they started to chat about planes, the man might possibly appear. If so, he could watch Harry for any indications that the boy knew he was there.

'And I found these.' Lucy took down two hardback books from a shelf. 'They were in a charity shop in Guildford. I thought I'd leave them on the table and see if they prompt a response from Harry. What do you think?'

Callum read the titles: *British Fighter Planes of World War Two* and *The Illustrated Encyclopaedia of Aircraft of World War Two.* 'Oh, perfect, Lucy.'

'I'd offer to let him keep them, but he once said that his mother thinks he's not ready for anything beyond *The Very Hungry Caterpillar.* Don't get me wrong, it's a great little book, but she has no idea of her son's capabilities.'

'Has no idea, or doesn't want to know?' said Callum.

Lucy made a face. 'I know she is under a lot of pressure, and my heart goes out to her, but part of me is angry at the way little Harry is pushed aside all the time. You've seen how he was today, Callum, he was almost overwhelmed by the attention he was getting, and we're not even family. I'm sure his mother and father love him really, but they never show him any affection.'

'I'm surprised he's so well-balanced. Most kids would try to get attention by throwing tantrums, even if it means getting yelled at. I've seen some pretty impressive temper tantrums in my time, all because the child concerned perceives a sibling is favoured over them. Harry seems to accept that little Jordan's disabilities mean that he takes precedence, doesn't he?'

'He does,' said Lucy. 'Do you know, one day when his mother was extra late collecting him, he said, "It's all right, Miss Reynolds, I don't mind. I'm the lucky one, aren't I? Jordan can't play, or go to school, or do any of the things I can." And what's more, it didn't sound like something his parents said, but as if he'd worked it out for himself.'

'Nothing about Harry would surprise me,' said Callum. 'But now I'd better let Michael know when he can come. I can hardly wait to hear what he says.' Having said that, Callum was also dreading what might come of it. What if Harry did have a serious problem, like the one Michael had described? What if neglect had given rise to some psychological disturbance? He told himself this was hardly likely to be the case. Hadn't he seen that dead airman watching over the little boy? That was no psychological disturbance, that was a spirit manifesting itself. Callum bit his lip. Maybe he should be more concerned about what it meant, why he was here. Was he a spirit guide, come to protect little Harry, or . . . what?

* * *

Arriving at the clinic, Alice went to the old cricket pavilion to meet Nelli in her consulting room, while Ellie hurried off to find Michael. Not finding him in his office, she decided to try his apartment.

'If you're looking for the Prof, Miss McEwan, I saw him heading for the car park a minute or so ago,' said one of the physios.

Ellie thanked him, swearing under her breath. She had forgotten that he was going to check out that little boy's aura. She raced to the car park, getting there just in time to see his car accelerating towards the gates.

Standing helplessly in the middle of the drive, Ellie let out a loud curse. Then she saw his brake lights go on, followed by the reversing light. He'd seen her! Oh, thank heavens!

'Ellie? What are you doing here? I thought you were spending some quality time with Alice. Nothing's happened, has it?'

'No, nothing's happened. It's just . . . Oh, Michael, I really need your help!'

'Jump in. I'll drive us back to a quiet spot and you can tell me about it. I'm early for my meeting with Harry anyway.'

They parked up in a corner of the staff car park under some trees. Ellie took a breath and explained her dilemma.

Michael said that it was indeed a delicate situation. 'This seems like the right moment to tell you that I've had a . . . well, a message, for want of a better word, from Carole.'

'Carole!' exclaimed Ellie. 'What? How?'

'Oh, you know Carole, bless her. It was a short addition to the shopping list on a pad in my kitchen. She says that this feeling we're getting of an impending crisis revolves around, and I quote, *Callum, the children, and the book.* By which I gather she means Christopher and his proposed novel, which, rather worryingly, is all about children. She stresses that the book is very important.' He gave her an anxious smile. 'So, you're right to insist that you cannot possibly go swanning around the Big Apple in a yellow cab right now, my friend.'

'So what do I do? How do I tell my lovely Alice that she'll be jetting off to the States alone because her partner is being called by the spirit world to aid a couple of possibly dysfunctional kids? I considered saying I'd mislaid my passport, but I keep it with hers, and they were both recently upgraded to machine-readable ones, so I can't even use the excuse that I won't have time to get a visa. I don't even need one.'

Michael narrowed his eyes. 'I think I have an idea. However, strange as it sounds, I'm not going to tell you what it is.' He turned and looked into her eyes. 'Ellie, go and enjoy what time you have with Alice. Make believe you are going to New York, and act delighted at your good fortune. And above all, make sure that Alice is totally assured of how thrilled you are by this amazing development in her career. Be happy, okay?'

Although she wasn't sure, Ellie had an inkling of what Michael was intending. 'And then?'

'I will come and see you both, and please, be shocked at what I ask of you. Okay? I mean, gutted. Act as if you are torn in two by my request. Oddly, I don't think it will take a lot of acting. If Alice reacts as I think she will, she will make the trip, not alone, but with either Nelli, or possibly Gordon, and it will be a resounding success. When she returns, she'll be so full of it that you'll be able to bathe in her reflected glory for weeks! Do you think you can do that?'

Ellie swallowed hard. 'I have to, don't I? Yes, Michael, I can do it.'

She was surprised to feel a wave of relief sweep through her. She now knew she was not imagining her concern that something bad was coming their way, and she knew too that this involved Callum and the two little boys, Christopher and Harry.

'Yes, Michael. We have our direction now. When we've got over this unfortunate hiccup, we'll turn all our effort to where it is needed.'

'Good girl! Now, off you go, and have a lovely time in what's left of the weekend. I'll go and see the boy, and I'll update you as soon as I know something. Do your level best to relax!'

Ellie leaned over and kissed his cheek. 'Thank you, Michael, and don't worry about my acting skills. Now we have a plan of action, it'll be "Eat your heart out, Angelina Jolie!"'

* * *

'Why do they call you Mole?' Oliver asked his new friend.

'Because I'm happiest underground.'

'Like in this place?'

Mole looked around, 'It's all right, I suppose, but you'll see what I mean when we've been collected and taken home. Now that's where I'm really happy. This is only a collection point.'

'Why are we being collected, and who by?' Oliver wished this odd boy would stop being so secretive.

'You'll find out soon enough.'

Seeing Mole squint at him in the torchlight, Oliver thought that the real reason for the nickname was the fact that Mole didn't wear glasses. He was short-sighted. Now he came to think of it, Mole bore a distinct resemblance to the mole in a book Oliver had loved when he was small, called *The Wind in the Willows.*

'Sorry, pal, but all I'm allowed to tell you is that you're one of us, and you've been rescued. We'll be picked up soon, and once we get home to the others, you'll be safe. That's when you'll be told why you're special.'

'Special?' Oliver was puzzled. He knew the other kids at school treated him differently, and he was pretty sure his parents did too — he saw the way other mums and dads treated their children. Most people treated him like a weirdo, and it made him angry. But special? No one had ever told him he was special before.

'We are all special in our own ways, Ollie. Now shut up and wait. You're starting to piss me off.'

'Sorry.'

Oliver sank back against the wall. It was cold in the cellar of the old derelict building. It had clearly once been a small inn or public house, and they had used a chute with a trapdoor to gain access. He guessed it was where they used to deliver beer in barrels, and there were fittings along one wall with pipes and tubes hanging from it. It smelled horrible and it was damp, but Mole had prised open the heavy lid of one of those plastic chests people used to store things like garden furniture cushions, and had removed some thick blankets to wrap themselves in. Oliver shivered. By now, special or not, he was wishing he'd never been talked into running away from home.

* * *

Looking up from his desk, DCI Bob Foreman saw DS Wendy Brown hammering away at her keyboard and wondered how long this one would last. Wendy had a reputation for causing serious damage to any keyboard she got her hands — or in this case fingers — on.

When she spotted him looking at her, she thumped the enter key, and sat back in her chair. 'Everything all right, sir? Only you look a bit perplexed.'

'That's because I am — perplexed, that is.'

'Oliver Cruise, is it, sir?'

'Not exactly, but, oh hell, yes, I suppose it is. The thing is, I can't stop thinking about Ellie McEwan.' He regarded her thoughtfully. 'You're the only person here who'll understand me when I say I woke up in the middle of the night to an overpowering scent of flowers. Lilacs, to be exact.'

Wendy drew in a breath. 'Now that's odd. So did I, sir. The smell was so strong it actually woke me up. I looked at my bedside clock to check that it really was the middle of the night, and the strange thing was, the clock display has the usual green numbers, but this time they were glowing with a bright mauvy, purplish light! It shook me, sir, I can tell you. Then I felt kind of . . . oh, how to explain it? Like I was being given a little nudge. You know, encouraged to do something. After that, all I could think about was Ellie. It bothered me so much that I rang her this morning and I'm calling by on Sunday evening. I'm going over to Snug Cottage when my shift finishes.'

Relieved, Bob smiled at her. Ellie and Wendy had become good friends after that last dreadful case in which so many lives had been threatened. A few feelers from Wendy might go down better than a call out of the blue from him.

'Was there anything in particular you'd like me to ask her, boss?' asked Wendy.

'Now that's a very good point,' said Bob, then he lowered his voice. 'Maybe you could mention that we're concerned about a missing boy. I have no idea if she will be able to help, but as we've both been "nudged", as you put it, it won't do any harm to ask her what she thinks. Be diplomatic about it, Wendy, but put her in the picture, okay?'

Wendy nodded. 'Leave it with me, boss. One thing's for sure, if anyone can explain the meaning of that smell of lilacs and that mauve glow in my room, it'll be Ellie.'

'Let me know what she says, won't you, as soon as you can. You've got my direct number. For some reason I get the feeling that we're going to be seeing quite a bit of the talented Miss McEwan in the next week or so.'

* * *

Harry thoroughly enjoyed the board game. It was a bit too old for him, but Lucy helped him with the answers and allowed him to put the pieces they won into the jigsaw puzzle. The idea was that the first team to complete their world map was the winner. As they played, Callum and Lucy added little snippets of information about the different countries, such as which animals live in Africa, and the like. To begin with, Harry asked the sorts of questions any bright five-year-old would, especially after he learned that Callum had travelled to a number of different countries. Had he ever seen a real lion? How tall was a giraffe? Did hyenas really laugh?

Callum tried not to be too didactic, keeping his answers light, and funny where possible. Then Harry asked him a question that stopped him in his tracks. Harry was holding one of the pieces in his hand, staring at it intently. 'Have you ever been to Germany?'

'Once,' said Callum, 'but not for work. It was a weekend break with friends.'

Still gazing at the piece, Harry said, in a voice that seemed to come from far away, 'I suppose it's rebuilt now. Nothing left of all those night flights, all those devastating raids.'

'Like London, it has regenerated,' said Callum, deliberately using a word that a five-year-old would not understand.

'Even Dresden? After the fire-bombing?'

'Yes, even Dresden. Although . . .' Callum stopped. He had once read the accounts of some of the survivors. It had given him nightmares for weeks.

'I know,' whispered Harry. 'Gomorrah.'

Before Callum could muster his thoughts enough to ask him what he meant, Harry had dropped the jigsaw piece. He smiled up at him. 'Anyway, did you see elephants when you were in Africa? I love elephants, don't you, Miss Reynolds?'

Lucy cleared her throat. 'Oh, yes, especially the baby ones, they're so cute.'

Now Callum could see why Lucy sometimes felt frightened. It was the rapid jump between the different personas that was most unsettling.

They finished the game, and Lucy went to make them all a drink. On her way to the kitchen she paused in the doorway and said casually, 'Show Harry those books I picked up, Callum, I'm sure he'd like to see them.'

With a slightly helpless glance at her, Callum retrieved the books from the shelf and put them down on the table. 'Look, Harry, Miss Reynolds got you these. Pretty cool, aren't they? With your amazing drawings, I should think you'll enjoy these.'

The little boy looked up at him, his eyes round in wonder. 'She got them for me?'

Callum nodded.

'Miss Reynolds is special.' He tilted his head to one side, and looked at Callum. 'Not special like you, but she is all the same. She cares.'

Out of the mouths of babes, thought Callum.

'Can I look at them now, please?'

Callum took them across to the sofa. Harry clambered up and lifted the first book onto his lap. He ran a hand over the cover, and opened it.

Somehow it wasn't a surprise that the book opened on a full-page photo of an Avro Lancaster bomber. It was a surprise to see the boy slide up a little as if to give room for someone to sit down next to him. The airman.

Callum froze, watching the spectral flyer drape an arm casually over Harry's shoulder and gaze with the boy at the image of the great warplane. Callum reminded himself that this was what he had come here to see, and that he must pay careful attention to what was happening. Dare he talk directly to the spirit? Not yet, he told himself. He still wasn't sure if Harry was really aware of the young man's existence. Yes, he'd deliberately moved up to let him sit down, but had he been conscious of doing so? He was fairly sure that Harry was unaware of that ethereal arm on his shoulders.

'Are those your favourite planes?' Callum said quietly.

'Easier to fly than a lot of others, and oh yes, they could withstand a great deal of punishment in the air.'

It was Harry who spoke, but the words belonged to the airman, whose mouth hadn't moved.

It's — his? — eyes still on the picture, he slowly said, 'Average age of death, aircrew, Bomber Command . . . twenty-three.'

Callum shivered, but he kept his eyes on little Harry. Despite having decided not to address the airman directly, he heard himself say, 'And you?'

'Twenty-five. I was one of the lucky ones.'

For the first time, the airman looked up. Their eyes met.

'Why are you here?' whispered Callum, still holding the gaze.

'For the boy.'

Before he could draw breath, before he could muster a response, Callum realised that Harry was alone on the sofa.

'These books are so cool!' Harry said, smiling happily

He has no idea, thought Callum. *Thank God for that. But what did the airman mean by saying he had come for the boy? Is he here to protect him? Or for something more sinister?* Callum desperately wished that Michael had been present for that brief exchange. Perhaps with his ability to see auras, he might have picked up something more from the airman. Callum frowned. He didn't even know if spirits still had auras. He'd never thought to ask. Auras surround all living things, but a spirit has no life force, so . . . Then he thought about Vera and the shimmering amethyst light that accompanied her.

While he was still trying to puzzle this out, Lucy had come back into the room. He only realised when he saw the mug of coffee she was handing him.

'Has he spoken to you?' she asked softly.

Callum nodded. He glanced at Harry, who was absorbed in an aerial photo of a Hawker Hurricane. 'Yes, the airman was—'

'Airman? What airman? What are you talking about, Callum?'

Dammit! Still, he supposed it had to come out sometime. 'I'll tell you later, Lucy, when we're on our own. Right this moment I'm wishing that Michael were here, while our little friend is still immersed in his warplanes.'

CHAPTER NINE

'Cavendish-Meyer Healing Centre, Janet speaking. How can I help you?'

Michael's secretary, Janet Cooper, listened patiently, wondering what, exactly, the caller was complaining about. When she managed to get a word in, she said, 'No, Mrs Saunders, that's perfectly correct. Someone has kindly offered to pay for any treatment you might require. There will be no cost on your part, none at all.'

'Well, there must be some mistake,' said the woman. 'Someone left a message on my Ansafone telling me to ring you to book an appointment, but I know nothing about your healing centre.'

Poor woman, thought Janet. 'Let me explain how we work . . .' She went on to describe the various stages a new client would be taken through from assessment to treatment.

The woman broke in. 'But I'm not ill! I cannot understand why someone thinks I should even visit you, let alone pay my expenses.'

Janet detected something underlying the woman's anger, so she said gently, 'We don't just treat physical illness, Mrs Saunders. We also offer a sympathetic ear. We listen, and if possible offer a solution that can help you move forward.'

Beth Saunders received this in silence. Since she hadn't hung up, Janet went on to suggest she come along and talk to them.

'After all, you won't be paying, so you have nothing to lose by coming over for a cuppa. There's absolutely no obligation on your part, and who knows, it might turn out to be of help.'

'Well, all right,' said Beth Saunders cautiously. Janet arranged an appointment for the following Monday morning at ten thirty. In fact, she had half expected Beth Saunders to phone, and was glad she had. When her anonymous benefactor had called a few days ago to arrange payment, he was adamant that Beth Saunders needed help badly, and he and the person on whose behalf he was calling feared for her safety. Having heard about the Cavendish-Meyer Centre, he and this other person felt sure that the clinic was 'where Beth needed to be'. This odd choice of words hadn't been lost on Janet. Most likely he, or someone close to him, had been treated here and had been favourably impressed. She checked their records for the name on his credit card, but couldn't find it. Obliged to divulge his name for the transaction, he made Janet promise not to give it to Beth. On no account must she be made to feel beholden to him, especially as he was only doing it on behalf of someone else. Janet promised to do as he asked, and would make sure that Michael and Ellie were aware of his rather odd request. None of them were certain that Mrs Saunders would actually turn up for her appointment. Janet hoped to goodness that she would. Something, she knew, was terribly wrong in the life of Mrs Beth Saunders.

* * *

When Michael arrived in Great Bookham, Lucy and Harry were in the garden playing with the next-door neighbour's cat, a large tabby that tended to spend more time with Lucy than its owner.

Callum met Michael at the door and took him to the lounge. 'Before you meet Harry there's a few things I ought to tell you. The thing is, his spirit airman appeared, and I inadvertently engaged with him.' He bit his lip. 'As far as I can tell, Harry is unaware of his presence. Although he cannot see him as I can, I get the feeling that on a subconscious level he knows that someone is with him. I saw him ease up on the sofa to give him room to sit down next to him.'

'Did he acknowledge the spirit in any way?' asked Michael.

'No, not at all. He seemed to move up quite unconsciously. Maybe I read too much into it, and he was just uncomfortable and shifted a bit, I don't know, but it seemed weird at the time.'

'So, tell me what this airman and you said to each other,' Michael said, frowning.

'Well . . . He quoted the average age of death for flight crew in Bomber Command. I asked him for his, and he said, "Twenty-five. I was one of the lucky ones."'

'Was that all he said?'

'No.' Callum looked grave. 'I asked him why he was here, and he said he was "here for the boy". Now I'm terrified of what that might mean. Was he watching over the boy, or had he come for him — in a bad way?'

Michael exhaled. 'I wonder. We won't know until we dig deeper. Do you think we might be able to get your pilot, or whatever he was, to make another appearance?' He gave Callum a wry smile. 'And when he does, you'll have to let me know. The only spirits I have ever had the privilege to see are two old friends and the odd dog.'

'I reckon if we get Harry back onto the subject of aircraft, his ghostly companion could well put in an appearance. If he does, I'll give you a nod, but you'll know in any case, because Harry's voice will alter. Be prepared, it's an unnerving experience to hear a male adult voice coming from the mouth of a five-year-old.' Hearing a door open, Callum looked up. 'Ah, here they are now. Ready for your aura reading?'

One of the greatest privileges of having auric vision is being afforded the sight of the aura of a child. The light is clear and pure, not yet contaminated by the negative energy deriving simply from having lived to adulthood. Today, Michael's eagerness to 'see' Harry bore a hint of apprehension. Would the child's aura change, as had that of his former patient, Lisa Trent?

Callum introduced Lucy, and then Harry. 'Harry is spending the day with Lucy because his mother had to take his brother to hospital.'

Michael beamed at the little boy and held out his hand. 'I'm very pleased to meet you, Mr Harry.'

Looking somewhat overawed, Harry took the hand of this rather portly gentleman towering above him, and whispered a quiet 'Hello.'

'Are you having a nice day out, Harry?' asked Michael. 'Or is Miss Reynolds making you do homework?'

'I'm only five, we don't have homework yet,' said Harry. 'I'm having a lovely time, thank you.' Then, enthusiasm overcoming his initial shyness, he said, 'Would you like to see the books Miss Reynolds got for me? They're awesome. Miss Reynolds is very kind, you know.'

'I'd love to see them,' said Michael.

Callum smiled, evidently relieved not to have to try and find a way to bring the talk around to flying. Young Harry had done it for him.

Michael waited until the little boy had settled himself on the sofa, and allowed his auric sight to open up. Immediately, waves of soft but clear rainbow colours began to radiate from the child. He was literally glowing, revelling in the attention that he was receiving from Lucy and Callum. Michael wondered whether it was the same glorious colour when he was alone at home, his parents busy attending to his needy brother. Would the aura then show the muted shades of a depressed life-light?

Michael sat beside him and took the proffered book. 'Callum says your favourite plane is the Lancaster. You'll never guess what, I rode in one once! We just taxied down the runway, but with all those engines thundering it was quite an experience, I can tell you! There's an aviation heritage museum in Lincolnshire, not far from where an old friend of mine used to live, which has a magnificent old plane called "Just Jane" you can ride in.'

'The Avro Lancaster NX691,' said Harry.

'That's right! She's the most famous heavy bomber of World War Two, so they told me.'

'Wrong,' said Harry.

Michael did not need Callum's nod to tell him that the voice belonged to someone else. Hearing it sent crystals of ice trickling down his spine.

'That bird was built in April 1945 and designed for the RAF's Tiger Force. She was intended to be deployed for operations in the Far East, but Japan surrendered and she never saw service. Instead, she was sold to the French and used for air-sea rescue and maritime patrol, but as you say, we have her back now. You were fortunate to get a ride in her, she's a beauty.'

Trying not to let what was being said distract him, Michael kept all his attention on Harry's aura. Initially, he struggled to comprehend what he was seeing. Above Harry's head, he signalled to Callum to take over the conversation, while he concentrated on the child's life-lights. Harry's aura *did* alter, but not as dramatically as that of the woman with two personas. When the airman spoke, the rainbow colours of Harry's aura became suffused with colours of a darker, stronger shade while remaining intact. Michael knew people who believed that little children lived within the auras of their parents, rather like an umbrella protecting them, until they ventured out and became individuals in their own right. Harry, it seemed, had his own distinctive aura already, but it was overshadowed with that of the spirit airman when he was present.

'I'd love to go on that plane one day!' said a small, enthusiastic voice beside him. 'Do you think I could?'

'I don't see why not, when you are a bit older, and if someone goes with you,' said Michael. The airman had gone. What remained was a lovely regenerated aura that had never given way to another, but had merely absorbed some extra colours for a while. Harry did not suffer with Dissociative Identity Disorder, and Michael was convinced that the boy was channelling from the spirit world.

He straightened up. 'Well, my friends, much as I'm enjoying myself, I really ought to get back to the clinic. I'll just have a quick word with Callum and then I'll be out of your hair. It's been good to meet you properly, Lucy, and you too, young Harry.'

Callum led the way to a small room off the hall that Lucy used as an office. He closed the door, leaned back against it and exhaled loudly.

'Phew! That was intense. It was the most powerful visitation — if that's what you call it — I've ever had! That airman was almost tangible. Before, he's been kind of wispy, sort of wraithlike. Which is what he is, I suppose — a wraith.'

Michael laid his hand on Callum's arm. 'Steady on, son. You see spirits all the time. How come this one has had such an effect on you?'

Callum looked almost embarrassed. 'It's the boy. Yes, I see dead people, but they are not using a child, a little boy like Harry, as a vehicle. I have no idea what this spirit's agenda is, and I don't want to see Harry hurt.'

Michael remembered Callum telling him he worried that Lucy was becoming too attached to her little pupil. Now Callum appeared to be making the same mistake. 'Listen, Callum. We haven't the time now, so I'll be brief. I'll just tell you what I believe is happening with Harry, then tomorrow, you and I need to have a long talk. I want you operating on full power, because . . . well,

Ellie and I think we are about to get embroiled in something rather dark. We don't know what it is yet, but whatever is about to break will call on the three of us to resolve. Which means we have to work in unison if we are to have any chance of success.'

'I won't let you down, but I don't want to let Harry down either. Although I've a feeling he'll have a part to play in this coming storm.' Callum gave him a rueful smile. 'I'd better get my head sorted out, hadn't I? And fast.'

Michael smiled warmly at the young man. 'You wouldn't know how to let us down, even if you wanted to. It's just that we don't yet know what form this . . . crisis will take, so we are in a bit of a quandary. Anyway, tomorrow you and I will have that talk. Ellie is back at work on Monday, so the three of us can try and map out a way forward. In the meantime, you will be relieved to hear that your lad does not suffer from DID. He has a beautiful clear aura. Yes, it changed slightly when the airman was speaking, but not even for an instant did it change in the way that of people with DID does. I firmly believe he's simply channelling thoughts from the spirit world, and as long as we are nearby, nothing will harm him.'

Michael paused, frowning. 'I could be wrong, but I think your airman is there to guide Harry, not to harm him. Furthermore, I have a good idea that before very long you'll be shown something to prove this.' He stopped speaking. What on earth had made him say that? It was as if someone had prompted him. Carole? Vera? He had seen no mists tinted with colour, had scented no flowers; nonetheless, he was certain that what he had said was the truth.

As Michael drove home, he decided he really should document what was about to unfold. He would start a journal, a record of all the incidents that involved them, but also, and especially, the children.

He would also pour himself a large whisky!

* * *

Having given Harry his tea — boiled eggs with soldiers — they drove him home to an emotional welcome. As soon as they arrived on the doorstep, Harry's mother flung her arms wide and embraced Lucy, weeping profusely. From what he could make out amid the fuss, Callum gathered that the other child was getting worse, and would require further stays in the children's hospital while they administered a new treatment. All the talk revolved around Jordan, and it saddened Callum to see Harry staring wistfully after them as they walked back to the car. After they drove away, neither he nor Lucy spoke for a while. Glancing at her, Callum guessed that she was again considering ditching her teaching job in order to look after Harry. This time he felt compelled to agree with her.

Forced by the winding lanes to concentrate on his driving, Callum was nonetheless very conscious of her next to him in the passenger seat. Reaching a long straight stretch between fields, he had just begun to accelerate away when he was overcome with a sudden foreboding. He took his foot off the accelerator and turned to glance at Lucy — and caught his breath.

Next to him, in full bomber command uniform sat, not Lucy, but the airman. The young flyer began to speak, but the voice that rang out in Callum's head was not the one he had heard earlier that afternoon. It was not even male. That deep commanding tone was that of Carole Cavendish-Meyer in one of her no-nonsense frames of mind.

'Callum! Brakes! Now!'

Callum braked hard, and the car slewed to a halt at the side of the road. Before he could even take a breath, a massive piece of farming equipment crashed through the hedge separating the field from the road, emerging inches from the front of his now stationary car.

Lucy put her hands to her mouth and screamed.

A harrow, armed with a row of huge metal discs, had sheared off from the main tractor and continued under its own momentum, coming to rest with its front embedded in the tarmac, feet from the bonnet of Callum's little Escort.

Callum sat back for a moment, breathing fast. Seeing that Lucy was unhurt, he released his safety belt. 'Lucy! I've got to check on the tractor driver. Something must have gone terribly wrong. Are you okay?'

'I'm . . . I'm fine,' she said shakily. 'Yes, you'd better see how he is.'

Callum fought his way through the hedge and raced over to the tractor. The driver didn't show any sign of having seen him, so Callum climbed up to the cab, and immediately understood what had happened. The driver was unconscious and unresponsive. Callum looked back and saw that Lucy was out of the car and heading towards him.

'Phone 999, Lucy! Ambulance! Patient not breathing! Cardiac arrest!'

Somehow — to this day Callum never knew how he did it — he managed to get the driver down from the cab and onto the road, where he immediately began CPR.

Fortunately for the tractor driver, Callum had once been a nurse in a field hospital. He recognised immediately what was wrong, and knew exactly what to do. He was also fit — another piece of good luck, as it took over fifteen minutes for the ambulance to reach them; CPR done properly and sustained for a period of time is tough on the first responder.

Surrounded by police and farm vehicles and a fire appliance, he and Lucy sat in the car watching the blue lights of the ambulance dwindle as it raced away. The flashing lights in the early evening twilight gave the scene a surreal, dreamlike appearance.

'I reckon he'll make it,' Callum said. 'He wasn't out long, and the paramedics got him more or less stable.'

'If he does survive, it's down to you,' said Lucy quietly. 'Not many people could have acted that fast.'

Callum shrugged. 'It's what we do. It becomes automatic after a while. A life was at stake.'

While chaos reigned outside as the rescue services tried to decide how to move the wrecked machinery, it was quiet in the car.

'You knew, didn't you? Knew what was going to happen.'

Callum swallowed. He didn't know how to answer her.

'Callum. You braked *before* that plough thing crashed into the road in front of us.' Her voice caught. 'We could be dead! By rights we should be!'

'I . . . uh. A premonition.' It was all he could think of. It was impossible to explain that a dead woman and a ghostly airman had warned him. 'Yes, that's it, Lucy, a premonition. It happens sometimes, doesn't it?'

When she didn't answer, he wondered how long it would be before he'd have to start telling her the truth.

'Let me get you home,' he said flatly. 'The police don't need me anymore, and you've had one hell of a shock.'

She nodded slowly. 'Yes, I think that's a good idea. And I think we need to talk, don't you? About what's going on.'

He couldn't disagree, things had gone too far for that. Callum manoeuvred the car away from the accident site and accelerated away. As they finally pulled onto the main road, Lucy said, 'By the way, how come your car smells of lilacs?'

'Er, air-freshener?' he suggested, hoping she wouldn't notice that he didn't have one. He would tell her about seeing the airman, and that he sometimes had these 'premonitions', but saying that he spent a lot of time around two dead women and their dead dogs might be a step too far.

CHAPTER TEN

His new friend Mole was a strange one all right, Ollie wasn't sure what to make of him. Ollie's mother would have said he had 'hidden depths', and he certainly had hidden somethings. What he found most difficult to take were the mood swings. One minute Mole was Ollie's best mate, the next he snapped his head off, leaving Ollie wondering if he liked him at all. Perhaps he was just pretending to be his mate in order to lure him away.

Looking around, Ollie wondered if he were in Wonderland — or was it a bad dream. Okay, it was better than that smelly cellar, but nothing in his new surroundings seemed quite as it should be. Was this where he was going to live from now on? In a church?

Right now he was alone, seated in what he supposed must have once been the main part of the chapel that he thought might have been called the nave. But there were no pews, just two very long old sofas with big cushions. A low, glass-topped coffee table stood between them, on which a number of books seemed to have been carelessly thrown, along with some spiral-bound notepads and a scatter of coasters. In the centre was a fruit bowl, filled with apples, pears and bananas. Against a backdrop of stained-glass windows this set-up looked incongruous, and very weird.

There were no electric lights, and the place was lit by lamps and candles. In fact, the only thing left of the church was the altar, still draped in a rich brocade cloth, a gilt wooden cross and two heavy brass candlesticks with altar candles burning in them. The stained-glass window high up behind the altar depicted an angel descending from heaven, beneath him an enchanted landscape with trees, fields and a river. The scene was decorated with flowers rendered in rich glowing colours.

The rest of the building had been partitioned off into rooms, whose doors were all closed. Curious to know what lay behind them, Ollie was tempted to go off and explore, but he had been instructed to sit tight and wait for someone called Gideon. Whenever Gideon's name was pronounced, it was in a tone of hushed reverence, and Ollie imagined him as a sort of modern-day Dumbledore, with a flowing beard and long, sweeping robes. Though come to think of it, if he was as wrong about Gideon as he had been about the person who collected them from the cellar, he would be about as far from Dumbledore as it was possible to get. Having been told by Mole that they usually sent a driver called Ray, Ollie had expected a stern, tough-looking bloke. When a motherly, smiling woman drew up in an estate car and bundled him inside, it dawned on him that the name must be Rae not Ray.

Rae had been kind. She had asked him if he was okay, and did he prefer to be known as Oliver or Ollie. Or perhaps he'd rather choose a new name for himself. Now he was in Gideon's care, he was free to be whoever he liked. 'In Gideon's care.' It made him feel special, as if he were among the chosen ones. Not being able to think of a new name, he said he didn't mind sticking with Ollie, and then summoned the courage to ask her what they were going to do with him. Why should Gideon, whoever he was, be interested in him in particular? All she would say was that everyone who came to Gideon was special. All would be explained when they got home.

So this was 'home'. He shifted about on the sofa, recalling a time when he was much younger, and his aunt used to take him to church. This aunt, now deceased, had been a devout Catholic, and he would accompany her to mass. He didn't get the service at all but he did love the building with its ornate fittings, the gilded statuary and the massive church organ that looked like it had come straight out of a horror movie. His blood ran cold when he learned that there were dead people beneath his feet. In spite of the dead people — or perhaps because of them — he had told his aunt he wanted to live in a church. Now her reply came back to him, and he shivered: 'Be careful what you wish for.'

He was still puzzling over her words when he heard a door creak behind him. He was about to find out.

* * *

Callum and Lucy sat on her sofa nursing mugs of hot chocolate. Lucy had taken some paracetamol, as her neck and shoulders were sore from having been thrown forward against the safety belt.

Lucy looked tired, but she wanted to talk. 'Please, Callum, tell me what's going on.'

He realised that he wasn't being fair keeping her in the dark like this. Lucy was part of it all, and she had a right to know what was going on, especially as little Harry was in her charge.

'It's like this,' he began, 'and I'm sorry if what I say shocks or frightens you, but you deserve to know. You see, it's something . . . well, something beyond normal reasoning.'

'I guessed that,' she said. 'From the moment I heard Harry talking about flying planes over Germany, I knew this wasn't some phase he was going to grow out of. I mean, you only have to look at those pictures . . .' She shook her head. 'I think my deputy head knew it too, but didn't know how to deal with it, so she didn't want to admit that she did.'

'It may well go deeper than you think, Lucy,' said Callum cautiously. 'It's my involvement that might upset you.'

'Oh, Callum, do get on with it!' Lucy turned to him. To his surprise, she was smiling. 'Why do you think I chose you to help me? Something — well, I suspect it was actually some*one* — guided me to you. Now it's up to you to explain why. And don't worry. No matter what you say, I'll believe you. Even if it's little green men sending messages from the planet Zog! All right? Whatever is going on around Harry, we are meant to deal with it together. So, come on, stop beating about the bush.'

So Callum told her. He told her about seeing the dead, about seeing the airman. About Carole and Vera, and even about Orlando. He told her about Rwanda and Bosnia, and how, on the verge of burning out, he had found the Cavendish-Meyer Healing Centre. How working there had revitalised him. He even told her how Ellie and Michael had saved his life. 'I'm beginning to believe that I was saved in order to be here for you and Harry when the drama unfolds.' At last, Callum fell silent, exhausted. After a few moments, he felt her take his hand. Everything was going to be all right, Lucy believed him.

'Now I know why I was directed to you,' she said, 'and who led the way. That was no air-freshener in your car, Callum, was it? It was the scent of lilacs.'

'Yes, it was. It's Vera's signature, sometimes accompanied by a mist the colour of amethyst. I am so relieved that she's watching over you. While Vera is around, or Carole, nothing will hurt you. They are very powerful spirits, especially Vera.'

'What was she like, Callum?' asked Lucy.

'I never met her, but Ellie knew her well, and she loved her. Ellie described her as powerful, but gentle. She said Vera was a spiritual woman with an uncanny sense of perception. In the course of their travels, she and her partner Carole had become acquainted with all kinds of different cultures that opened their minds to many things, including the paranormal. I wish I could have known them. I'm sure I would have learned a lot from them. Ellie told me that if Carole hadn't been there to see her through the aftermath of her car crash, and then to teach her how to manage her new gift of auric sight, she would be dead by now.'

'They sound like quite a pair!' said Lucy. 'Is it true that the healing centre is the result of a legacy Carole left to Ellie and Michael?'

'Yes, it is. And through them, the rest of us have been enabled to help and heal others.'

As he spoke, Callum became aware that Lucy was still holding his hand, and that a force like an electrical current was passing between them. They had made a very powerful connection. Where it might lead was for the future to determine. 'It's strange, Lucy, but I get the sense that Carole's presence is becoming more pervasive, and that soon she will be as forceful a power as Vera. Carole died more recently, so I guess she has needed time to reach that same level of energy.'

'I can see that,' said Lucy thoughtfully. 'We in the physical world need time to recover, maybe it's the same in the spirit world.' She giggled. 'Listen to me! I've always prided myself on being down to earth and practical, but I'm starting to understand that there really are more things "in heaven and earth", and that's not a bad thing.'

They sat for a moment in contemplative silence.

'Where do we go from here?' said Lucy.

'There's one other thing I haven't told you, Lucy. It seems there might be another child who is "special", though not in the same way as Harry.' Callum told her about Christopher and his wish to write 'a very important book'.

'Listen to this: "Clover and her mother, Lori, live in a commune. She has never seen her father, and her mother never speaks of him." '

She shivered. 'I see what you mean. I've seen plenty of eight-year-olds' attempts at writing, but never anything like that.'

'Michael thinks he's channelling, just like Harry is channelling his airman.'

Lucy whistled. 'And do you think the two are connected? The boys are being, well, *used*, by someone or something?'

'Ellie and Michael think it's a possibility,' Callum said. 'I'm seeing young Christopher tomorrow, and I'll tell you what happens.' He turned to her. 'You look exhausted. I'll let you get to bed now, our narrow escape on the road was one hell of a shock.'

Lucy smiled. 'You know I'd almost forgotten about that after what you've been telling me. Unfortunately, I have work to do, and it can't wait. Most people have no idea of how much administrative work a teacher has to do. All that paperwork on top of the actual teaching!' She looked into his eyes. 'And thank you, Callum. Thank you for saving my life.' She brushed his cheek with her lips. 'See you tomorrow?'

'I'll come over as soon as I've finished work and have seen Christopher, if that's okay?'

'Keep in touch. And Callum . . . Stay safe.'

He smiled at her. 'You too, Lucy. And let me know if there's anything that worries you, or you don't understand, okay? Day or night, I'm here for you, and for Harry.'

In the brief moment that passed before he stood up to leave, a shower composed of particles of light descended over their two figures. Then it was gone. Shaking his head, Callum left the room, closing the door behind him. These were strange times indeed.

* * *

Despite the comforting warmth of Alice's embrace, Ellie couldn't sleep. All she could think about was Christopher and the book he wanted to write. If, as Carole had insisted, what was about to descend on them concerned the children and the book, what part did that book play? And why Christopher? He was a perfectly normal little boy. But was he? What normal eight-year-old miraculously survived the death of his sister and the subsequent breakdown of his parents' marriage without coming out of it totally unscathed? Maybe the book was an outlet for his pain, although if that were the case his aura certainly didn't show it. For one so young he had a strong aura that radiated determination and self-contentment. There was no indication of sickness or debility, and unless her auric powers were letting her down, he was psychologically healthy and well-balanced. Which brought her back to the question, why him?

Alone, she would have got up and made herself a hot drink, but Alice had been so over-tired that she had struggled to get to sleep, and now she had finally succeeded Ellie was reluctant to disturb her.

Having come to a dead end with her thoughts about Christopher, she turned her mind to the clinic. She was suddenly reminded of a conversation she'd had with Michael's secretary, Janet, about a woman with a mysterious benefactor who had apparently insisted that the centre was only place that could help her, adding that 'people' were concerned for her safety. That could mean any number of things. Was she self-harming? Suicidal? They had dealt with several cases of clinical depression since the healing centre had opened, all with successful outcomes.

Ellie snuggled closer against Alice's sleeping body. Maybe someone was threatening this woman. Was it a case of domestic abuse? She hoped not. Such cases belonged in DCI Bob Foreman's department, not in the centre, but what did she know? Maybe the woman just needed a sympathetic ear and some sound advice from a neutral observer. Whatever the case, she would no doubt be able to deduce much from this woman's aura, and then—

Children!

The word sounded in her head with such force that Ellie almost jerked upright.

She had no doubt as to who had spoken.

'Okay, Carole,' she whispered, 'I hear you, but next time, maybe a little less volume, if you wouldn't mind.'

Oh, tut tut! Yes, it was Carole all right. She'd know that muttered disapproving grunt anywhere. She squeezed her eyes shut.

'All right . . . so our new client — Beth Saunders I think her name is — is somehow connected to the children, Christopher and Harry. Am I right?'

A feeling of peace drifted over her from above, and the room was suffused with a soft blue light. Despite the disturbing nature of the message that had just been conveyed to her, Ellie knew that now she would find sleep. It was reassuring to know that Carole and Vera were getting through to them, and that the information they were relaying from the spirit world was strong and would help them.

After all, was her last waking thought, *we are fighting on the side of the angels.*

* * *

If at that moment Ellie had looked out of the window, she would have seen two swirling spirals of coloured mist spreading throughout the orchard, where they lingered for a moment among the branches of the old apple trees before sweeping up to encircle the house, casting Snug Cottage in a gentle light. Spinning up into the night sky they came together, forming a braid of vivid blue and violet . . . Then they were gone.

* * *

Ollie had been right about Gideon, but only in that the man was a tall, imposing figure with a beard. That was where the resemblance to the headmaster of Hogwarts ended.

Sitting down next to Ollie on the sofa, Gideon apologised for the lateness of the hour. 'It's far too late now to start on any explanations, or to show you around your new home. I've instructed Rae to bring you some supper and make you comfortable for the night.'

Ollie gathered from this that he'd be sleeping on the sofa, but that was okay, he'd slept on worse. He was exhausted, and not a little scared, anxious about just what he'd got himself involved in. Gideon had been kind enough. From the way he spoke he seemed like an educated bloke, and he had a posh accent that made Ollie think of universities. However, he still had no idea of what went on here. And why a church?

Gideon laid a hand on his shoulder. 'I know you must have all sorts of questions, Ollie. First thing tomorrow, I'll come and explain everything. Just know that you are safe and that you will be well cared for. Bear with me tonight. Tomorrow you will be given your own room, and your new life as part of our family will begin.'

Gideon got to his feet and stood for a moment, smiling sympathetically down at him. 'Poor lad, you must feel so confused. Rest assured that from now on, your talents will be appreciated, and you will be treated as a valued individual. There'll be no more bullying, no more name calling. You are special, very special, Ollie, remember that.' Gideon looked up as the front door opened. 'I'll leave you with Rae. I'll be back to see you first thing. Enjoy your food, sleep well — and welcome.'

Rae bustled in and placed a tray in front of him. There was a large bowl of soup, its delicious smell suggesting that it could only be homemade. There were also two warm bread rolls filled with cheese, ham and tomato. Only when he saw the food did he realise how hungry he was.

'Eat up, Ollie, I'll be back shortly. I'm just going to make sure your bed is aired. It's only for tonight, and please, don't worry if you see me lock the doors. We're not keeping you prisoner, it's just to make sure you're safe and no one gets in.'

'What is this place?' he asked softly.

'Home. That's all you need to know for now. Don't worry, Gideon will answer all your questions tomorrow. Now, eat up before it gets cold.'

The food was delicious. He'd just finished when Rae returned.

'Come this way. Like I said, it's only temporary, but it's better than the sofa.' She went over to one of the series of closed doors and unlocked it.

Ollie followed her into a small cell-like room. Inside was a fold-up bed and a few pieces of heavy wooden furniture. On the wall was a cross and a small plaque so old that the writing had faded. High up in the wall, too high to see out of, was a narrow window. An inner door stood open into a bathroom with a shower, a handbasin and a toilet.

'It's not exactly the Ritz, my love, but it will do for one night. The church is heated, but if you get cold, there are extra blankets in that old chest. You'll find toiletries in the shower room, oh, and if you want a shower, you need to leave it running for a while for the water to get hot.' She gave him a motherly smile. 'I know this must all feel very strange to you, but you could not have come to a better or a safer place. You'll find love and understanding here, and none of the ill-treatment you've suffered in the past.'

'How do you know how I've been treated?' Ollie asked. 'Gideon said the same, he said there'd be no more bullying. It's true I've been bullied all my life, but how does he know that?'

She laughed softly. 'Oh, we know everything there is to know about you, my lovely, more than you know of yourself. You have an exciting future ahead of you, Ollie, but right now, you must try and get some sleep.'

'You won't lock my door, will you?' Ollie said anxiously. 'It's just that I don't like being shut in confined spaces.'

'Of course not, sweetheart. We know about that too. I'll leave your door slightly ajar, all right? But you must promise that you won't wander about at night. The outer doors will be locked, but the church is alarmed, so we don't want you setting them off and waking us all up, do we? Promise that you'll stay in your room until someone comes for you in the morning?'

He nodded. 'I promise. And thank you.'

'There's water by your bed, and some biscuits. I'll be back early tomorrow morning with some breakfast, and then Gideon will come to see you. You can ask him all your questions then, and he'll show you around your new home.' Her smile broadened. 'Wait and see, you'll love it. Now, settle yourself down, my cherub. Sleep well.'

After a quick wash, he curled up under the duvet. The bed was surprisingly comfortable, and he soon began to doze off. His last waking thought was that in all his life he'd never been spoken to so affectionately as tonight. It made him feel good.

CHAPTER ELEVEN

Somewhat overwhelmed, Christopher had been silent throughout most of his tour of the healing centre. When Michael led him into the Orangery, he wandered around wide-eyed, touching the plants and finally coming to a stop in front of a magnificent specimen.

'That's a palm tree!' he exclaimed.

'Sort of,' said Michael, 'though not quite like the ones on the beach in tropical countries, it's an indoor palm.'

'Cool,' murmured Christopher. He glanced down at the pool and gasped. 'What is *that*? It's huge!'

'That's a giant Koi carp,' Michael said. 'Its proper name is *Cyprinus rubrofuscus "koi"*. It can live for twenty-five to thirty-five years . . .' About to launch into a lecture, Michael brought himself up short, remembering the purpose of this visit. 'Anyway, we have work to do, don't we? It's time we met Jason Adamson so we can have a chat about writing and books.'

Reluctantly, Christopher took his gaze from the glorious gold and black koi. 'Yes, of course. Sorry, Michael, but I didn't expect this place to be so big, and so, well, awesome. It's a lot better than Daddy or Granny said. And it all belongs to you and Aunty Ellie! That is just amazing!'

'It belongs to us, but it also belongs to the people who come here. It's for everyone really. We want to help people, and make them better, and happy again.'

Christopher regarded him thoughtfully. 'It's a shame, isn't it, that not everyone feels that way. There's plenty of bad people around who don't want anyone at all to be happy.'

Simple words, but it was sad that a child of eight should already be aware of that side of humanity. 'It's true, Christopher, there are bad people around, but if you just stay on the side of the good guys, you'll be okay. Shall we go and find Jason?'

Jason was waiting in his office for them, and after the introductions, he asked Christopher how he'd got on with copying out sentences from other books.

'Pretty well, I guess, and I think I've started to understand what Michael was talking about,' said Christopher. 'And I decided to try something else too, apart from writing out the sentences.'

Jason tilted his head to one side and cocked an eyebrow. 'Oh yes? And what was that?'

'My dad let me borrow his Pearlcorder. It's a thing where you record what you're saying and then play it back. I say the words I want to write into it, then I play it back and write down what I've said. My spelling is rubbish, and it's a bit of a mess — I don't get all that stuff about splitting things up and using those comma things — but the idea comes out all right. Once I get the comma stuff right, it will make sense, won't it? What do you think?'

'It certainly will,' said Jason. 'I don't suppose you brought any of these things you wrote with the Pearlcorder with you, by any chance?'

'Oh yes.' Christopher was already rummaging around in a folder commandeered from his grandad's office that he'd been carrying around with him all morning.

This was the first Michael had heard of this new 'work' the boy had embarked upon. It wasn't a total surprise that the lad had taken up his suggestions so readily, but he was surprised that he had even taken them further. He wondered where Ellie and Callum had got to, he really wanted Ellie to hear this for herself.

He was just thinking he might phone Ellie when she and Callum burst in through the door. 'Minor calamity — the power went down in Alice's pavilion, but it's all sorted now, thanks to Callum.'

'Christopher was just about to read out some sentences he's written down for us,' Jason said. 'Go ahead, Christopher, if you're ready.'

But the four pairs of adult eyes fastened upon him were too much for Christopher. 'I don't know . . . it feels like I'm having an exam or something.' He fell silent and sat staring at the floor.

Callum went to the boy and squatted down in front of him. 'I know what you mean, exams are horrible, I hate them too. We're just excited about your book, and we'd like to hear more about it. We're hoping for a sneak preview, that's all. So how about it?' With a wink at the little boy, he sat cross legged on the floor, as if he himself were a kid.

Christopher giggled at this un-adult behaviour. 'Oh all right then. Here goes.' He took a breath. ' "Because they have been travelling for so long, Clover has never been to school. But she is far from stupid. She has gained immense knowledge and learned a myriad of skills from a multitude of different teachers who are all the kind people around her." '

The four adults were silent. *Multitude?* thought Michael. *Myriad? What boy of eight would know such words?*

Christopher regarded them anxiously. 'You didn't like it, did you?'

'No! It's not that at all,' said Callum, the first to regain the power of speech. 'We think it's remarkable. We're just quiet because we're all so gobsmacked. That was brilliant, Christopher. Well done.'

'I can see it's going to be a very interesting book, Christopher,' said Jason. 'I suppose you can't tell us the whole story? Not as if you were writing it, but as if you were describing one of your favourite books.'

'That's a bit difficult,' said Christopher. 'I . . . we haven't finished it yet.'

'He writes with his friend,' said Michael quickly, to save the boy from having to explain about his imaginary companion. 'How about a few words, just to give us an idea. You know, like if you were describing Harry Potter, you'd say it's a book about a very special boy who goes to an amazing school for wizards, and he and his friends have lots of adventures fighting the dark lord Voldemort.'

His brow creased in concentration, Christopher said slowly, 'It's about special children. Clover's one. She's so special that to keep her safe, her mother keeps running away. Well, one day, Clover decides she wants to stop running and face the thing her mother's so scared of. Clover knows that where they are now is full of people who will help to protect her, so here is where she'll stay. Together with her new friends she will face the darkness that's out there threatening her. Then the battle begins . . .' His voice trailed away.

'I'm sorry I'm not a publisher instead of a nurse,' said Callum. 'You're right, Christopher, you do need to write your book.'

Michael agreed. Noticing how exhausted the child looked, he proposed a break. Perhaps he'd like a dip in the pool before lunch? There were no hydrotherapy classes until two, and there were swimming trunks he could borrow if he wanted.

Christopher's face lit up. He turned to Callum. 'Would you come with me?'

Callum smiled. 'If these two slave-drivers can do without me for half an hour, I'd be delighted.'

'Be our guest,' said Ellie with a wink. 'Just don't get used to it!'

Amid the general laughter, Callum ushered the boy out of the office. Passing Michael, he fell behind and whispered, 'I'll let you know what he says when there's just the two of us.'

Michael touched his arm. 'Of course. And take good care of him, Callum. He's very precious.'

'Oh, I know. See you later.'

* * *

'Well!' Jason said, looking troubled, 'I get the feeling there's a whole lot more going on here than I'm privy to.'

'Sorry, my friend,' replied Michael. 'But we haven't much more of an idea than you.'

Jason pulled a face. 'Look, I know that you guys have, well, rather different skills to me, but there's little I can do to help without the whole picture. I'd like to help, and if I can I will, but can you at least tell me why you are both so concerned about this extraordinary little boy with a wish to write a book. From what he said, his story isn't so different from the Harry Potter books, and I'm sure hundreds of kids have read those and believed that they could make up similar stories of their own. Yes, he quoted some very "adult" words, but if, as you said, Michael, he's working with a friend, he probably had help.'

'There is no friend, Jason,' said Michael. 'It's that imaginary one I told you about.'

'Ah, I should have realised that. I see your point now. And if it all stems from the traumas he's suffered, what he says about good and evil makes a bit more sense. Is it about his sister dying? Or about the parents? Does he see them as light and dark? If it is, as a behaviourist I have to say it runs very deep.'

Ellie leaned forward. 'To be honest, Jason, we think we are looking at something very different to mainstream childhood psychology. Going by his aura, Christopher appears to be a remarkably well-adjusted boy who has weathered his traumas brilliantly. This strange insistence on writing a book has seemingly come out of nowhere. It's as if someone, or something, is exerting extreme pressure on him, and is using him to tell us something of immense importance.'

'Ellie is right, Jason,' Michael said. 'And there's another thing. If you recall, we sent Callum to see you because a young teacher, a friend of his, needed his advice on another child, an even younger boy, who appears to have an inherited memory of flying Lancaster bombers. Well, we think a similar thing is happening with him.'

Jason's brow furrowed. 'You said some*one* or some*thing*, Ellie. Are we straying into the esoteric here? You think it's something . . . paranormal?'

Ellie nodded slowly. 'Yes, Jason, we do, and we badly need you on board to help us keep our feet on the ground and point out those aspects that arise from more earthly causes.'

'Since he saw you, Jason, Callum has been doing some more work with that little five-year-old lad,' Michael added. 'He says that the child has an artistic ability way in advance of his years. Not only that, whenever the subject of aviation comes up, he speaks in a totally different voice. I've heard him myself, and believe me, it's pretty unnerving! We are all of the opinion that the boy is being used as a channel to pass on information.'

'Channelling! My goodness!' Jason said. 'I've heard of it, but always in the context of séances. You know, a spirit who visits Auntie Gladys to tell her that her husband passed over safely, and is happy in the spirit world. I'm not being derogatory — even Arthur Conan Doyle used to attend séances — it's just something I know nothing about. I root out deep-seated psychological problems arising from real events and help children to move on from them, hopefully to better futures. As to what you are describing, fascinated though I am, I can't quite see where I fit in.'

His bewildered expression made Ellie want to smile. Instead, she said, 'We totally understand, Jason, but I think the more you see of these children, the more you'll come to realise that there's something broader than psychological issues going on with them.' She glanced at Michael. 'And I hate to say this, but I suspect we are about to hear of another child with inexplicable behaviour.'

'What, a third child!' Michael exclaimed.

'So far I'm just reading between the lines, but don't be surprised if one of tomorrow's new clients is a woman with a problem child. Anyway, back to Christopher. Are you on board, Jason?'

'Oh yes, count me in. Though I doubt I'll be of much help.'

'You will be,' said Ellie. 'Setting aside the paranormal for a moment, we are still left with two children from troubled backgrounds. Your job — no, your *calling*, is to help such children. You work with them all the time, Jason, whereas we do not. Believe me, you could be invaluable.'

* * *

True to his word, Gideon arrived after breakfast. He seemed different this morning, slightly on edge. Although he wore the same smile as before, it didn't quite reach his eyes. Always straightforward, Ollie asked him if there was anything wrong.

Gideon apologised. It was nothing, he said, just a small problem that he would deal with after he'd shown Ollie his new home.

'First, a guided tour,' Gideon said. 'So far, you've only seen the inside of the old chapel. That particular building serves a variety of purposes, one being that of a temporary stop-over for newcomers while their permanent accommodation is being made ready for them.'

Ollie liked listening to Gideon. He spoke in a deep, sonorous voice with a cultivated accent, yet he didn't talk down to him. Ollie thought he'd make an excellent teacher. Maybe he was. So far, Ollie knew nothing about the people he was joining.

Gideon strode off down the aisle to the back of the church, and pushed open two heavy wooden doors at the far end. To his amazement, Ollie found himself looking out upon a breathtaking landscape instead of the churchyard he'd been expecting.

'Where are we?' he breathed.

'This is our forest,' said Gideon with some pride. 'Beautiful, isn't it? But come, let's get you to your room so you can see what you might need to make you comfortable. With time, you might want a different kind of living space, in which case we'll do all we can to provide it for you.'

Ollie remained standing where he was. 'But why me? I don't get it. Are you sure you're not mixing me up with someone else? You're treating me like royalty, while I'm nobody, nothing but an ungrateful little oik. I should know, I've been called it often enough.' His voice trembled.

'By ignorant people who cannot — or don't want to — see what's in front of their eyes,' Gideon said softly. 'Yes, Oliver Cruise, it's you we are thinking of, and no one else. Just be patient a little longer. Everything will be explained to you as soon as you are settled in. First, you need new clothes, and a few other personal necessities. You came to us with only the clothes you stand up in, and I think you've been wearing them for a while now.'

Part of Ollie remained unconvinced. After all, as his dad used to say, there's no such thing as a free lunch. What would be expected of him in return for all this largesse?

As if he'd read his mind, Gideon said, 'Ollie, we meant what we said about being safe here. Nothing bad will happen to you within our boundary. Misfortune lies without. So, cheer up. Embrace your new beginning.'

As they continued their tour, Gideon told him a little more about the place. 'The property extends over four hundred acres, about half of which is forested, a gift bestowed by a generous benefactor. First, I expect you'll be wanting to know about us, why you are here and the part you will play.'

'I want to know that right now. Wait, what is that place over there?'

Gideon laughed. 'That's a tree-house. As I said, you might one day feel you need a different sort of place to live in rather than the one you've been assigned. That tree-house is Luna's, where she lives with her cat, Sprout. You'll meet her in a moment. She will help you find your way around while Rae sorts you out some clothes and whatever else you might need.'

The wooden house that so fascinated Ollie was built on the branches of two massive trees growing so close together that they seemed to form a single trunk.

They were now walking along a wide sandy path. Ollie began to notice other dwellings half hidden among the trees. Some were simple log cabins, while others resembled giant toadstools springing up from the forest floor as if they'd grown there. Perhaps he really was in Wonderland!

'And this is the main house.'

Ollie gasped. He was looking at a building that resembled a small French chateau surrounded by a moat. With its turret rising up from the thick canopy of trees, it could have been a castle from a past age, imposing but not dark or threatening. It sure was different from the two-bed semi-detached with on-road parking where Ollie came from.

'This is where you'll be staying while you get used to things here,' said Gideon. 'If it suits, you might choose to stay, it'll be entirely up to you. Or you might choose to live elsewhere — set up home in the forest, out in the fields, or the gardens. The house also has an annexe that accommodates three or four people. Some people prefer having their own room within a shared environment. Not everyone likes living alone.'

'Are there many of us, Gideon?' Ollie asked, surprised to hear himself already saying 'us'.

'Twenty at present, not counting Rae and me. Five are . . . what you might call mentors. Guides, perhaps? Yes, guides is better. They are older people who will guide you until you reach an understanding of your life and its meaning. Three are carers whose task it is to look after your material needs. Two are in charge of the upkeep of the house and gardens. The remaining ten are our special charges — children and young adults, of whom you are one.'

They were now halfway across a wide causeway that spanned the moat. Ahead of them lay an expanse of lawn and well-tended gardens that extended to the front of the big house. Ollie followed Gideon like a boy in a dream. When Mole convinced him to quit his miserable life and join people who lived a different kind of existence, he had imagined some kind of commune. He saw himself roughing it in a caravan or a decrepit mobile home, or perhaps one of those self-sufficient farming communities where he'd have to work the land and milk the cows. Never in a million years had he conceived of somewhere like this. Unless it was all a front, and he was about to be trafficked abroad as a boy slave.

They passed through the gardens and up to the ornate front door. Gideon was about to push it open when a man ran out, closely followed by Rae.

'Gideon!' Rae shouted. 'I need to talk to you. Now.'

The tall, bearded man regarded Ollie with a wry smile. 'Looks like you and I are to be interrupted again.' He turned to a tall, slim young man who had emerged behind Rae. 'Mark, would you find Luna, please, and ask her to take Ollie to his room and show him where everything is. She can take him around the two floors he'll have access to before Rae comes back to take over.' He turned back to Ollie. 'Ah well, perhaps later we'll be able to have our long overdue chat. I'll see you at lunch anyway.'

He and Rae sped off around the side of the big house.

Mark held out his hand. 'Good to meet you, Ollie. I'm one of your helpers. I'm not sure, but I might even be your new buddy.

Let's hope so.' He gave Ollie a dazzling smile. 'We have the same sort of buddy system as they do in scuba diving — you know, when they watch each other's backs. Basically, what it means is that I'll be there for you while you settle in. If you need help, or if there's anything you want to talk about, your buddy is never far away.'

Although he didn't say so, Ollie wasn't sure he liked the idea of someone watching over him that closely. Instead, he said, 'This place is going to take a bit of understanding. So far, I'm totally in the dark.'

'We all were, Ollie. Believe me, I was the worst. Talk about a Doubting Thomas. It took me ages to realise that coming here was the best thing that ever happened to me. You'll soon see what I mean.' His smile faded, his expression became anxious. 'Um, there's a bit of an issue going on right now that Gideon needs to sort out, but he'll be back as soon as he's dealt with it.'

'Is it serious?' asked Ollie.

'Nothing that Gideon can't handle. Anyway, let's go and find Luna, shall we? She's probably up in your room. Gideon's put you in Willows, it has a great view right over the forest. All the rooms have the names of trees — if you need me, I'm in Aspens, a bit further down the hall.'

The door marked 'Willows' stood open, revealing a large room with French windows that opened onto a narrow balcony with a wrought-iron railing. The windows were hung with heavy taupe-coloured drapes. There was a double bed covered in a white quilt. The furnishings, all in the same pale wood, consisted of a wardrobe, a chest of drawers, an Ottoman and two comfortable chairs positioned on each side of the window, looking out.

'All the rooms have en suite shower rooms,' Mark said behind him, 'and yours has a little study with a desk and bookshelves.'

'A study? What, like to do schoolwork?'

'We all have work to do, Ollie, but don't worry, there's no exams and no one standing over you or anything. We simply work on what makes us special, for the greater good. But don't worry about that right now, it'll all be explained. Now, here's Luna.'

Ollie had been so amazed by the room that he hadn't noticed the girl. She was holding a vase of flowers that she was just about to set down on one of the bedside tables. She was about sixteen, dressed in jeans and a sweatshirt, and her shoulder-length dark hair had a strip of silvery white running the length of it.

She turned and smiled at him, and for the first time in his life, Ollie Cruise was in love.

* * *

'I sense a different kind of darkness out there tonight, Rae. We need to take especially good care of the children.'

Standing next to him, Rae followed his gaze into the forest. 'Of course I will, that's what I'm here for . . . but we still have two to bring in. I just hope we're not too late.'

'We'll get them here. I swore we would, and I will keep to my promise.' *If I can*, he thought. This recent problem had sown a seed of doubt in him. Were matters escalating too fast for what they planned to achieve? 'I suppose there's still no news from him?'

'Nothing. That's what I wanted to talk to you about.' Rae bit her bottom lip. 'Brendan rang me a few minutes ago. Another appointment has been missed. Brendan had to go out in person and pick up the pieces. Something has happened, something serious. I fear for him, Gideon.'

'So do I,' whispered Gideon. The two of them fell silent, gazing into the dark. A breeze had sprung up, causing the trees to sway slightly, and the leaves to rustle. Normally a soothing sound, tonight it had an ominous quality. Gideon turned to her. 'Will you look after everything here? And take especial care of Oliver? I need to go out in search of them. I'll ask Serena for help. She'll point me in the right direction.'

Rae squeezed his arm. 'They'll be safe with me. If you're away for some time, I will gather the others together each night, just as darkness begins to fall, and we'll put a ring of white light around our home. We'll be safe then. Just find him, and bring him back.'

Gideon nodded. 'I'll spend a little time with Oliver before I go, I owe him that much. Then I'll seek out Serena. I'll be back as soon as I have an answer.'

'Keep yourself safe, Gideon. We all rely on you.'

She was right. The weight of responsibility lay heavy upon him. 'And, Rae, whatever you do, you must stick to the rules. No one, absolutely no one, is to cross the perimeter line, not by a single step, especially at night. Do you understand?'

'No one need leave. The storerooms are full, we have everything we could possibly want. Just come home safely, and bring him with you. As you said, the darkness is building. It's growing stronger. The . . . the thing we feared. It's starting, isn't it?'

'It is, Rae. But we always knew it would happen. Now it is, we need to complete our mission, gather the children and fight for what we believe.'

'Amen to that.'

CHAPTER TWELVE

DI Jon Leatham had hit a wall. Despite it being Sunday, he'd got in early that morning he'd been chasing up possible leads on their missing boy, Oliver Cruise, but they had all come to nothing. Just as he was about to take himself off to the car park for some fresh air, Wendy approached his desk.

'Um . . . sir, I've been thinking. This might be nothing, but . . .'

'Welcome to the club. I've had a whole bloody morning of nothing! So, what's your nothing, Wendy? I hope it's better than mine.'

'Well, a friend of mine is a sergeant at Reigate. A little while ago they had a girl go missing. I don't know if you remember the case — a fifteen-year-old called Daisy Hilton?'

Jon didn't recall it, but he hadn't been at the station that long.

'She was never found, but the strange thing was, her parents received a letter about three months after she disappeared. They were convinced it was from her. Forensics compared the handwriting with her schoolwork and confirmed it was indeed Daisy's, so the search was scaled down somewhat, although it remained open. Daisy wrote that she was safe and happy. She was sorry for all the trouble she'd caused, but she wouldn't be returning home. The experts studying the handwriting said that it exhibited no indications of stress, and they were certain the letter had not been written under duress.'

'And the connection to our case?' asked Jon.

'Two things. One, Daisy was an odd child, very much a loner. There was talk of ADHD, although it was never officially diagnosed. Whatever, she was a bit of an outsider at school.'

'Like Oliver Cruise?'

'Exactly like Oliver Cruise,' said Wendy. 'What interested me about it is that when she first went missing, the only lead they ever had was that she'd been seen with a strange boy — a lad with longish dark hair and, wait for it, a pronounced limp.'

'Bloody hell!' breathed Jon. 'Our little Brummie!'

'Looks that way. They had a witness who was able to give them a better description of him than the one we have; so good, in fact, that they had one of their artists produce a composite sketch from it. I thought we might show it to your lady down at the community centre, what do you think?'

'Ah, good old Kimberly Clack. Absolutely, Wendy. Have you got it yet?'

'Annie's faxing it across now.'

Jon rubbed his hands together. 'Well, DS Brown, looks like you and I are about to hit town.'

'It'll be a pleasure, sir.'

They found Kimberly at the centre. She was in the kitchen, loading a dishwasher with crockery. 'Hello, officers! Any news of Oliver?'

'I'm afraid not, Kimberly,' said Jon. 'We've come to see you about that young man you saw with him — the lad with the limp.'

'Sorry. I've been keeping an eye out, but I haven't seen hide nor hair of him.'

Wendy showed her the identikit sketch her friend from Reigate had sent. 'Have a look at this. Would you say that's a good likeness of him?'

Kimberly squinted at it. 'I'll say! Yes, that's him all right, that's Mole. I'm not sure about the eyes, though, but the rest of his face is spot on. Here, give us another look.' She stared at it, biting her lip.

Jon and Wendy shared a glance.

'Ah! It's just dawned on me. He had something wrong with his eyes, like he was short-sighted. He'd screw up his face when he looked at you, sort of peering.' She nodded to herself. 'I got the feeling he'd never been looked after properly, what with that limp, and probably he needed glasses. That's the problem when they won't talk to you. How can you help when you don't know what they've been through? We do our best here, but there's only so much you can do when they won't say how they're feeling.'

Jon said that he and his fellow officers often felt the same way. It was so often hard to get through to kids, and you could only watch helplessly as they took the wrong paths.

Leaving Kimberly with a copy of the identikit picture, they made their way back to the station.

'It doesn't bode well, does it?' said Jon after a while.

'It does not,' said Wendy grimly. 'Sounds to me like he's procuring kids for someone — traffickers, maybe?'

'As soon as we get back, would you contact your friend in Reigate, and find out how far they got in their investigations into this boy Mole, if indeed they investigated him. I think we should be concentrating our search on him, don't you? After all, if we find him, he could well lead us to Oliver Cruise.'

'And possibly Daisy Hilton,' added Wendy, 'if she's still alive. If you think it might help, I can drive over to Reigate and talk to Annie.'

'Go for it, Wendy,' said Jon, quickening his pace. 'I'll get hold of the boss and let him know about this new development. If nothing else, at least we now know that Oliver didn't just do a runner because he was fed up with the way he was being treated. Mole's connection to another unsolved disappearance shines a whole new light on it. Oliver was lured away.' He grimaced. 'But where to?'

* * *

After a lunch that Christopher pronounced 'epic', Ellie drove him home. He was no sooner through the door than he began to regale his father and grandmother with stories about the amazing place Ellie and Michael lived and worked in. 'It's like a stately home, Dad, only a lot more fun. And I had a beef burger!'

Daniel laughed. 'But did you learn anything about writing? I thought that was why you went.'

'Oh yes! Jason — he's really nice and dead clever — told me lots. We had a chat after I had a swim in the pool.'

Ellie noticed a shadow pass briefly over Daniel's face at the mention of swimming. She hastened to add, 'Our nurse Callum swam with him.'

'Callum's a great swimmer!' said Christopher. 'I like him a lot.' He grinned at his father. 'Jason liked my writing, and Michael's going to help me, too.'

Ellie glanced at her watch. 'Sorry to dash off, but I must get back.'

At the door, Daniel gave her a hug. 'Thank you for doing that for him. He's clearly had a brilliant morning. I really appreciate it.'

Ellie sped back to the clinic, itching to discuss what was unfolding with Michael and Callum, and also hoping that Alice hadn't been looking for her. An earlier call had assured her that Alice would be tied up for some while, as Gordon had been held up, and she was tackling a mountain of paperwork that had built up during her absence.

Flipping her brain back to the children, Ellie realised that a pattern was beginning to emerge from the different strands, brought together by Vera and Carole. That alone was worrying.

If the spirit world were expending this much energy in contacting them, what was about to occur must be important, possibly extending much further than the healing centre itself and the people therein. The last time they had been called upon to intervene, it was to save lives and stop a murderer. What would be wanted of them this time?

It was half two by the time Michael and Callum were free. Ellie decided they should meet in the less formal environment of her consulting room.

As he always did when he came here, the first thing Michael did was gaze for a few moments upon her Louis Comfort Tiffany posters, losing himself in the intricate patterns formed by the branches of a tree, a peacock's tail. With the aid of some strategically placed lighting, Ellie had designed the room so as to give her clients a feeling of calm and well-being, and if the effect on Michael was anything to go by, she had succeeded.

'Okay, my friends, let's see what we have,' she began. 'Hopefully from there, we can proceed to a plan of action. But before we start, there's something I want to throw at you both.' Ellie looked from one to the other of them. 'I didn't make too much of this in front of Jason, for fear of discouraging him with too much metaphysical talk. Last night . . . Last night I had a very clear message. Not from Vera, this time it was Carole, and there was no mistaking it, believe me! It was as if she were in the room with me, and not only that, but she was positively yelling at me!' She turned to Callum. 'You probably won't have heard, but tomorrow — as long as she turns up — we have a woman booked in who has a mystery benefactor who has offered to pay all her costs. His very words were, "This is where Beth needs to be." Not only that, but he fears for her safety, but he gave no further explanation. Her name is Beth Saunders.'

'What did Carole say about her, then?' asked Michael.

'Well, I couldn't sleep last night, and as I lay awake I kept wondering what kind of trouble this Beth was in, which is when Carole made her presence known, in the form of a single word: "Children". I knew at once where she was directing me, and I asked her if she meant that this Beth Saunders woman was connected to our anxieties about Christopher and Harry. As soon as I asked that question, she stopped browbeating me. I suddenly felt very peaceful, and I went to sleep almost immediately.'

'There's no doubting what she meant, then,' said Michael. 'Let's hope Mrs Saunders doesn't get the heebie-jeebies and misses her appointment. Do you want me to be there when you meet her, Ellie?'

'Maybe not the first meeting, Michael. No offence, but we have no idea what her circumstances are, so perhaps to start with she might feel more comfortable talking to another woman. What do you think?'

Michael nodded. 'You are right. Assess her, and we can take it from there. Personally, I can't wait to hear what she has to tell you.'

Ellie winced. 'Don't get your hopes up too high. She might not feel confident enough to reveal all in one visit, although her aura will help me to see what's going on, even if she struggles to put it in words.'

'And, thankfully, Carole has given you a way in,' added Callum. 'That's a massive help.'

'She has indeed,' said Ellie uneasily. 'I'll get back to you both the moment the interview is over. Now, where are we? Callum, you first. How did it go with Harry at Lucy's yesterday? And then Michael can tell us what he found from the lad's aura.'

Callum ended his report by describing the heartrending look of sorrow and loneliness on the child's face as he and Lucy drove away. Then he told them what had happened on their way back to Lucy's.

'You were nearly killed!' exclaimed Ellie in horror. 'Why on earth didn't you ring us!'

He shrugged. 'I didn't think of it. We weren't injured, neither of us were, thanks to the airman and your Carole.'

'Thanks to them, *and* your quick reflexes, Callum! What if you hadn't understood what they were telling you? Or you had hesitated.' She shuddered.

'No one could misunderstand Carole Cavendish-Meyer! I didn't meet her when she was alive, but blimey, talk about forthright! I reckon she would have stamped on the brake for me if I hadn't understood her!'

'He's got a point there,' murmured Michael.

'Anyway,' said Callum, 'the upshot was that I told Lucy all about myself, including my visitations. She was fine with it, and what's more, you'll never guess what — she told me she felt that someone or something had led her to me. Not only that, she has caught the scent of lilacs around her recently, so I guess Vera is watching over her too.'

Ellie wondered if Michael would tell Callum about the lights he'd seen when the young man and Lucy were together, but he said nothing.

'Do you think this means that the spirit of the airman is on our side?' Michael said. 'Funny, I had a feeling something would cause you to think that was the case.'

'I remember you said as much when you were at Lucy's house,' Callum said, 'and, yes, now I'm convinced he means Harry no harm. In fact, I find his presence quite reassuring.'

'And the boy's aura, Michael?' asked Ellie.

'Oh, simply beautiful. And I'm pleased to say that when the airman was present, especially when he was speaking through Harry, the lad's aura just seemed to absorb different, more dense lights but did not wane. Which means I can confirm that he does not suffer from any form of identity disorder.'

'Which, in turn, confirms that we are involved in something not of this world, and that it revolves around these children.' Ellie was silent for a long moment. 'The problem is, we have no idea where to go from here.'

Michael nodded slowly. 'Watch and wait, that's all we can do. And be prepared. And on that note, I urge you both to take good care of yourselves in the coming days. We must all eat well, sleep when we can, and use every tool available to us to make ourselves strong. Ellie, get out into that lovely summer house and enjoy some quiet time out there for meditation. I'll continue to work with Christopher on the book. And you, Callum, spend as much time as you can with Lucy, and whenever possible, little Harry. But — and this is important — be careful how you go about it. I'd hate anyone to get the wrong impression from your interest in the boy. Apart from ruining your careers, you could lose your opportunity to keep him safe.'

'I understand,' said Callum. 'We are both very aware of that.'

'Good. Now, what do you think about the three of us getting together, just for a few minutes, before we leave for the day, to update each other and air any concerns we might have?'

'Sounds good to me,' agreed Ellie.

'Absolutely,' added Callum.

'Then the next step — unless any of us gets another violent prod from Carole — is to find out everything we can about Beth Saunders,' Ellie said. 'Oh, by the way, I almost forget, I'm seeing Wendy Brown tonight. She's calling round after work for a coffee and a natter.'

'Give her our best,' said Michael, 'and tell her we don't see nearly enough of her. We'll all have to have supper together one night in the new café at the centre. What do you think?'

'I'll tell her,' replied Ellie. 'I'm sure she'll jump at the chance. You know Wendy, she loves her food.'

Michael stood up. 'If we are done here, I need to go and check tomorrow's appointments. Stay alert, my friends, and take good care of yourselves.'

'And I have to go help Maureen Shaw with a new in-patient,' said Callum, getting to his feet. On his way out, he paused at the door. 'Carole's getting much stronger, isn't she, Ellie? And now I have her to thank for saving my life — yet again! If it wasn't for her we'd have died when that piece of farm machinery crashed through that hedge. It's pretty mind-blowing to realise that both Lucy and I are only breathing because of the intervention of a . . . well, a ghost.'

'I don't think of Carole in that way,' mused Ellie. 'I just feel her presence, as if she's still alive. And, yes, Callum, I think Carole is becoming stronger, and more significant too. And I'm so glad of that! If I could choose anyone to be by my side in a fight, it would be Carole.'

* * *

Mark and Luna had left Oliver alone in his room for a while to rest. He lay down on the bed and closed his eyes, trying to assimilate everything he had seen that morning. To say he was overwhelmed was an understatement, yet he still wavered between being thankful for all that was being offered to him, and suspicious of it. He'd heard about any number of crazed religious fanatics, and the lengths some of them went to in order to attract wide-eyed innocents in search of some meaning to their lives. Gideon didn't seem mad, but he had charisma and authority, and the people here obviously revered him. Rae spoke of him not in mere admiration, but with something approaching love.

A voice startled him out of his reverie. 'Oliver, I'm sorry. You must think I'm abandoning you here. Please believe me when I say that your arrival here has coincided with an annoying development that I have to deal with before I can explain more fully the reason why you've been brought here. It's not my wish, but I have no alternative, I really must go out for a while.'

'Sorry, Gideon, I was miles away,' Oliver mumbled.

Gideon chuckled. 'I think you were right here, and wondering what you'd got yourself into.'

He closed the door behind him and sat down heavily in one of the chairs facing the window, gazing out into the swaying trees. 'I've always made it my policy to speak to every newcomer in person, and explain what this place and the work we do here. As I said, I've been called away urgently, but I can't just leave you here not knowing what's going to happen to you, so I have asked Rae and Luna to do it for me. They will be able to answer all your questions. Is that all right with you?'

Ollie nodded. 'Oh, yes please. Dead right I'm confused, so if they can tell me, that's fine.'

Gideon stood up, placing a gentle hand on Ollie's shoulder. 'That's good. Now I must go. And, Oliver?'

Ollie looked at him enquiringly.

'Welcome, son. Welcome to the Eleventh House.'

CHAPTER THIRTEEN

Later that evening, Wendy arrived at Snug Cottage. Walking into the hall, she said, 'I'm so pleased to be here, I just love this place.'

'It is lovely, isn't it,' said Ellie, giving her friend a hug. 'Although somehow I don't feel as if it's mine, but that I'm taking care of it for Carole. It sounds weird, I know, but it feels as if every inch of the house is impregnated with her presence.'

'I don't think it's weird,' said Wendy. 'She played such a big part in your life, especially your recovery. You must miss her terribly.'

'I do, Wendy.' Ellie hesitated. 'Would it surprise you if I said she's still around?'

Wendy laughed. 'After what we all went through, nothing would surprise me again!' She glanced around her. 'Is she here now?'

'No, silly!' said Ellie. 'Unlike some people I could mention, I don't see spirits. It's just that every now and again, she makes her presence felt. Now, back to the real world. Have you eaten?'

'Not exactly. I went to see an old friend this morning, another detective sergeant over at Reigate, and had a snack lunch with her. But don't worry, I'll make myself supper when I get home.'

'Oh no you won't. Come into the kitchen. Alice and I have already eaten, but it's still warm. So, sit yourself down and I'll get it out. Oh, and Alice said to say "Hi" but she's trying to catch up with her emails and phone calls. Her practice is getting busier all the time, and now she and her assistant, Gordon Lamont, are being pursued by any number of big companies that are interested in AZSEE — that's the diagnostic computer software they've developed. It's an exciting time for her, but I'm afraid she's getting snowed under again, even though she now has people working for her.'

'Tricky, isn't it? If it's your baby, it must be hard for you to let any of it go by farming it out to others,' Wendy said.

'You have to, though, if you're to have any sort of home life,' said Ellie. 'You need that so as not to burn out, but we seem to have less and less time to relax and be together.'

Wendy raised an eyebrow. 'Do I detect a note of sadness, or maybe even resentment there, our Ells?'

Ellie gave her a wry smile. 'I'm a fine one to talk, aren't I? But in my case I lost a partner because I let work take over my life. The experience taught me how easy it is to tip the balance and start neglecting the people who matter most to us. Anyway, dinner is served, and there's some fresh crusty bread as well.' She took cutlery from the drawer, and dished up the food. 'How's Bob — oh, and Jon Leatham, is he still working with you?'

Wendy looked hungrily at the chicken satay. 'They send their best wishes, and they are both fine. Jon has settled in well, and he's great to work with. But, hey, one piece of news regarding the boss. He doesn't know that we know — no one dares bring it up — but he's been told to make a decision about his future. It's crunch time for the DCI. The mess room lads have even opened a book on it: will he stay, or will he go?'

'Oh no!' Ellie exclaimed. 'The place wouldn't be the same without Bob, would it?'

'It certainly wouldn't, and who knows who we might get next. Still, he's done his time. And I can't help thinking that his wife might welcome a break from preparing those famous packed lunches he brings every day.'

Poor Bob, Ellie thought. He was so utterly dedicated to his job, but he also loved his wife. She wouldn't want to be in his shoes.

Wendy was eating appreciatively. 'This is delicious, Ellie. I wish I could cook like you. Most of the time I exist on microwave meals, or something that requires only one or two brain cells and very little time to prepare.'

'Are you very busy at the moment?' asked Ellie, passing Wendy a bottle of spring water and a glass.

Her friend paused eating for a moment, her fork raised. 'Well, since you ask . . . I've been meaning to talk to you about a case we're working at present. But don't worry, it's not some grim murder. In fact we aren't totally sure if it's even a crime.'

'Sounds intriguing.'

'It's worrying more than anything. We have a missing boy — well, he's fourteen, a teenager.'

Ellie frowned. Right now, any mention of a child made the hairs on the back of her neck stand up.

'You might have seen it on the news. They are calling him the "Boy in the Red Jacket".'

'I haven't listened to the news in days,' admitted Ellie, 'or watched TV for that matter. What's the story?'

'He's a strange boy, Ellie. We can't quite work him out. His name is Oliver Cruise. His parents and his teachers say he's a bright, intelligent lad, while his contemporaries call him a weirdo. The parents are making a big show of acting distraught, but Bob thinks there's something they aren't telling the police. Not only that, but they suspect the school — or one teacher at least — are in on it too. Either Oliver's involved in some sort of trouble at school, in which case why aren't they telling us what it is — or there's something about him, or that's wrong with him, that neither parents nor his teachers are prepared to share. Whatever, we think Oliver is kind of different in some way. Now we have a witness connecting him with another boy, who was also seen with a girl who went missing months ago. As I said, it's a weird one.'

Ellie bit her lip. Surely not . . . this was not what she wanted to hear.

'The fact is, Ellie, both the DCI and I had a bit of a strange experience the other night. We both woke up to a very strong smell of lilacs filling our rooms, and in my case, it was accompanied by a distinct mauve glow close to my bed. Afterwards, all I could think of was you. I told the boss, and as he had experienced the same thing, we decided we were being nudged in your direction.'

Ellie looked anxiously at her friend. 'I think you are right. I have no idea what it means, but there have been some . . . odd phenomena to do with some children we are acquainted with, and if you are being guided in my direction, I'm guessing there's a connection to your missing boy somewhere.'

'I knew it!' Wendy shook her head. 'The moment I smelled flowers, when there were none in the room, I thought of what you'd said about Vera and Carole and their messages.'

Ellie sighed. 'And believe me, those messages are coming in thick and fast at present. What's so damned annoying about it is that we have no clue as to what we are actually dealing with.' A sudden thought occurred to her. She lowered her voice. 'Look, Wendy, can you please not mention this to Alice? I haven't told her anything about it yet. Michael and I believe we are on the brink of something very — what shall I say — serious, even dangerous. All we know is that we are needed, Callum too. We are needed for the children. The thing is, Alice wants me to go to New York with her to attend an important symposium. It's a major step for her, Wendy, but I just cannot go, not with everything that's going on. I'm trying to work out how to tell her.'

'Oh shit! You really are between a rock and a hard place, aren't you? I'm so sorry. Of course, I won't say anything to Alice.'

'Thanks. Michael says he'll find a way around it. He sounds pretty certain, but I'm still dreading the fallout. I'm letting her down in a big way, and frankly, if she did go ape, I wouldn't blame her in the slightest. I'd be devastated if the boot were on the other foot.'

'I can understand why you haven't said anything,' said Wendy softly. 'She was beside herself when you had such a close call last time, and she'd be doubly worried about your safety if something, well, something bad happened again. And I hate to say it, but Alice is a bit like us coppers; very down to earth, and has little time for the paranormal. We've seen too many scams and confidence tricksters to countenance, well . . . clairvoyance, for instance.'

Ellie smiled ruefully. 'And don't I know it! Although, thank heavens she has come to accept my ability to read auras.'

'As have we in the police. The guys and gals at the station all love you, and have nothing but admiration for your gift. You really are the exception to the rule, and as you know, after that run-in you had with DCI Foreman and his poorly son in that supermarket, he is your greatest advocate.' She laughed. 'Not to mention your invaluable help with those two horrible murder cases! He still talks about that incident with his little boy as if it happened yesterday.'

Ellie smiled broadly. 'So do I, actually. That's where it all began. I knew immediately what was wrong with the little lad, I could see it as clear as day, and thank heavens Bob didn't ignore me and write me off as a flake. Do you know, Wendy, I really believe that my encounter with his boy was preordained. Call it fate, or destiny, or whatever you like, but it was meant to happen.'

'I hate to admit it, but even this hardened and cynical detective agrees with you one hundred per cent, as does her even harder and tougher boss!'

While Wendy finished her supper, Ellie told her a little more about Christopher and Harry. She didn't mention the spectral airman, just that both boys were displaying talents and using language that was way beyond their years.

Surprisingly, Wendy accepted her account quite easily. 'Some little kids are like that. One of my cousin's daughters was very different to her brother and her sister. When she was still very small she'd come out with these random statements that seemed to have no bearing on anything, which later turned out to be true. I was quite creeped out!' Wendy gave a dry laugh. 'Once, she said to me, "Shame about that scar on your face, Auntie Wendy." I didn't have a scar. Two days later, I got into a fracas with a couple of junkies, and guess what,' she touched the side of her jaw, 'I received a deep cut from jaw to cheekbone. It's faded now, but I had a scar for years. I can still see little Jasmine touching the side of her face as she spoke to me, exactly where I got cut a few days *after* she mentioned it. She stopped making these predictions as she grew older, and she has no memory of it now, but her family all remember the things she used to say.'

While Ellie was making coffee, Wendy received a call on her mobile.

'Wendy Brown . . . Sorry, caller, it's a bad signal, can you say that again?'

Ellie watched a look of distress flood her face.

'I'll be there. Can you give me that location again, please? I need to make sure I got it right. Okay, got it. Thank you.'

Wendy pushed her phone back into her pocket and stood up. 'I'm sorry, Ellie, I have to go. That was Jon Leatham. They've had a report of a boy's body, found on the edge of Abinger Forest.'

An ice-cold hand clasped Ellie's heart. It was beginning. The thing that had been haunting them for so long was finally starting to manifest itself.

'Go! But, Wendy, keep me updated. I, no, we — Michael and Callum and I — are in this with you. Understand?'

With a quick nod, Wendy made for the door.

* * *

Wendy knew the road the boy had been found on. As a schoolgirl, she had had a friend whose mother ran a stable in the forest, and she'd often visited her there. She had enjoyed going but had been too afraid of the horses to ride.

A blaze of flashing blue lights ahead told her she had arrived at the scene. As she slowed down, a uniformed policeman signalled to her to stop. She flashed her warrant card and was waved through the cordon.

She parked behind the assembled vehicles and made her way over to the DI, who was standing talking to the boss. She passed a waiting ambulance with its back doors wide open and assumed the body must still be *in situ*.

Drawing closer to her colleagues, she noticed their puzzled expressions.

Jon Leatham beckoned to her. 'Ah, Wendy. Glad you made it. We've got a very odd situation. Have a word with that guy over there and tell me what you make of him.' He pointed to a tall man in a fleece jacket who was talking animatedly to an ambulance driver.

'Sure, sir, but where's the dead boy?'

'Wouldn't we like to know,' grumbled the DCI, hands thrust deep into the pockets of his long grey overcoat. 'According to that chap in the fleece jacket, he is driving home from work and sees something lying by the side of the road. Sticks his hazards on, goes to investigate and finds a boy, dead. He covers him over with a blanket from his car, and waits for a car to pass by — sod's law, he has no mobile phone, and we all know this is a rarely used road, so no one comes. Finally, he drives on to the next house with lights on, and gets the owner to ring us. Goes back. Blanket still there, boy gone.'

Wendy shrugged. 'Obviously, the boy wasn't dead at all, just stunned, and he wandered off.'

'Just go and talk to the chap who found him, Wendy,' said Bob.

'All right, sir,' she said, beginning to sense there was more to this than met the eye. 'Has someone made sure we have that blanket? There might be DNA on it, it needs bagging and tagging.'

Jon winked. 'All done, Sergeant, but good on you for mentioning it.'

The man, who said his name was Will Harrison, looked genuinely worried.

'I know you've probably been over this half a dozen times, sir, but could you tell me what occurred, from the time you spotted something beside the road.'

With a shaky sigh, the man started to tell his story all over again. 'I thought it was an animal. We get a lot of deer killed on these back roads, and on the main ones too, but it looked too dark for a deer, and I was afraid it might be a dog.' He shivered and drew the foil blanket he'd been given closer around him. 'I soon realised it was no dog. It was a kid — oh, I don't know, about fifteen, sixteen, something like that. He had on a dark bomber jacket, and those black sports jog pants that boys like. Naturally, I thought he'd been hit by a car or something. I mean . . . all in black, in the dark. Maybe he was hitchhiking.'

Wendy nodded.

'Well, the thing was, Officer, there was no blood. Not a drop, and if he'd been hit — well, surely . . . Anyway, I could see he was dead, but even so, I got a torch from my car and checked his pulse and everything. There was nothing. And the worst thing . . . the worst of all, was his face! Officer, I've never seen anyone look so terrified. If I didn't know better, I'd swear he'd been literally frightened to death.'

'You're certain there's no chance that he'd either passed out, or maybe had a fit of some kind and was unconscious, not dead? He might have come to when you were off looking for help, and wandered off.'

He gave her a resigned look. 'Officer, I'm the first responder and safety officer for the company I work with. When I say he was dead, I bloody well mean it!'

'I'm sorry, sir, I didn't mean to sound rude, or upset you,' said Wendy. 'I'm only looking for a reason for the boy to have vanished within such a short space of time. You didn't go far, am I right, before you found a house and phoned 999?'

'A quarter of a mile, certainly no more. And the householder reacted immediately, so I was able to get back fast.'

'Look, let me take you over to the ambulance. You're frozen, and you have had a shock. You can sit there for a while, and I'll be back with you soon.'

Wendy returned to the others.

'The verdict?' asked the DCI.

'Pound to a penny, he did see a boy, and I'm fairly sure that he really was dead, sir,' she said.

'So, what happened in the ten minutes or so Mr Harrison was away looking for help?'

'The only thing I can think of is that he was killed, either deliberately or accidentally, and whoever did it came back for the body,' suggested Wendy. 'Did the witness tell you that there was no blood on the boy?'

'He did, so it wasn't a hit and run. We all know the carnage one of those—'

Just then Jon ran up to them, calling, 'Got something, sir! It's not easy to make out by torchlight — we'll have to check again in the morning — but there are definite drag marks, stretching from inside the treeline to the side of the road where Harrison says the boy was lying. From what we can tell it looks like the boy was hauled out of the woods, dragged to the edge of the road and dumped.'

'So maybe the intention was to get the lad into a vehicle, but they saw Harrison's headlights and just jettisoned him,' offered Wendy. 'Then, when Harrison drove off, they came back for the kid and scarpered.'

'It's possible,' said Bob slowly. 'You don't think this is some kind of elaborate hoax, do you?'

Jon made a face. 'I wouldn't rule it out completely, but my gut tells me it's for real.'

'You should have seen Harrison's expression when he described the look of terror on the boy's face. I swear that was no act. It'll be giving him nightmares for months,' Wendy said firmly.

'Right. Get uniform to close off the road, seal this area, and tomorrow we'll do a fingertip search through the surrounding woodlands, concentrating on those drag marks and where they came from. We'll also get Forensics to check the area where the body was found, although I'm guessing we'll have contaminated most of it already.'

'What about Mr Harrison?' Wendy asked.

'Make sure we have his details, and then get him home. He can give a full statement tomorrow.' Bob turned to go. 'I need to get back and report this to the super. I want everyone back here at first light.'

Having made the necessary arrangements with uniform, Wendy and Jon asked Harrison if he was okay to drive, and when he said he was, offered to follow him home, just to make sure that he was okay. By this time he had calmed down considerably and politely refused her offer.

'You do believe me, don't you, Sergeant?' he asked as he was about to drive away.

'Yes, sir. I do.' She took her card from her pocket and handed it to him. 'Seeing as you live fairly locally, sir, if you should hear anything about a teenager having been seen heading this way earlier in the evening, would you ring me?'

Harrison agreed to contact her immediately, and if he remembered anything else that might be of help.

Wendy watched him drive slowly away, thinking that Mr Harrison wouldn't be driving along this stretch of road anytime soon, especially after dark.

CHAPTER FOURTEEN

Marie Littlewood's home had been in her husband's family for many years. The house had undergone much renovation and extension in its long life, but it still retained its olde-worlde charm. For much of that time the local GP had had his surgery there; three generations of Dr Littlewood had come and gone before a smart new surgery was built in the village, and Marie's husband now saw his patients there.

That night Marie, who hadn't been sleeping particularly well, heard footsteps on the stairs. She looked at her alarm clock and saw the time was a quarter to two. She wasn't unduly worried; you don't live in a house with two men and a boy and not get used to their nightly trips to the bathroom. She lay snuggled beneath her duvet and waited for the return trip, wondering vaguely why whoever had answered his call of nature hadn't used the upstairs bathroom or the en suite.

With a grunt of mild annoyance at having to leave her warm cocoon, she slipped her legs over the edge of the bed and felt around for her slippers. Her husband, who was often called out at night, slept in an adjoining room so as not to disturb her, so she went there first. Easing open the door she peered in, but there was the shape of his large frame, still sleeping soundly.

With a frown, she pulled on her dressing gown and stepped out onto the landing. No lights were on, and all was quiet. Dan's door was closed, but the door to Christopher's room was wide open, the bed empty.

She smiled to herself. He was probably raiding the fridge. It had happened before, which was why she always left out a few tasty snacks for the lad.

When she found the kitchen in darkness and the downstairs toilet empty, she began to worry. She checked the outside doors back and front, but both were locked. Next she tried the new conservatory, a generous gift from Ellie and Michael, but that too was securely locked, the windows all closed.

Her anxiety grew. 'Christopher?' she hissed into the darkness. 'Christopher, where are you?'

No answer came, instead she heard more footsteps coming down the stairs.

'Mum? Is that you?' Daniel appeared in the hallway. 'Where's Christopher? He's not in his room.'

It was then that Marie noticed a chink of light underneath the dining room door. 'I think he's in there,' she whispered, pointing.

'What on earth is he doing in there?' muttered Dan.

He pushed the door open, and she followed him inside. Christopher was sitting at the dining room table, writing industriously on an A4 notepad.

'Come on, son,' said Daniel. 'Back to bed. You need your sleep, young man. Looks like we've been a bit too encouraging about this book of yours. We can't have it taking over your life. Now . . . upstairs.'

Christopher kept writing.

Marie touched her son's arm. 'Dan, I think he's asleep. Believe it or not, you used to sleepwalk when you were little, so he's probably got it from you. I don't think he heard a word of what you just said.'

'But he's never walked in his sleep before.'

'Well, I'm pretty sure he's doing so now, so don't shout at him. We need to coax him back to bed and not frighten him awake. All right?'

Marie tiptoed over to the small figure, still hunched over the table, writing furiously. Peering over his shoulder, she saw he'd covered two pages of an A4 notepad, but she couldn't read what it said.

She straightened up. Time for that later. She tried to recall how she had cajoled Daniel back to bed on the nights she found him wandering the house in his sleep. 'Christopher, darling. Time to stop now. You must go back to bed. It's very late and you've done enough, okay? Bedtime, Christopher.'

The hand slowed its feverish pace, coming gradually to a stop.

Without acknowledging their presence, the boy closed the pad and pushed back his chair. With unseeing eyes, he walked past his father and his gran, out into the hall and up the stairs.

'Get behind him, Daniel!' urged Marie. 'If he wakes up he could fall.'

Like an automaton, the boy returned to his room, climbed into his bed, pulled the duvet over his head and lay still.

Marie sighed with relief. Noticing her son's anxious expression she smiled at him. 'Don't worry. The first time is always the worst. Although you did once try to climb out of a window — an upstairs one. Your father almost had apoplexy.'

'But why start now, Mum? This has never happened before.'

'Maybe it has,' said Marie, 'and Della didn't tell you. I don't think it's too surprising. After all, Christopher has been through a lot.'

'I suppose so,' said Daniel. 'I'll be lying awake every night now, listening out for him.'

'It could well be a one off and will never happen again. Ask your father about sleepwalking in the morning and see what he thinks. Anyway, Christopher will sleep soundly for the rest of the night — you always did. Just don't be surprised if he's a bit tired tomorrow. Now, get back to bed, son, or we'll all be like zombies in the morning.'

But before returning to her room, Marie went back downstairs and took the notebook from the dining room table. Back in bed, she looked at what the boy had been writing. What she saw almost caused her to let go of the book.

The writing was that of an adult. To Marie's untutored eye it looked impeccable: grammatically sound and structurally polished. The vocabulary was way beyond that of a boy of Christopher's age. Yet he had written it. She had watched him.

Should she read it? Marie hesitated, almost afraid of what she might see. Her eyes travelled down the page, until the last few sentences, at the point where she had intervened to persuade him back to bed.

> *He found the boy lying on the roadside. Someone had thrown a blanket over the still form, and he felt that his heart would break when he pulled away the covering and saw the look of deathly terror, etched permanently on the teenager's face. 'You'll pay dearly for this,' he hissed into the night sky. Then, gently, he slipped his powerful arms beneath the inert figure and lifted him up. 'I'm taking you home, our beloved son.'*

And there it finished.

Every last vestige of sleep gone, all Marie could think of was that she had to talk to Ellie McEwan. She was tempted to ring her there and then, but stopped herself. She would ring first thing in the morning — no, she would go over to Snug Cottage and catch Ellie before she left for work. She didn't quite know why, but

Marie was certain that this piece of writing was vitally important to something Ellie was involved in. She had no idea what this something was, or why little Christopher was involved, but Ellie had to read this thing he'd written.

Having decided on this course of action, Marie laid the pages aside, suddenly drowsy. As her eyelids closed and she drifted into slumber, the heady scent of flowers filled the room.

* * *

In spite of the comfortable bed and the soft duvet, Ollie lay awake for hours thinking over what Rae and Luna had told him. He found it hard to believe that he was being offered something so perfect. Nothing less than a new life, full of promise, with a brilliant future before him — if he was prepared to work for it. Great sacrifices would be asked of him, it seemed. The place where he was now — which Rae called the Eleventh House — was being subjected to malign forces. Just what these were she was leaving to Gideon to explain. All she would say was that from time immemorial, dark Satanic forces had threatened to overwhelm all that was good in the world. Now evil had come to their door, and they must fight it with everything they had. That said, he was not to worry. They had powerful friends on their side. Right now he was safe, and would remain so, along with all the others Gideon had taken under his wing. As she left him to sleep, Rae made him promise never to set foot across their boundary. Tomorrow, Mark would show him exactly where the perimeter lay, so that he wouldn't cross it knowingly, thereby exposing himself to the dark forces beyond.

Of all the things Rae and Luna had told him, the most important was why he had been chosen. It had taken a while, but slowly he was coming to realise that it explained all the years he had dwelled with the feeling that he was out of place, an outsider.

In light of what they had told him, he understood now why his parents and his teachers — one in particular — had put so much effort into convincing him that he was 'not right in the head'. He was special, not 'weird' at all. Not only that, he had gifts that, nurtured and used wisely, could be immensely powerful. Hitherto, the adults in his life had dismissed the abilities that made him different as either of no importance, or just plain ridiculous, when in truth, they were his greatest strengths.

It was no wonder he couldn't sleep. Eventually, he decided to get up and try to find the kitchens and get himself something to drink. He was about to do so when he was overtaken by a sudden overpowering weariness, and he sank back against the pillows.

It had all been a bit too much to take in, and he still had so many questions . . .

'Ask anything you wish, but tomorrow. Sleep now, Ollie.'

He recognised the voice at once, it had been Luna's. But he was alone in the room.

He smiled, and closed his eyes.

* * *

While Ollie slept, the other inhabitants of the Eleventh House gathered in the old chapel.

A little way in front of the altar, laid out on the mosaic tiles, was the dead boy. A rich brocade cloak, formerly the proud vestment of an archbishop, was draped over the body. Only the face, the ravaged face, remained visible.

Around him, a circle had formed. Outside it, and a little apart, stood Gideon. None but the figure on the floor wore any special garment. All were dressed in their everyday clothes.

No one spoke. After several minutes, Gideon approached the dead boy, bent down and gently cradled his face in his hands. His eyes on the boy and speaking in a deep, sonorous voice, he told them to place a ring of golden light around the boy, and ask that he be guided to a place of peace.

Someone watching from the doorway would have seen the darkness within begin to recede, while the nave where the boy lay shimmered with the golden light of an evening's sunshine.

Still holding the boy's face, Gideon repeated the mantra, which gradually rose into a reverberant hum. *'Om Shanti, Shanti, Shanti.'* Peace, peace, peace. Like the ripples moving across a pond, the others joined in and the gentle glow became a glorious golden light.

Gideon looked up at the others, and a slow smile spread across his face. 'They are with us,' he whispered. 'They've come for him.'

Their faces turned to the arched ceiling, they watched swirls of rainbow light that danced and drifted, and then a mist the colour of amethyst descended, enveloping the body lying on the floor.

In moments, the mist had dissipated, the glow faded, and the chapel was dark once more.

Gideon looked down, and with a sigh of relief, brought his hands from the boy's face.

All the anguish had gone from it. The boy was at peace.

'Our son, you have come home to us. Rest in peace, child, safe in the arms of the angels.'

Silently, one by one, they turned to leave. Finally, Gideon was alone in the chapel. There he would remain, keeping vigil, until the new day dawned.

CHAPTER FIFTEEN

Ellie felt as if Monday had taken off leaving her struggling to catch up. She had barely left her bed when Marie Littlewood was on the phone to her. Thankfully, Alice was in the shower, and didn't overhear what was said. The upshot was that Ellie went to work via Marie's house. Again, she was lucky — Alice had left early to await a call from the CEO of a new medical software company, yet another one interested in AZSEE. Apparently, this company was prepared to make a very generous offer. Ellie hated resorting to so much subterfuge, but as Alice was full of their proposed trip to New York, as well as the business deals flowing in, Ellie was able to play it cool, saying as little as possible about her own life. She arrived at Marie's house to find her clutching an A4 notepad, which she thrust at Ellie before she could even say hello.

Now she was at work, the notepad open on her desk in front of her. She had shown it to Michael as soon as he arrived for work. They discussed what it might mean, and to say it gave them cause for concern would be an understatement. Meanwhile, they were still having to deal with the everyday running of the centre while trying to fathom out a way forward.

Ellie glanced at the wall clock and closed the pad. In five minutes time she would be meeting Mrs Beth Saunders.

For some inexplicable reason, the prospect frightened her. She couldn't understand why, but she would have given her eye teeth to be able to cancel the appointment. Was there just too much going on at present, or was it some kind of premonition? Whichever it was, she had no choice, so she might as well get it over with.

They had arranged for Janet Cooper to wait in reception, so that Mrs Saunders would be greeted by a friendly face. They had spoken before, so might help put Mrs Saunders's mind at ease.

One minute, two minutes. Three minutes late. Ellie wondered if she might be getting a reprieve. Just as she began to dare to hope, there was a knock on her door.

Getting to her feet, Ellie painted a smile on her face.

'Mrs Saunders, lovely to meet you. Please, do come on in and take a seat. Can I get you a cup of tea or coffee?'

Evidently somewhat overawed by the plush Art Nouveau room she found herself in, Beth Saunders shook her head at the offer of a drink. She cleared her throat. 'I confess I am utterly in the dark about why someone would insist on me making this visit, and even more so as to their offer to pay for it.' She spread her hands. 'I mean, it must be costing them a fortune!'

Ellie laughed. 'Not so much as you might think, Mrs Saunders. We are here to help the people who come here achieve better health or peace of mind, we're not out to fleece them. No one who needs it is refused treatment. Indeed, some have left here without even reaching for their credit card.'

Beth Saunders raised an eyebrow. 'I'm not sure what a financial advisor would think of your business strategy. And if that's the case, how do you keep the place afloat?'

'It's a long story. Let's just say we are no ordinary healing centre. Now, let me introduce myself. The truth is I have a rather unusual gift that enables me to heal the people who come here, such as yourself.' Beth opened her mouth to protest that she had no problem to heal, but Ellie held up her hand.

After a few minutes of further explanation, Ellie was able to tune in to Beth's aura. Her life-lights, Ellie saw, were in a terribly poor state, so much so that Ellie wasn't sure how she was managing to go on. The brightness and placement of the colours in her energy field were all wrong, indeed, they were almost negligible, and instead of radiating outwards, they flickered feebly, close to her body. Just looking at this tired and dispirited aura made Ellie want to cry. This poor woman.

'Oh, Beth,' she breathed. 'We really do need to talk.'

* * *

Beth wasn't the only person in the clinic with depleted energy. Accustomed to channelling his energy to where it was needed, particularly when undertaking a session of aura healing, Michael now felt considerably under par. One look at the words in the A4 notebook Marie had brought had sent his energy levels plummeting and his concentration elsewhere. He and Ellie had agreed that they should show the book to Callum, and to Jason, although the latter would not be in until the afternoon. It was a significant development, and a worrying one.

Instead of doing what he ought, and arranging his appointment list for the next few days, he was sitting in his office with a 'Do Not Disturb' sign on the door. He had informed Janet that he needed thirty minutes of uninterrupted quiet to meditate. Janet knew him of old, and he could be assured that no one would break in on him, not while his faithful Rottweiler was on guard.

Michael slid a relaxing CD into his recorder, adjusted the volume and sat back in his chair, closing his eyes. Offering up a prayer for safety and guidance, he slowly opened up his seven inner energy chakras to cleanse them and allow spirit to enter.

He had a very specific way of doing this, and as he followed this well-trodden path, he began to feel better. He saw each centre as if it were a beautiful rose opening up in the sunlight. He started with the root chakra, situated at the base of the spine, and visualised it as a blood-red flower unfurling its petals. He then moved up to the sacral chakra, and saw a flower of vivid orange. He moved on up his gradually relaxing body, opening each chakra in turn. He saw the solar plexus as yellow, the heart green. The throat was blue, the third eye in the middle of his forehead was indigo. Finally, he reached the powerful crown chakra, whose colour was deep violet.

Soon, Michael was walking along a sunlit beach with his wife on their favourite Greek Island. Everything was as it had been in the time before she fell ill, before her subsequent death.

As they walked, he confided in her. 'I do wonder if I have taken on too much, my darling. What with the healing, and the strange and sometimes frightening world that Ellie and I seem to have been thrust into.'

'You will be given no more than you can deal with, Michael,' said his wife gently. 'And you know you are never alone. Spirit guides you and will always intervene whenever you need help.'

'I suppose the worst that could happen, should things go terribly wrong, would be that I meet my death. And as that means I'll be with you again forever, perhaps it's not such a bad thing.'

'Michael Seale! Much as I love you, I really must chide you for talking like that. You should treasure every day you are given and be thankful for it. A life well lived, that's what you must aim for, and make sure you hang onto it for as long as you can.'

'I stand corrected, although I can't help being fearful of this thing that is out there threatening the children. We know very little as yet, but what we might find ourselves up against could be something very powerful.'

'Then take your own advice, Professor, and make yourself ready to meet it. And now, my darling one, come, take my hand and sit with me on the sand. Drink it all in, my love — the scent of the olive groves, the glitter of sunlight on the waves. Take energy from such moments, and always remember that you have a good heart, and that you are not alone, never.'

Gradually, Michael's world re-established itself around him — his chair, the desk at the window. With a sigh, he one by one closed down his chakras, murmured a 'thank you' and opened his eyes. In those first few moments he could still hear the waves lapping the shoreline and the earthy scent of olives. He was ready now to face whatever was to come.

* * *

Fully expecting to have to coax Beth Saunders's story from her, Ellie instead was confronted with a woman in floods of tears, while the difficulties facing her poured out of her in a tidal wave of emotion. In essence, Beth had been the proud mother of a delightful child, who from being a little angel had suddenly and inexplicably changed into a monster.

Beth went on to say that the child's malicious behaviour was only directed at her, and her husband could detect no change. As far as he could see she was the same sweet little girl as always, and it was his wife who was at fault. She was being neurotic, he said, and accused her of ill-treating the child. What had once been a happy home was being ripped apart, and Beth could see no way out. No one believed her; indeed, she hardly knew how to repeat some of the terrible things that came from her little girl's mouth. As her situation grew from bad to worse, Beth had come to the realisation that this child she had struggled so hard to conceive and had considered a blessing from heaven, had become a curse.

Ellie listened with a growing awareness that what was happening with this woman could not be resolved with a cup of tea and a session of aura healing from Michael. One thing she did know for certain was that Beth Saunders was not lying. Ellie could easily spot a liar by observing changes in their aura. This was no story concocted to excuse a child's bad behaviour. Something more was going on here.

The first thing she had to do now was take a look at the child's aura, and this had to be done while the child was alone with her mother. 'Where is Izzie now, Beth? At school?'

Beth nodded, wiping the tears from her eyes. 'She goes to the primary school near where we live. She finishes at three. I collect her every day except Friday when my husband picks her up.'

Ellie knew from the message she had received from Carole that Beth's daughter was in some way connected to the other children. All three were 'possessed', it seemed, and she was concerned that in the case of Beth's daughter, the spirit was malign and not, like Harry's, a force for good. She thought fast; she must not let this woman walk away. 'Having heard your story, Beth, the first thing I have to say is that I completely believe you. Secondly, I'm asking you to put your trust in me and my colleagues at the clinic. You don't know us, but you were led to us for a reason, and we will do our utmost to help you.'

Beth looked down. 'Thank you. Thank you so much.'

'I think you could probably do with that cup of tea now, couldn't you? While I'm organising that, I'd like to ask Michael, who is the co-owner of this centre, to come and join us. Is that okay with you?'

Beth managed a weak smile. 'That's fine. I'll be glad of anyone's help right now.'

A few minutes later, Ellie returned with tea and Michael, and Beth described how Izzie behaved towards her when the two of them were alone together. Ellie thought she sounded cunning and hurtful in ways that were far beyond her six years, but couldn't understand why this behaviour should be directed solely towards her mother, who loved her so dearly.

'We need to see Izzie as a matter of urgency,' said Michael softly.

Ellie nodded in agreement. 'I'm thinking the best place to do that would be right here at the clinic.' She looked at Beth. 'Could you get her here, as soon as possible — without causing a problem with your husband, of course?'

'He'll be late home tonight. He has to attend a meeting in Haslemere, and he's not likely to be back until about ten. I could give Izzie her tea, and then drive back here with her at around four, or four thirty, if that's not too late for you.'

'That's perfect for me,' said Michael. 'How about you, Ellie?'

'Yes, that's fine. The sooner the better. Then we can offer Beth some concrete help.'

Beth looked worried. 'I just hope it won't be a waste of your time. You've been so kind, even just being able to talk to you has been a help. The trouble is, I know what she's like, she'll be the perfect little angel with you, and you won't see what I've been talking about.'

'Don't be so sure,' said Ellie. 'We have a way around that. What we'll do is this: Michael will bring you both in here, then he'll go out for a while on some pretence, leaving you alone with Izzie. What she won't know is that I will be in the inner office,' she pointed to the far end of the room, 'and I have a carefully placed mirror there which allows me to watch what's going on. I can also hear everything that is said, so I will be able to observe Izzie's behaviour towards you.'

As Beth got ready to leave, Ellie took another look at her aura. It shone a little more brightly than when she first came in. Not a lot, but Ellie knew she was looking at a glimmer of hope shining through the darkness. Somehow they must find a way to help this poor beleaguered woman, because she was approaching rock bottom.

* * *

DS Wendy Brown shook her head in despair. They had combed a huge expanse of woodland spreading out from the place where the boy had been dumped, but had found nothing. Yes, the ground had been disturbed, but nothing had been dropped, and there was no discernible trace of shoe or tyre prints. The more they looked, the more despondent she became. She was absolutely certain that Will Harrison, the motorist who had spotted the dead boy, had been telling the truth. She had even spoken to the person who had rung 999 for him, and had been assured that the man who knocked on their door was truly distraught. Wendy's hopes now rested in an old car blanket that was currently being analysed by Forensics. Such tests are not an overnight job, even though Forensics were doing their best to rush them through. In desperation, she had requested sniffer dogs to be brought in to trace the scent of the dead boy from the blanket. The response was a resounding 'no'. Given that there was no hard evidence to suggest that there had even been a boy in the first place, they weren't about to waste more time and resources on a chimera.

Late that morning, they gave up, took down the cordon and opened up the road. Having spent hours thrashing about in the margins of the forest, all were agreed that there was nothing to find. Not only that, rain was forecast for that afternoon and evening, so even if Forensics did find something on the blanket, the crime scene, if that's what it was, would be washed clean.

Wendy drove back to the station, Will Harrison's voice ringing in her ears. Why did the dead lad look so terrified, she asked herself. Why?

As she parked her car, she decided that after hitting the vending machine for hot chocolate, she must phone Ellie McEwan, and ask her opinion. She might not be able to help, but at least she wouldn't laugh, as her colleagues probably would. A terrified young man didn't just die, only to be magicked away in a matter of minutes after having been discovered. That sort of thing just did not happen in Wendy's very practical world, although it did happen in Ellie's. At the very least, Ellie wouldn't tell her she was barking mad.

Back at her desk, Wendy dialled Ellie's number and prayed she wouldn't get her ansaphone. When she heard Ellie's voice, she almost cheered. She said she was sorry to phone her at work, but there was something she had to tell her about that had occurred the previous night. When Ellie didn't answer, she assumed her friend was busy, and hoped she wasn't too annoyed. When the silence continued, she began to worry. 'Ellie? You still there?'

'Wendy,' Ellie said at last. 'Can you come here? Straightaway? And if he's available, please bring the DCI with you.'

* * *

Ellie sat staring at the open notebook on the desk in front of her. There was no doubt in her mind that young Christopher's 'novel' was a record of actual events. The boy was simply recording information as it was given to him. He had had 'ideas' before, which generally came to him from his imaginary friend — doubtless his version of the airman — but where the book was concerned, something far more powerful had intervened.

She closed the notebook and hurried out of the office. No matter what Michael had planned for this morning, she wanted him with her when Wendy, and hopefully, Bob arrived. This was a sudden and unexpected turn of events. She had not foreseen the involvement of the police in the matter of the children. Now it seemed it had suddenly become a police investigation.

As she hastened towards Michael's office, she had a sudden thought: Alice! She was here at the C-M Centre today, working with Gordon and Nelli Kuiper. Yes, her Azimah clinic was situated away from the main house, in the renovated cricket pavilion, but she and the others regularly came across to either the café or the main reception area. If Alice caught sight of the DCI's ubiquitous grey suit, she would be inside Ellie's office like a rocket, and she wouldn't be happy. This could force Ellie into confessing that she would not be travelling to New York with her, something she dreaded. Well, there was nothing to be done about it now. All she could do was pray that Michael had his escape plan hatched. If not, she might just have to resort to telling her partner the truth and risk a major falling out. More than anything, she dreaded losing her beloved Alice.

Michael listened to her, his expression more serious with every word. 'This is it, Ellie, the ball is rolling. There's no going back now.'

'Yes,' she said, 'though we've known it was coming.' Oddly, she felt almost relieved. Her only worry was Alice.

She was just about to ask Michael what he thought she should do, when there was a knock at the door, and Alice burst in.

'Am I interrupting anything serious,' she said, 'or can you spare me a minute?'

'Go ahead, Alice,' Michael said quickly. 'Uh, is everything okay? You look troubled.'

'Oh gosh, I hardly know how to tell you this,' she said miserably. 'But I guess it's best to just come out with it. Ellie, would you be distraught if our trip to New York was cancelled? I'm *so* sorry, honestly, but I've had an emergency call from one of our colleagues in the States. He has a serious case, and he's at his wits' end trying to save a young woman with the Azimah Syndrome. He's begged me to go, taking Gordon and the AZSEE program with me, to see if we can help the girl. The thing is, we need to go soon, like tomorrow. We can then stay on for the symposium next week. The trouble is that's far too short notice for you to sort out all your clinic appointments and I'm sure you wouldn't want to be away that long.' She gazed at Ellie, wide-eyed and beseeching. 'I don't know what to say to you, Ellie, other than I'll make it up to you. And, oh I don't know, maybe we could get away, a proper holiday, just the two of us, when this is all over?'

Ellie's shock at being thrown this lifeline must have looked to Alice like disappointment. Trying not to smile, she said, 'Well, obviously I'd have loved to have been with you in your moment of triumph, but I'm the last person to stop you helping someone going through Azimah. Of course you must go, and yes, I'd love to have a holiday with you. So don't feel bad, okay?'

Alice ran to Ellie and hugged her, making Ellie feel so guilty she almost told her that she wouldn't have been able to go anyway. Luckily, common sense kicked in.

Alice stepped out of her embrace. 'I have to get back to Gordon, and prep Nelli about next week's appointments as she's going to be holding the fort in our absence.' She gave her a final squeeze and kissed her. 'Bless you for being so understanding. I'll see you later. I'll probably head off early and pack.'

'Then I suggest we get a takeaway from the village for supper. I'll pick something up on my way home.'

Alice nodded and thanked Michael. 'And look after this precious woman in my absence, won't you?'

'There's nothing I'd rather do, Alice,' said Michael with a beatific smile.

When the door had closed behind Alice, Ellie let out a groan. 'I feel like a total heel!'

'And I feel eternally grateful. Talk about being saved by the bell.' He laughed at Ellie's crestfallen expression. 'Oh, Ellie, don't you realise that there's a very good chance our celestial friends orchestrated this? They knew you couldn't go when you are needed here. This was meant to be, and you didn't have to lie to your partner. You *would* have loved to be with Alice when she gives her address at that symposium, and you *would* move heaven and earth to help another young woman going through what you went through. So rest easy, my friend.'

'I suppose so.'

'That's my girl. You can wave your Alice goodbye with a smile and a clear conscience. Frankly, she wouldn't understand what we may be delving into, anyway, so she's better off not knowing about it, especially if it's as dark as we fear.'

'Since you put it like that,' said Ellie, somewhat mollified, 'I guess I should thank my lucky stars for a narrow escape. Now, let's head down to my office and wait for Wendy, and possibly Bob Foreman. They should be here any time now.'

By the time Wendy and Bob arrived, Alice was safely back in her clinic taking Nelli through her additional tasks. Despite the reprieve, Ellie didn't want to have to answer awkward questions about the DCI's presence.

Bob strode in and enveloped her in a bear hug. 'It's been far too long, Ellie, and it's all my fault, but you know what the job's like. How are you, anyway?'

'I'm good, Bob, thank you. It's so lovely to see you.' *He looks bigger and greyer than ever,* Ellie thought. *Perhaps his indecision about whether or not to retire has been weighing him down.* Quickly, she checked into his aura, but saw little that was new. The arthritis in his knee was a bit worse, but his general health appeared to be fine, although she had doubts about his emotional state. Colours that were usually bright had dimmed somewhat, an indication of stress somewhere. She reminded herself to ask him about it before he and Wendy left and find out if she or Michael might be able to help.

She pointed to the sofa. 'Please, take a seat. I apologise for dragging you out here, but we really had no choice. The thing is, Michael and I believe that something very serious is happening, and we thought you should know about it. It has to do with this dead boy that was found.' Her two visitors immediately leaned forward expectantly. 'But before I go any further, I must ask you to keep an open mind, which may not be easy for a couple of detectives accustomed to seeing everything in black and white, as it were. But bear with me, listen to what I'm about to say — and trust my judgement.'

Bob gave her a wry smile. 'If anyone else but you had said that, I'd be shifting around in my seat and looking for the exit. But since it is you, we'll listen, and we won't dismiss you as a couple of cranks.'

Ellie gave a fleeting smile. 'Before I start, I'd like you to take a look at this.' She picked up the pages covered in Christopher's handwriting and handed them to Wendy. 'You rang me earlier and told me of a strange incident on a back road near Abinger Forest. Read this, and tell me what you think.'

Wendy read a couple of sentences and looked up at Ellie with a puzzled frown. 'I don't—' Ellie motioned her to continue. When she looked up again, Wendy's puzzled expression had turned to one of shock. She handed the pages to Bob.

When Bob had finished reading, Ellie said, 'This was written by an eight-year-old boy — whom you've both met, by the way. He was asleep at the time — that is, he was sleepwalking, something he doesn't normally do.'

Neither Bob nor Wendy spoke. Michael gave them a few seconds to digest this, and then he said, 'I'd better give you the background — such as it is. Wendy says that you and she have both experienced waking up to the smell of lilacs, and for some reason Wendy immediately thought of Ellie. The scent of lilacs always accompanies a visitation from Vera. It means that the unusual events we have been observing lately involve you. You've been led here for a reason.'

'Given the inexplicable nature of what went on during that terrible killing spree you were trying to bring a stop to, neither of us is going to dismiss what you're telling us,' Bob said.

'The DCI is right,' Wendy said. 'From that piece of writing you've just shown us, and the mysterious disappearance of that dead boy, clearly this is going to be no normal investigation.'

'We hoped you'd say that,' said Ellie. 'Now you understand what we're up against, we'll give you a more detailed account of a series of apparently random incidents that have occurred lately, and which we now know to be interconnected.'

Between them, she and Michael recounted the story of Callum and Lucy, little Harry and his airman, and young Christopher's strange compulsion to write a book, the latest and rather disturbing episode of which had been written in his sleep. Ellie told them about the interview she had just had with a distraught mother whose adorable little child had become all at once and for no apparent reason, suddenly malevolent, as if she were possessed. She told them too, of Carole's sudden manifestation, and of the message she had conveyed — that what was happening concerned the children, and the book. She glanced at the two police officers, wondering how they would take all this talk of spirits manifesting themselves, but they merely nodded, apparently unfazed.

When they had finished, Bob sat back and ran his fingers through his hair. 'I'm wondering how we should play this.' He looked at Wendy. 'I'm going to have to be very careful about which officers I assign to this, aren't I?'

'You are,' she said. 'Might I suggest you include DI Jon Leatham, and PC Paula English, if you can get her seconded to

CID for a while. Both had first-hand experience of the last, er, "unusual" case that Ellie and Michael had been involved with.'

Ellie nodded, pleased with the choice. She remembered how, when called upon to confront the paranormal, both officers had responded without turning a hair.

'Excellent suggestion,' Bob said, 'plus young DC Trevor Grant.'

'Trev? Oh. He's fairly new, isn't he, sir, I haven't had much to do with him yet.'

'Let's just say he has an interesting background. His previous posting didn't last long because some bright spark found out something from his past which made him a laughing stock with his fellow officers.'

'So that's why he's so quiet,' murmured Wendy.

'Exactly. Keeping himself to himself,' Bob said. 'But don't let that fool you, he's a very astute young man, and since he's not averse to thinking outside the box, I think he'd do well in an unorthodox case like this one. Anyway, I'll add him to the list and see how he copes. And I think that will be enough. A small but carefully chosen team.'

Now they had their team, Ellie sent out for coffee. While they sipped, she and Michael told Bob and Wendy about Harry's sad home life, the little boy neglected by parents struggling to cope with a severely ill brother. Listening, Bob's expression became positively thunderous. He was a loving father and found it hard to countenance the neglect of a child, however unintentional that might be.

'Huh,' he said. 'If it was me I'd go the other way and *over*-compensate for what he's missing out on. Poor little tyke. I can understand why Callum and his teacher Lucy feel the way they do about him.' He shook his head. 'So, it's the children, I get that much. But how do we join up the dots?'

'That's what we are trying to work out,' said Michael. 'Having heard about that dead boy, along with what Christopher has written, I've come to the conclusion that it all hinges on that mystery man who called the dead lad "son". I don't think he meant it literally, as in flesh and blood, but he obviously cared deeply for that boy.'

'That's what clinches it for me, too,' said Wendy. 'The way that poor guy who found the boy described the look of terror on his face still haunts me. And now I've seen what young Christopher wrote about the look of terror — what was it, "permanently etched on the teenager's face . . ." Well, it proves to me that we are not looking for someone who terrorised and killed the boy, but someone who was looking out for him and cared about him.'

'Is it possible the lad was your missing teenager?' asked Michael. 'It's all over the news.'

Bob shook his head. 'No, we showed the man pictures of Oliver Cruise, and it definitely wasn't him.'

'Which means you now have two missing boys, one dead, and one — hopefully — alive,' mused Ellie. 'I wonder . . .'

'You think there's a connection?' asked Wendy.

'If what Michael suggested is true, and the man who spirited the boy's body away is at the heart of all this — well, could he be the key to it all, including the missing Oliver Cruise?'

'I think I need a bit of time to get my head around all this,' Bob said. 'One thing I do know for certain is that we have to work together. So, are you up for being part of another investigation? Ellie? Michael?'

'We were part of it from the very start, Bob,' said Ellie. 'It's just that none of us knew it at the time.'

'Except Carole and Vera,' added Michael dryly. 'And they certainly knew about it. As they kept on telling us.'

'Speaking of Carole,' Ellie said, 'we've forgotten to tell Wendy and Bob about the near miss Callum had with that tractor.'

After listening to the story, Bob said he'd seen it in the log sheet at the station, but hadn't recognised the name. 'One of the officers who went out to that said it could have been a triple fatality. He wondered how the hell the driver of the car had managed to stop.'

'Now you know,' said Ellie. 'It was thanks to Carole Cavendish-Meyer, a dead airman and a bit of déjà vu!'

'Ellie McEwan! Please' Bob said. 'I'm prepared to be open-minded, but don't push it too far!'

Ellie grinned. 'Just saying. Anyway, how are we going to approach this combined operation?'

'Do you think you guys could put down what you know about these children in writing?' Bob said. 'Add as many names, locations, dates and other relevant info as you can think of. I'm going to need to prep our new team, and we need to give them as much information as we can. It's a big ask, I know, on top of all your other work, but it would help us enormously.'

'Of course we will, Bob,' said Ellie. 'Michael and I are planning to cut our workload to a minimum, and we'll only be seeing urgent cases while this is going on. We'll get onto it at once. And you must let us know of anything that you think is relevant, especially any sightings you have of this mysterious person who took the dead boy away.'

'Don't you worry about that,' said Bob. 'The minute I've briefed the others, I'll organise a house-to-house in that area, and we'll scour that part of the forest and the surrounding villages.'

'And please let us know the moment young Christopher writes any more of his book,' added Wendy.

'We'll be watching him like a hawk, believe me,' Michael said.

'As soon as I have seen Beth Saunders and her daughter, I'm going to go and see Marie and Daniel,' Ellie said. 'They are both aware of Vera's presence in our lives, so it won't come as a complete shock to them that Christopher's sudden literary brilliance is probably being channelled by her.'

'That's quite a lot to take on board,' said Bob dubiously, 'even if they are more, well, more spiritually aware.'

'Do you recall when Daniel went through that terrible time and became so depressed? Well, he often went to sit in our summer house at night.'

Bob and Wendy both nodded.

'It was Vera who sat with him and offered him consolation. What's more, she manifested in a corporeal form, despite having died several years previously. Daniel will believe me, don't worry about that.'

'Ah, I see,' Bob said. 'Corporeal form, eh? I guess it'll take me a bit of time to get used to thinking of things in that way.'

As Bob and Wendy left, and seeing that Bob's aura looked a little brighter, Ellie decided to postpone her quiet chat with him. He had quite enough to take on board for the time being.

'We are out of the starting blocks, old girl!' said Michael when the door closed behind them.

'I'm just waiting until Alice's flight is in the air. Then I will be one hundred per cent committed to this, you can be sure of that.'

Michael winked at her. 'Now, my friend, let's go and get Janet to clear our diaries. Urgent cases only for the time being, we have other work to do!'

CHAPTER SIXTEEN

His mind in turmoil, Ollie set out with Mark and Luna to walk the perimeter of the land which he was being told to call home. His thoughts full of all the information he had been given, he paid scant attention to the surrounding landscape or the terrain through which he was passing.

Luna, pausing to allow him to catch up, regarded him with sympathy. 'Overload, eh? Don't worry, we all felt like that at first.'

'I feel as if I've wandered onto the set of some weird film starring teenage superheroes, all under threat from an evil power. It's mental! One minute I'm all stoked about it and can't believe my luck, and the next I'm scared shitless!'

'Just go with it, Ollie. It'll all work itself out.' Luna looked up into the trees and smiled. 'You *are* lucky, you know. Luckier than you think. I could be wrong, but I think we got you just in time. There are two more out there whom we need to find and bring in. There should be twenty-two of us here, if we're to remain safe.'

'Shut up, Luna,' said Mark. 'He's got enough to take in. Ollie's lucky, let's leave it at that, and get on with what we're meant to be doing, showing him where the boundary is.'

Luna smiled equably. 'Okay. Ah, here's the lake, I'll let you carry on from here.'

The path they were on suddenly opened out to reveal the still waters of a large lake. Between the reeds and the bushes that fringed the shoreline were a number of small bays, on one of these a short wooden jetty jutted out into the water. Ollie thought it would be a great place to fish from — not that he'd ever gone fishing, but he liked the idea. At the far side of the lake, the forest was considerably thicker, crowding upon the shore and casting the water in shadow. Ollie found it sinister.

Mark rested his hand on Ollie's shoulder. 'You never go over to that side. Never.' He pointed. 'If you look closely, you'll see a rope extending from one shore to the other, cutting the lake in two. That is the perimeter line. You are free to go where you like on this side of the lake — there's some boats over there, and canoes you can go rowing in. But you must never go beyond the rope.'

Following Mark's pointing finger, Ollie noticed a small, incongruously ornate boathouse on the bank, half hidden by trees.

'That's where Josh lives,' Mark said. 'It's his job to keep a watch on the perimeter, and he reports directly to Rae or Gideon.'

'Reports what?' asked Ollie.

Mark shrugged. 'Anything he sees.'

Luna looked up at the sky, where the sun was now almost directly above them. 'We should get a move on. Gideon wants to see Ollie before lunchtime, and we have a way to go yet.'

After another half hour they were approaching the chateau, having completed a full circuit.

'Gideon will meet us in the hall.' Luna glanced up at the sky again. 'In ten minutes.'

'How come you keep looking up at the sky, Luna?' Ollie asked.

She smiled enigmatically.

'You'll notice she doesn't wear a watch,' said Mark with a grin. 'She doesn't need one. She's in tune with nature, is our Luna. She can tell the time from the sun, knows all about plants and animals.

Other things too, like the weather. Things you and I don't even notice.' He gave Ollie a nudge. 'Don't worry, you'll learn about our different abilities as you go along. We're all very different, and every one of us has some rare gift or talent.'

'Rae told me the same thing, but I still don't get what it's all for,' said Ollie.

'You must ask Gideon when you meet him,' Luna said. 'He'll explain it better than us.' And she gave him a tender, reassuring smile, which he thought the most beautiful thing he had ever seen in all his life.

As the three of them entered the chateau, it suddenly felt to Ollie like he was coming home.

* * *

With a smile, Gideon watched the three figures crossing the bridge over the moat. 'Look at them. What a motley crew. But each one of them so precious.'

Rae looked at him affectionately. 'We won't lose any more of them, Gideon. What happened yesterday was not your fault. He stayed away too long. He was very good at what he did, but he underestimated the dangers he faced out there. I'm not completely sure that he didn't sometimes court the dark forces that followed him.'

What she said was true, but he still felt responsible for the boy's death. Hadn't he thought the same thing on any number of occasions? What weighed heavily on him now was, that in that case, why hadn't he brought the boy in, and employed his talent in some other task?

As if she had read his thoughts, Rae said, 'He wouldn't have listened to you, Gideon. He did what he wanted, in his own way. I think he came to believe that he was invincible.'

'Until he was proved wrong,' said Gideon bitterly.

'I'll leave you now,' said Rae. 'I think you should be alone with Ollie.'

'Thank you. You are right. Poor Ollie is in a state of confusion right now. Hopefully, I shall be able to put his mind at rest, and then he can start to live properly.'

Rae rested her hand on his arm for a moment, and was gone.

'Ollie! Hello! At last we have a few minutes to talk. Come with me, and we'll go to my rooms.' Gideon led the way through the house to a door at the rear. His apartment was on the ground floor, with big French windows that opened into the gardens. This was his quiet place, and he rarely invited anyone inside, but he felt bad about having left the boy adrift with no guidance, so for once, he made an exception.

'Now you've seen the grounds and walked the perimeter, what do you think of your new home?'

'It's awesome, sir. It's like a . . . a world within a world.'

'It is, Ollie, and I'm Gideon, not sir.' Indicating a tapestry-covered sofa, he invited Ollie to sit. 'Make yourself comfortable there, and ask away. I'll answer all your questions, and this time we won't be interrupted.'

* * *

Looking around the room, Ollie saw dark paintings in heavy gold frames on the walls, and ornate furniture that might have come straight from a museum. The shelves lining the walls held more books than a library.

'Awesome!'

Looking slightly amused, Gideon said, 'When our benefactor brought us here, I left this room just as it was; a tribute to his kindness, you might say. The other two rooms are much simpler, more in keeping with my own inclinations.'

For some reason, Ollie found this reassuring. This opulent room didn't sit well with his impression of Gideon and his selfless band of followers.

'Well then, ask away.'

Ollie took a deep breath. Where to start? 'What *is* the Eleventh House? I mean, what is its purpose? And why am I being treated so well? Rae and Luna told me all of us here have talents and gifts that make us special in various ways, but what for?'

Gideon, who had taken a seat in a matching armchair, was silent for a few moments as if considering his answer. 'In essence, the Eleventh House is a safe haven, one of several scattered in different parts of the world. They emerge when the time is right — that is, when the universe believes there is a need for them. As to their purpose, they exist for the good of mankind in dark times.' Ollie opened his mouth to speak, but Gideon raised a hand to forestall him. 'Let me explain. I was chosen to look for twelve young people, all of whom had had difficult lives. They were misunderstood, their qualities mocked. A Higher Power recognised that these young people, of whom you are one, would be capable of great things as they grew into adulthood. Their actions would benefit mankind in different ways. They might alleviate suffering, or develop a means to end violence and bring about a more peaceful world. Some might even take up arms and do battle with evil . . . if they were allowed to live to maturity.'

'If?' Ollie interjected. 'What, you mean they might be, well, killed or something?'

'You are still young, but you should know that evil does indeed exist. There are dark forces abroad whose interests do not lie in a peaceful world without suffering. This morning you were shown our boundary. Beyond that boundary lies Evil, whose sole desire is to unleash the apocalypse and bring about the destruction of everything that is good in our world.'

Ollie felt a trickle of icy water run down his spine. Had he really been in danger 'out there'? He didn't recall any evil forces, nothing more dangerous than the school bullies and the disparaging remarks of some of his teachers. His life had certainly never been threatened. 'I don't know, I just felt different. I knew I wasn't like the other kids, but I was more unhappy than scared. I was called names, but no one really threatened me.'

'It would have happened, Ollie. You didn't know it but you were already living in a dangerous place, with people around you who meant you harm. People who knew that you must not be allowed to thrive, who would do everything in their power to prevent that happening.' He smiled at the bewildered boy. 'But that can't happen now. Here, you will reach your full potential, and achieve the purpose you are meant to fulfil. By the time you leave this place, as one day you will, you will be beyond their grasp.'

Ollie pulled a face. 'I can't see me doing anything to benefit the whole of mankind. I'm no genius, that's for sure!'

Gideon laughed. 'Oh, Ollie, you don't have to be a genius — although it's true we do have one or two budding Einsteins in our midst. You could simply be here because you are destined to do something amazing. Rae has already remarked on your photographic memory. She says you can recall faces and even incidents with uncanny accuracy.'

Ollie shrugged. 'Oh yeah. That. I thought everyone could do it. Rae called it something else, and she said the way I remember is different.'

'Yes, many people have eidetic memory — that is, they have total recall of an image, but that's just short term, only lasting a few seconds. Yours is not like that.'

'I know I can remember anything I see written down, even if I don't know what it says — like another language — but what use is that if I still don't understand it?'

'Well, for example, let's say a scientist shows you a paper with an extremely abstruse formula — like one of Einstein's, say. You'd be able to reproduce it afterwards with one hundred per cent accuracy, right?'

Ollie shrugged. 'Yeah, I could do that.'

'So, what if this valuable paper, that the scientist had taken years to perfect, was stolen, or got lost or accidentally destroyed, and there was no other copy? You'd have it right here, wouldn't you?' Gideon tapped his head. 'Now, suppose that formula was a cure for cancer or something. You might not have been the genius who discovered it, but without you and your memory, any number of people might have died before it was rediscovered.' He held Ollie's gaze. 'So you see it's often just a chance action on your part that results in something much bigger. Imagine grabbing hold of someone who has tripped and is about to fall on a busy railway line. Your quick reflexes might save a woman who would go on to give birth to a great leader, or a heart surgeon. It's not all about creating some ground-breaking invention, it can also be something as simple as preventing someone from falling over and thereby changing the world.' Gideon looked at him affectionately. 'When you come to us we don't always know what the future has in store for you, but we do know that you are here for a reason, and that you are to be protected.'

He kind of got that, but he also knew, though he didn't know how or why, that there was something else, something Gideon wasn't telling him, though his intuition told him not to press him about it. Instead, he asked, 'Can you tell me more about these evil forces? There's something in the darkness on the other side of the lake. Is that the evil you were talking about?'

When he mentioned the lake, Gideon seemed startled for a moment, as if the question had taken him unawares. Then he smiled again. 'Well, evil comes in many forms. There are bad people with dark hearts who will do anything to bring down those who want to live in peace and harmony, and who want the same for others.'

'If these bad people got in here, what would they do?' asked Ollie uncertainly.

'They won't get in, Ollie, they can't. But to give you an idea of how they work, I'll tell you about another place where bad people did get in.' Gideon sat back in the tapestry chair. 'A long time ago, I spent some time trying to help a friend who had started a small community in Cornwall, growing their own food and selling honey in the local market. Someone among them turned against what they were trying to do and began sowing discontent and causing arguments. It started with the little ones, who became fretful at night, waking up from nightmares. Friend turned against friend, food went bad, the bees abandoned their hives and children began to see things in the shadows, which became more numerous, casting places that had previously been well lit into deep shade. Eventually, we traced the corruption to its source and cast him out. After he had gone, the sun shone again, and children slept soundly at night.'

'So, is it real people threatening this place, like the one you just told me about, or is it something else? Luna said you'd found two more special children, and that time was running out for you to bring them here.'

'Some are real people, Ollie, but others are evil spirits that interfere in people's lives and cause bad things to happen. Normally, I would advise a newcomer not to trust anyone, but your case is rather different. I mean the other gift you have, your ability to sift what people say and winnow the truth from it. Now you are free to live the life you were meant to, no one will be able to lie to you, because you'll see through them at once.' Gideon suddenly looked tired. 'Luna's right. There are two more children to bring in, but we will find them. It's what we are here to do. And one of the two is very important indeed. We have trusted friends out there, and I have every faith that one of them will find a way to bring her home.'

'People like Mole, you mean?'

'Yes, people like Mole.'

'This girl . . . why is she more special than the rest of us?' Ollie asked.

'Young as she is, she is immensely powerful. With her help, we might be able to finally end the war against the forces of evil. When that happens, we will no longer need that perimeter line, and we will all be free to roam where we like.'

Listening to Gideon speak, Ollie began to realise that he was part of something immensely significant, far beyond anything he could possibly have imagined in his previous life.

'What's her name?' asked Ollie, not quite knowing what else to say.

'Clover,' said Gideon softly. 'Her name is Clover.'

CHAPTER SEVENTEEN

Just as Lucy was finishing her lunch, she heard someone call her name. She threw her sandwich wrapper into the waste bin and hurried across to where the deputy head was waiting for her in the doorway.

'Come along to my office, Lucy. I've asked Amelie to look after your class for you.'

'Is something wrong, Mrs White?'

'We have a bit of a situation, I'm afraid, Lucy. It's Mrs Davison, Harry's mother.'

God, thought Lucy. *What now?*

Closing the door behind them, the deputy head seated herself at her desk and pointed to the chair opposite.

Lucy sat, and waited for her to speak.

After some deliberation, Mrs White began to explain. 'Mrs Davison rang a few minutes ago. She was in a terrible state. Crying — no, sobbing — she begged me to call you to the phone so she could speak to you. It appears she tried your mobile, but there was no reply.'

'I turn it off during class, Mrs White, we all do. But I can call her now.' Lucy started to get up from her chair.

'Just a minute, Lucy.' She hesitated. 'You've, er, you told me once that you thought there was something . . . how can I put it, something *unusual* about little Harry. At the time, knowing about his brother's medical condition and how much of his parents' time and attention was taken up with caring for him, I may have chosen to rather, er, play down your concern regarding Harry. I genuinely believed that beyond his exceptional artistic talent, any other odd behaviour on his part could only be a call for attention.' She looked directly at Lucy. 'Well, this call from Harry's mother has made me think you were right to worry, and I was wrong to dismiss what you were trying to tell me. What's going on with that boy, Lucy?'

What to say? No way could she tell this woman the truth. 'Mrs White, could I just ask you what his mother was so upset about this morning? She's always in dreadful rush, and hates leaving little Jordan with others. She's at the end of her tether most of the time, and she's always emotional, but to call the school . . . what has happened?'

The deputy head frowned. 'She won't tell me. She says she will only speak to you. According to her, you are the only person who understands that her son is not like other little boys. What does she mean by that?'

'Goodness knows I'm no psychologist, Mrs White, but I've observed a number of aspects of Harry's behaviour that lead me to the same conclusion. Until now, his parents have either refused to admit, or honestly don't believe, that there's anything different about him. Dawn Davison even referred to his paintings as "scribble", and that says a lot, doesn't it?' Lucy shrugged. 'Maybe all he needs is a bit of love and attention, but the child needs help, and I've tried to be there for him as much as my role as his teacher permits.'

Nicole White pushed her telephone across the desk. 'Ring her. Then we'll discuss how to proceed.'

Lucy was gripped with sudden panic. If she got this wrong, the result could be a nightmare for Harry — if the school involved social services, for instance. Oh, if only Callum could be here to help her.

Slowly, she reached for the receiver and dialled the number Mrs White had written down. As, offering a silent prayer for help, she waited for a reply, she was overtaken by a sudden peaceful sensation, and she smelled the heady scent of flowers.

Telling Callum about it later, she said that she hadn't even been certain that it had been herself speaking, that it was someone else calmly reassuring the distraught mother that all would be well.

She put down the receiver, meeting the deputy head's enquiring gaze. 'Do you think Amelie could cover my class for an hour or so? I think I should go and see Mrs Davison in person. This isn't something that can be dealt with over the phone, and it's not for Harry's ears. Would you keep Harry safe until I return?'

'Is he in some kind of danger?' asked Mrs White, surprised at Lucy's choice of words.

Lucy hesitated. 'I honestly don't know . . .' Then she thought about the airman and the scent of flowers. 'No, I don't think so, not while he's here at school. But, please, just in case. I'll tell you what Dawn has to say when I get back. Is that all right?'

'This is very unorthodox, Lucy, but in the circumstances . . . I'll sort out your classes for you. And make sure you report to me the minute you get back. Oh, and Lucy, I thought you handled that call particularly well. Good for you.'

Closing the door behind her, Lucy offered up another prayer, this one in thanks.

When she drew up outside the Davisons' house, the door flew open before she was even out of the car.

'Oh, thank God you've come!'

Dawn Davison looked in a worse state than ever, and Lucy began to fear that something terrible had happened — could it be Jordan?

But when they entered the lounge, Harry's brother was there, strapped into his wheelchair. Not Jordan then.

'He's left me! He's left *us*!' Dawn gestured dramatically toward the boy in the chair.

'Bryan?'

'Bryan. He's gone! Oh, Lucy, what are we going to do?'

'Hold on, Dawn. Now, you just sit down and I'll make you a cup of tea, and then you can tell me all about it.' Gently, Lucy led the agitated woman to a chair next to her son. 'You sit there, and don't worry, I'll find the tea things. While I'm in the kitchen take a few deep breaths and try to calm yourself. Don't forget Jordan's here, we don't want to upset him, do we?'

'No, of course not.'

Five minutes later, Lucy was back with two steaming mugs of tea. She pulled up a chair close to Dawn and asked her to tell her exactly what had happened.

Dawn's tears gave way to rage. 'He never even had the decency to talk it over with me. My God, when I think of what we've both suffered over the last few years, but we've always struggled on. Then all at once he's grabbing his clothes from the drawers and cupboards, yelling that he's had enough, that he's taken more than any man can be expected to. The bastard! What about me? And the mess he's left behind him? But more than anything, what about the children?'

Yes, what about them? Lucy thought. 'Are you sure he didn't just have a meltdown? I mean, you've both been under a lot of stress. Don't you think he'll realise what he's done and come back once he's thought about it?'

Dawn looked exhausted. 'No, Lucy, he's gone for good. I think it's been coming for a while, and I wouldn't be surprised if there isn't someone else involved. He told me to expect a letter from his solicitor. I can only think that means divorce. But what worries me most is how I'm going to cope on my own, what with Jordan in the state he's in, as well as his five-year-old brother. I can't do it! Nobody could.'

How could anyone be so callous as to just walk out on his wife and kiddies, thought Lucy, not when one was chronically ill and the other . . . well, she wasn't sure how to describe Harry. But it seemed that Bryan had done just that. What selfishness! 'What about your family?' she asked. 'Could one of them come and help out for a while?'

Dawn sighed. 'There's no one. We always prided ourselves on being self-sufficient. I have no immediate family, and the few friends I have left are in no position to leave their own families to come and support me and two needy children.' She broke down again. 'Jordan, well, I could just about cope with him. I'm used to his needs, and with carers and my lovely neighbour for emergencies, I think we'd manage, but . . .'

Lucy swallowed. 'Harry.'

Tears pouring down her cheeks, she said, 'I don't know what you must think of me and the way I treat my darling little boy. I love Harry so much, but I just don't have the energy to cope with both children, and I have no choice but to care for Jordan, he relies on me for everything. All my energy goes into him, leaving nothing for Harry.' She looked directly at Lucy. 'I *do* know that he is different, Lucy. I *do* know that he has enormous artistic talent. As for his knowledge about aeroplanes, well, it terrifies the life out of me. I'm not denying any of that, like Bryan used to, I just don't have the strength to deal with it. Can you understand that? I never wanted to, but I was forced to choose between them, which, when it came down to it, was no choice at all. Look at Jordan, Lucy! Just look at him! And then tell me I had a choice.'

Lucy looked at the helpless little boy, vaguely trying to focus on a multicoloured mobile dangling above his chair. An oddly contorted small hand reached up to it, then fell back again.

Biting back tears of her own, she asked, 'What do you want me to do, Dawn?'

'You are the only person I know who sees Harry for what he is. You probably know more about him than I do. And . . . you are the only person I trust. My beloved husband's parting shot was that since I was never going to cope, there was always social services, and in any case, Harry might be better off in care.' Her eyes narrowed. 'Well, no child of mine is going into care.'

The thought of it turned Lucy's stomach over. 'I need to make a call, Dawn. No promises, but I do know what you are asking, and,' she drew in a breath, 'I'll do my best, I promise.'

She pulled out her phone and dialled the direct number for her deputy head. 'Mrs White, I'll explain everything when I get back, but I need to ask for your help, and to ask you to trust me.'

'Go on.'

'Could you arrange for me to have a week's compassionate leave, as from tonight? Uh, a family emergency, maybe?' She lowered her voice. 'This is a very serious situation, Mrs White, otherwise I wouldn't be asking.'

There was a long silence. 'I'll put the wheels in motion, and the moment you get back here, come to my office and we'll discuss the reason for your sudden need to take leave of absence.'

'Oh, thank you,' Lucy whispered. 'Thank you, Mrs White. I'll be back in half an hour.'

Lucy ended the call. 'Okay, Dawn, here's what we'll do. You concentrate on Jordan, but promise me you'll get all the help you can, because unless your husband sees the light and relents, you could have a whole load of legal issues to deal with. But right now, pack a case for Harry, and fill it with all the things he loves — teddy bears and the like — along with the toiletries he might need. After school, I'll bring him home to say goodbye to you. Make a big fuss of him, tell him you love him but I'm taking him for a little holiday as you have a lot to deal with right now.'

'Oh, I hope he understands,' Dawn murmured.

'Your son understands far more than you know, Dawn. He once told me he considers himself lucky compared to Jordan, which is quite something coming from a five-year-old.'

'Did he really?' Dawn shook her head. 'After all the times we've put him second to his brother . . .'

Sensing more tears coming, Lucy got up to leave. 'Right, I must be off, but I'll be back as soon as school is over. One more thing before I go, my friend Callum will help me. You met him the other day, if you remember. He's a nurse and he gets on well with Harry. Your son is in safe hands.'

'I remember him. Harry couldn't stop talking about him after you so kindly had him for the day.' Dawn actually managed a smile. 'He says you should marry Callum, so watch out, you could have a pint-sized matchmaker on your hands.'

Suddenly hot, Lucy laughed and began fussing with her jacket and bag.

At the door, Dawn put her arms around her. 'You're an angel, Lucy. I can't thank you enough for everything you're doing. You have no idea how much it means to me, and Harry, and little Jordan too.'

Although she knew he was working, Lucy couldn't wait to ring Callum and tell him what had happened. To her surprise he answered immediately, explaining that he was having a late lunch. She gave him the gist of the morning's events and asked him if he would be free to meet her at her house after work. Without the slightest hesitation he said he'd be there, but wasn't she putting her job in jeopardy by giving one of her pupils so much attention?

'Callum, I'm certain we have the deputy head on our side. She's already granted me a week's grace by permitting me to take compassionate leave. Something Dawn said must have made her change her mind about Harry. If we can keep her on side, at least until we find out what happens next, it'll give me time to decide what to do about him.'

She drove back to the school, her mind full of plans for the coming week, and how she could accommodate her little lodger in her tiny semi-detached cottage. First, however, was the immediate problem of sorting out her classes. She just hoped she had been right about Mrs White, because she was relying on her to straighten things out with the headmistress. To that end, Dawn was to ring the school tomorrow and explain that Harry was unwell and that she was keeping him at home until he recovered. Unless he was away too long, it was doubtful that the school would require a doctor's certificate — they'd worry about that later. If it had only been a case of a husband walking out on his wife and children, Lucy would have continued to teach, and Harry would attend school as normal, but this was no normal situation, and Harry was no normal boy. She and Callum had been handed a perfect opportunity to try and get to the bottom of why this little boy was being watched over by a dead airman.

* * *

Ellie, Michael and Callum had got together and devised a strategy whereby Ellie could observe Izzie Saunders's aura without the child's knowledge. With ten minutes to go before the child and her mother were due to arrive, Ellie felt the same reluctance to go ahead with it as she had prior to meeting Beth for the first time, and she couldn't understand why. Having spoken to Beth, she felt nothing but concern for the young mother, and she very much wanted to help her. So why this strange apprehension?

'Are you all right, my friend?' Michael asked. 'You look troubled.'

'I don't know,' she said, and told him about the sense of foreboding she had experienced that morning, and that it had suddenly come over her again.

They were sitting in the Orangery, from where they would be able to see Beth's car drive past on its way into the car park. His eyes on the window, Michael said, 'I feel it too.'

Worrying as it was, at least it made Ellie feel better knowing that someone else was feeling the same way.

'Maybe it's because it involves a child, and we know children are central to what is happening right now,' suggested Michael. 'And what Beth Saunders told you was pretty disturbing, wasn't it? Or am I just trying to convince myself that this bad feeling is of no great consequence?'

'Sorry, Michael, but I think it's what Beth told me, don't you?'

'Oh well, we'll soon know, won't we?'

'There's her car now,' Ellie said. 'Is Callum all prepared?'

'Yes, he's in reception, he's just given me a thumbs up. Do your thing, Ellie, and I'm going to be very interested in your observations.'

Ellie stood up. 'Well, right now I'm more anxious than interested, but here goes, let's try out our acting skills and get this over with.'

Michael and Ellie arrived in the foyer just as the main door opened to admit Beth and Izzie. Ellie was struck immediately by the child's dark beauty.

Izzie had long wavy hair so black it was almost blue, and the biggest, darkest eyes that Ellie had ever seen. As soon as she caught sight of them she drew closer to her mother's side, smiling a little nervously. A perfectly natural reaction in a child meeting adults she didn't know.

Mother and child hesitated in the doorway. 'Ah,' Michael said approaching them with his hand outstretched, 'you must be Izzie. Lovely to meet you. I'm Michael, and this is Ellie, the doctor who is going to have a chat with your mummy.'

Izzie's dark eyes darted around the reception area, taking in the comfortable seats, the houseplants. There was a vase of flowers on the desk. 'This doesn't look like a hospital. I had to go to one once when I cut my hand, and I didn't like it. It smelled funny.'

'That's because this isn't exactly a hospital, it's called a clinic, but we do the same thing, we make people better.' Beaming at her, Michael said, 'Let's go and sit in the Orangery for a bit, shall we? We just need to fill in a few forms before Ellie has a look at your mummy.'

They had agreed beforehand that they should tell Izzie that it was her mother seeking advice, and that having been unable to find a childminder at short notice, Izzie was coming along too.

As they made their way to the Orangery, Ellie tuned in to Izzie's aura. What she saw puzzled her. Yes, there were the bright vibrant colours so typical of children, and as the child chatted to Michael, she saw the colours of the clothes she wore. This too was to be expected because a child's aura often reflects the colours of their favourite things — toys, clothes or just colours they like. But beyond this, there was something else that Ellie couldn't quite make out. Then she realised that amid the various colours that glowed and pulsated, there was one that was missing. The colour pink was completely absent, to the extent that none of the other colours had even a slight pinkish hue.

Reluctantly, she turned her attention back to the others. There would be time to delve deeper into this unusual phenomenon later, after Michael had observed the child's aura while she and Callum staged their award-winning performance. As Michael was jotting down their details for the clinic's records, Ellie saw Callum approaching. The show was about to begin.

'Miss McEwan,' he called, looking suitably flustered, 'I'm so sorry to interrupt, but we have a problem with a referral. It's Mr Catterall — you know how difficult he can be. He is insisting that the London hospital who are to treat him is too far away and he can't make the journey. He's causing quite a fuss. Could you spare a few minutes to speak to Janet in the main office?'

With an annoyed tut, she apologised and stood up to follow Callum. 'Michael, perhaps you'd take Beth and Izzie to my consulting room after you've finished here. I won't be long.'

Two minutes later, she and Callum were in her rooms, where she carefully stood the inner office door very slightly ajar, allowing her an unimpeded view of the consulting room couches, praying that no one would knock against or close it.

'Give me five minutes to observe how the child's attitude and her aura change when she's alone with her mother. Then go in and take the girl to the café for a hot chocolate or something, while I supposedly examine her mother, okay? Beth, Michael and I will join you shortly after that.'

'Got it, Miss McEwan, and good luck.'

Ellie concealed herself and took several deep breaths. She hadn't said anything to Michael or Callum, but she was actually afraid of what she might see. Part of her hoped that poor Beth was making a terrible mistake, and that her daughter was simply going through a phase so many kids went through when they got to about six, testing the boundaries of parental authority with back-chat and impertinent remarks.

'*Come on, McEwan, who d'you think you're kidding,*' she muttered to herself. '*That's not the case, and you bloody well know it.*'

She heard the sound of voices, and the outer door opened. Michael invited them to sit down, the chairs having previously been arranged so as to give Ellie a clear line of sight across the room to Izzie.

This was it. Ellie took another deep breath and waited for her auric vision to open up.

Beth's appeared as it had on their first meeting, dull and depleted, while the child's resembled that of any child of six, except for that peculiar absence of the colour pink.

Michael chatted affably, until his phone was heard, buzzing in his pocket. 'So sorry, Beth, it's an important call. I'll have to leave you for a couple of minutes, but Ellie will be back any moment.'

Mother and daughter were alone.

Ellie held her breath, her eyes on the mirror and the child reflected therein.

Almost instantaneously the child's aura underwent such a dramatic transformation that Ellie almost gasped aloud.

Hardly believing what she was seeing, she watched the child's pretty face contort into an expression of pure malice. She seemed to pin her mother with her dark eyes, causing Beth to shrink back in her chair.

'What did you bring me here for?' Izzie hissed. 'You've tricked me, haven't you? This is no clinic, and that woman isn't a doctor, and you're not ill. Are you?'

Even the voice had changed. It certainly wasn't that of a six-year-old being cheeky. No ordinary child of six would even know how to express such malice. Ellie could only think of it as evil. However, the transformation in her manner was as nothing compared to that of her aura. Sickened, Ellie forced herself to examine it minutely, so that she could describe it accurately to Michael.

The colours were still there, but faint, as if she were seeing them through a tinted window. The phrase 'through a glass darkly' came into her mind. The childish bright colours were mixed with those of a muddy hue that was not quite brown, and that she found somehow repulsive. Gradually, it seemed to seep through the original colours, which began to shrink before her gaze like the flame of a gas cooker as it is turned down.

Beth's response was admirably controlled, her tone even. She must have learned never to rise to the child's provocations. Ellie wasn't sure she herself could have managed such restraint, and regarded Beth with a new respect.

'I'm sorry you don't like it here, Izzie, but no matter what you think, Mummy does need help, and these kind people have offered to see what they can do for me.'

The child laughed derisively. 'Oh, come on, you're beyond help, and you know it. In fact, instead of wasting your time in clinics, why not just go down to the river and do what you failed to do the other day?' Her eyes glittered. 'I can't wait to tell Daddy about you wasting his money on a bunch of crackpots.'

'You can tell him what you like, darling, because it's not costing him a penny.'

Izzie responded with a glare at her mother, but said nothing. By now, Ellie was wishing that Callum would hurry up and relieve her. She'd seen all she needed to, all she could take.

Finally, the door opened, and Callum stuck his head inside. 'Miss McEwan is on her way, Beth, sorry for the delay.'

He transferred his gaze to Izzie, and for a moment Ellie thought she saw him flinch. Did his smile seem forced?

'Well, Izzie, suppose I take you to the café for a treat while Mummy is being seen by the doctor. Fancy an ice cream, or a hot chocolate with sprinkles? What do you say?'

Izzie hesitated, and then threw him a bored smile. 'Okay, I guess an ice cream would be nice.'

From her hiding place, Ellie watched the child's auric colours burn brightly again and the darkness recede. Suddenly, the child was smiling happily. 'Do they have lots of flavours? My favourite is cookies and cream, what's yours?'

'Anything with chocolate in it,' said Callum, appearing to gather himself. 'Let's go and see what they've got, shall we?'

Ellie waited while their chatter receded down the corridor outside before emerging from her hiding place.

Beth, who was sitting slumped back on the sofa, sat up as soon as she saw her. 'Now do you see what I mean?'

Before Ellie could answer, Michael hurried in. Beth looked at their faces and burst into tears. 'You have no idea what a relief it is to know that someone else has seen what I am faced with day in, day out.'

Ellie hurried over and put an arm around her. 'Oh, I saw it all right, and I have to say I think you were amazing with her.' The two women glanced at Michael, who was regarding them anxiously. 'Our Izzie put on a stellar performance, Michael.' She shook her head. 'I don't know how Beth copes with such . . . vitriol.'

'I don't, is the answer. You heard what she said about the river? Well, the other day I was moments away from throwing myself in. I would have too, but for this lovely old man and his dog who happened to be passing and stopped me.'

'Oh, my dear,' Michael said, 'it sounds awful. I'll just ask Janet to get us some refreshments, and we can talk while Callum is looking after Izzie. But, Beth, are you sure you're okay to carry on? If you prefer, I can get our nurse practitioner to administer a sedative, just a light one, and one of us can drive you home.'

Beth shook her head and blew her nose. 'No, it's thoughtful of you, but I'll be fine. I think it's just relief, to be honest. Ellie has now seen Izzie as I see her, and I don't feel so alone, or that I'm going mad.'

Michael went to find Janet, and Ellie tried to decide how much to tell Beth. After some deliberation, she settled on a brief description of what she had observed. She could give Michael the full Technicolor version later.

'Her aura does look rather dark, but I'll have to discuss it further with my partner. One thing I do want to ask is, does her voice always change when she's being so detestable — forgive me for using that word, but—'

'There's no need to apologise,' Beth interjected. 'She is detestable. But when she's like that she's no longer my daughter, and I so want my daughter back. Yes, her voice, her whole demeanour changes. She's not Izzie, but at the same time she is her, if you get what I mean.'

Ellie assured her that now she'd seen it first hand she understood perfectly, but as she had previously mentioned, she would value her partner's expertise and opinion, in order to get a better idea of what they were dealing with. She hoped she sounded convincing, because as things stood, she was at a loss to understand what she'd just witnessed. Unless . . . No, it could not be. Was she on the threshold of another confrontation with the forces of evil?

Meanwhile, Beth was saying, 'I know this sounds like something out of a bad horror story, but I'm beginning to believe that my daughter has become possessed. Please don't laugh, but I just can't think of any other explanation for why a beautiful, loving child should suddenly start acting like she does.'

'I'm not laughing, Beth,' said Ellie, who had had the very same thought. 'Tell me, how did Izzie know about that time you were at the river, and what you intended to do?'

'That's the thing, she didn't! I didn't tell a soul, partly because I was ashamed of my weakness. But I felt so alone, Ellie, cut off from everyone because I couldn't get them to believe me. People were starting to give me odd looks, whisper about me.' She shook her head. 'If it hadn't been for that old man by the river that day, who took what I said seriously, I swear I'd be dead by now.'

Ellie had forgotten about the mysterious person who had offered to pay for Beth's treatment. If everyone Beth knew refused to believe her, who could it be? Like a lightning bolt, an image flashed through her mind, only to fade as soon as it had struck home. An old man and a dog, following Beth along a tow-path, both man and dog encircled in a halo the colour of amethyst. If ever she had needed a sign that this child was connected to their own haunted children, one had just been granted her.

'Beth, listen—'

At that moment the door opened and Michael backed in carrying a tray of steaming mugs of tea. 'Janet was stuck on the phone, so I brought them myself. I hope I haven't missed anything important.'

Ellie puffed out her cheeks. 'Frankly, Michael, I have no idea how to go about it, but we need to keep a very close eye on Beth and her daughter. If I told you Vera thinks they need our protection, what would you say?'

'I'd say, in that case that's what we need to do,' Michael said.

'Vera? I'm sorry, you've lost me. Who's Vera?' said Beth.

'You'd better have some tea,' said Ellie, 'because it's a long story.'

CHAPTER EIGHTEEN

To DS Wendy Brown's disappointment, PC Paula English was in the middle of another case and unable to join their small team. With no Paula around, Wendy was having a lot more to do with DC Trevor Grant, and was beginning to see another side of him. She had always regarded him as a loner, which had somewhat set Wendy, a team player herself, against him. She now knew that this reticence was a defence mechanism, his way of warding off the piss-takes of his fellow coppers. Once the team was in place, she made a point of having a quiet word with Trevor and was glad she'd made the effort. It soon became clear that the young officer was hugely relieved to finally have someone to talk to who would not hold him up to ridicule.

'I'd always dreamed of becoming a detective, Sarge, and I've finally made it, but it's been a rough road. Now, please don't laugh, but I'm truly coming to believe that it was all preordained. And I mean all — my burning ambition to get into CID, all the flak I've taken along the way, and now being part of this special team. I know I can make a contribution, and I'd really appreciate a chance to go out to the Cavendish-Meyer Centre and meet Ellie McEwan and the professor.'

The young man regarding her so eagerly through narrow, dark-rimmed glasses looked nothing like the usual image of a copper.

For a start, he had a sensitive, almost bookish look about him. He was smartly dressed, and his light blond hair was cut in the latest spiky style. She asked him if he was willing to work extra hours, including evenings, and he said that he was; indeed, he had expected to be asked to do so. He lived at home with his mother, his father having been killed in a road traffic collision a few years ago, and he had no dependants. His mother, he added, had fully supported him in his decision to become a police officer.

Wendy had been wondering how to broach the tricky subject of the taunts and snide remarks of his fellow officers at his former station and what lay behind it. She needn't have worried, Trevor pre-empted her question.

'And, Sarge, if I'm going to be working closely with you, I guess I should put you in the picture regarding the reason why I was transferred. You see, my mother is clairvoyant, and the guys at the station found out about it. I was raised in a Christian Spiritualist church — and before you say anything, I had one of the happiest childhoods you could possibly imagine. The people around me were kind, and even as a child I found the services uplifting. They often spoke about death, and the land of eternal summer that awaits us all in the afterlife. So I was never afraid of death. I don't know how much you know about Spiritualist worship, but towards the end of the service there is always a speaker, a medium who invites the spirit world to join the gathering and bring messages from the other side. Mum was often the medium called upon if there was no Spiritualist National Union representative available. I remember how delighted everyone was when she stood up to receive the messages from the other side.

'To give you an example of what I mean when I say Mum was clairvoyant, I'll tell you about something that happened before we moved here and were still living up in Northumberland. It also explains why I was laughed at so much at my former station. At the time there had been a series of attacks on young women in the area. One night, my mother was driving home from visiting a friend when something compelled her to stop the car. She was on a long stretch of deserted road across the moors. She pulled into a lay-by and stepped out of the car. A young woman was walking away from her in the direction of the nearest town, weeping. Mum knew that someone had dumped her out there, leaving her to walk home alone. She was about to go after the young woman and ask her if she could help when a car passed. The driver slowed to a halt beside the young woman and said something to her, then the passenger door opened and she got in. Suddenly, the road was empty. Mum realised that what she had just 'seen' was a message. The thing was, she knew who the man was. He was an important figure in the neighbourhood, and she knew what the reaction would be if she reported it. However, when the following day she heard that the young woman had disappeared, Mum felt obliged to go to the police.'

Wendy vaguely remembered this story, for a while it had been the standing joke in the police mess rooms. The man Trevor's mum had reported was well-connected, some of those connections being high-ranking police officers. The family was subjected to harassment, which became so unbearable that they moved south. In a cruel twist of fate, the man himself later departed for another part of the country and the attacks and disappearances ceased. It was too late for Trevor's mother, however. Her name was never cleared, and Trevor became known as the guy whose mum was an attention-seeking nutter, a waster of police time.

Wendy asked him if he too was clairvoyant.

Trevor nodded. 'Sometimes, though nothing like Mum.'

Wendy waited, but he didn't explain further. 'So, how come, if she was treated so badly by the police, did she so strongly support your decision to join the force?'

Trevor shrugged. 'Because she realised that it was my calling. She also believed I might make a difference, and that one day I might be able to prevent someone going through what she'd had to. In her words, "we do not go against that which is decided for us."

'And there's something else, Sarge. About my mum . . . The thing is, I never involve her in my job, and I never ask her help. After what happened up north, it wouldn't be fair on her. And if in the unlikely event that she did become involved in this investigation, spirit would direct her, not me, nor anyone else.'

'I totally understand that, Trev. And who knows, there might turn out to be a rational explanation for the things that are happening.' Even as she spoke, she was sure that both she and Trevor considered that about as likely as pigs sprouting wings. 'At the end of the day, we're still down-to-earth coppers, and we always put hard facts first. The boss in particular still struggles with some of the inexplicable things he's witnessed, search *Butterworths Police Law* as he might!'

Trevor nodded. 'I find it refreshing to think that not everything in life is black and white.'

'I guess we can't be anything but grounded in reality when we see so much of the bad in people. It takes a personal experience like your mum's to make you realise there's something more out there.' She gave a little shake of her head. 'Anyway, back to the real world. Any updates from the house-to-house around where the dead boy was found?'

'I just bumped into a couple of uniforms who were coming off their shift out there. They reckon it's a nightmare. The houses are scattered all over the place — in the woods, down unmarked roads and dead-end tracks, and when they eventually get to them, the owners are out. Like I said, nightmare.'

'Yes, I've been there,' said Wendy, recalling her visits to her friend's stables. She had wondered then how anyone ever found their way home, especially at night.

'Anyway, the bottom line is there are no leads. No one has mentioned having seen anyone acting oddly, or any strangers hanging around.' Trevor lifted his glasses and rubbed his eyes. 'Isn't it more likely to be a local, though? From what you told me, it sounds like this mystery man knew the area well. I'm wondering if he lives there somewhere.'

'Won't uniform have realised that?' said Wendy.

'It didn't sound that way to me, but maybe the guys I spoke to were just tired after their shift. But now you mention it, maybe I should take a stroll downstairs and ask the duty sergeant what their remit is for the search, just to be sure.'

As he was about to leave, Trevor turned back. 'It's a bit weird, Sarge, don't you think, that if what that boy wrote is what actually happened, how on earth did that mystery man know where to look for the dead boy? And the timing was spot on. Our guy drives away to get help, mystery man arrives, then is gone before he gets back. Bit too convenient, wasn't it?'

'That's what we thought,' admitted Wendy. 'And if I didn't know Ellie and Michael so well — hellfire, Trev, I even know Christopher, the lad who wrote that prophecy or whatever it was — I'd be shouting, "Hoax!" from the rooftops. At the time, it was thought that whoever took the kid was responsible for killing him, either deliberately or accidentally, and was trying to conceal the death. Then Ellie showed me that piece of writing. It even described the look of terror on the dead boy's face. Everything Christopher wrote corresponded with what my witness told me. I'm telling you, it shook me rigid.'

'That tells me that he didn't come upon the lad by chance. He knew where to look because . . . he had help.' As he spoke, Trevor stared into the distance, a faraway look in his eyes. 'He was guided there . . . to that . . . very spot . . . Yes, that's it. He was guided. Someone . . . someone close, told him where he would find the boy.'

Suddenly, Trevor turned his gaze upon her. 'He's a local, not close to that lay-by, but not too far from it either. He had help, Sarge! He didn't stumble across the boy, he wasn't searching for him, he was led there.' Fixing her with his eyes, he said, 'Trust me, I know this. He had a guide, a spirit guide, or possibly someone with second sight.'

How do you know that? Wendy thought. 'It seems our DCI was right to choose you for the team, Trevor. Get downstairs and ask the sergeant to tell his people that we are looking for someone who lives within . . . Well? What radius, Trevor?'

'Five miles, not much more than that.'

'Off you go then, Detective. And then I reckon we should go out and join them, don't you?'

'Is there anyone at the station who knows that particular spot, Sarge, who knows it really well? I've hardly ever been there.'

'Me, I guess,' said Wendy. 'I spent a large part of my youth in and around the forest.'

'Perfect. Then can we get a map, like a walking map or an OS one? If we look at it before we go, it might save us some time.'

'Ask DI Leatham. He's always off hiking, and he has loads of maps of the area. See what he's got, and ask him if he fancies a walk.'

* * *

Deputy Head Nicole White regarded the young teacher seated on the opposite side of her desk with a thoughtful expression. Lucy had just finished telling her about Harry's distraught mother and the quandary she was confronting.

Nicole had a lot of time for Lucy Reynolds. She had noticed how well she communicated with the children in her charge, and appreciated her handling of them. She reminded Nicole of herself when she first began teaching, though she had to admit that Lucy was more perceptive than she herself had ever been. On a number of occasions, Lucy had pointed out an issue concerning one of her pupils that no one else had been aware of, prompting a quick resolution of the situation before it got out of hand. Knowing all this about Lucy, Nicole was ashamed of the way she had dismissed her concerns regarding Harry Davison. It was true that she had been under considerable pressure from the headmistress about new administrative procedures that were being implemented, but that was no excuse for neglecting a pupil. It was the first time in her career that she had failed to put a child's welfare before her administrative duties, and she wasn't going to let it happen again.

'So, let me make this clear. You are aware of the possible risk to your career should anything go wrong in the course of the action you're proposing?'

'Absolutely, Mrs White, but I don't think I have a choice. It's your position that concerns me.'

Nicole White gave a dismissive wave of her hand. 'I'll deal with that if the need arises. To be frank, I let you down when you first came to me about Harry, so the least I can do now is offer you as much help as I can from now on. However, I need a few more details. I seem to remember you indicated that Harry might be in some kind of danger. Danger from what, exactly? Or from whom? I don't have to remind you that we are obliged to bring in the authorities in the case of a threat to a child.'

'Oh, it's nothing like that,' Lucy said quickly. 'We — that's me and my friend Callum — are just concerned about how Harry has come to know things a child of his age could not possibly even have heard about. This, and his exceptional artistic talent could make him vulnerable to exploitation, and we want to prevent that. Even his mother is afraid for him. As I think I told you, Dawn always denied there was anything special about him, but she's now admitted that she always knew, but was unable to deal with it.

That's one reason why I want to have some time off, so I can look after him while his mother sorts her life out.'

Why did she get the feeling that Lucy was holding something back from her? Nicole was the kind of woman who liked to know exactly where she stood, especially now, since her own job could be on the line.

'And?'

'Sorry?'

'Come on, Lucy. There's more to this than you're saying. Much more. If you want me to cover your back, it's only fair that I have the full picture.'

Lucy looked down at her hands in her lap. 'I haven't lied to you, I just left parts of it out. To be honest, I'm afraid that if I tell you everything you'll think I'm being paranoid.' She swallowed. 'And if I'm not there to take care of Harry, what will become of him?'

Nicole noticed how close to tears the young woman was. 'Why don't you just tell me, my dear? I know you're not someone who gets over-emotional, and I also know that you are doing this in the belief that you can help a child. And don't worry about how I might react — believe me, at this stage in my life, there's not a lot that can shock me.'

'Well, it started with the pictures . . .'

It took Lucy a good ten minutes to tell her the whole story, including the appearance of the airman, Harry speaking with the voice of a World War Two pilot, and how her fears had led her to share her concerns with one of the male nurses at the healing centre, who had become her friend and ally.

'Strangest of all is that Harry is not the only child displaying unusual behaviour. It appears there is something very weird going on, but we have no idea what. The owners of the clinic are working with another of these little boys, and are doing everything in their power to get to the bottom of it, and make sure these children are protected.'

As Nicole listened to Lucy's account, a memory rose into her mind. So immediate and vivid was it that she almost cried out. It happened when she had just seen a drawing Harry had made while he'd been waiting for his mother to collect him at the end of the day. It featured a squadron of propellor-driven planes flying in formation, out of the daylight into a night sky. She remembered telling Lucy that, yes, the child showed exceptional talent and should be encouraged, but reminded her of the school's policy not to single any one pupil out as being 'better' than his schoolmates. Lucy opened her mouth to speak, but appeared to think better of it, and said nothing. Nicole then left the room, but remembered something she'd forgotten to tell Lucy, and turned back. From behind the closed door she distinctly heard a man's voice, although she knew for certain that there was no one in the room besides Lucy and the boy. What was it the voice had said? Ah, now she remembered: he had been reciting a list of statistics. She heard him say quite clearly, 'That's how many young men died serving with Bomber Command in World War Two. That's more than the entire RAF in the present day.'

Lost in the memory, Nicole glanced absently down at a notepad on her desk in front of her. Scrawled across the open page was a number.

55,573

She knew immediately what it meant. This was the number of airmen who had died serving in Bomber Command in the Second World War.

She realised that Lucy was staring at her. 'Are you all right, Mrs White?'

'Oh, er, yes, I . . . I'm fine.' Pulling herself together, she looked back at Lucy. 'The fact is, I think I heard Harry speak in the way you describe. Only once, and from behind a closed door. At the time I thought I'd imagined it, or it was a radio on somewhere . . . But now I know. It was Harry.' She shook her head. 'I'll help you, Lucy. Your compassionate leave has been approved, and I'll easily be able to organise a supply teacher to cover your lessons, so don't worry about your other pupils. You can tell Mrs Davison that I'll accept her excuse that her son is unwell, and I won't demand a doctor's letter. Please do stay in touch and let me know how things are going, and if I can do anything to help. You can rely on me.'

Lucy's face positively glowed with relief, and Nicole hastened to dismiss her before the tears started. 'Good luck, Lucy. Take good care of your special little boy, and remember I'm here for you.'

As the door closed behind the young teacher, Nicole looked down at the notepad. The page was blank.

CHAPTER NINETEEN

'The time has come for you to meet the others,' Gideon said. 'I will introduce you tomorrow, so each of them can tell you about their particular skill. You might find some of them surprising, they might even seem somewhat esoteric, but try and keep an open mind. Use your own gift and pay close attention to what they say, and you'll discern the truth in it.'

'Oh, okay,' said Ollie dubiously, unsure what 'esoteric' meant. Gideon raised an eyebrow. 'Well, it's just I'm a bit kind of anxious. I mean, they all sound so amazing, like they have these really ace skills. And what do I have? A good memory. They'll probably laugh at me.'

'Ollie, you could save them all if it's in your destiny to do so. Be yourself, and you'll soon find out what you have. Both Rae and I believe there is more to you than you yourself are aware of. Your special qualities were never allowed to flourish in the life you were living before you came here. Indeed, the people around you were trying to stamp them out. Now there's no one to hold you back you can become the amazing person you really are.'

Feeling quite overwhelmed by this man's belief in him, Ollie managed a grin. 'I'll do my best.'

'I know you will. Now, to business. Rae will spend some time with you this evening, and before you see her, I want you to think about what kind of life you envisage yourself living once you've settled in. What I mean by that is, whether you think a simple life would suit you, out in the natural world. If so, we would provide the means to that end — a view of the night sky, for example, a place amongst growing things, with books, scented candles, and even a source of relaxing music. Or you might have a scientific bent, in which case you'd need a computer, access to scientific data and learning, and a personal space that's more hi-tech and functional. It could also be that neither of those options attract you, and you just want to be a kid, a teenager who enjoys films and music, and just having fun. And that's fine too.' Gideon gave him a reassuring smile. 'But don't worry if after a while you change your mind. Nothing is set in stone. All we ask is that you agree to abide by a few simple rules, or perhaps I should call it a code of behaviour. Basically, you are asked to treat everyone you meet in the Eleventh House with respect. Honour their dignity, and look out for them, for they are your family, and they will do the same for you.'

Ollie thought that was pretty fair, considering what he was getting in return. But how was he to choose how he wanted to live? He'd had few expectations, and little in the way of realising them anyway, certainly nothing like Gideon was offering — books, computers . . . And his parents had always made him feel as if he owed them big-time for the few basic necessities they *had* provided.

'Don't fret over it,' added Gideon. 'Rae will advise you, and you don't have to make a decision immediately. Take your time, look at some of the living spaces the others have chosen. Now, one last thing, Ollie. There are two things we need to discuss before we go any further. One, is that I need to be sure that you are willing to leave your old life behind. Before you answer, there is something you should know. It might be hurtful, but it's a fact. You will believe me, won't you? You'll know I'm not lying.'

Wondering what was coming next, Ollie nodded. 'I will.'

'Your parents, Ollie, have been heavily influenced by one of the teachers at your school — I'm sure I don't need to tell you which one — who wished you harm. In fact, if we hadn't got to you when we did, he would soon have exerted his influence over you, and depleted as you were at the time, I don't think you'd have survived. I'm sorry to have to tell you this, but it's the truth, and you deserve to know it.'

Indeed, Ollie knew exactly who this teacher was.

'I believe you. But if I have this great ability to read people like you say I do, how come I didn't know he meant me so much harm? I mean, everyone lies. At least until I came here, I thought that was just the way people were. Adults especially, they lie to kids all the time. Why wasn't I aware that the lies I was being told were so dangerous?'

'Your parents and the teacher had the power to suppress your ability, tamp it down if you see what I mean?'

Ollie nodded. 'Yeah, I do. Like I was depressed, kind of, well, flattened. You're right!'

'And do you feel different since coming here?' Gideon asked.

Come to think of it he did! Despite being so gobsmacked about it all, it was true, he was starting to feel more alive than he ever had before.

'I can see your answer in your face, Ollie. You're feeling that way because we — this place — are here to nurture you, not drain your energies. That said, I want to make absolutely sure you are firm in your decision and won't change your mind at some later date. For that reason I'm giving you a week in which to consider whether you want to stay with us, or go back to your parents. If you decide to stay, you will make one call to your parents, telling them you are safe and well, and will never be going back. Do you understand?'

'I understand, Gideon.' Ollie didn't say so, but he had already made his decision. He knew which family he would choose, and he didn't need a week to make up his mind.

'One final thing, my young friend. There is something I have to show you. I would rather you didn't have to see it, but it's important that you do. I think you will understand some things better afterwards.' Gideon stood up. 'Come with me.'

Ollie always felt safe around Gideon, sort of peaceful. He'd never felt like that with anyone before, and he supposed this was what it was like to trust someone. So, he followed the tall figure without hesitation, despite Gideon's heavy tread and grim expression.

He soon realised they were heading towards the old chapel where he had spent his first night. Maybe they were about to meet a new special child, but why then was Gideon's face so set?

Gideon opened the wooden doors and came to a halt in the entrance. He placed his hands on Ollie's shoulders and looked him full in the eyes. 'This will upset you, my son, but you need to know that the work we are undertaking in this place is no game. Outside this small parcel of land that is our sanctuary, there is much evil. With that comes deeds such as I pray you will never have to confront.'

He turned slowly, and began to walk towards the altar.

Following behind him, Ollie smelled incense. Somewhere, soft music was quietly playing.

Arriving at the altar, Gideon stepped aside.

Lying on a low dais, draped in a golden embroidered cloth with his head and shoulders uncovered, was a dead boy.

'Oh no! Not Mole,' whispered Ollie.

'We are burying him at first light tomorrow, Ollie. I hope you'll join us to say goodbye.'

Ollie turned to Gideon. 'What happened?'

'He was murdered, son. As you would have been had you remained out there much longer.'

'Was he very special?' whispered Ollie. 'Was that why he had to die?'

'Not in the way the rest of you are. But he had an amazing ability to . . . find people.'

'Like me?'

'Like you,' said Gideon. 'We owe him a lot.'

'So, wasn't he part of the group? Why was he out there if it isn't safe?' Ollie asked, his eyes on the dead boy's face.

'Yes, he was one of us. The thing about our Mole was that he was a free spirit. He came and went as the mood took him, and no one could predict where he would go next. He was one of several seekers we have out there, and in general they remain safe, but Mole . . .' Gideon shook his head sadly. 'He came to us from the streets. He never would say exactly what had happened to him in the past, but he grew up angry and defiant. He found peace here for a while, but then his wanderlust reasserted itself, so he became a valued helper on the outside. Sadly, we cannot always protect those souls who are beyond our boundaries, and as for Mole, I think he believed he was invincible.'

'Until his luck ran out.' Ollie sighed.

'Indeed. But we should go, you've seen enough.'

'Would you let me stay with him? Just for a while? I'd like to thank him for finding me.'

Gideon regarded him fondly. 'Of course you can, son. I'll wait outside for you and we'll walk back together.'

Watching his retreating figure, Ollie realised that no one had ever looked at him that way before — with affection.

* * *

Ellie was beginning to feel sorry for Beth Saunders. Someone so basically down to earth and sensible must be finding it difficult to come to terms with the strange world she was suddenly being faced with. Yet she seemed to be taking it all on board, even if she struggled with some of the concepts.

When they had finished explaining what they believed was happening, she looked almost relieved. 'I can't quite get my head around some of what you've been saying, but it does make a kind of sense, and it's certainly an improvement on some of the things I've been imagining.' She looked from Michael to Ellie. 'So, what it comes down to is that something strange is going on, and it's to do with young children. Have I got that right?'

'You have,' said Michael. 'Each of the children we've been talking about is acting strangely, and I'm sorry to say that Izzie's behaviour is possibly the most problematic. It hurts me to even think of what you have endured from the daughter you love so much. How frightened and alone you must have felt!'

'By far the worst part was that no one saw her when she was acting that way,' Beth said. 'Everyone who came into contact with her found her charming, a delightful child who was never grizzly or fretful and always affectionate towards the people around her.'

'Tell me,' asked Ellie. 'Can you pinpoint exactly when this sudden change in her came about? Did anything happen that seemed to prompt it?'

Beth shook her head. 'I don't know how many times I've gone over that question. I know exactly where and when she first said something really mean to me, but I can't for the life of me explain what caused it.'

'So, what happened?' asked Michael.

'Well, nothing really — nothing that I can recall anyway. It was almost a year ago. Izzie had been invited to a birthday party near Gomshall. The house was in an out-of-the-way spot in a densely wooded area. It was the usual thing — you know, games and prizes and cake to eat. The birthday girl's mother had organised a treasure hunt in a little copse at the bottom of the garden, so the kiddies all pulled on their coats and headed off to search for the prizes. Izzie found one under a tree. She ripped off the paper to find a soft toy in the shape of a toadstool. I'll never forget that toadstool, nor Izzie's face as she looked from it to me.' Beth fell silent.

'What happened next?' Michael prompted gently.

'She said, "If this was real, I'd make you eat it. And then you'd die."'

Ellie gave an involuntary shiver. 'And that was the start of it? Did she behave that way towards you from then on?'

'No. After the party she was just the same as ever, and I assumed she'd probably heard it from someone, or it came from a television programme. It must have been about a month before it happened again, then it gradually became more frequent. Now it's every time we're alone, and the things she says are becoming more and more spiteful.'

'I heard her, Beth,' said Ellie. 'She was positively venomous. And the change in her when Callum came in was instant. In the blink of an eye she was a sweet little girl deciding which flavour of ice cream to choose.'

Something, or someone, had to have caused it. Something at that birthday party? Was it someone who had been there that day? Some predator who had found their ideal victim in Izzie? None of it was tying up. Three children, all possessed by some spirit, but all manifesting it in different ways — one writing prophecies, one playing host to a dead airman, and now a little angel with a noxious tongue. Another child, too, found dead at the side of the road only to vanish into thin air minutes later. What in hell's name was the connection between them? Her head aching from all these conundrums, Ellie realised she was being asked a question.

'What should I do now?' Beth asked.

What indeed? Despite having vowed to help this woman, Ellie had no answer for her. Izzie Saunders was yet another piece in a puzzle, and Ellie had no idea where she fitted.

Thankfully, Michael came to the rescue.

'The main thing is that you're no longer alone. Now we know about Izzie, Ellie and I will discuss the way forward. Rest assured, we will get to the bottom of what's causing this.'

'Do you think I'll ever get my darling daughter back?' Beth whispered.

'We'll do everything we can to make that happen,' Michael said. 'It may take some time, but we are here for you. If you need us for anything — if something else happens, or you are anxious about anything — you can always come to the centre, or phone us, day or night. And, Beth, stay strong. You've been directed to us for a reason, and we won't let you down.'

Ellie wished she felt as confident. Yes, they would do everything in their power to help, but what, exactly? Where would they go from here? The truth was, Ellie was still reeling from what she had heard coming from the lips of a pretty little six-year-old girl. Thank goodness Beth was unable to read auras. If she could, she would probably be shocked at the sudden diminishing of Ellie's life-lights.

After Beth and her daughter had finally left, Ellie, Michael and Callum were back in her consulting room, the door firmly closed.

'I'm sorry, Ellie,' said Michael softly. 'I hadn't expected it to take so much out of you.'

She smiled at him. 'It's me who should be apologising. I hadn't prepared myself for so powerful a manifestation. It took me right back to the past, and I . . .' Her words trailed off.

'No one could have prepared themselves for that,' Michael said. 'We've encountered evil before, but none of us expected to meet it in this way. This is a more serious matter than we thought.'

'Yes, it is.' She sighed. 'Well, if nothing else, it was one almighty warning of what is to come.' She turned her gaze on Callum. 'And as for you, I could be wrong, but I've a feeling you didn't have the best experience with sweet little Izzie, either?'

Callum was endowed with dark good looks and a mischievous air that was at the same time perfectly sincere. Now, he was pale, his features drained. Ellie had never seen him look so afflicted. 'Callum? Talk to us.'

He bit his bottom lip. 'I've seen plenty of savagery in my life — in Bosnia, Rwanda — but nothing like this. War brings out the worst in people — violent rage, thirst for power and so on — but all those things are still recognisably human, and in a way they're to be expected. What I sensed today — and even caught a brief glimpse of — wasn't human at all.'

Michael regarded him steadily. 'Can you explain what you mean? Describe what you saw — from the first moment you set eyes on the child.'

Ellie recalled Callum's involuntary flinch when he was first introduced to Izzie.

'Initially, I thought that she was like any other little girl, although given how fair her mum is, I was expecting a cute blonde kid, not someone as dark as me.'

'Maybe even darker. That hair of hers is raven black,' said Ellie.

'I was surprised too,' added Michael. 'But we know nothing about Beth's husband, of course. Maybe she takes after him. But, sorry, we're interrupting you, Callum . . . Go on.'

'It was when I first came in, after you'd been observing her aura, Ellie. For a moment I didn't know what I was looking at . . .' He frowned, as if he were searching for the right way to describe it.

'I saw you look startled,' said Ellie, 'but so briefly I thought I'd imagined it.'

'Oh no, it was real all right! I may even have recoiled. Then I couldn't believe I'd actually seen . . . what I saw.'

'What did you see?' asked Michael.

'For a split second, Izzie was both the pretty little girl I'd seen in the Orangery, and someone else. It was like two faces in one. And the second face was all twisted and malevolent. And the eyes . . .' Callum shivered. 'Black as pitch, and so baleful. I froze, pinned by their gaze. Then she looked away, and when she looked back she was just Izzie again.' He looked helplessly at them. 'I might have convinced myself I'd imagined the whole thing if it hadn't been for what happened later, in the café.'

Ellie wasn't sure if she really wanted to hear what was coming next.

'I believe that there is some evil spirit around that child,' Callum said. 'Harry has the airman, but he is a benign spirit, and when he appears he looks no different to any other young man. But Izzie, even when she's being an "ordinary" little girl, has something deeply unpleasant keeping watch over her. It didn't take shape, like Harry's airman, but it was there all right. I felt rather than saw it, and it sickened me.'

'It took no form at all?' queried Michael.

'There did seem to be something there, but it was more like . . . like something was leeching the colour out of one particular area just behind the child. It seemed to hover there, rather like a shadow, but more fluid and shapeless.'

'And how did the child behave while it was there?' asked Ellie.

'There was no change in her behaviour. She acted just like any other child who'd been given an ice cream as a treat. In fact, she was rather funny, and really quite sweet — or she would have been if I wasn't constantly on edge waiting for that wicked, black-eyed apparition to reappear.'

'I'm sorry you had to go through that,' said Michael. 'And was that it? Nothing else?'

Callum took a breath. 'A few minutes before you and Beth arrived, Izzie put down her spoon and stared up at me. It wasn't disturbing, there was no change in her face or expression, she just said, "You're different, aren't you?" I can't remember exactly what I said, something like, *No, I was just a plain, ordinary nurse, nothing different about me, ha ha.* But she gave me a very knowing look, as if to say, *If that's the way you want to play it, then fine, but you don't fool me.* The thing is, Harry said the same thing to me when we first met, and I still don't know if it was Harry, or the airman who said it. Now I'm not sure if it was Izzie who remarked on it, or someone . . . or something else.'

Ellie opened her mouth to make a remark, but there was more to come.

'Apart from all that, what scared me most was what happened just as you walked into the café.' He glanced at them both. 'Seconds after I saw the three of you approaching, that vile shadow thing withdrew, away from Izzie. I saw it kind of drift towards the window, almost as if it had seen you too, and wanted to get away. If you remember, when we all left the café, I stayed behind for a minute, and joined you outside?'

They nodded. 'That's right,' Michael said, 'I thought you'd left something behind.'

'No. I was confirming something.' Callum's face was set. 'When the café was refurbished, whoever did the decor introduced a line of planters with houseplants. You've seen them, they divide the café into two areas. Well, the shadow thing passed over these planters on its way out. In the places where it had crossed them, the plants were withered and dying. A brief instant of contact with that thing had been enough to kill them.'

Seconds passed, then minutes. No one spoke. Finally, Michael voiced what they had all been thinking. 'Evil has returned to the clinic. I think we can all feel how the temperature has dropped since that child was in this room. Wherever Izzie Saunders has been present will have to be cleansed. I doubt it's the child herself, but there is a malevolent entity that has attached itself to her. We must rid the place of its presence, and we need to do it fast.'

Ellie stood up. 'You are right. I'll go and see if Janie is free. If she is, I'll take her to all the places where that child has been and see if she picks up any remaining bad energy. If she does, I'll know that in a few hours she'll restore the original harmony of our precious clinic.'

'I saw her earlier,' said Callum. 'She was just about to enter the café, but stopped and walked away. Now I'm wondering if she'd picked up on something.'

Following a trauma in her late thirties that changed her life, Janie Morris spent years in remote locations studying the ancient spiritual practice of shamanism. Back in England, she followed the path of a modern shaman. No one was better suited to the task of cleansing bad spirits from a home or workplace than Janie.

'Go now, Ellie,' insisted Michael. 'We can't leave things as they are for much longer, especially in here. This is a haven of tranquillity, your special place, and right now . . .'

He had no need to continue. Ellie hurried from the room. Luckily, she bumped into Janie in the foyer, escorting a smiling young couple out of the clinic.

'Glad I managed to catch you, Janie. I need your help.' Ellie briefly explained that they'd had a visit from a child with a bad spirit.

'So, that's what it was!' Janie exclaimed. 'Twice today I've sensed an atmosphere, an almost stifling oppression, but then it disappeared and I thought I must have imagined it. Give me a few minutes while I go up to my room to prepare, then you can show me exactly where in the clinic it has been, well, contaminated. Then I can call on spirit to help me cleanse and purify those areas.' Janie smiled. 'Don't look so worried, Ellie, think of it as taking out the garbage and dumping it.'

But Janie hadn't seen Callum's face. Picturing that look of utter horror, Ellie doubted it would really be that easy.

CHAPTER TWENTY

'Gideon! It's Brendan on the phone.'

Rae held out the receiver to him as if she were presenting him with an award, and he knew Clover had been located. They were one step closer to achieving their aim.

'Brendan! You have news for us?'

'We have her, Gideon, and her mother. They're both well, and for the time being are safe, but I'm not sure how long we can keep them that way. I'd really rather they didn't have to be here after dark.'

'Give me your location and we'll head over to collect them, and this time I'll come myself, along with Rae and one of the others.'

'We are at the Ten of Pentacles,' said Brendan. 'Got that? Ten of Pentacles.'

'Perfect. We'll be there in less than an hour.'

'May the Great Spirit be with you,' said Brendan, and the line went dead.

'And with you and your precious charges,' whispered Gideon. As she took the phone from him, he noticed her hand shake slightly. And no wonder. This was a momentous day. Even the place where Clover was awaiting collection was propitious. Each of the collection points was named after one of the cards in the Tarot. The Ten of Pentacles symbolised family, stability and a firm foundation. That had to be a good omen.

'This is it, Rae. Grab the car keys. You and I are about to set off on the ride of our lives!'

* * *

It felt strange to be tramping along the woodland paths again. Wendy recalled the fun she and her best friend, Maggie, had had running along these same paths when they were kids. They had remained inseparable throughout their adolescence, until Wendy went off to start her police training and Maggie became a student nurse. Life intervened, as it so often does, and they gradually saw less of each other. Their friendship finally ended when Maggie fell in love with one of her patients, a young airman from Canada, and flew off to start a new life across the Atlantic. Now it was down to a card at Christmas and a vague promise to keep in touch.

By the time she reached the house where she had spent most of her weekends and school holidays, Wendy was feeling quite nostalgic. She had decided to start her enquiry with Maggie's family, the Keeles, as they had lived in that house for generations.

Perhaps it was nostalgia that had prompted her to leave the car at the end of the lane leading up to Heathersett and proceed on foot. She had also left Jon and Trevor hunting down the residents of two neighbouring woodland cottages.

Unaccountably nervous, she rang the bell and stepped back. The covered porch, the name plate and the ornate door knocker were so familiar that she might have been ten years old again, calling in for ginger beer, and if she was lucky, a piece of Mrs Keele's homemade Victoria sandwich.

'Little Wendy Brown! As I live and breathe!' The old man regarded her in amazement. 'But, lass? Where's that smart uniform of yours? Don't tell me you're not in the police anymore?'

'Hello, Grandpops!' With a proud smile, she held out her warrant card for him to see. 'I'm a detective now. A sergeant, no less!'

'Oh, lass, that's grand! Come on in! I'll tell Helen you're here. She'll be thrilled to see you again.'

As Wendy followed Grandpops Keele through the hall and into the big living room, another wave of nostalgia washed over her. All those rainy afternoons playing Cluedo, Maggie getting in a huff because Wendy always won. She smiled to herself. Back then she would never have dreamed that one day she'd be solving real-life murders.

'Wendy! Oh, this is lovely! My dear, it's been far too long, and we've been missing you!' Helen, Maggie's mother, hustled across the room and threw her arms around her. 'Did you hear the news? Maggie and Connor are expecting a baby! Imagine — me a granny! Who'd have believed it?'

As they chatted and reminisced, Wendy thought of her own family, and how different they were from this one. The Keeles were open and friendly — their 'welcome' mat meant exactly what it said. Her own parents, on the other hand, were what you might call reserved. They were stiff with their few visitors, and life at home could never be described as fun. Consequently, she'd spent as much time as possible at Heathersett.

After a while, Wendy realised that time was getting on and she really must get down to the real purpose of her visit. A pause in the chatter gave her an opening.

'Well, if there's anything we can do to help, you just say, dear,' Helen Keele said.

'Well, we'd like to know more about the properties within, say, a five-mile radius from here, and who owns them. No one knows this area better than you and Grandpops, which is why I thought of asking you.'

'Well, most of this area is part of the Surrey Downs, and then there's the forest, of course. So there's not many residential homes.' Helen began to look rather anxious. 'I hope nothing serious has happened, only we're pretty isolated out here. I don't want to be fretting about the two of us being alone at night. It's a big house, and Duncan is away a lot, so it's often just me and Dad — oh, and then there's the horses. You don't think there's any danger to them, do you?'

'No, you don't have to worry,' Wendy said quickly. 'It's a rather strange case. I'm not allowed to give out too many details, but I can tell you that last night a young man was seen lying by the side of that back road people use as a short cut between the main road and the village. He was spotted by a motorist, who went to call for assistance, but by the time he got back, someone had taken the body away. We are trying to discover exactly what occurred, so we're asking everyone in the vicinity if they saw or heard anything that might help.'

'That's a rum 'un, by no mistake,' muttered old Mr Keele. 'If you ask me, it's someone playing a joke. You know, like the things students used to get up to. Get your mate to lie down in the road and play dead, then when someone goes for help, you pick him up and drive away, laughing yer heads off.'

'Dad! The police would hardly be combing the neighbourhood if they thought it was a practical joke. Now, be sensible and go and fetch the map book. Wendy's right, we know everyone who lives round here, so let's try and help her.'

Duly chastised, Grandpops left to find the map book, giving Wendy a wink as he passed her chair.

Smiling, Wendy turned back to Helen. 'I don't suppose any of the people round here have a teenage boy of around sixteen, do they?'

'Oh dear, so young! His poor mother.' Helen shivered. 'There's not a lot of young people here these days. Most of them move to the towns as soon as they can get away. There's not much to do in the forest. Or like my Maggie, they marry and go and live abroad.'

'So, who does live around here?' asked Wendy. 'My colleagues are checking the cottages just off the road leading up to here, but I remember some pretty big old houses, some of them right in the middle of the forest.'

Grandpops returned with the map book. 'Here. I've marked all the properties with red crosses. If I put a little number next to each one, we can tell our Wendy what we know about it, and she can write it down in her notebook.'

'Smart thinking,' said Wendy. 'As long as I can pinch your map book for reference. I promise to return it.'

'Please take it,' said Helen. 'It'll be a good excuse to get you back here for another visit. It's been a breath of spring to see you again, my dear.'

'That it is!' exclaimed Grandpops. 'Does my heart good. Weren't you and our Maggie a right pair of mischievous little monkeys! I remember that time when—'

'Dad! Wendy's got work to do. Next time, okay?'

'Sorry, love.' He placed the map on Wendy's lap and sat next to her. 'Right then, now this one here lies back just off this lane, about half a mile further into the wood. It's called Woodlands.' He rolled his eyes. 'Owners are a couple who have a flat in the city. Business people, they use it as a weekend cottage, but they look after it well. Name of Hallam — James and Connie.' He looked across at Helen. 'Right so far?'

She nodded. 'They have no children, and there's an older husband and wife from Abinger who look after the garden and do a bit of cleaning for the Hallams.'

Wendy wrote this all down.

'Next is this one here.' Grandpops jabbed a finger on the map. 'Flood Lane, about a quarter of a mile after the Woodlands Trust access road on the left.'

'Big property that,' added Helen. 'It's a retreat, with I don't know how many acres of land. It used to be owned by the Cross family, but they downsized and sold it to some organisation, I think.'

'It's called White Gates,' Grandpops said. 'To be honest, I've never actually seen it. There's a long drive and it's surrounded by trees and a high old wall along the front. It'd make a very good retreat, I should think.'

'Okay, I can get the details later, as long as I have the location,' Wendy said.

'Number Three is in this area here,' said Grandpops, pointing to another area illustrated with little drawings of trees. 'Old property, bit rundown now, but then so is its owner.' He gave a throaty chuckle. 'Benjamin Hackforth. Local eccentric, and collector of stray cats! It's called Shepherd's Cottage, but don't be fooled, there's not a sheep in sight, just cats!'

Wendy made a careful note of that, and given her allergy to cat fur, determined to send either Jon or Trevor to that one.

There were three more smaller dwellings and finally another large property.

'I'm going to leave that one to you, love,' said Grandpops to Helen. 'You know more about it than me.'

'Hardly,' replied Helen. 'I've never managed to get past the Lodge House. All I know is that it's basically an old manor house hidden in the trees. That nice Howard Fenton who lives in the lodge told me the family who owned it have dwindled to one old boy and his nephew. He reckons the old chap is losing it, as he's turned into something of a recluse, and without the nephew to look after him he'd have long since been consigned to a nursing home, or be pushing up daisies.'

'So how on earth does he look after the estate?' asked Wendy.

'Oh, because he's stinking rich,' said Helen. 'Yes, the nephew does everything for the old chap, but they employ scores of people to look after the grounds.'

'And the house?' asked Wendy.

'Oh no, no one gets into the house, apart from the nephew, and in a dire emergency, Howard. Howard said the old guy will die there one day, because he'd never let a doctor through the door, let alone a couple of paramedics.'

'Do we know his name?'

'Nancarrow. Philip Nancarrow.' Helen frowned, 'Cornish name, I believe. But I don't rate your chances of getting to talk to him, Wendy. If he won't even let a doctor in, I can't see a detective getting much of a welcome.'

Wendy closed her notebook and got to her feet. 'Thank you, this has been an amazing help. You've saved us a whole lot of time. Now I suppose I'd better go and see where my colleagues have got to.' She picked up the map book. 'But I'll return this very soon, and next time I'll come when I'm off duty.'

'You do that,' said Helen, enveloping her in another hug. 'In fact, ring us when you next have a day off and come to lunch, if you can bear Grandpops regaling you with stories from your misspent youth!'

Wendy smiled. 'I'll risk it. And thanks again. See you soon!'

Still smiling, Wendy walked back to the car. This visit had felt like going home. It gave her a good feeling to know that if she were ever to need anything, the Keeles would always be there.

* * *

Christopher was puzzled. All day long, his gran and his dad had been giving him anxious looks, and he couldn't work out why. Eventually, with another hour to go before tea, he decided to hide somewhere and ask his friend what was going on, because he certainly didn't understand.

It hadn't been easy, as after a while he had begun to suspect that he was being actively watched, so he had to resort to some serious escape tactics. Luckily it was an old house — not huge, like the one his friend Jack lived in. That one had, well, like a squillion rooms at least. Nevertheless, he knew of various nooks and crannies here where a little boy could easily hide away.

Now he was sitting on an old upturned barrel at one end of an outbuilding that according to his gran had been used to store fruit and vegetables over the winter months. It smelled a bit weird, but not totally stinky, like the windfall apples he used to pick up in Ellie's orchard after she told him they weren't good for the dogs' tummies. Since Ellie's spaniels weren't too bright when it came to what was good for them, he and his dad often went into the orchard to collect the fallen fruit.

'So. Any ideas?' he asked his friend. 'Have I done something I shouldn't?'

'Nothing that wasn't absolutely necessary, Christopher.'

'Why all the looks, then?' He frowned. 'And if you don't mind me saying, that was a pretty rubbish answer. You make it sound like I *did* do something, but I'm sure I didn't. I like being here, as you well know, so why would I be naughty?'

'You weren't naughty, really you weren't. It's just that adults . . . well, they operate on a different plane.'

Christopher's frown deepened. 'Plane! Talk sense, will you. What have planes got to do with anything?'

He heard a soft laugh. 'Sorry, I meant a different level. They don't see things as we do.'

'You can say that again,' muttered Christopher, kicking his heels against the wooden barrel. 'Oh, and there's another thing. I don't suppose you know where my notebook has gone, do you? The one with my exercises in? I don't want Jason to think I'm not doing my homework.'

'It's safe.'

The voice in Christopher's head was fainter now.

'Please don't go! I want to know what's going on.'

'Listen to me, Christopher. Go back into the house and stay there, especially tonight. Promise me you won't come out again, and keep close to your dad or your gran. You're right, something *is* going on, but you'll be safe in the house. Don't be afraid, I won't leave you, but I have some very important things to do right now. And don't forget, you have a book to write. So go to your room, find another notebook and write this down . . .'

Christopher listened. He had no idea how, but he knew he'd remember every single word, exactly as his friend told him, and he would write it all down, word for word.

When his friend at last fell silent, Christopher leaped off the barrel and raced into the house.

* * *

In a different part of the garden, Marie Littlewood and Scrubbs, Ellie's faithful retainer, were puzzling over one of her favourite *Viburnum tinus* shrubs.

'Well, dang me if I know what's happened to it,' said Scrubbs, scratching his head. 'How very odd. Never seen the likes o' that before in all my years as a gardener.'

'It's such a robust and hardy plant,' said Marie, 'yet it looks like it's been burned.'

'I've seen plenty of frost damage,' said Scrubbs, 'along o' plants in the fields that have been sprayed. They do it to potatoes, spray the foliage so it dies off and the potatoes grow stronger. But no one sprays here, do they?'

'No, not at all,' Marie said. 'The only thing I ever use is a fungicide to control mildew and black spot on my roses, but nothing else.'

They considered the plant in silence. One side of the attractive dark-green foliage had become withered and blackened, as if someone had aimed a flamethrower at it.

'Sorry, Mrs L, but this one's got me beat,' admitted Scrubbs, looking annoyed with himself. 'The only thing I can think of is some kind of blight, but 'eaven knows what's caused it. All I can advise you is if you see it anywhere else, give me a call. It might just be notifiable.'

On her way back to the house, Marie found herself looking around uneasily. She was devoted to her garden, and spent as much time as she could in it, especially in the early mornings and late in the day, but this afternoon it gave her an unpleasant feeling. The shadows seemed to have deepened much too early, and there was a chill in the air that made her shiver.

Marie increased her pace. She had a sudden urge to look back over her shoulder, but was too afraid to do so, and almost ran the final stretch to the back door.

CHAPTER TWENTY-ONE

Janie was exhausted. It had taken her much longer than she had anticipated to clear the negative energy from the clinic, but she had pushed on, knowing how important it was to remove every last trace of this thing that had pervaded the healing centre. Ellie had warned her that it would probably be powerful, but Janie hadn't expected to encounter such an oppressive atmosphere.

She was an expert, and never doubted that she would eventually succeed in ridding the clinic of what had invaded it, but the effort had drained her. Everywhere she sensed its presence she had stopped and prayed to her spirit guides for assistance. Chanting softly, she seemed to float from place to place, carrying like a chalice her fragrant smoking smudge stick of herbs, sage and *palo santo* wood. She finished by inviting all the good spirits back into the space she had cleansed, filling it with peace and love once again.

Satisfied that not the smallest trace of this malignant spirit remained, she reflected on the task she had just completed. Certain phenomena she had encountered in the course of her ritual cleansing still puzzled her. From time to time, a vivid blue light descended upon her and drew her to a particular place, usually in the corner of a room, and invariably she would find some negativity lurking there which would otherwise have gone undetected.

Her last action before declaring the cleansing complete was to ask Callum to remove every single dead plant from the containers in the café, emphasising that every leaf, flower and root must be taken outside and burned. Any remaining ash should be buried, and white sage scattered over it to purify the ground. He complied with her request without asking a single question.

Finally, she was able to go to her room and perform a cleansing ritual on herself. She was just bringing it to an end when someone tapped on her door.

Her visitor smiled at her with understanding and compassion. 'I was just wondering if you might be feeling the need of a little aura regeneration. You went through a lot doing all that, so if you'd like me to, I can bring some extra colour back into your energy field.'

She accepted gratefully and sank back, allowing the professor to shower her with a stream of colours that she could feel penetrating every fibre of her being. She bathed in this refreshing burst of energy for over ten minutes before finally turning to him with a grateful smile.

'Oh, I needed that. Thank you so much for thinking of me.'

'Your energy wasn't nearly as depleted as I'd expected,' said Michael, 'but nevertheless you can consider yourself recharged. And it's we who should be thanking you — the whole place feels full of love and light again, just as it ought to.'

'What *was* that, Michael? It was so powerful.'

'We don't know,' he said. 'But it had attached itself to a six-year-old child.'

Janie gave an involuntary shudder. 'Well, whatever it was, I just pray it doesn't come back.'

'Unfortunately, there's no guaranteeing that it won't. Ellie and I are going to hold a meeting with all the healers who work here, or visit regularly. We need to build up a ring of protection around this healing centre, and in order to do that, we'll have to use every available energy and spiritual belief we can. If nothing else, we'll make it very difficult for the forces of evil to find their way in.'

'Well, you can count on me,' said Janie. 'And if you think it's appropriate, I have a powerful friend I can call. She's a formidable shaman who's often called upon to protect different communities from harm, disease, misfortune and evil spirits. Should this manifestation make a reappearance, I urge you to enlist her help.'

'I won't forget your suggestion, Janie. As soon as we have a clearer idea of what we are up against, we can decide if your friend's help is needed. And once again, thank you.'

When Michael had gone, Janie decided she might as well re-establish contact with her friend right now, if only to discover whether she was in the country. She was often away, going wherever she was needed, often to far-flung, out-of-the-way corners of the globe. She would be a powerful ally, and after her experience this morning, Janie had an uncomfortable feeling they might be needing all the help they could get in the days to come.

* * *

Callum knew nothing about shamanism, but he admired Janie Morris. She was always so calm and serene. While some people drained you of energy, Janie had the opposite effect. She always made him feel as if he'd just stepped out into the garden on a sunny summer morning. Today, however, there was a new urgency in her manner, and having seen for himself what had been done to those plants, he had no need to question her about her instructions, he simply followed them to the letter.

Now he was standing in an overgrown area of the garden, some way from the house itself, staring down at a small rectangular patch of freshly turned earth. He had done as she asked, and burned the dead plants and buried the ashes. For some reason, he found this dead plant matter repellent, as if he were handling something putrid, like rotting meat. He had sprinkled the contents of the container Janie had given him over the ashes prior to filling in the hole, and had been amazed at the transformation wrought by the aromatic white sage. The air became fresh again, and he let out a sigh of relief.

His phone rang in his pocket, making him jump.

Lucy sounded excited. 'Can you talk?'

'Yes. Are you all right? Harry?'

Lucy launched into an account of her meeting with Harry's mother, and her subsequent interview with the deputy head. Callum listened with growing concern. So far, events were working in their favour, but how long would their luck hold out? The image of those withered and blackened plants rose into his mind, and he swallowed, hard.

'Listen, Lucy, where are you now?'

'At Harry's home. I told Dawn to spend a few moment alone with Harry, to reassure him that he was loved, and wasn't being packed off somewhere because he was in the way.'

Callum chuckled. 'I bet that won't fool our Harry in the slightest.'

'I'm sure it won't, but right now, all I want to do is get him away from here so I can keep my eye on him. Callum, are you still free to come to my place when you finish work?'

'Of course. I'll let Michael and Ellie know what's happened, and I'll be on my way.' He hesitated, not quite knowing how to put what he was about to suggest. 'Lucy, um, don't take this the wrong way, but I think the three of us should stay together from now on, until we have a better idea of what kind of danger Harry, and us for that matter, could be in.'

'I was going to say the same thing, Callum. As soon as you get here, we'll discuss how to go about it.'

'All right. I'll see you very soon. And, Lucy? Please, take care.'

Callum pocketed his phone, deposited the tools back in the shed and ran to the front door.

He caught up with Michael in the foyer, and told him what he and Lucy had decided. Michael pursed his lips thoughtfully. Then he said, 'Right. All three of you must move in here. I cannot have you stuck all the way out at Great Bookham. It's just too far, especially if we have to act swiftly. We've only one in-patient at present and she leaves tomorrow, so I suggest we temporarily close that floor off to patients.' He nodded to himself. 'Yes, that will work, and if necessary, we'll make that area our command centre.'

'What about Sister Shaw?' asked Callum. 'She lives on that floor.'

'I'll talk to her. I can always offer her the option of taking some paid holiday if she'd like — there are no patients to look after — or she can stay on and be the voice of reason, as she so often is. She's one of us, Callum, and just because her skills lie in the practical rather than the psychic realm, she can still be of help. After all, she has a great deal of understanding.'

'Which is a valuable commodity,' said Callum. 'I hope she does stay.'

Michael winked. 'Ten to one she will. I've never known her to back off and leave her friends if she can be of help.' He grasped Callum's arm. 'I'll update Ellie, while you get away as fast as you can. Tell Lucy to pack what she needs for a stay at the C-M Centre.'

* * *

As Ellie dished up their dinner, she could hear the thump of Alice bringing her cases down the stairs. She had managed to get hold of two seats on a British Airways flight to JFK leaving at eleven thirty-five the following morning. It was an eight-hour flight and she would arrive in the States at fourteen twenty-five. Ellie had told her to book a taxi to Heathrow, but Alice had insisted on driving. She'd have plenty of time to sleep on the plane, she said, and having her own vehicle in the long-stay car park meant that no matter what time her return flight got in, she could drive straight home.

'Ready!' Ellie called out. For their last meal she had chosen a Chinese takeaway from their local restaurant. For one thing, it was Alice's favourite, and would be lighter than Italian, and less spicy than Indian considering her long flight.

'I'm going to leave at just before six tomorrow, babe,' said Alice, helping herself to rice. 'I'll pick up Gordon, and we'll hit the road straightaway. I wanted to travel light, but with this important symposium, and the reception that always follows, plus travelling to wherever the AS patient is, it was hard to decide on the right clothes to take.'

Ellie wished that selecting the most appropriate outfits for a trip away was the only thing she had to worry about, although she, too, would be packing a few items of clothing in case she found herself staying at the centre. Thoughts of the centre and the possible danger they might face prompted a wave of anxiety, and she bent over her food to hide her face from Alice.

Alice didn't notice a thing. Her head was full of last-minute details. 'I've got all the essentials together — passport, credit cards and all that. We are collecting the tickets at the airport, so that's one less thing to worry about. The biggest problem is Gordon and his precious AZSEE. Okay, he's got the software on his laptop, but there's the headset, the scanner and all the other peripheral stuff that he daren't entrust to a baggage handler. We're going to pay extra so it can go as hand luggage in the cabin with us—' She stopped speaking and laid down her knife and fork with a clatter. 'Listen to me, I'm such a heartless prat! Oh, Ellie! This should have been our special trip, not another work-related drama that has me rushing off to the other side of the Atlantic. No wonder you're quiet. I'm so sorry.' She reached across and took Ellie's hand. 'Really I am.'

'Oh, Alice, I'm not quiet because I'm upset. Of course I'd love to hear you give your address at Mount Sinai Hospital, and I'm sorry that I won't be there to support you, but just think: I wouldn't be here now if someone hadn't gone out of their way to help me when I needed it. If you can do the same for this American girl, then that's all that matters.' She mustered a warm smile. 'And don't forget, when all this is over, you and I are going away together, somewhere warm and sunny, and neither of us will even mention work for a whole week. Okay?'

'That sounds like heaven,' said Alice. 'So how about if while I'm away, you do a bit of research and choose where you'd like us to go. And make it somewhere special. Okay?'

Ellie smiled. Thankfully, Alice hadn't the slightest idea what 'when all this is over' actually signified. This time she felt no guilt. She was now seeing the bigger picture, and was only relieved that Alice would be safe, thousands of miles from Surrey.

* * *

Sometimes it seemed to Gideon that he'd been waiting a lifetime for the day when they would finally bring Clover home. Now, as they drew near the Ten of Pentacles, it dawned on him that it was really going to happen. There had been various obstacles placed in their way — a broken-down vehicle blocking a narrow lane, lights stuck on red, slow-moving vehicles on narrow roads where it was impossible to overtake — but none were insurmountable. Foreseeing that they would try to stop him, he had sent out several vehicles from the Eleventh House, all at the same time, and all heading in different directions so as to confuse those who wanted to interfere. He was also banking on them not expending too much energy on the pursuit, on the assumption that he'd send one of the others to pick up their special girl.

All at once the cottage was in sight, and almost before Rae had drawn to a halt, he was out and running up the path.

The front door flew open, and Brendan was racing towards him, a woman and a child at his heels. 'Go! Fast as you can. They are close, Gideon, too close!'

In moments, Rae was off, roaring away from the tiny cottage. Their two passengers were silent, both shocked at the speed of events, and probably aware of the danger they were in.

'It'll be okay,' said Gideon softly. 'We are going home. It might be a rough ride, but we will make it.'

'And only just in time,' said Clover's mother. 'Look behind you.'

Gideon looked in the wing mirror. Behind them, he saw a thick column of smoke rise up into a sky lit with an orange glow. The Ten of Pentacles was burning.

He's safe. It was Serena, who had been watching the scene unfold from her tree-top home in the forest.

He gave thanks to the good spirit watching over Brendan.

He'll be coming home too. As soon as he can.

Yes, it was time Brendan was back where he belonged. He had been an enormous asset to them on the outside, but he'd done his part and now he should come in from the cold.

'There are blankets on the back seat next to you. Wrap up warm and make sure your safety belts are fastened. Don't worry, Rae is a pretty good rally driver, and she'll get us all home safely.'

'Oh, I know she will,' said the child confidently. 'And I can't wait to see our new home. Neither can Mummy. She's been having to protect me all on her own for much too long — now she won't have to, will she?'

'No, Clover. Lori can share that honour with us. From now on, everyone in the Eleventh House will be protecting you.'

As the day drew to a close, the colour slowly draining from the surrounding landscape, Rae gritted her teeth and put her foot down.

* * *

Christopher stared at the sheet of paper and screwed up his face in perplexity. Surely he didn't write that. But he had, he'd written it all down just as his friend had told him, and it had come out in proper writing. Grown-up writing, with grammar and all that, as . . . well, as good as a book! Had he fallen asleep and his dad had somehow written it for him? No. Christopher was one hundred per cent certain that he'd been awake all the time. He remembered going up to his room, finding some paper to write on and laying it on top of an old *Beano* annual so he could press on it. He sat down on his bed, and the next thing he knew was that the sheet of paper was covered in neat handwriting. There! He hadn't dozed off . . . or had he? One of Christopher's most treasured possessions was a wristwatch just like his dad's, only smaller. Like his father, he had developed the habit of looking at it every now and again. Looking at it now, he realised that over half an hour had passed since he entered his room, so had he written it, or . . . ?

Christopher sighed with realisation, he really could be an idiot sometimes. His friend had written it! Well, obviously he, Christopher, had *actually* written it, but his friend had guided his hand. Now that was sorted, the question was, what to do with it? He needed to get it to Michael. After all, Michael had said that the book was *very* important, and that they must keep it to themselves, which included Ellie, and Callum, of course.

So now he had another dilemma. His friend had made him promise not to go out at night, but surely if he just slipped out and ran through the orchard to Snug Cottage he'd be safe enough? There was no danger in the orchard, he played there all the time, and being out in the dark didn't frighten him. If he put the sheet in an envelope, which he could get from his grandfather's office, he could run across, pop it through the letter box and be back before anyone missed him.

Yes, that's what he'd do. He felt bad about breaking a promise, but if the book was as important as his friend and Michael said, he was sure he'd be forgiven.

CHAPTER TWENTY-TWO

'If we carry on much longer we'll be out all night,' said Jon, ticking off another of the properties on their list. 'The only two remaining are the big estates, so why don't we leave them till tomorrow? It'll be dark soon, and I confess to not feeling totally comfortable being out in the wilds.'

Wendy smiled. 'Well, sir, I never thought I'd hear you say that. If your collection of maps is anything to go by, you must have walked every path in the country.'

Jon gave a slightly embarrassed laugh. 'Well, not quite all, but I've been in some very lonely places over the years, and I've never felt like I do here. It just doesn't feel right, I don't know how else to explain it. One thing I do know is that if I'd been on my own, I'd probably have legged it by now. And did you notice, the birds have stopped singing.'

'So they have,' said Trevor, glancing around uneasily. 'I agree with Jon, we should leave those two bigger properties until the morning.'

'Well, I'm quite happy to call it a day,' said Wendy, closing her notebook. 'Actually, it's a good idea, because it'll give me a chance to do a bit of checking up on them before we visit.'

They lost no time in returning to the car and making their way back. Wendy couldn't help noticing that the further they were from the forest, the more relaxed Jon and Trevor became. By the time they drew into the station, they were their normal cheerful selves again. It was odd, all she'd felt was pleasure at being back in familiar surroundings.

By now, Wendy's shift had ended, and Jon urged her to go home. Tired as she was, she was eager to find out more about the retreat and the recluse, Nancarrow. When she said she would stay, Trevor, whose curiosity had been piqued, said he would too.

Wendy was glad of the company. Not only that, Trevor turned out to be worth his weight in gold when it came to research. While Wendy bashed at her keyboard, cursing every time she struck a wrong key, the pile of printouts on Trevor's desk steadily mounted. They had divided the search between them, with Trevor concentrating on the retreat called White Gates.

'They don't seem to advertise much,' said Trevor, looking at some of the results he'd printed. 'As far as I can tell, it's not your typical wellness and healing retreat, but neither does it focus on meditation and yoga and all that. It seems to be simply a place to go to escape from the stresses and hubbub of daily life, and spend time in nature, with an emphasis on physical exercise and nutritious food. They also hold classes in various arts and crafts, and since these run for several weeks, it looks like they cater for some quite long stays. I wouldn't mind betting it's where high-flyers go when they burn out.'

'Anything about who owns it?'

'A couple calling themselves Alistair and Nancy. They don't give a surname, but I get the impression they're not a couple it sounds like they're business partners. Both have travelled extensively so it says here. According to one of the brochures I did find, "We bring together a wealth of knowledge from many different cultures to help you rejuvenate mind, body and spirit. We offer a range of therapies aimed at reducing stress and anxiety, and provide a friendly and supportive environment during your stay with us. We always do our best to make our guests feel at home, be it for a few days, or longer."'

'Well, that's a definite for tomorrow morning,' Wendy said.

Trevor laughed. 'I might even check in, especially after a stressful week of late shifts.'

'I think it'd take more than hugging a tree and a bit of exercise to calm me after a bad week,' said Wendy. She regarded him curiously. 'Trev, can I ask you something?'

'Sure.'

'Out in that wood. Why were you and the DI so twitchy? I didn't get any of those weird vibes Jon was going on about.'

Trevor smiled at her. 'If you don't mind me saying so, Sarge, you are a pretty down-to-earth kind of person, aren't you? And that's not a criticism. The DI has a heightened awareness of danger, maybe because of the job, or it could be because he's out in nature a lot, on his own.'

'Ah . . . like the birds,' said Wendy.

'Exactly.'

'I wonder why they stopped singing,' she said. Now she thought about it, it was rather strange.

He considered the question for a moment or two. 'Birds sense danger too, they're much more sensitive than us. Their lives depend on it. If it's a predator, keeping still and silent is the best form of protection.'

'Yes, I know all that,' said Wendy. 'But there were no predators in that wood, and it still doesn't explain why Jon — and you too — were so paranoid. You're not birds, are you?'

'No, we're not,' said Trevor, amused. 'Nevertheless, there *was* something out there, Sarge. Okay, not a predator in the way you are thinking, but something bad nevertheless. The DI was uncomfortable for the reasons I just explained, but I was picking up something on a different level altogether. There were powerful negative energies washing around us. More than that, there was rage. I could feel it swooping through the trees around us, like a huge dark bird. No, that's not it either, it was like someone searching for something and not finding it, then is eaten up by frustration. I would not have wanted to get in its way.'

'You felt all that?' Wendy shook her head. 'And all I felt was . . . well, nothing really. I suppose I am down to earth, but I've got good instincts. Like Jon, I'm trained to pick up on subtle indications that something is wrong. I mean, back when that terrible thing occurred at Ellie's clinic, I felt the evil there, and I was terrified. So, why not now?'

Trevor thought about that. 'All I can think of is that for some reason you weren't supposed to feel it today. Maybe it wasn't you being warned off, just the DI and me, but don't ask me why that should be.'

Wendy gulped. 'Bloody hell, Trev, what is all this?'

'Dark doings, Sarge. Dark doings. And on that happy note, I'd better get off, as I've promised to get Mum fish and chips on my way home, and I can hear her stomach rumbling from here. Sorry to dash off like this.'

'No, that's fine, you get away, and thanks for what you've done. I'll give Mr Nancarrow another half hour, then I'll head for the chippy myself. The thought of fish and chips has got my taste buds working. See you tomorrow!'

There was no regular night shift in CID at present, although a handful of officers were on call in case the need arose, so Wendy was alone. Even the boss seemed to have gone.

Philip Nancarrow. The name sounded like something from a novel or film, like *Jamaica Inn*. Sadly, the real world provided scant information, and she began to wish that Trevor hadn't gone home. According to Helen Keele, Nancarrow was stinking rich, but no matter how widely she searched, the source of his money remained a mystery. She kicked herself for having omitted to ask what the nephew's name was. She had been so happy to be back at Heathersett with these warm and welcoming people that she'd forgotten to put her copper's hat on. The only name in her notebook was that of the lodge keeper, Howard Fenton. Perhaps if she managed to get him on his own, and threw in the fact that at one time she'd practically lived with the Keeles, might she get more from him? Her thoughts on how she might approach him, she put his name into the PNC and was amazed when she got a result.

'Aha! So, what have you been up to, Mr Fenton?' she whispered. It turned out that he had been arrested for theft, five years ago. The single conviction had earned him a suspended sentence, and since no further convictions followed, it appeared that he had learned his lesson. Even so, it made Wendy wonder why Helen Keele had spoken of him so cordially, calling him 'that nice Howard Fenton'. It also appeared that he was the sole employee. Funny that. Wendy reminded herself to have another word with Helen the following day.

'I've just heard from Professor Michael Seale.'

Wendy jumped. Engrossed in Howard Fenton, she hadn't heard the boss come in. 'Flippin' heck, sir! You don't half move quietly for a big man.'

Bob laughed. 'It comes in handy when you have kids, helps you keep up with what the little beggars are plotting next. Anyway, Michael rang me to say that the little Davison boy — er, Harry is it? — is now with his teacher, Lucy Reynolds, and Callum. Michael has suggested they stay at the C-M Centre for the time being, as this strange situation feels as if it's escalating.'

'Sensible move, but how did that come about? Isn't it a bit risky when she's his teacher?'

'Apparently, the deputy head has approved it, on the grounds of extenuating circumstances. The kid's father has done a bunk leaving the mother with her other son, who's disabled, and she can't cope with the two of them. The next step would have been social services.' Bob looked grim. 'And knowing the situation with the boy, they saw this as the best way to keep him safe.'

'Well, sir, I'm not going to disagree with that.'

'Anyway, I filled Michael in on the house-to-house we've been conducting in the area around where our dead boy vanished.' Bob raised an eyebrow. 'So, what's keeping you glued to your desk so long after the end of your shift?'

'There are two properties remaining from the house-to-house, sir. I wanted to run some searches on them before we wade in tomorrow. Forewarned, and all that. Trevor found plenty of info on the first one, but the other isn't proving so easy.'

'And which one is that?'

'It's called Knightswood House, on a huge estate adjoining the forest. It's at the end of a long drive, past a lodge house, and belongs to a—'

'Nancarrow,' said Bob.

'You know him?' asked Wendy, surprised.

'Not personally. Nobody does. But I know *of* him.' Bob pulled a chair up and sat down. 'And I can tell you right now it's no use even trying to get to see him.'

'I heard that he's a recluse, sir. A friend of mine's mother lives nearby, and she told me he refuses to see anyone.'

'She's right. You'd have more chance of meeting Lord Lucan. However, you could give his nephew a try. He's the old man's carer. I have met him a couple of times, he's a nice bloke, name of Jago Nancarrow.' He gave a little shrug. 'Although I can't see anyone at Knightswood having anything to do with our dead boy. They are far too self-contained. That estate is like a miniature kingdom ruled over by a monarch who has incarcerated himself in a tower. Sad, really.'

'Have you seen the house for yourself, sir?' asked Wendy.

'No, I met Jago in the gatekeeper's lodge; I didn't get to see the house itself. I suspect it's pretty rundown by now, given that no decorators or builders have been given access for many a year.'

'Were you aware that the gatekeeper, Howard Fenton, was once arrested for theft?'

If Wendy had expected Bob to be surprised by this she was wrong. He just nodded. 'Bit of a strange one, that. I always suspected that he was covering for someone else. I would swear he wasn't a thief. Clean as a whistle, good references, and then he nicks a woman's handbag? I don't think so. Nevertheless, he wouldn't budge. Said he'd done it, and copped a suspended sentence.'

'Sounds like I'm going to have an interesting morning, what with a retreat that is possibly intended for overworked business-people and the curious occupants of Knightswood House . . .'

'If I were you I'd get myself off home for a rest,' said Bob, getting to his feet. 'Oh, and before I forget, at some point tomorrow we should get over to the clinic, as I want to meet young Harry.'

'Me too,' said Wendy. 'Even if I am going to be expecting a ghostly airman to appear at any moment.'

Bob opened his mouth to respond, but closed it again and glanced around, frowning.

'Where the dickens is that cold draught coming from all of a sudden? Has someone been opening the windows?'

Wendy looked around. 'Not that I can see, sir, and I hadn't noticed any draught.'

'It's bloody freezing!' exclaimed Bob. 'Don't say the damned air conditioning is playing up again — that's all we need at this time of year. Look, you get home, Wendy. I'm going down to leave a message for maintenance. See you tomorrow.'

Wearing a puzzled frown, Wendy watched him hurry off. It wasn't even remotely cold in the office. Maybe the boss was coming down with something. With a sigh, Wendy shut down her computer and gathered up her things. Fish and chips were calling.

* * *

Finding an envelope for his writing had been a piece of cake. On entering his grandfather's office, Christopher saw a whole stack of envelopes in a posh leather stationery rack on the desk. One would certainly not be missed, and Christopher was soon back in his room, carefully folding the precious sheet in two and sealing the envelope. Very carefully, he wrote the name ELLIE on the front in big letters.

Now he needed to get out and back again without his absence being noticed. This part wasn't so easy, with his dad and granny watching him so closely. He sat on his bed to think it through. He daren't take his outdoor coat. If it was missing from the hook in the hall, they'd know immediately that he'd gone out. So, he'd have to run as fast as he could to keep warm. It really wasn't far. Down the back garden path, into the end of the orchard, and along the grassy path through the trees and the meadow to Snug Cottage. He'd need to sneak through the big gate and around the side of the house to the front door, but unless he knocked against something and made the dogs bark, he'd do it easily. Then run home, and hope he hadn't been missed. Anyway, what was the worst that could happen? A strict telling-off from his dad, and some disapproving looks from his gran? Well, he'd just have to find a good excuse and hope he got forgiven before supper, because he was hungry already.

He slid off the bed, pulled on his warmest jumper and pushed the letter into the back pocket of his jeans.

He even thought of leaving a CD playing, and chose a kid's spy thriller. Brilliant! He left his room and tiptoed down the stairs to the hall, where he stopped and listened. Gran was in the kitchen, cooking their supper with the TV on, and he knew his dad was doing his homework for that Open University degree he was studying for.

He bit his lip. This was the best chance he was going to get.

The cold hit him as soon as he closed the side door, and he wished he'd chanced sneaking the coat out. Well, he hadn't, and that was that. There was no point dithering now.

Christopher sprinted down the path, reaching the orchard in minutes. It was much darker than he'd expected this early in the evening. But he'd come prepared. He switched on his pocket torch and shone the beam onto the path. No problem. This was going to be what his dad would have called a doddle!

'Go back into the house, Christopher, and stay there, especially tonight. Promise me you won't come out again.'

The warning issued by his friend suddenly filled his mind, and he slowed his pace. There had been an urgency about that message, hadn't here? But he'd ignored it.

He looked around warily. Why was his torch beam so weak all of a sudden? He'd put new batteries in before he came out. And his feet! How come they felt so heavy, as if he were wading through mud?

For the first time, Christopher wondered why on earth he was doing this.

Nevertheless, he pressed on, trying to convince himself that he wasn't getting colder with every step. And now the path. It seemed all overgrown suddenly, and there were brambles snagging at his socks. Mr Scrubbs would never leave it like this. He'd never seen brambles in the orchard before, and how come the trees seemed taller and more dense? It was more like a forest than the place where he played with the dogs.

Christopher stopped in his tracks. He heard a deep, throaty growl coming from somewhere behind him. That was no spaniel. What was it making that noise?

He turned round slowly, but all he could see was darkness. Or . . . what was that!

Shaking with terror, he saw two blood-red eyes fixed on him. Then another pair joined the first. They seemed to crackle like the embers in a fire.

This had to be a bad dream. He'd fallen asleep on his bed. That's what it was, it was a nightmare. He'd wake up any minute now. Any minute! He must just hold on and he'd wake up! Trembling now from head to foot, he told himself not to cry, he was a big boy now. But it was no good, the tears were seeping down his cheeks. He wanted to call for his father, but he knew he wouldn't hear. So he cried out, 'I'm sorry I broke my promise! Please help me!'

'I've got you.'

The voice was deep, but also soft and kind.

'Now, look down at the ground, Christopher, and keep looking at your feet. Don't look up. I will guide you. Just walk, and think of home, all right?'

He sniffed and said yes.

'But most important of all is that you listen only to me. Trust only my voice, and none other. Do you understand?'

Christopher nodded.

'Christopher! What on earth are you doing out here?'

Dad! Christopher was on the point of looking up, calling out to him, when the first voice spoke again. 'Only me! Remember! Do not look up! That is not your father. They will try to trick you. Trust me, Christopher, and *keep* walking.'

Though his feet felt like he was wearing diver's boots, he did as he was told — he was too scared not to — and with every step closer to home it felt easier.

'Christopher, darling! Why are you in the orchard? Is everything all right?'

Ellie's voice, followed by that of Michael.

'Goodness me, lad. You gave us a fright when we saw you out here in the dark. Come on back to Snug Cottage. Ellie will make you a hot drink and I'll ring your dad.'

'Only my voice.' The words echoing in his head, Christopher, eyes on the ground, walked on.

'Good boy. Not far now.'

'Who are they?' he managed to whisper.

'No one. Just don't look up.'

Christopher struggled with the urge to just take a peek. What if those voices *were* Ellie and Michael? What if his friend was not his friend at all, but something wicked leading him away from the people he loved?

'Stay strong, Christopher. They are tempting you, that's all. They can't reach you, so they are slipping nasty little lies into your thoughts. Think of home, and your dad and your gran, and don't look up!'

He seemed to have been walking forever, but then he felt concrete beneath his feet, and the cold was suddenly less intense. At last, he dared to look up, and the porch light ahead told him he had made it. He was home. All at once, he heard a howl of rage coming from somewhere behind him, and he fell to his knees, clasping his hands to his ears.

'You are safe now.'

He felt instantly warm, and he saw that he was cocooned inside a ball of lavender-coloured light. In front of him stood a beautiful old lady. Shimmering slightly, she held out her arms and lifted him gently to his feet.

'Are you an angel?' he whispered.

'In a way,' she said, and gave a little tinkling laugh like the windchimes in the orchard.

'Are *you* my friend? Is that what you look like?'

'I've always been your friend and I always will be, even though we won't talk so much in the future. Even so, I'm always here when you need me. Just ask for my help, and I'll be there.'

'Like back then?'

'Just ask, that's all.'

Her eyes shone with so much love that he felt awful for having broken his promise. Stuttering, he attempted to say how sorry he was. Then he remembered why he'd gone back on his word and left the house. 'The letter! I needed to give Ellie what you helped me write! That's why I broke my promise. You said the book was very important, so—'

'It's all right, Christopher. But things are different now. That letter must not go to Ellie, or Michael, or anyone. I know how they work, they will have changed it while they had you under their control. It will no longer be my words, and it could do a lot of damage if Ellie or Michael were to see what's written there now.' She held out her hand. 'May I see it?'

He hesitated before taking the envelope from his pocket, and handing it over reluctantly. How could writing that was sealed in an envelope possibly have been altered? It didn't make sense.

She read it. 'As I thought. Do you remember what we wrote?'

He nodded. 'Of course. I always remember everything you tell me to write down.'

'Read this.' She handed it back.

He screwed up his eyes and started to read. 'But this is all wrong!'

'Very wrong, but luckily we found it in time and it's no longer a danger to anyone.' She gave him an extremely mischievous smile for someone so old. 'Or it won't be in a minute. Watch.'

She took it from him. At the touch of her hand, the paper crumbled to dust, so fine it didn't even fall to the ground. He watched it waft away, until it was gone.

'How cool is that!' he exclaimed. Then his face fell. 'Oh boy, am I going to be in trouble! I've been gone for ages, Dad is going to kill me.'

Again, that melodious laugh. 'No, he won't, I promise. Now, listen, before you go in, I have something to tell you about your writing. We'll carry on with your story, but if you can't get what you've written to Michael or Ellie, you must always give it to your gran, and she'll make sure it gets safely to Ellie. Okay? And don't worry, I'll make sure the same thing doesn't happen to her. From now on, your gran will be our secret postwoman.'

He nodded solemnly. 'Right. And I'll never break a promise to you again, cross my heart and hope to—'

'I know you won't, so we'll leave it at that. Now, you'll have to be brave and try to forget what happened tonight. Don't be afraid to go back into the orchard, it's just the same as it always was, somewhere to have fun playing with the dogs. I'll help you not to think about it, but there'll be times when it comes back to you. When it does, just push the thought away, and remember they cannot hurt you again.'

As he gazed back at her, the shimmering lilac light grew brighter, so bright that he was forced to close his eyes.

When he opened them again, he was in his room, his CD playing. His father stuck his head around the door, and Christopher saw that he was smiling.

'Gran says supper's ready, son. Looks like you've been asleep too. I nodded off over my books — that's a first, I must say. Anyway, shake a leg. Grub's up!'

Christopher followed his father out of the room, surreptitiously patting his back pocket. It was empty. Briefly, he wondered why this should come as a relief. The truth was, he felt distinctly odd. It was probably because he'd just woken up, and he'd been having this really weird dream . . .

'Christopher! Are you hungry or not?'

'Coming!' Christopher ran after his father. 'Yes, Dad. I'm starving!'

* * *

Ellie went up to their room to make sure Alice hadn't forgotten something in her rush to pack. Right now, her partner's head was all over the place, and no wonder — she was about to deliver the presentation of her life. Ellie groaned. She should be with her, supporting her. Instead, all she felt was relief at having been let off the hook.

She went over to the window and looked out at the orchard, just visible beyond the garden wall. It would be easier once Alice was safely in the air, then she could focus all her energy on what lay ahead. She would spend some time in the garden room, her sanctuary, and gain strength from meditation.

As she turned away from the window, she caught sight of a movement in the shadows at the far end of the orchard. Could it be Orlando? The dog had often been seen lately . . . She opened the window and leaned out. Whatever it was had stopped moving, in its place was a swirling mist the colour of violet. Vera. It had to be. But why out there now, in the evening? It was pure chance that she had looked out at that particular moment. It didn't make sense, and for some reason it bothered her deeply.

With an effort, she dragged herself away and carried on searching. Almost at once her eye fell on Alice's phone charger still plugged into the wall socket. Now that really would have upset her if she'd gone without it. Ellie unplugged it, and with a final glance around the room, hurried downstairs. This would be her last evening with Alice for a while, and she was determined to make it count.

On reaching the bottom step, she froze. The sudden thought that she might never see Alice again rose into her mind. She had no idea what they were about to walk into, but whatever it was, she knew it was terribly dangerous. The insidious words uttered by a six-year-old child. The dead plants, and the evil that had permeated the clinic until Janie had cleansed it. What if . . . what if this time good didn't prevail over evil? What would Alice come home to? Ellie stood there, her mouth dry, her head full of dark thoughts.

'Hello! You're miles away, aren't you. What's going through that head of yours?' Alice was smiling at her from across the hall.

'Sorry! I was thinking of things you might have forgotten, and one of them's *this*.' She held up the charger. 'Or were you planning on remaining incommunicado?'

God, Ellie thought to herself, *how forced, how stilted I sounded.* But Alice reached out for the charger. 'Oh shit! How could I forget something that vital! Thanks, babe. My phone's all charged up, so I'll put it in my hand luggage straightaway.'

Alice carried it off, giving Ellie a few moments to pull herself together. She told herself she must make tonight count. Be happy for Alice, so she went away content, and keep that promise to make plans for a holiday together. In fact, it would be something positive to work towards. There was a rough ride ahead, with new and unforeseen challenges to face. This would be something to keep her grounded. What could be more unexceptional than a holiday in the sun with the one you love? It was something solid to aim for, and no one would know just how precious a target it was.

Ellie found herself smiling.

'That's better!' Alice was standing the lounge doorway.

'Just so you know, I'm already thinking about holiday destinations. So don't hang about, we have shopping to do. There's swimming costumes to buy, and suntan oil!'

CHAPTER TWENTY-THREE

Leaving Harry's things in the car, Lucy began gathering her own belongings. The plan was for Callum to go straight home from work and pack a bag, then they would take both their cars to the C-M Centre. She glanced at her watch. He should be here any time now.

At first she had worried that being whisked away so abruptly would upset Harry. Instead, he seemed happy and excited. He told her it made him feel special, and assured her that he would try not to be a nuisance. *Oh, Harry*, she thought. *You wouldn't know how to be a nuisance.* It made her realise that this wasn't going to be easy for her, and she had a feeling it would be hard for Callum too. There was still a line that must not be crossed, which meant that she wouldn't be able to get as close to her little pupil as she would have liked. She would have to remember that she was only his teacher doing a favour for a distraught mother.

Almost angrily, Lucy began to shove various items of clothing into her bag. She had to get a handle on her emotions. Hopefully, in the clinic, with other people around, it would be easier to maintain her perspective. Above all, she wanted Harry to enjoy himself, while at the same time being safe.

Fortunately, Lucy wasn't the type to go to pieces in a crisis. Despite having none of her own, she enjoyed being around children, and had an easy rapport with them. She knew teachers who, having spent years dealing with little ones day in, day out, vowed never to have any of their own. Not Lucy. She was looking forward to the day, not too far in the future, when she would have children. Hopefully, her years of experience would give her a head start on those who embarked on parenthood having had little or no contact with the young.

By the time the doorbell rang, she was more or less organised, telling herself that she didn't live too far away and could always pop home if she'd forgotten anything important. By that time Callum would be with her, so Harry wouldn't be left alone.

Ah, that must be him at the door now. She glanced out of the window and frowned. That car she'd heard draw up wasn't Callum's, so who was ringing the bell? She hesitated, not knowing whether to answer, and then she heard him calling her name.

Callum stood on the doorstep, grinning broadly. 'Sorry, slight change of plan. On reflection, I didn't like the idea of you two driving alone, even with me following, so I've borrowed Dad's estate car for the duration. There's bags of space in the back, and it means we'll all be together. I've even got hold of a child's car seat from our neighbour, whose boy has outgrown it.'

Lucy felt considerably reassured. After that horrible incident with the tractor she was concerned about driving Harry anywhere. At least Callum appeared to have an early warning system in the form of spirit. 'Brilliant! Let's get Harry's things out of my car, and then I'll bring mine. I'll sort Harry out while you pack the car.'

Soon they were on the road, Harry bouncing in his seat with excitement. 'Is there a TV there? Can I watch cartoons?'

'Sure is,' said Callum. 'You can watch as many cartoons as you like — within reason. But we'll find all sorts of other things to do — hey, they have a studio there, with paints and pencils, and a lady who teaches people art to help them relax.'

'Wow! Do you think she'd let me draw something too? Do *I* need to relax?'

Callum chuckled. 'Don't worry about relaxing, Harry, that's just for us stressed adults. And I bet you can draw better than any of them, including the teacher.'

As they chatted away, Lucy noticed Callum's eyes constantly darting about, on the lookout for any sign of trouble. He was taking no chances with their precious cargo.

Michael was waiting for them at the front door. He helped them offload their belongings and stood with her and Harry while Callum parked the car.

'We have selected two adjoining rooms for you,' said Michael. 'One has two beds, a double and a single, and a small lounge area, which I thought would suit you and Harry. The adjoining room has a double bed, so if Callum takes that one, he's close at hand. Both are en suite, so you won't need to leave your rooms at night. Is that all right?'

'Perfect,' said Lucy gratefully. 'I really appreciate what you're doing. I confess that although I was delighted to be able to look after Harry, I was beginning to wonder if I was up to it — you know, living alone . . .'

'It's best this way,' said Michael. 'We're all here for you. Including this lovely lady.' Lucy saw a tall, smiling woman approaching them. 'This is Sister Maureen Shaw, our resident night sister. She lives on the same floor as you, but further along the landing in the adjoining wing. If anything worries you, or you need any medical help or advice, just ask Sister.'

At once, Lucy felt as if she'd known this kind and motherly woman for years. She smiled at her and had just started to speak when Callum arrived. As soon as he saw Maureen, his face lit up.

'You've got VIPs with you this week, Mo. They'll be needing the red-carpet treatment, especially the young gentleman. What do you say, Mr Harry? Reckon you're a VIP?'

'Um. What's a VIP, Callum?'

'A Very Important Person, and yes, you are.' Maureen beamed at him.

'Gosh. I've never been one of those before! I really like it here!'

Amid the laughter, Lucy thought that anyone seeing them now would never guess the strange circumstances that had brought this bright little boy to the clinic. The thought made her smile, but only briefly. The laughter, she soon saw, was all on the surface, and beneath the jollity ran an undercurrent of tension.

'Why don't I take you up to your rooms and let you get settled in,' said Maureen. 'It's getting late and this little man needs to eat. We can have something brought up from the café if you like.'

Callum shook his head. 'Don't worry, Mo. We'll take our things up, and go down and get some food. We can unpack when we've eaten, and get Harry off to bed. It's been a long day for the lad, and I reckon he'll sleep like a log.'

Lucy hoped he would. As for her, she'd be sleeping with one eye open, watching her little ward like a hawk — or a night owl.

* * *

Michael watched them go. He had just seen, for the second time, a shower of coruscating light cascade like a silver snowfall around Callum and Lucy. Callum had taken a bag from her to carry up the stairs, and when his hand brushed hers for a moment, the air between them shimmered with tiny glittering droplets. No one else seemed to have noticed, and Michael was sorry now that he hadn't made time to ring some of his colleagues and ask them about it. He'd never heard of this amazing phenomenon and wondered why not.

He realised he hadn't eaten either, and stopped at the café on his way back to his apartment. For once, it was almost empty, so he decided to eat there rather than cook a meal for himself.

The two head chefs, Si and Charles, were on duty, so he took the opportunity to tell them they had two extra guests who would need feeding for a week or so.

'Ah, yes,' said Charles. 'The young teacher and the kid. We heard they were coming.'

'Well,' said Michael, 'they are to order whatever they want, the bill's on us. Just keep a tab of the costs, and don't let that young teacher pay for a thing.'

'Got it, boss.' Si gave a gracious bow — that is, as gracious as you can be when you're as small and round as Si.

It always amused Michael to see the two chefs together. They were such an unlikely pair, Si short and — well, fat — and his partner Charles tall and hollow-cheeked, despite his habit of tasting every dish they served up, and with a lot more than a spoonful.

'Oh good,' exclaimed Charles. 'I adore cooking for children, you can have such fun with it, can't you, Si?'

Si rolled his eyes. 'Faces. I ask you! A master chef and he spends hours in the kitchen making faces out of the food. His speciality is clowns; he really goes to town on them, makes them out of mashed potatoes, with baked beans for eyes and mouths done in ketchup.'

Michael laughed. 'I'm sure young Harry would be delighted with a mashed-potato clown. But in the meantime, do you think you could rustle me up a mushroom omelette and one of your delicious mixed salads?'

'Is that with or without a face?' asked Si, solemnly.

'I'm tempted,' replied Michael, 'but maybe I'll give it a miss tonight, thank you.'

Charles gave a resigned shrug. 'Your loss. Pity, though. I do a brilliant owl, with cucumber, peppers and olives.'

They went off to the kitchen, while Michael found himself a table. Si and Charles had wrought enormous changes to the café since they had taken over its management. Their mere presence brought a smile to people's faces, and the food they served was both nutritious and tasty. Si's Thai meals were very popular, so much so that people from outside the centre had started to frequent the café. This had worried Michael initially, but it had since turned out that those who came to eat often went on to book treatments or became clients.

Waiting for his food to arrive, Michael was tempted to ring Ellie to let her know that Callum, Lucy and Harry had arrived and were safely ensconced on the first floor. Then he remembered that tonight was Alice's last night before she flew off to the States. It could wait until tomorrow. Whatever tomorrow brought.

'One omelette, and an owl-free salad,' said Si, setting the plates down in front of him. 'Although Charles couldn't resist adding this little dessert, so you can see what you were missing.'

With a flourish, he whisked a serviette from a side plate, to reveal a perfectly fashioned sheep made from banana slices and black grapes.

Michael laughed. 'That's wonderful! How on earth did he do it, and so fast?'

'I told you he was artistic. What that man can do with a boiled egg and a slice of spam is quite beyond belief.'

Still laughing, Michael told Si that the sheep had made his day, and to pass his thanks to the creative genius in the kitchen. 'While you're here, there's something I'd like to ask you.'

'Of course, Prof. Ask away.'

'It's about the teacher, Miss Reynolds, and the little boy. Would you mind keeping an eye on them when they're in here, just in case anything, er, unusual seems to be going on.'

'Like someone watching them, for instance?' said Si.

'That sort of thing,' said Michael, 'or anything else that doesn't seem right. And if you do, would you let me know?'

'You got it, Professor. I'll tell Charles.'

Michael was glad that he'd thought to ask. They could not have too many people watching out for Harry.

* * *

Rae sat on a wall outside the chapel and stared up at the stars. The drive back had been perilous, but they had made it, and now the precious child was sleeping in the safety of the Eleventh House.

Rae was utterly exhausted, more drained of energy than at any time in her life. Yet she could not sleep, not while there was still one more child out there. If the dark ones turned their wrath on him, she and Gideon might fail in their mission to bring every child in, the boy might die and she would never forgive herself for not having reached him in time. She pictured the terror on the face of poor Mole. That other child must not meet the same fate.

Immersed in her thoughts, she hadn't heard Gideon approach. 'I've news for you, my brave friend.' He lowered himself onto the wall beside her.

She blinked. 'News?'

'While we were away on our rescue mission, the others laid Mole to rest. They knew that if we were successful in our mission, Clover and her mother would be brought to the chapel, and they didn't want the first thing they saw to be a body. He was consigned to hallowed ground, Luna led the interment, and according to her, Ollie said some very moving things about Mole. Now he is away from that poisonous home of his, and the clutches of that evil teacher, Ollie is already starting to blossom. That lad is going to be an asset, Rae.'

Rae was glad that Mole was now at rest. In her exhausted state, she had completely forgotten that he was still in the chapel.

'Brendan is also back,' Gideon said. 'He's tired and shaken. Right now Serena is with him, and he'll be fine in no time. You'll be interested to hear that there is a "For Sale" sign outside Ollie's parents' house. Furthermore, Brendan was told that his teacher failed to turn up at school this morning, and wasn't answering his phone, so the police were alerted. They went to his house and found him lying on the kitchen floor, dead. It would seem they had displeased their masters in allowing young Ollie to escape.'

'Which suggests that he might be more valuable than we realised,' said Rae. 'Thank God we have him.'

'Indeed.' Gideon unfolded his long frame and stood up. 'Now, I think you could do with some help.' He held out his hand. 'Come with me, and we'll restore some of your energy.'

He led her to a shady, moonlight-dappled corner of the gardens. It had been planted so as to form a series of concentric circles, in the centre of which stood a bench seat of weathered wood. Slender trees and flowering shrubs made up the outer ring, beneath which ran a circular path. Within the outer ring was another ring of low-growing evergreen shrubs, predominantly winter-flowering daphne, whose fragrance filled the entire garden. A circular stone pathway ran around the bench, which sat in a bed of winter-hardy herbs and purple pansies. There were two such circles in the grounds, the Winter Circle, and the Summer Circle. Both were a source of natural energy and served as an aid to meditation and for cleansing troubled souls of negativity.

Rae sat on the bench while Gideon stood behind her, his hands resting lightly on her shoulders. He began to chant. It was a familiar litany, one they often recited, in which he called upon their guiding angels to join him in restoring new life to this weary soul.

'Keep us safe, keep us whole, keep us healthy, keep us wealthy, keep us wise, keep us happy. Prayers like silver arrows, breathe energy into our sister.'

An immense calm spread throughout her body. Eyes closed, she saw herself surrounded a by soft glowing light that seemed to shimmer like a heat haze. Gideon continued to chant for some fifteen minutes before giving vent to a long breath. He thanked their spirit guides.

Rae opened her eyes and turned her face to the night sky. Above the Winter Circle, the heavens were lit up with an *aurora borealis* of breathtaking hues — blues and mauves, greens and crimson, waves of colour blending into one another. She caught her breath. 'Gideon! Look!'

'We have powerful helpers, my dear friend. Remember those who came and restored peace to our son Mole? They are rejoicing, and thanking you for bringing Clover home.'

Rae felt tired, but comfortably so, nothing like the drained exhaustion of before. She would sleep easy now, and when she woke, she would be ready to take on their final task. One more child. One more boy. With that boy safe, they would be powerful enough to do battle with the forces of evil and vanquish them. The special ones would be safe. Each one would go forward in safety, and in accordance with his or her special ability, make a difference in a failing world that so desperately needed them.

'Come. Rest now.'

Gideon helped her to her feet and led her back to the house.

'Sleep soundly. You did well today, Rae. Not many people could have driven like you. They threw a lot of obstacles at you, both mental and physical, but you brought us home safely, and the heavens are grateful.'

She lay down on her bed and fell asleep at once.

CHAPTER TWENTY-FOUR

Despite having been awake half the night listening out for noises, Callum woke at six, feeling surprisingly rested. Just knowing that Lucy and Harry were close by was immensely reassuring — for once, he didn't have to worry about where they were or what was happening to them. 'Come on, Callum, be honest with yourself,' he muttered. 'Just knowing she's there, just metres away, is a good feeling, never mind the rest of it.'

He blinked. The airman was sitting at the bottom of the bed, regarding him in silence.

'Shit!'

Callum grinned sheepishly.

The airman was smiling at him, evidently amused by his reaction. 'Sorry, I didn't mean to startle you. I get so used to people not seeing me I sometimes forget that there are a few of you who can.'

'Yeah, I can see that being kind of difficult for you.'

'I wanted to thank you,' said the young airman. 'I'm charged with watching over Harry and knowing you are also looking out for him in the material world makes it a lot easier for me. I'm glad you have brought them here. It's a good place. Even so, it has been tainted with evil, and you must tell the people who run it to cleanse it thoroughly, not just once, but regularly.'

Callum recalled the dead plants that he had so carefully buried. 'What *was* that thing?'

'Something you never want to meet, Callum. I know you sensed it, but fortunately, you didn't meet it head on.'

'It's attached itself to that little girl, hasn't it?' Callum asked.

'In a way. It doesn't mean the child is possessed in the accepted sense. It's just using her as a sort of go-between. Even powerful entities cannot always manipulate a strong adult, but children are very malleable, and that little girl is unusually open to spirit.'

'Is that why Christopher has been chosen to pass on messages to us about special children in the form of a book?' asked Callum.

The airman nodded. 'Spirit can talk to a child as easily as I'm talking to you, but adults, even the most receptive, can be difficult to reach. It drains us of our strength, and we can't afford that, because it makes us vulnerable.'

As he spoke, Callum noticed that the airman was becoming less clear, his outline vague as if he were turning to mist. 'Am I draining you?'

'A little, I'm afraid. I should go, but once again, thank you.'

Callum was left staring at an empty space at the bottom of the bed. He cursed himself for not having the presence of mind to ask him about the things that had been puzzling him. The airman had said he had been 'charged' with looking after Harry, which confirmed his impression that the airman was protecting the boy. But on whose behalf? And why was Harry in danger? He could hardly wait to speak to Michael and Ellie.

He got up and went to the bathroom. As he stood under the shower, he realised that other than the few questions about Dresden in Lucy's house, this exchange with the airman was the first time he'd communicated directly with spirit. Even Vera and Carole and the dogs hadn't actually spoken in the way another person might, but the airman had, and it felt a little surreal.

As he dressed, he began to hear movement in the adjoining room, and childish laughter, and turned his mind to the coming day. It was going to be quite a task making it fun for the lad while remaining alert to danger.

Whether it was this thought, or something else that caused it, Callum was overtaken by the conviction that something was going to happen today. He had no idea whether it would be good or bad, but it was a warning. He must not let Harry out of his sight.

* * *

Ellie had known that saying goodbye would be difficult, but when Alice began loading her baggage into her car, it took all of her strength not to cry out and beg her not to go. Her heart breaking, she put on a smile and told Alice to imagine that she was there in the audience when she gave her presentation. She told her she was proud of her, that she loved her, and was still telling her so as the tail-lights disappeared around the corner, and Alice was gone.

Ellie was left staring at the empty lane, with tears in her eyes and an ache in her heart. As she stood, unable to break away and face what was to come, she felt a damp muzzle push into her hand.

Without looking down, she stroked the familiar silky fur of the dog now leaning against her, just as Orlando used to do when he wanted a tickle.

'It's best this way, my girl, and you know it. Now, take a deep breath, go and get yourself a big mug of tea and thank your lucky stars that your precious Alice is well away from here. And stop moping, it doesn't suit you one bit!'

The voice she heard was not just in her head. It rang in her ears.

Ellie turned towards the house. Standing in the doorway in her trademark baggy cords, the only unfamiliar thing about Carole was the expression on her face, which was soft, and full of compassion.

'All you need to know is that we are here for you, my dear, and above all, that we are here for the children. It was right that Alice should go. You are now free to go forward. A lot is at stake, Ellie. Stay strong, and tell that old duffer Michael from me that he's to use every scrap of knowledge in that big old head of his, and not to ignore the messages from spirit. Ever!'

On the word 'ever', her outline grew fuzzy and began to dissolve into the surrounding mist.

'God bless.'

Nothing remained of the woman and her dog but a soft blue mist that was gradually extinguished in the early morning light.

Ellie took a deep breath, marched resolutely into the house and put the kettle on. It didn't do to argue with Carole Cavendish-Meyer.

* * *

'My friend said I'm to give you this — it's for Ellie.'

Marie Littlewood accepted the sheet of paper without asking a single question. 'Thank you, Christopher. I'll take it over right now.'

With a relieved smile, Christopher raced back up the stairs to get ready for breakfast.

It's like two worlds colliding, thought Marie. There was the earthly, day-to-day world where a smiling child in PJs went charging up the stairs to change for breakfast. And then there was the other, difficult to grasp and tenuous, where strange things happened and knowledge was acquired through intuition. Like now. She didn't know how she knew it, but it was an accepted fact. She was now the designated go-between, passing messages between Christopher's 'friend' and Ellie and Michael. It was something she didn't even think to question.

Marie knew that Alice was leaving very early, indeed, she had probably already gone, meaning that Ellie would no doubt go into work earlier than usual.

She took a warm coat from the rack in the hall and slipped it over her nightdress, pulled on her boots and hurried over to Snug Cottage.

When she saw her on the doorstep, Ellie stared at her, her face full of concern. 'Marie! Is everything okay? Is Christopher all right?'

Marie hastened to reassure her that everything was fine. She held out the sheet of paper, looking much as Christopher had done when he placed it in her hand. 'I brought it straight here. I haven't read it, but the writing is the same as the last one.'

Ellie held the door open for her. 'Come in, let's go through to the kitchen and we'll have a look at it.'

After a boisterous welcome from the dogs, she sat next to Ellie at the kitchen table. In an elegant hand, the story seemed to follow a new trajectory:

Winter sun shone down on the child's hair, so that it glowed like gold.

'Why am I called Clover?'

'Because you are a child of light. Even your name is built around LOVE.' The man gave her broad smile, 'C . . . LOVE . . . R, right?'

'Oh, yes. That's nice, isn't it? Tell me, why is this place called the Eleventh House?'

'In astronomy, the eleventh house brings you allies and friends. It's the part of the heavens that is governed by the sign of Aquarius, and the planets Saturn and Uranus. This house is about strength within a community, Clover. It's about how a group of people with a collective goal can achieve their dreams and aspirations. Do you understand what that means?'

Clover thought for a while. 'I think it means I'm home.'

The man looked at her affectionately. 'It does.'

'But there are two more to find, aren't there? Two more children.'

'Just one. We are hoping that very soon he'll be here with us.'

'No, you are wrong,' said the child. 'The girl must come as well.'

'What girl?'

'You know who I mean. Of course you do,' chided the child whose name was "love". 'She has to come here too, or it will never be over.'

The two women looked at each other.

'Well, I don't know,' said Ellie eventually. 'This needs some thought. I'll have to show it to Michael and Callum and see what they say. I have no idea what this is about, Marie, and from the look on your face, you don't either. All I can say is that I promise to tell you when we get to the bottom of it.'

'Ellie?' Marie said shakily. 'You don't think that the boy it says they're looking for is my Christopher, do you?'

'No, I don't, Marie. I can't tell you why, but I'm pretty certain that someone, some — let's call it a being — is using Christopher to communicate with us. I'm also certain that they're a force for good, and that they're using these rather cryptic messages as a means to help us.'

'Well, I hope you're right. Whatever it means, one thing's for certain — from now on, that my grandson isn't going to be left alone until this is over.' She stood up. 'I'd better get back. Oh, and don't worry about the dogs, we'll look after them. Just keep in touch. I feel a bit isolated not knowing what on earth is going on.'

Ellie promised she would, and gave her friend a hug. 'Just take care, won't you?'

Marie hastened home, terrified that she was already too late and would arrive home to find that Christopher had been whisked off to this mysterious Eleventh House.

* * *

Wendy was glad that the boss had decided to accompany them on their return to the woodlands. She hoped his down-to-earth presence would calm Jon and Trevor's nerves.

Rather than go as a group, which might be intimidating, they decided to work in pairs. Jon and Bob would go to the retreat at White Gates, while she and Trevor would try and gain access to the mysterious Knightswood House.

'Hope you have better luck than I did,' Bob said as they set off. 'Although that Jago chap tried his best to be as helpful as he could. I reckon he's got his work cut out looking after his uncle. Oh, and Howard Fenton at the Lodge — cut him some slack, Wendy, would you? He never nicked that handbag, I'd bet good money on it. I think all he was guilty of was misplaced loyalty to someone he cared for.'

The weathered plaque affixed to the front wall of the stone lodge house declared that the building had guarded Knightswood House since 1798. Wendy hoped it didn't guard it too fiercely because they had no option but to try and get an answer here, as the ancient iron gates straddling the entrance to the long straight drive were padlocked.

Trevor, who had been happily chatting all through the journey, grew increasingly silent and pensive the nearer they were to their destination.

About to knock, Wendy dropped her hand and turned to him. 'All right, Trev. What's bothering you?'

'I, er . . . It's . . .'

She put her hands on her hips. 'Hello . . . ?'

He gave her a rueful smile. 'Sorry. It's just . . . What would you say if I told you this place has the strangest atmosphere I've ever encountered?'

'I'd say what the dickens are you talking about.'

'I wish I knew,' he said. 'I don't mean it's a bad atmosphere, nothing like what Jon and I felt yesterday evening. It's just, well, confusing.'

Wendy shook her head. 'Confusing. Right. Well, we'd better see if we can get a bit more sense out of Mr Fenton, then, hadn't we?'

Trevor grinned sheepishly, 'Sorry, Sarge. Yes, of course.'

She lifted her hand again, and gave the heavy iron knocker a hearty thump.

It swung open. The two men in the hallway broke off their conversation and smiled at them enquiringly.

'Can we help you?' asked the shorter, stockier of the two.

'Surrey Police, sir. I'm DS Wendy Brown and this is DC Trevor Grant. We were hoping to have a word with Mr Nancarrow — it's about an incident that took place the night before last, not far from here.'

The taller man stepped forward, holding out his hand. 'I'm Jago Nancarrow, how can I help?'

They shook hands, and Wendy continued. 'It was actually Mr Philip Nancarrow we needed to talk to, if he's available.'

'I'm very sorry, but that's not possible. And anyway, he wouldn't be able to help you, he hasn't left the house in years. He's severely agoraphobic, you see.'

It was the answer she'd expected, but she couldn't help feeling a little disappointed. 'Then perhaps you two might be able to help. You must be Howard Fenton, is that right?'

'I certainly am,' the second man said. 'Come on in. I was just going to make coffee, or perhaps you'd prefer tea?'

Inside, the old lodge was like something from a distant era. Some of the interior walls still retained the original stonework, while others had been rendered and painted. The arched windows were deeply recessed and framed in stone, the glass etched with leaves and climbing plants. The open fireplace, in which a log fire was burning brightly, was large for such a small room.

'I'll leave you to talk to Jago,' Howard said. 'I'll just get some drinks together.'

Jago pointed to a couple of comfortable-looking old armchairs. 'Take a pew, Officers, and tell me what this is about.'

Wendy told him about the body which had so mysteriously vanished. 'I'm afraid that if the young man's body doesn't turn up, we're most likely looking at a crime having been committed, possibly a serious one. In which case—'

'You will want to search the surrounding properties.' Jago looked slightly nervous. 'Believe me, if this was my house, I'd throw the gates wide open, right now . . .'

Wendy waited for the 'but'—

'Look, I saw nothing untoward that evening. As for Howard, you must ask him when he comes back with the tea, but he would have told me if he'd seen any suspicious activity. It's what he's here for, to look out for intruders so that my uncle is never disturbed. I said he was agoraphobic, but it's rather more serious than that. It's not just a case of not liking to go out, but his mental condition is such that the slightest change in his daily routine could tip him over into madness. I cannot afford to let that happen.' He shook his head sadly. 'However, you have your job to do, and I don't want to be obstructive, so here's what I'll do. I still won't be able to let you into the house, but he might allow you to look around the grounds, and maybe the outbuildings. Would that help?'

'Thank you, sir, that would be a great help,' Wendy said.

'Before I go and ask him, I ought to warn you that he'd never agree to teams of policemen in uniform stomping around in the grounds. It would have to be just you and your colleague, accompanied by either me or Howard.'

Wendy said she understood. They had no wish to upset Mr Nancarrow, and in any case it wasn't a question of a search party but a quick look around for any traces of the missing dead boy, and where he might have been taken.

'I'll go and see what I can do. Oh, and the locals may have misled you into thinking that my uncle lives in a great rambling mansion and is nothing but an old miser who spends his days counting his huge stash of loot.'

Wendy could well imagine the rumours that would inevitably have sprung up about the old recluse.

'He is fairly wealthy, it's true, but he spends all of it on wages and accommodation for his staff, a group of trustworthy retainers who dedicate their efforts to the endless task of maintaining the grounds and gardens and preventing them from becoming a jungle, and keeping the fences secure.'

Howard entered, carrying a tray of mugs. 'As for the house itself,' he added, 'it's little more than a ruin.'

'He's right,' said Jago. 'And it is far from being a mansion, it's just a nice rural property — a Tarrant House, if you know what that is.'

'Yes, sir,' said Trevor, causing them all to look at him in surprise. 'Walter George Tarrant, master builder and developer. He was Surrey's most prolific builder in the early nineteen hundreds.'

'He was indeed,' Jago said, evidently impressed. 'He designed a number of quite magnificent properties such as the elite St George's Hill Estate, as well as more modest buildings like Knightswood House.'

'It's a sin, the state it's in now,' said Howard, handing round the drinks. 'I fear it'll be beyond redemption by the time Philip passes through the Pearly Gates.'

'To put it bluntly, it's downright dangerous,' said Jago. 'Howard and I have managed to keep one wing reasonably safe to live in, so my uncle spends his days there, and where I, too, have my rooms, but the rest of the house . . .' he spread his hands, 'is closed off and left to the mercy of the elements. Anyway, I should go and see if I can get these good people inside the Inner Sanctum. Sorry about the tea, Howard, but I shouldn't be long.'

Hearing the front door close, Wendy glanced out of the window and saw his tall figure pedalling furiously down the drive on an old bicycle.

'He's pretty devoted to his uncle, isn't he?' she remarked.

'Oh yes,' said Howard. 'Back in his heyday, Philip Nancarrow was a notable philanthropist who helped any number of people get back on their feet when they were in trouble. He still does, as far as he's able. He's given the people who work here a roof over their heads and food to eat, without which they'd be on the streets. Thanks to Philip, they're safe, and have some money in their pockets. They can go into town, pay their way and hold their heads up.'

She didn't say so, but Wendy found it rather an odd set-up. 'I think you know a friend of mine — Helen Keele from Heathersett?'

Howard broke into a smile. 'You know Helen? Lovely woman. I've got a lot of time for that lady.'

'Her daughter and I were best friends when we were kids. I spent more time at the Keeles' home than I did in my own. I loved the woods. In fact, I was happier here than in the town.'

'Are you a local too?' Howard asked Trevor.

'No, sir. I come from up north. I'm a Northumbrian.'

'So, where's the Geordie accent?' Howard asked.

'I've been living down south for years, sir, although I'm new to this district.' Trevor shrugged. 'I guess I just acclimatised.'

Or lost it deliberately, so as not to draw attention to his mother and her damaged reputation, Wendy thought. She turned to Howard. 'How long have you been here, Howard?'

He looked up at the ceiling. 'Let me think. Coming up to eight years, I reckon.'

So, Howard Fenton had been working here when he was arrested for theft. And as her boss swore it was because he'd been protecting someone, it was most likely someone around here. Interesting. 'A long time,' she said. 'And the others employed on the estate?'

He smiled. 'Oh, we all know when we're well off, Detective Sergeant Brown. Most of the others have been here as long, or longer, than I have. This is our home.'

'What would become of you if anything should happen to the old man?' she asked. 'I mean, he's pretty old, and if he won't let a doctor into his house . . .'

'*Que sera sera*, Sergeant. Although I have every confidence that Jago will honour his uncle's promise that we will all be looked after. Jago is a good man, and I don't think we have anything to fear. It's going to happen one day, in fact I'm surprised the old boy's still with us. Nevertheless, none of us wants to move on, so you might say every day is a blessing.'

What a weird set-up, thought Wendy, *it sounds positively feudal.* She hoped she might get an opportunity to speak to some of the 'staff' on their own, without Howard or Jago being there. Were these others as grateful for their lot in life, and as trusting of the Nancarrows, as Howard seemed to be?

'You are very honoured, you know,' said Howard suddenly. 'I've never known of anyone having been allowed inside the gates before.'

'Well, we aren't actually in yet,' said Wendy grimly. 'Jago could easily come back and say that Philip has gone into meltdown, and we'd be back outside those gates of yours.'

'Well, we're about to find out,' said Trevor, who had been looking out of the window. 'Here's his bike now.'

'Officers, you're in luck. My uncle didn't sleep well last night, and has gone back to bed. It looks like he's taken something to help him relax. So, if you're ready? Howard, can you unlock the gates, please, and lock them again after them? Then, if you wouldn't mind going with the detectives, you can take the car to about three quarters of the way down the drive, then park and go the rest of the way on foot. I'd better stay and keep an eye on my uncle. And if you could try to keep your visit as short as possible, and do not on any account try to approach the house.'

Having assured Jago that they would do as he asked, they hurried out to the car.

Finally, the rusty old gates swung open with a metallic shriek. Wendy was looking forward to telling Grandpops and Helen that she'd actually been to Knightswood House, even if she hadn't gone inside.

'He's very anxious that we don't go near that old house, isn't he?' whispered Trevor. 'A bit *too* anxious, don't you think?'

Her eyes on the rear mirror, Wendy watched Howard lock the gate behind them. 'Yes, I do. In fact I reckon this whole set-up stinks to high heaven.' She glanced at Trevor. 'Are you still getting that same confused feeling? You know, like when we first arrived?'

'Damn right I am, only it's worse now,' said Trevor. 'Much worse.'

'Then you'll be pleased to know I'm feeling it too. And when we've had our look around, we'll go back to base and have a good look into the Nancarrows.'

CHAPTER TWENTY-FIVE

'Oh, I'm so glad you're in, Ellie,' Michael said. 'There's something that's been troubling me all night. I can't stop wondering if Beth is in actual danger from her child. I know it sounds preposterous, but it was the utter venom in Izzie's voice when she addressed her mother. I'm terrified that we've sent Beth Saunders away unprotected.'

Ellie, who had been about to show Michael the latest offering from their little author, was somewhat knocked off her stride. Apart from that, she was surprised at his sudden apprehension regarding Beth Saunders.

'Listen, Michael, don't assume that Beth is unprotected. I am absolutely certain that it was Vera who directed her to us, and don't forget her Good Samaritan, whoever that is, who offered to pay for her treatment. Between them, they are watching over Beth, so you can be sure that nothing will happen to her. I also believe that she is receiving help with dealing with "Bad" Izzie. You should have heard the way she spoke to her, she was so calm and sure of herself. It was quite an eye-opener. Oh, and Beth does realise that she needs to spend as little time alone with her daughter as she can, and to try and always be in the company of other people. Don't ask me why, but whatever that evil entity is, it can't use the child when other people are around. Nor do I have any idea why it didn't sense me hiding in my inner office, but it didn't.' She gave her friend an encouraging smile. 'Look, Alice has gone now, she phoned me a few minutes ago from the departure lounge where she's waiting to board. So, I'm now one hundred per cent focused on the children, and what's going on with them. Which means that if anything bothers you, you can talk to me, day or night.' She paused. 'Now that's out of the way, I have some news for you. If you're up for it, that is?'

'I'm sorry. I don't often get anxious like that, but that poor lass was giving me a touch of the cold sweats.'

'Well, listen to this. It'll make you forget all your anxieties. Would it surprise you to hear that I met Carole today?'

'Pardon? Did you say you *met* her?'

'Standing on the front doorstep of Snug Cottage, in the obligatory corduroy slacks — complete with dog hair, of course. Oh, and Orlando turned up for an ear tickle.'

'Hang on. You describe it as if you actually saw her, not just her signature blue mist.'

'Because I *did* see her, Michael. Just like I'm seeing you, but only for a few moments. But while it lasted, it was truly amazing, as if she was back at home, like she always was.' The last words caught in Ellie's throat.

'Did she tell you off about something?' asked Michael.

'Oh yes, she certainly did.' Ellie told him exactly what Carole had said, including what an 'old duffer' he was.

'Well, that confirms it, doesn't it? She obviously hasn't changed her opinion of me.'

'But that's not all,' said Ellie. She took the folded sheet of paper from her shoulder bag. 'Marie Littlewood came over at the crack of dawn — in her nightie, would you believe — to bring me this.'

'Another sleepwalking episode from young Christopher?' asked Michael, taking the paper from her.

'No. He said he just wrote it, and that his "friend" had done it with him, "guiding my hand", as Christopher put it. Go on, Michael. Read it.'

Having read it through twice, Michael leaned back in his chair and closed his eyes. 'Now, let me get this straight. The first time Christopher spoke to me about his book, he said it was about three children, called Clover, Zillah and Finn, and about good and evil. So, now we meet Clover, and she seems to be talking to someone she trusts, wouldn't you say?'

'Yes,' Ellie said. 'He says the man looks at her "affectionately".'

'So, according to the original storyline, Clover and her mother arrive at a place which sounds a bit like a commune. The people there are good people and they want to protect her. This last episode confirms this. The place Clover has arrived at is called the Eleventh House which she believes is her home. Right so far?'

'Absolutely,' said Ellie. Suddenly, the story was beginning to make more sense. 'And the people who run this place are out hunting for a boy. Now, could that be Finn?'

Michael nodded. 'That's what I'd say.'

'And Clover also says there's another girl who needs to be found, although this man in charge, whoever he is, doesn't appear to realise that. Maybe that's the girl, Zillah.'

'Very possibly,' murmured Michael. 'Now, on reading this, two things stand out for me, the first being the word "special". If you remember, Christopher said they were special children. The other word is "home".' Michael grasped her arm. 'Ellie! I don't think we're the only people who are trying to protect special children! I think whoever runs this Eleventh House is doing exactly the same — finding these children and taking them to a place where they will be safe.'

Yes! thought Ellie. This was exactly what was happening. For some reason, another group of good, caring people were out there gathering up special children to protect them, perhaps from entities like the one that had chosen Izzie to attach itself to.

Then another thought hit her. The word 'home'. 'Oh my God! Michael! We need to talk to Bob and Wendy! I think I know what happened to that dead boy who was found in the road. In Christopher's sleepwalking message, the man who found him and called him son, said he was taking him *home*. I swear it's the man Clover is talking to in today's message. I think he took that dead boy to the Eleventh House. The police have to find that place. If they are gathering in those children, it means they believe them to be in serious danger, and if that disgusting entity that used Izzie to get in here is anything to go by, the people trying to save them could be in danger too.'

Michael held up his hand. 'Hang on a moment. Yes, of course we must get in touch with Bob, but first, let's try and get it straight in our own minds. And I really think Callum ought to be in on this, don't you?'

Ellie's thoughts were racing so fast she was having trouble reining them in. But Michael was right, they must share this with Callum. She stood up. 'I'll go and find him.'

'And, Ellie, make sure Lucy and Harry have someone with them while he's away. This could take a while, and we need that child watched constantly.'

She found them in the Orangery, and as luck would have it, Jason Adamson was with them. He agreed to be chaperone for half an hour, and said he would bring Lucy and Harry to Michael's office when his own first appointment was due.

On their way back to her office, Callum told her of the airman's advice to have the C-M Centre regularly cleansed, and she said she'd have a word with Janie as soon as they had finished their discussion.

'So you actually saw the airman this morning. Well, *I* saw Carole, and that's a first for me. It was . . . she was so real. I wanted to rush up and give her a hug. I still miss her terribly. I suppose I always will.'

'We said she was coming through stronger, didn't we,' said Callum, 'and I guess that proves it. And you're getting stronger too, Ellie, otherwise she would not have been able to reach you in that form. It's not only your gift of auric sight, you are also becoming far more open to spirit. You and Carole were very close, so it doesn't surprise me that it's you she has chosen to appear to.'

Dear Carole. Ellie felt a rush of affection for her old friend, a fondness that was as strong as ever, even when they were literally worlds apart. 'Do you know, she still had that same wonderful blue aura. I couldn't help tuning into it despite my awe at seeing her so clearly manifested. Now I think about it, it has changed; it's a deeper cobalt blue of immense brilliance. In fact, it's almost as intense as Vera's glorious purple and lavender.'

'I think we could be very glad of so much power as the dark forces start to gather.' Callum stopped in his tracks and turned to face her. 'Ellie, is it okay to be frightened? Because I am. Perhaps I'm not strong enough for this?'

'Yes, it is okay to be frightened, Callum. After all, we're only human. It means we won't make the mistake of underestimating what we are up against. Fear warns us not to go blundering blindly into danger.'

They walked on in silence for a few minutes, then Ellie said, 'It's always worse when people we care deeply about are involved, and I know how much you care for Lucy and little Harry. But always remember that you're not alone, we're there for them too. For as long as it takes.'

They found Michael pacing the office. 'Ah! Good, good. We'd better start by putting Callum in the picture. Will you do the honours, Ellie, or shall I?'

'You do it, Michael, you'll probably put it better than me.'

First, they showed Callum the sheet of paper from Christopher, and then Michael told him what they thought it meant. He sat for a while in silence, thinking over what he'd heard. 'There's a lot I don't understand, especially concerning that child, Izzie. One single visit to the centre, and wherever she set foot was polluted.' He ran his hands through his hair. 'I may be way off the mark here, but it takes me back to a mercy dash I was involved in not long after I joined MSF. We were in Israel, and I was working with an amazing doctor called Zillah. She told me it's an old Hebrew name, meaning "shadow" or "shade". She had these dark eyes, and she fastened them on me, saying that yes, it sounded very poetic, but fortunately it did not reflect what was in her heart.'

At first Ellie didn't understand what he was getting at. 'You mean, like Izzie?'

He nodded. 'She still needs our help, doesn't she? After all, she was sent to us. But the thing is, how? Dare we bring that dark force back to the clinic and risk it violating what we have here?'

'Perhaps,' Ellie said slowly, 'we aren't meant to bring her here. Perhaps our task is to get her to the Eleventh House. That's what Clover is saying in the message Christopher's friend sent. She's destined to go there, not here.'

'I think you're right, Ellie,' Michael said. 'We know next to nothing about the people at this Eleventh House, but if it is a place of safety for the special children, they are probably well protected and have more understanding of these dark forces than we do. We have our gifts, and the guidance of Vera and Carole, but we are far from adept in all matters of spirit.'

'Basically, what it comes down to is good versus evil,' Callum said. 'Christopher's story is about a group of people fighting a battle to protect special children. If we accept that, then the people at the Eleventh House must be the good guys—'

'But who are the bad ones?' Ellie demanded. 'And why are they hell-bent on going after these children?'

Neither Michael nor Callum had an answer.

'And where do Harry and Christopher fit in?' Michael said. 'They are also special, but according to Clover only one boy and one girl remain to be found. Yes, the boy is apparently called Finn, but is that his real name? Could he possibly be Harry?'

Suddenly, Ellie heard herself say, 'Christopher is *not* special. He's just acting as a messenger, no more than that.'

The two men stared at her. 'What?' she said. 'Why are you looking at me like that?'

'You sounded a bit, er, forceful, Ellie,' said Michael. 'Rather like another old friend of ours, in fact.'

Ellie shrugged. She'd just stated a fact, that was all.

'I think Ellie's right,' said Callum. 'The airman said children are much easier to communicate through than adults.'

'Which leaves us with Harry,' Michael said.

Neither Ellie nor Callum had an answer to that.

* * *

Now visible across a stretch of grass, Knightswood House looked even more of a ruin, and probably as hazardous, as Howard and Jago had described it to be.

'I guess that's the part the old guy lives in,' said Trevor, pointing to the left-hand side of the old house. 'At least it doesn't look in danger of imminent collapse like the rest of it. It's such a shame, it must have been really nice back in the day.'

Howard was talking to a young man in oil-stained overalls who had been tinkering with a big petrol mower. Wendy went over to join them.

Howard introduced him as Seb, adding, '. . . and he's not seen or heard anything either.'

Seb's look of open curiosity made Wendy want to smile. Clearly, visitors were something of a novelty at Knightswood. 'Sorry, Detective. A couple of us went down to the local that evening, but we didn't see anything suspicious either on the way there or back. Not that we ever do, mind.'

'And nothing in the outbuildings, garage or sheds has been disturbed?' she asked, already knowing what the answer would be.

'Nope. And let's face it, you can't just stroll into the grounds, can you? Place is locked up tighter than a duck's arse, plus there's cameras all around the gardens and they are checked every day. It's like Fort Knox in here, miss. You'd be best trying some of the smaller houses.'

She thanked him and went back to Trevor, who was still standing where she'd left him, gazing up at the old half-derelict building.

'Don't tell me it's haunted too,' she whispered, with a glance back at Howard, still chatting to Seb.

'It just doesn't equate,' he said quietly.

'What doesn't?'

'The house. It doesn't feel like it should.'

'Trevor! You're not making sense. What exactly should a sodding great pile of brick and timber "feel" like in the first place?'

He groaned. 'Sarge, I can't possibly explain now. It's just . . . Look, I know you think it's a dead end, and it might well turn out to be one, but I'm convinced that we really do need to look closer at the owner, *and* the house. But not here.'

Wendy shrugged resignedly. They continued to wander around the grounds, and managed to speak to one of the other gardeners, but he more or less repeated what Seb had said.

'And that wall over there is the boundary?' asked Wendy, pointing to an ancient stone wall.

'That's right,' Howard said. 'Goes all the way round. The only entrance is the one at the end of the drive where you came in. I suppose there must be about two and a half acres of garden, certainly plenty to keep our little workforce busy.'

'Where are the others?' asked Trevor.

'One has a day off today, and two are dredging a small stream that runs alongside the west wall. It flows through a culvert that goes under the wall and the road, and feeds into a bigger stream on the common land opposite.'

Wendy did not point out that this represented a weakness in the defences of Knightswood House. Not that anyone could have brought a dead body into the grounds that way. It was time to bring their visit to a close. She apologised to Howard for wasting his time, and asked him to thank Jago for allowing them inside. 'We are sorry about his uncle's poor state of health, and I do hope we haven't disturbed him.'

'He'll be asleep for hours, most likely,' said Howard, 'he usually does when he gets like that, but I'll pass on your message. Would you like me to contact you if any of us see or hear anything?'

'By all means, sir.' Wendy took a card from her bag. 'We'll be grateful for any help you can give us. This is a very distressing situation for everyone. The thought of a young man dying alone is bad enough, let alone having his body disappear like that.'

As they drove away from Knightswood, she said to Trevor, 'As soon as we are back, I want you to dig up everything you can on Philip Nancarrow, and I'll go and see what the boss has to say about the retreat. After that, I'll see if I can trace the history of Knightswood.' She stopped. 'On second thoughts, you can do that when you've finished with old Nancarrow. You're faster than me — and I'll thank you to keep any comments about the way I treat my keyboard to yourself!'

'As if I would, Sarge,' said Trevor, all innocence. 'Although, now you mention it—'

'Trevor!'

* * *

'Ah, back at last. I've been waiting for you.' Bob pointed to a chair. 'I hope you had more luck than us, Wendy, though from the look on your face, I'd guess that's a "no". You don't look like you're bubbling with excitement.'

'You first, sir. Was the retreat a non-starter?'

'I'd say so,' said Bob glumly. 'As you thought, it is a kind of rehab centre. Nicely laid out, lovely grounds, and very discreet. We gathered that a few high-profile names often go there, so we weren't exactly flavour of the month. We had a quick gander around, but the people we spoke to hadn't even heard about what happened, even on the local grapevine. Jon and I are pretty sure the place is kosher, and that no one is trying to hide either an abducted teenager, or a dead boy anywhere there.' He leaned back in his chair, which groaned ominously. 'So, how did you get on?'

Saying that the supposed mansion was little more than a derelict ruin, and as expected, they hadn't been admitted into the house itself, she told him that they had actually managed to get inside the gates and take a look at the grounds.

'Blimey!' exclaimed Bob. 'How on earth did you manage that?'

'Well, Jago made a bit of a drama about the uncle's condition, but I think he was going to let us in all along, almost as if he wanted us to see what a dump it was so we would give up on it as not worth a second visit.'

'And what else is bothering you? Come on, Sergeant, I've seen that look on your face before.'

'Well, I have my suspicions about Philip and Jago Nancarrow. And don't ask me why, because even he can't explain it, but Trevor's policeman's nose is twitching like fury. He kept saying how the place didn't feel right.'

'Sounds a bit like Jon yesterday,' said Bob. 'He told me the forest gave him such a bad case of the heebie-jeebies he couldn't wait to get out of there and back to the station. Weird. So, what's the plan now?'

'I've got Trevor tied to his computer hopefully digging up some background on the Nancarrows, and we'll take it from there. Personally—' She looked at her phone, which had started vibrating. 'Mind if I get this, sir? It's Ellie.'

Bob straightened up. 'Sure. Go ahead.'

The call was brief. 'They're asking if we could go to the Cavendish-Meyer, sir. Christopher has written another message, and they want to share their thoughts on what it might mean. Are you free to come along, sir?'

Bob was already on his feet. 'You drive, Wendy. I'll just let Jon know, and we'll go right away.'

CHAPTER TWENTY-SIX

No birds sang in here. Deep in the woods, down where the shadows encroached on the lake, a vicious wind raged through the trees, whipping the bare branches into a frenzy, sending leaves spiralling into the air as if churned up by the blades of a helicopter. The conifers, black against the stormy sky, thrashed about like tall figures in agony.

Squirrels and field mice fled, or cowered, twitching, in holes, their tiny hearts beating visibly.

Despite the absence of fences and warning signs, few ramblers or dog walkers ever ventured into this part of the forest. The mere presence of the watchers who kept vigil here was enough to deter even the most brave — or foolhardy — walker from crossing the invisible boundary protecting their domain. Day and night, these watchers surveyed the land on the other side of the water, alert for the slightest breach in the divide that separated them from the place where the children were being kept.

Red eyes fixed on the opposite bank, the entity seethed with impotent rage. The golden girl had been taken from them, and now it seemed that the blind boy would be lost to them too. This could not, must not happen.

All at once, a birch sapling snapped with a crack like a shot being fired. In a last tremendous gust of wind, it flew across the lake and plunged into the water.

As the ripples spread, the wind gradually dropped. Terrified woodland animals dared to raise their heads and look about them.

From behind the watchers, a low, throaty chuckle was heard that grew louder, culminating in a wild demonic howl of laughter. Ha! Let them have the blind boy. He still had the other. He had Zillah, child of shadows. The axe that would smite the Eleventh House and rip it asunder.

* * *

Back and forth, Gideon paced his room, seized with a terrible indecision. Clover was right, the other girl must be found and brought here, but, oh, the risk! One wrong move, the slightest hesitation, and they would lose everything, including the precious children they had fought so hard to rescue. Should they fail, all the years of struggle and painstaking toil would have been for nothing, and the world would be a darker place.

To and fro, Gideon paced, bowed down by the weight of the decision he had to make. Unless they brought that girl to the Eleventh House, they would never achieve their objective. The children they had found would be safe, but they would never go out into the world and fulfil their destinies, and what would happen when he, Rae and the others no longer had the strength to continue protecting them? After all, they were only mortal.

Gideon stopped pacing. Only mortal. Yet he was acting like God. Saving this one girl would change the lives of millions all over the world. Who was he to make this momentous decision for all of them? It wasn't right not to give them a say.

He hurried off in search of Rae.

* * *

Ellie met Janie just as she was coming out of her room.

'It's safe, Ellie, your rooms are as peaceful and tranquil as ever. If rooms had auras, yours would be bright and powerful.'

Ellie thanked her friend. 'And the rest of the place?'

'Unfortunately, the same can't be said of the entire building. Whatever that . . . *thing* was, it was deeply unpleasant, and it's left tiny pockets of darkness where there were none before, despite the help I had with my initial cleansing ritual.'

'Help?'

'Don't ask. It was certainly new to me. Something guided me to certain areas, and it was spot on every time. I found small patches that would have festered and spread if they hadn't been cleansed.' Janie shrugged. 'Spirit, I guess.'

'What form did this "help" take?' Ellie asked.

'A patch of blue light, almost like a reflection. It bobbed along ahead of me and stopped at certain places, refusing to go any further until that particular spot had been cleansed.'

A smile spread over Ellie's face. 'Well, Janie, it looks like you had the pleasure of meeting Carole Cavendish-Meyer herself. And from what you say, she's taking the care and upkeep of the centre that bears her name very seriously. Oh, and a word of warning if she helps you again. She likes things done her way. Indeed, she practically wrecked my kitchen once because I was slow to catch on to one of her messages.'

Janie laughed. 'In that case, I promise to be good and pay attention!'

Just then, Callum's voice echoed along the corridor. 'Bob and Wendy are here!'

'We'll see them in my office, Callum,' Ellie called back. 'Janie has declared it good to go.'

'Okay, then would you mind if I go back to Lucy and Harry? I'm getting a bit antsy about being away from them.'

'Of course. Then could you bring them down to meet Bob? He particularly asked to see Harry while he's here. Just give us half an hour or so.'

Soon, Callum was back with Bob and Wendy, and Michael followed a minute or two later.

Once they were all inside her room, Ellie showed them the latest draft from Christopher. She was just about to explain what they thought it might mean when her desk phone rang in the inner office.

Sounding somewhat on edge, Marie Littlewood told her Christopher had been behaving strangely. 'He had a kind of, well, I don't know how to describe it. It was as if he were asleep and having a bad dream, except a moment before, he'd been pulling his boots on ready to go to the orchard with me and Dan. It . . . oh, I'm sorry, Ellie, I'm not making much sense, am I?'

'It's all right. Just take your time, Marie. A bad dream, you say. Did he speak, or did he just seem frightened?'

'Yes, he was muttering all the time, but it didn't make much sense. I can't remember everything he said, except that the orchard was all overgrown, and he felt lost, and, oh yes, he felt bad about breaking a promise. But he didn't say what the promise was or who he'd made it to. Then he started shivering, and I was afraid he might have a seizure or something, but he didn't; he just kept saying that eyes were watching him, red eyes. And that he must not look up, he had to keep walking — walking home.'

'It must have been a bad dream, then,' Ellie said.

'I'm not so sure,' Marie said dubiously. 'Anyway, next thing I knew, he had snapped out of it and was back to normal. Said he was looking forward to playing with the dogs. He had no memory of what had just happened to him.'

'I don't know what to say to you, Marie,' confessed Ellie.

'And that's not all,' Marie said, more evenly now. 'Yesterday evening, something odd happened. We were all in the house; I was getting supper ready, Christopher was in his room and Dan was doing his course work for university. Anyway, I was listening to the radio, as I do when I'm cooking. It was all underway, the food in the oven, when I must have gone to sleep. Suddenly, I found that I'd lost almost half an hour. It was most strange. Dinner was practically ready, and I'd missed most of my programme. Then Dan came down and said he'd nodded off at his computer. He went up to call Christopher for supper, and came back saying the lad must have dozed off as well. Apparently, Christopher looked kind of confused when Dan told him to go down to the kitchen.' She took a breath. 'Later, after Christopher had gone to bed, I went up to his room to collect his clothes for the wash, and the hems of his jeans were filthy, all covered in mud, and his trainers were caked in it. I didn't notice it at dinner, but I think he'd been out, and it must have been while we all slept, or whatever it was that came over us.'

'And this was late afternoon, early evening?' Ellie said. A memory came back, of the previous evening. She'd gone upstairs to make sure that Alice hadn't forgotten anything. She'd gone over to the bedroom window and seen a movement in the orchard followed by the familiar mauve glow that meant Vera was out there. Had she been there because of Christopher? Was it Vera who had been telling him to look at the ground and keep walking home?

'Ellie? Are you there?'

'Yes, sorry, I was just thinking. Look, I think Christopher was having a flashback to something that happened yesterday evening. How did he seem when you went into the orchard?'

'Fine. Just as usual. He was having fun with your boys, and showed no sign of any distress,' Marie said.

Vera! It had to be. 'What could possibly have made him go out to the orchard in the dark?'

'And what was this promise he broke?' mused Marie. 'Oh! I remember now! He said the *letter* had made him break his promise!'

It all fell into place. The letter Marie had brought to her that morning had been written the day before. Christopher had thought it important enough to brave the dark and deliver it himself . . . Then something had tried to stop him! That was why Vera was out there! It had nothing to do with her at all, Vera had been out there to guide the boy home. How much should she tell Marie? 'It sounds like he was in a hurry to deliver a message to me and something spooked him. Luckily, Vera brought him home, so no harm was done, other than getting his trainers muddy.'

Not wishing to frighten Marie, she added, 'Tell you what, just keep an eye on him, and if anything worries you — if he has another of those flashbacks, say — bring him over here, and we'll all have a talk about it. How does that sound?'

'Oh yes, thank you, Ellie. I didn't want to bother you, but it seemed quite serious.'

'You didn't bother me in the slightest. Call any time you like, okay? In fact, you don't even have to ring, just get yourselves over here if you are really worried. Scrubbs will always look after the dogs for me.'

Marie's call had her head spinning, but she couldn't think about it now. Bob and Wendy were here waiting to be updated.

'I've given our friends a rough idea of what we have concluded,' said Michael, 'and they've just told me there's been a very strange turn of events regarding the hunt for Oliver Cruise. His parents seem to have suddenly upped sticks and moved elsewhere, and Oliver's teacher has been found dead in his home. In the light of what we assume from Christopher's message, Bob and Wendy are now thinking that Oliver is probably at this Eleventh House too.'

'It's a most odd state of affairs,' said Bob. 'Imagine doing a moonlight flit when your child is missing! The whole thing stinks.'

'We've contacted the estate agent,' Wendy continued, 'and even they can't get hold of the Cruises. Apparently, both their phones are unavailable. Jon Leatham got the estate agent to let him into the house, and on their ansaphone was a message from Oliver. I have it written down.' Wendy took out her notebook. 'Here we are: "This is Oliver. Please don't worry about me. I am safe, well, and happy, and I won't be coming home." Exactly the same thing happened to a girl named Daisy Hilton a while back. She was from Reigate. She disappeared without trace, and then her mum and dad received a letter saying that she apologised for the trouble she'd caused, but she was safe and happy, and she wasn't going home.'

'What I don't get,' said Bob, rubbing at his temples, 'is where this place is. I mean, dammit, if it's taking in children hand over fist it's hardly going to be some little cottage or house in town.'

'And it can't be that far away from here,' said Wendy. 'It has to be somewhere pretty close since it seems to be connected to this healing centre.'

Michael scratched his head. 'Trouble is there are so many big properties around here. This part of Surrey isn't called the Stockbroker Belt for nothing. They like it because it's so close to London, only half an hour on the train.'

'Which means that most of these big places are owned either by very rich individuals or big companies for their managing directors and the like,' said Wendy. 'To me, the Eleventh House sounds more like a commune than that sort of residential property, but we've never heard of the existence of such a place.'

Bob grunted. 'And the two properties we pinned our hopes on as likely places our mystery man might have taken the dead boy have both turned out to be non-starters.'

Ellie noticed that Wendy didn't look totally convinced of that, and she said so.

Wendy bit her lip. 'I'm not so sure, though I have nothing to back it up. The one place that my colleague Trevor and I checked out is certainly not somewhere you'd take kids to keep them safe, in fact quite the opposite! You'd not let a kid within a million miles of the house itself, it's falling down. But . . . There's just something about it that doesn't feel right.'

'Can it be followed up?' asked Ellie.

'Trevor's doing that right now, although to be honest, Ellie, even if there is something fishy going on there, I very much doubt it has anything to do with this case, and there's no chance of it harbouring the missing children.'

'It'll probably turn out to be something much more basic,' added Bob, 'like drug-related crime, or somewhere to stash stolen goods. Something far more criminal than what you are looking at, anyway.'

'We need to find it. We *have* to,' Ellie said passionately. 'We are connected to this Eleventh House in some way, and we need to know why, because I'm certain it's for a very important reason.'

Bob broke the silence that followed. 'From a law enforcement perspective, we have the missing boy, Oliver Cruise, along with reports of the removal of a teenager's body from what could have been the scene of a crime, or a hit and run. This last incident has given rise to a large police presence in the area around where the body was last seen. If there indeed was a commune or somewhere like that, or even a house with an unusually high number of young people in it, one of our officers would have come across it, but so far, nothing of that sort has been reported. I even considered sending up a police 'copter with a thermal camera, but they are costly, and because your part of the investigation is still off the record, I didn't want to draw too much attention to what we are doing.'

'Mmm, I see your dilemma,' said Michael. 'Wendy has mentioned the place she went to, but weren't there two properties?'

'Oh yes, White Gates,' Bob said. 'We were told it was a retreat, and as there wasn't much information about it, Jon and I went to check it out. It turned out to be a place the rich and famous go for rehab. Very exclusive and very discreet. We enquired further, and it seems to be exactly what it says in the brochure. So, at the official level, there's not much more we can do other than keep searching the area. However, we have our little team of four working at a rather different level.' Bob shook his head wonderingly. 'Who'd have believed it? Me, the most hard-nosed plod-hopper south of the Smoke, conducting an investigation that involves a child unconsciously writing messages from a dead person, and another who creates detailed pictures of World War Two aircraft *and* is being chaperoned by a dead airman!'

'Talking of unconscious messages, that's what that phone call I just took was about.' Ellie told them what Marie Littlewood had said.

Bob's smile left his face. 'Does this mean you think Christopher is still in danger? Because if so, is it safe to leave him in your village? It's not exactly a hive of activity out there. He only has an older woman and his father around to watch him — I'm not counting Dr Littlewood as he spends more time working than at home. Is that sufficient protection?'

'For a start, never underestimate the love of a grandmother for her grandchild,' said Ellie, 'and Daniel would walk over hot coals for that boy. So, in my opinion, if you add Vera to the equation, Christopher is safe at the moment, and if they are worried about anything, they'll bring him here post haste.'

'And from the looks of it, that book still isn't finished,' said Michael. 'In which case someone, very probably Vera, is taking care of our little author, and will continue to do so until he writes 'The End'. At which point, he will cease to be of interest and return to being a normal eight-year-old who is probably more inclined to play outside with Ellie's dogs than pen a bestseller.'

Bob still didn't look convinced.

'So, where the hell is this place and it's enigmatic leader?' Wendy asked. 'And who is this mysterious person removing certain children? Hell, he could go down for child abduction, big style. And why? What is his end-game for these "special" children?'

'Actually, said Ellie, 'there's a veritable *Who's Who* of such persons. Who is Clover? And her mother, Lori? Who is the dead boy? Then there's a blind boy who has just surfaced, who is he? Who is the person paying for Beth Saunders's treatment?'

'And who is this "other girl" in Christopher's latest missive?' Michael waved the paper in the air. 'We're assuming she's probably Beth's daughter, Izzie, but if that's so then why is she called Zillah? And if we are wrong in our assumption, who is Zillah?'

'And I need to add a very big "what" to that list of "whos".'

The others looked at Ellie.

'What on earth has little Harry got to do with it all?'

She knew there was no answer to that question. Yet. But what she did know was that Harry, along with his two guardians, Callum and Lucy, were very important indeed. And something told her it wouldn't be long before they discovered just how important they were.

She turned to Bob. 'Harry will be along shortly. I told Callum you wanted to meet him. He, Callum and Lucy are staying here for the time being.' She explained that Harry's father had left suddenly, and his mother was unable to cope with both Harry and his chronically ill brother.

Bob virtually swelled with indignation. 'How could he do such a thing? Has the man no feelings? It's his family, for God's sake. His children!'

He was still shaking his head when a tap on the door announced the arrival of Harry and Callum.

The next ten minutes were a welcome antidote to all the anxieties her conversation with Bob and Wendy had aroused. Bob turned out to be a natural with children, and Harry's shining face when he looked up at this great bear of a man was a delight to behold. Listening to them chatting away like two old friends, it took Ellie a while to realise how cleverly Bob was eliciting responses to some pretty probing questions.

'I'm going to meet a *real* art teacher in a minute,' said Harry proudly. 'She's got a funny name, so Callum says I can just call her Frankie.'

'Well, now, that's a coincidence! My daughter's called Frankie, but she can't paint for toffee. Callum tells me you're very good at drawing, would you show me your picture when it's finished?'

'I suppose . . . I don't know if I'm allowed to keep it, though. It might have to stay here.' Harry looked hopefully at Callum.

'Oh, you'll be able to keep it, don't worry. And I'll make sure Bob and Wendy get to see it.' He held out his hand. 'Come on, Champ, Frankie is waiting to meet you. She says she's looking forward to it, you're the youngest artist she's ever taught.'

Harry said a polite goodbye, leaving the four adults smiling after him.

'What a lovely kid,' said Wendy. 'He's got better manners than most children twice his age — oh, and what's the art teacher's name, by the way?'

'Françoise Duplessis,' replied Michael.

'Ah, I see. That is a bit of a mouthful for a five-year-old.'

'So, Bob,' Ellie asked, 'Where did you acquire your child analysis skills?'

Bob laughed. 'From the kids. We came late to parenthood, and I took it very seriously. I still do, especially as, hell, you need to be at the top of your game with three canny offspring to deal with.'

'Well, I'm seriously impressed,' said Ellie. 'And what did you make of our Harry?'

'Almost too well-adjusted. Talk about an old head on young shoulders.' Bob glanced at his watch. 'Oh dear, we'd better get back. And after our discussion this morning we'll redouble our efforts to find a possible location for this Eleventh House. And Wendy and Trevor will have another look at Knightswood House. Rest assured, you are our priority. If you, or anyone else connected to the centre, receives any sort of threat, just give us a ring and we'll be here — along with half of Surrey Constabulary on blue lights if necessary. Okay?'

Ellie hugged them both. 'I'm so glad you are with us, it means a lot, really. And if you, or any of your colleagues come across anything you can't explain, something that's beyond the normal, you must call us immediately. We both feel that there's something out there with evil intentions with regard to those children and the place where they have been taken. And if you do encounter it, be warned, it won't be anything like the bad guys you normally go head to head with. Take care, both of you, and trust your instincts. And trust Vera. She's around you, I know she is, and if you need her help, ask. She can only help if you ask for it.'

As both police officers, nodding slowly, took in her words, Ellie detected the faint perfume of lilacs wafting in the air around where they stood.

CHAPTER TWENTY-SEVEN

They were less than half a mile from the centre when Bob's phone rang.

'Sir? It's Jon Leatham. Are you far from base?'

'We're on our way back from Ripley, ETA fifteen minutes. Has something occurred?'

'Sir, could you go back to the C-M Centre, and we'll meet you there? Trevor has come across a piece of information that we think should be shared with Miss McEwan and the Professor.'

'Understood. We haven't long left the place, so get there asap.' He ended the call. 'Turn the car around, Wendy. We're going back. Looks like you'll soon be getting that information you were hoping for.'

* * *

It was rare to see every member of their community together in one place. The one exception was Josh, the lookout who lived in the boathouse, who remained on watch. Sinister forces lurked across the dark waters of the lake beyond the rope divide, waiting for an opportunity to make an incursion. Fortuitous indeed that Josh wanted nothing more than to be beside the lake in peaceful solitude. Josh had an important role to play in the security of the Eleventh House and its children, and he performed it with pride.

As he had once told Gideon, not everyone is cut out to be an active member of a social community, but there are other ways to contribute to the greater good.

So, with the exception of their lakeside brother, the rest of the family congregated in the chapel. No one had explained to them why they were there, yet they all knew. Some had learned of it through clairvoyance, others intuition, still others simply because they always knew it had been coming. Gideon was about to take his place before the gathering when he heard someone gasp. Serena was staring at him, her eyes wide in amazement.

'Yes? What is it, Serena?'

'He's on his way. Finn is coming to us at last.'

Gideon was taken aback, although he didn't for a moment doubt the truth of what she was saying. But how? Everyone was present for this crucial meeting, including those from the outside, the seekers and rescuers. 'How, Serena? How is he coming here? Who is bringing him in?'

In a faraway voice, she said, 'He's coming alone.'

'Serena. Finn is blind. How . . . ?'

Her expression full of a rapturous joy, Serena said, 'Have faith, Gideon. He has invisible guides walking with him every step of the way. Now, he has an old man and a dog with him. They are on a tow-path beside a river. Further along that path are two old women, who will lead him to the next village. And from there, others will help him until he reaches our gates. One by one, they are stepping out of the mist to bring Finn home!'

Gideon had no doubt that what Serena was seeing was coming to pass. She was a true visionary, and he believed every word she spoke. By some miracle, Finn was on his way home at last.

But now he had an important question to put to the assembled community members. He told them the future of the Eleventh House was in the balance. He told them they must listen carefully to what he was about to ask them, discuss it among themselves, and then go away to meditate upon it in silence.

'Search your souls, my good friends, for we must arrive at a consensus if we are to move forward. We must be united, with a single goal. The fate of the Eleventh House, and of all who live here, depends on what you decide. Put your trust in the power of good to guide you to the right decision.' He looked into the eyes of each one of them in turn, and took a deep breath. 'This is what I want you to consider . . .'

* * *

'Wendy! You are not going to believe what I just heard.'

It was a surprise to get a call from PC Paula English, who was currently up to her neck in a complicated case.

'It's only just come in,' Paula said. 'Another child has gone missing.'

Wendy groaned. 'Does this mean it's coming our way? Is that why you called?'

'I don't know yet, my lovely. I was just giving you a heads up. But here's why I had to phone.' Paula's voice went up an octave in her excitement. 'The boy has gone missing from a home for the blind! And what's more, he did it without help. The staff are aghast. Apparently, he tagged along with a group of visitors on their way out of the premises. If it does come your way, his name is Ryan Findlay, but everyone calls him Finn.'

Finn . . . Now where had she come across that name recently? Of course! Christopher. His letter had spoken of *'a blind boy named Finn'*. This could only mean that this blind boy had been 'collected' in some way, and was probably either en route to, or already safely ensconced in the Eleventh House. She must tell the others at once! She thanked Paula, hoping she would overlook the abrupt way she ended the call, and raced back to Bob, who was standing where they'd been waiting for Jon and Trevor.

'Another piece to the puzzle just fitted in, didn't it?' said Bob when she told him. 'But it's like doing a jigsaw with no picture to follow. I suggest you go and tell Ellie and Michael. I'll hang on here for the others, they won't be long.'

She found Ellie and Michael standing in the doorway to the large brightly lit room that was used as an art therapy studio.

Michael pointed silently to the small boy sitting a little apart from the others, working industriously on his picture. 'Callum and Lucy are in there too, they're talking to Frankie. Callum just told us he's seen the airman standing right behind Harry, watching every stroke of his brush.'

Wendy stared hard, trying desperately to get her first glimpse of a spirit. Failing miserably, she gave up and told her friends the news about Finn.

With a glance at Michael, Ellie said, 'It seems like it's all going according to plan, doesn't it?'

'And if our Christopher's words are correct, their revered leader is now going to be thinking very hard about that "other girl" and trying to decide whether or not to bring her in,' Michael said.

'And I'm having nightmares about it being Izzie,' said Ellie. 'Even though I believe our role in all this is to get Izzie there somehow, it terrifies me to think of them inviting that child inside their precious sanctuary with that evil thing attached to her. I just hope the protection we are assuming they have is as strong as we think.'

Wendy was rather glad not to have been at the clinic at the same time as that child. She might not be sensitive like the others, but she reckoned even she would have picked up on an atmosphere as awful as the one they described.

'I think I should get Callum to join us, don't you, Michael?' said Ellie. 'If what our detectives have to tell us is significant, he should hear it too.'

'You're right,' Michael said. 'Lucy and Frankie are with Harry, and our budding Picasso looks like he's in for a nice long session, so he's fine for now. I'll go in and fetch him.'

Calling to Lucy that he wouldn't be long, Callum emerged from the art room, and they all took the stairs down to the foyer, arriving just in time to see Bob and two other officers coming in through the doors.

'You know our DI Jon Leatham, don't you?' said Bob. 'And this is the newest member of our little team, DC Trevor Grant. Knowing her two friends, Wendy guessed they were probably reading the young detective's aura. She noted their interested expressions, and the way their gazes lingered on him while they chatted. She couldn't wait to quiz Ellie on what she'd seen.

'Let's all go and sit in the Orangery,' suggested Michael. 'There shouldn't be anyone there at present.'

As they made their way through the miniature jungle, between the beautiful plants and indoor trees, Wendy glanced at her companions. The expressions on their faces, Jon's stern and Trevor's anxious, told her that what Jon had to tell them was of major importance.

Michael showed them to a small cluster of seats in a far corner, and Jon explained what had prompted him to call this impromptu meeting.

'It was something Trevor said to me after his visit to Knightswood, one of the properties we were interested in. He said that he left the place with a strong feeling that something was, well, *wrong* for want of a better word. Perhaps I should explain that Trevor is very, er, susceptible to atmosphere, and he . . . well, he . . .'

'It's all right, sir,' Trevor said. Smiling at his DI, he turned to Ellie and Michael. 'Sometimes I receive messages from beyond, and I sense, or perhaps I should say *know* things. It's not always easy to explain how. Anyway, whenever I've been in the forest, or close to Knightswood House, I've had this strange sensation, and not a good one either.'

'You are clairvoyant?' asked Michael, interestedly.

'I'm not really sure what to call it, but yes, something like that.'

Jon took up the thread. 'Anyway, Wendy asked Trevor to go online and search for background information on Knightswood and Phillip Nancarrow, its owner. He got zero results, which seemed a bit odd, so we looked at the Land Registry maps for the area. It took us a bit of time, but we finally managed to work out where the Knightswood House boundaries lay, and they didn't correspond to what the gatehouse keeper, Howard Fenton, had told the sarge.'

'Are you sure?' Wendy said. 'But he showed us an old wall that he said ran all the way around the perimeter.'

'But we never actually followed it all the way round, did we, Sarge?' said Trevor. 'We saw it from the front, and the beginning of it along the sides of the property, but we didn't want to disturb the old man by going too close to the house, so we never got to see the rest. Fenton made such a thing of it completely enclosing the grounds, with no rear entrance, that we took him at his word.'

'Unless we are completely wrong about it, and I don't think we are,' said Jon, 'there is a massive piece of private land behind that house, containing fields, woods and a big chunk of the forest. According to the maps, there's even a small lake there.'

'And it all belongs to Knightswood House?' asked Wendy.

'Ah, here's where we find another anomaly,' said Trevor. 'I know people often change the name of their properties, but still, that whole area is marked down as belonging to a house called Belcastel, and we're damned if we can trace either the house or its owner.'

'And I assume it's not Philip Nancarrow,' said Wendy, a shiver of anticipation making her catch her breath.

'No,' said Jon quietly. 'Go on, Trevor. Tell them what you discovered.'

'There is no Philip Nancarrow. He does not exist. Neither does Jago Nancarrow, so I don't know who we spoke to that morning. If there is an old recluse in that house, which I doubt, he's certainly not Philip. Philip Nancarrow died on 14 February, 1945. Flying back to England in his Lancaster bomber after the bombing of Dresden, his aircraft went down over the channel, and he was killed.'

A lengthy silence followed this revelation. Finally, Callum said, 'Correct me if I'm wrong, but I've a good idea that at this very moment Philip Nancarrow is sitting in the art room, guiding the brush as Harry paints.'

* * *

Ellie was first to recover her wits following this bombshell. So this was the link between the airman and the special children. There was still a lot they didn't know, but the most important question had just been answered.

'Now we have a problem,' she said. 'How can we get to see that land behind Knightswood House without alerting its inhabitants? I think we all realise that you have just found the Eleventh House. And if it is as special as we think, it's going to be protected. We cannot go barging in through their defences and possibly exposing ourselves to danger. Something vile is abroad out there — we have seen the harm it can do right here; Janie is still trying to rid the centre of it after one brief visit. If it is a place of safety for special children, we cannot afford to compromise their security.'

How, then, should they proceed? Jon volunteered a possible solution. 'I've a friend who owns a small light aircraft. He uses it for sightseeing and introductory lessons. What if I asked him to fly over that area and take some aerial shots of it for us? Or even better, I could go with him and take a look for myself.'

For some reason, this frightened Ellie, though she had no idea why it should. On the face of it, it was a perfect solution.

Trevor glanced at her as if he sensed her reluctance. 'It sounds good, sir, but I don't think we should draw attention to that area, and we should definitely not fly over it.'

Relieved, Ellie agreed with him.

'What if we just skirt around the perimeter,' persisted Jon, 'even if it's only to estimate the size of the plot, and see whether there's a house there. Perhaps there is, but it's hidden in the trees. I've got some powerful binoculars, and my friend often flies over that part of Surrey, so we wouldn't be conspicuous.'

'Well, I don't see much harm in that,' Bob said, 'as long as you don't go too close. I saw the look of alarm on Ellie's face when you brought up the suggestion, and if she doesn't think it's advisable, that's good enough for me. What we can do, however, is keep a watchful eye on the comings and goings at the lodge, because it could well be the means of access to the land behind the main house. I'll post a surveillance crew at the gates, and they'll log everyone going in or out. I very much doubt it's the main entrance, but until we know more about that stretch of land and who owns it, it's all we have.'

'If I might make a suggestion, sir,' said Trevor. 'Using the Land Registry maps, we can identify all the properties surrounding Belcastel and mark where their boundaries end. Once we have those, we can get an idea of the extent of the Belcastel estate and map it out for ourselves — always bearing in mind that maps are incredibly useful, but you have to see the actual terrain for yourself to know what you're dealing with.'

'That's going to be a time-consuming job, Detective, but it could give us some definitive answers,' Bob said. 'Okay then, as soon as we get back to the station you, Jon, contact your friend and see if you can get a glimpse of what's going on out there, but tell him on no account must he fly over it but just skirt around the edge. Trevor, get back to your maps and I'll organise you some uniforms to assist.'

Ellie felt better knowing that a 'no fly zone' had been ordained, but she still couldn't help feeling anxious about Jon taking to the air. A quick glance at Trevor's aura told her that he too was worried. She also had a strange feeling that all these procedures would turn out to be unnecessary, and access to the Eleventh House would come about in a very different way. For some unknown reason, she saw an image of Harry, with Lucy and Callum on each side of him, holding his hands. The image burst into her mind; so clear was it that she almost gasped. She glanced at the others, but no one seemed to have noticed. Except Trevor.

Their eyes met, and he gave her an almost imperceptible nod. Either he had seen the same image, or it was he who had sent it. She nodded back.

'If it's all right with you, sir,' Wendy was saying, 'I'd like to pay another visit to my friends at Heathersett. The family has been living in the forest for generations, and I'll bet you anything you like Grandpops will know about Belcastel or at least have heard stories about it.'

'Good idea, and if you don't mind me tagging along, we'll go as soon as we've finished here. And, Trevor, while you're on your rounds, talk to the owners of the other properties. Some of them might be like Wendy's friends and have been in that area long enough to either know or have heard something about it. Keep your ears open.'

'Yes, sir,' said Trevor.

Throughout this exchange, Michael had been unusually quiet, regarding Ellie in a rather odd way. She wondered if he too had seen that strange vision of Harry with Callum and Lucy. She was almost relieved when he transferred his attention to the others.

'Please do keep us informed of anything you discover about this mysterious place, because I'm beginning to realise that we must make contact with these people without delay,' he said.

Bob assured him that they would.

When the detectives had gone, Callum said he ought to get back to Harry. They hadn't yet decided how to spend the rest of the day, but he assured them he'd let them know as soon as they made up their minds.

'Please do,' Ellie said. 'And if by any chance you get to speak to the airman, try and get him to tell you where the Eleventh House is located. Michael is right, we have to make contact with them, and I doubt it will come about through the house-to-house enquiry the police are conducting.'

'One more thing, Callum,' added Michael. 'I'm very curious to see the picture Harry is painting today. I assume Françoise knows she's to keep whatever that boy does under wraps?'

Callum nodded. 'I've had a word with her about it, emphasising how important it is.' He headed off towards the art room, leaving Ellie and Michael alone.

Michael watched her narrowly for a couple of seconds. 'Okay, out with it. What exactly is going on with you?'

Ellie didn't know how to answer. What *was* going on? 'I feel . . . I don't know . . . different. I can't put it more clearly than that.'

Michael regarded her sympathetically. 'Don't worry, I understand. It's confusing for all of us, but we are receiving help. What would you say if I told you your aura had changed?'

Ellie frowned. 'Changed? How?'

'Suddenly, there's a lot of blue in it, and blue has never been your signature colour in the past.' He raised an eyebrow. 'However it *is* the signature colour of someone who was — is — close to us.'

'Carole.'

'Carole. Exactly. Now you may not have noticed, but you've been much more assertive of late. Having given it some thought, I've come to the conclusion that since Carole has become stronger in spirit, she is passing on what she knows through you. I also think she's sharing it with others as well.'

Trevor! 'I think I get what you mean. It answers something that happened when everyone was here.'

'That young detective?'

'Yes. This very clear image came into my mind, almost a vision, and I'm certain that he either saw the same thing, or sent it to me. It was extraordinary, nothing like it has ever happened to me before.'

'I think Carole sent it to you both,' said Michael. 'I could see at once that Trevor is extremely sensitive, more so than anyone I've come across in a while. Our Bob did a very smart thing when he brought him into their little team.'

'He is sensitive, isn't he? He picked up on my concern about the wisdom of flying over the Eleventh House at once.'

'Yes,' Michael said thoughtfully. 'I didn't see that at the time, but on reflection, I think you're right. Who knows what powers they have, and if they have managed to create a zone of protection over their property, it could be harmful to them if someone attempted to penetrate it. It could also be catastrophic for the plane. Oh dear. I hope Jon doesn't do anything silly. He did look pretty excited about his idea, didn't he?'

All at once, Ellie was gripped with a feeling of absolute certainty. 'He'll be fine. If he does try to be clever, he'll be stopped, end of story.'

Michael shook his head, bemused.

Ellie chuckled. 'From the way you're looking at me, Michael, I'd say you're not sure who you're talking to right now. All I can say is that I feel very much more confident now we have our Carole putting in her two penn'orth. Actually, I'm humbled that she's chosen me to be the receptacle for her pronouncements. I finally understand what channelling really means.'

Michael began to get to his feet, having noticed a small group of people trickling in among the foliage. 'Looks like Will Ryan is bringing his yoga students in. I guess it's time for us to beat a retreat.'

'If it's all right with you, I'm going to go to my rooms for a while. I have a couple of calls to make, and I'd also like a bit of time on my own to think, and prepare myself. Things are beginning to move, and I want to be ready.' She smiled affectionately at Michael. 'And maybe you'd like to do the same. We are going to need all our strength for what is to come.'

CHAPTER TWENTY-EIGHT

The members of the Eleventh House had made their decision. They were to wage war with the forces of evil and bring Zillah into the fold. Initially, one or two of them had expressed their opposition on account of the risks involved, but after further discussion, they too had agreed. The next step was to draw up a battle plan.

After some deliberation, Gideon had chosen three of the special children and one of the guides to form the vanguard of their small army. None dissented. All recognised that their particular talents were admirably suited to the task. His first choice was Serena. Her clairvoyance, the ability she had to see across time and space, was essential to the success of their campaign. She was also able to direct spirit forms to where they were most needed. She was by far the most spiritually connected of all of them, including Rae, and even Gideon himself.

His second choice was a teenager who had chosen the name 'Roku', meaning 'six' in Japanese. He was the sixth special child to arrive at the Eleventh House, and considered six to be his lucky number. His strength lay in his extraordinary ability to make people believe in the impossible. You might walk into the garden and see rhododendrons flowering in November. Then there would be Roku, laughing at you, the blooms would be gone and it was winter again. His talent for inducing confusion would be invaluable when they were forced to confront the enemy.

The final two were Luna and Mark. Gideon chose Luna for her almost-primitive connection to the weather, nature and the earth, Mark for his ability to communicate telepathically. Better than any radio or telephone, he could pass messages or collect information from the children or the guides. He would be able to communicate even in the absence of a radio or mobile phone signal, and should things get difficult, Gideon knew Mark would never leave his side.

Now he and his loyal lieutenant Rae sat in the Winter Circle, in silent meditation. Looking deep into their souls, they asked spirit for guidance, for protection against the evil forces waging war against the Eleventh House, and everything it stood for. Gideon asked especially to be shown a path, a way forward. Rae asked for the strength to do what was required of her, and to do it well.

Slowly, they opened their eyes and returned to the Winter Circle.

'So, we are not alone in the fight,' murmured Gideon almost dreamily. 'We have friends on the outside, friends with powerful connections. With their help, we will make it through. And I now have a plan.'

'And I now have the courage to see it through,' said Rae.

* * *

When Callum entered the art room, Françoise Duplessis and Lucy were gazing down at Harry's painting. Françoise, in particular, seemed barely able to contain her excitement.

He went over to take a look for himself. Fully expecting to see another aircraft, he wasn't prepared for what he now saw. He drew in a breath. 'What *is* that?' Although deep down, he already knew.

Harry had been given a canvas board and a selection of acrylic paints. He had never used acrylics before, his primary school art materials didn't extend beyond wax crayons, which were perfectly adequate for the pictures that adorned the fridge doors of most family homes and bore titles like 'My Mummy and Daddy'. Harry, however, was far beyond making stick figures and splodges of something that might be a cat or a dog.

'He just picked up a brush, chose the colours, and started painting,' said Frankie, her accent considerably more pronounced than usual. 'I have never seen anything like it in my life.'

The painting was a boiling mass of colour — swirls of inky black, smoky grey, vivid reds and oranges, and flashes of sulphur yellow. It gave Callum the impression that he was looking at a vision of hell.

Which it was. This was a pilot's eye view of a city in flames. Trevor's words rang in his ears: *'Philip Nancarrow died on 14 February, 1945. Flying back to England in his Lancaster bomber after the bombing of Dresden, his aircraft went down over the channel, and he was killed.'*

Slowly, Callum raised his head. Just behind Harry, his hand resting on the child's shoulder, stood the airman. Their eyes met.

Despite all the suffering he had been witness to — in Rwanda, in Sarajevo — Callum had never seen such utter grief. Suddenly, he understood. This airman's guilt over the atrocity he had participated in, resulting in the deaths of thousands of innocent civilians, was keeping him earthbound. In order to expiate his crime, he had committed himself to saving a life rather than taking it, even if it were only that of one little boy. The airman would protect Harry to the very end. He had no life to lay down but he did have a soul, and Callum believed he would risk even that if it would keep Harry safe.

As the airman continued to gaze at this mortal, he seemed to sense something of his compassion, and the sorrow left his eyes, to be replaced with a look of firm resolution. He raised his free hand in a smart salute. Harry had a very important task in front of him, and together, Philip and Callum would make sure he succeeded, that he came through.

'I know artists who would be proud to have painted that,' whispered Frankie. 'But this *enfant* . . . *Incroyable!*' She threw up her hands.

Lucy laid a hand on her arm. 'Frankie, I know it's amazing, but, please, you won't tell anyone else, will you?'

'No, don't worry,' Frankie said. 'It's just that it's so . . .'

'We should give it to Michael for safe keeping,' Callum said to Lucy. 'I'll do that now, if you stay with Harry. As a matter of fact, it confirms something we were suspecting, and he and Ellie need to know.'

Callum was glad that his spectral airman now had a name. Perhaps when this was over, he would write the story of Philip Nancarrow. Like it or not, the two of them had a connection, and he felt he owed it to this lost soul to keep his memory alive.

* * *

Grandpops's eyes lit up with pleasure at the sight of Wendy back again so soon. He ushered her and Bob inside and offered them tea, which they accepted gratefully. 'Helen's at the hairdressers,' he called from the kitchen, 'she won't be long.'

'It's all right, Grandpops, it's you we wanted to talk to,' Wendy called back. 'You've got such a good memory, we thought we'd pick your brains about the old days in this neck of the woods.'

As soon as he'd set a tray of tea down and handed round the mugs, Grandpops lowered himself into an easy chair, displaying his remaining teeth in a broad smile. 'Well, wouldn't you know! I was of a mind to ring you myself, young Wendy. You had me thinking about that Nancarrow place, an' I did a bit of diggin' around in the old newspaper cuttings I keep in my drawer.'

'You didn't come across any mention of a house named Belcastel, I suppose?' asked Bob hopefully.

'Oh, that old place,' said Grandpops dismissively. 'No, that's long gone.'

Wendy sat up straighter. 'You know about Belcastel? What's the story behind it?'

'Well, most of it is likely hearsay, but a bit of it is true. Do you remember when you asked about Knightswood House before, and Helen said it had a massive amount of land attached to it?'

'Yes, I do,' said Wendy.

'Well, originally — and I'm talking about way, way back — that piece of land was bought by a wealthy businessman. He built a kind of fantasy house, and called it Belcastel. Knightswood didn't exist back then, and the whole area was owned by the Belcastel estate. Knightswood was built later, somewhere around 1925, I think, for one of the owner's daughters.'

'But that can't be right,' said Wendy. 'I saw a plaque on the wall of the lodge house with the date 1798 on it.'

'Ah,' said Grandpops, 'that's because it was the lodge house to Belcastel, not Knightswood.'

'You said Belcastel was long gone,' Bob added. 'What happened to it?'

'Now here's where it gets a bit complicated,' said Grandpops, his forehead wrinkling. 'Let's see if I can get it straight. Back in the days when my dad was still young, it was supposed to be owned by the Nancarrows, a wealthy family from the West Country, but the estate was registered under a different name. It was rumoured that it was put in the name of the eldest daughter who had been widowed very young, and her late husband had no family, so they thought that the estate would remain in the family if anything happened to the father. Though it's likely he was just avoiding having to pay tax.'

Very likely, thought Wendy, but she was still puzzled that they hadn't been able to find anything at all about the name Nancarrow. 'The thing is, Grandpops, we can't find any mention of a Nancarrow. The old man who supposedly lives at Knightswood with his nephew doesn't exist, nor does the nephew. The only Philip we could trace died in 1945, towards the end of the Second World War.'

'And this Philip, did he happen to be one of those poor young pilots who never came back from the war?' asked Grandpops.

'Well, yes,' said Wendy, wondering where this was leading.

'He's the reason there's no longer a Belcastel House,' said Grandpops. 'Philip was the youngest son of the last surviving members of the Nancarrow family — the father, mother and two daughters — who all doted on him. His parents never recovered from his death, especially his father, who, upon hearing the news, had the Belcastel family home torn down in a fit of insane grief.' Grandpops shook his head. 'My dad said there was lorries coming and going for weeks on end, carrying away every brick and every piece of timber. All that was left was Knightswood House and the lodge, and the shattered remnants of the family moved in there.'

'So how come you said someone called Philip Nancarrow still lives there?' asked a very confused Wendy.

'We were told he was the son of one of the daughters, named after her dead brother, Philip. Other than his nephew, Jago, he was the last in line, so they said, the rest of the family having died.' Grandpops shrugged. 'And we had no reason to believe otherwise, although, as none of us ever set eyes on him . . .'

'And I met Jago,' mused Wendy, 'or at least I met someone calling himself by that name.'

Bob shook his head in frustration. 'We really need to get into that old house and see if this old guy exists, but—'

'We dare not,' added Wendy. 'Not after what Ellie told us. We are caught in a cleft stick.'

'You can say that again!' Bob said. 'The only thing I can suggest is that you ring Ellie or Michael and tell them what Mr Keele has said. Then it's up to them to decide what to do next.' He turned to Grandpops. 'And although another cup of your delicious tea would make my day, we ought to be getting back to the station.'

'Before you go, I found this in my old papers.' The old man handed Bob a yellowing and much-faded newspaper cutting. 'It appeared in the local paper at the end of the war. It's all about Flight Lieutenant Philip Nancarrow. You can keep it if you like, it's time I got rid of some of these old things. He was a hero, you know. That cutting tells you a lot about him, there's even a photo of him there.'

'We must show this to Callum,' Bob said to Wendy.

Grandpops looked at them enquiringly, evidently wondering who this Callum was. Neither felt like enlightening him — how could they begin to explain that this friend of theirs saw Philip regularly, eighty years after his death.

* * *

'You caught me at just the right moment, Jon. I've just had a last-minute cancellation, so if you're quick, I've got half an hour to spare and I'll take you up for a shufti.'

Vincent Collins kept his light aircraft, a Cessna 172, at a small aviation centre some five miles from the station. Jon drove straight there, and just over half an hour later they were in the air, heading for Belcastel.

'I really appreciate this, Vincent,' said Jon, gazing down at the Surrey countryside unfolding beneath them. 'It's a whole lot easier than trudging through people's gardens in the mud.'

'Not only that,' said Vincent, 'you get a proper perspective from up here. Patches of land that at ground level looked perfectly rectangular suddenly reveal themselves to be quite asymmetrical. So how big is this estate, do you reckon?'

'We really aren't sure, that's the problem. So much of the land is forest and woodland. If we start at the gates to the Lodge House, we can follow a wall for a short way, then we should see an old, rundown house. The land I'm interested in is behind that house. I've got a vague idea from a Land Registry map, but there's such a lot of common land it's hard to see where the boundaries are.'

'And we can't fly directly over it, you say, just skirt round the edge?' said Vince.

'Yeah, that's right. Orders from the boss. On no account must you cross into their air space.'

Vince laughed. 'Very cloak and dagger, I must say. Is your boss afraid we'll get shot down?'

'No, nothing like that,' Jon said, a little embarrassed. 'It's sort of covert, we don't want anyone on the ground to know we are poking around. I'm sorry I can't tell you what it's about, ongoing investigation and all that . . . You know what it's like.'

'Say no more, I'm just glad to be of help.'

Jon gazed up into a cloudless sky. 'This is awesome! You've got one hell of a job, my friend. But then you've always loved flying, haven't you?'

'Nothing like it, mate. You can breathe up here, and the freedom it gives you! You're literally on top of the world. You really should learn to fly, Jon. I think you'd be a natural. Just imagine, you're working a really shitty case, so you take off into the blue and it all melts away. It sorts *my* head out, I know that.'

'Maybe I'll take you up on that one day,' said Jon. He looked down. 'Ah, there's the main road leading to where we want to go. We are not far from the lane and the gates to the estate.' He took out his binoculars. 'When we reach the gates and the Lodge House, veer left and follow the wall.'

'Affirmative,' said Vincent. 'Now what the hell is *that*?'

Ahead of them, Jon saw what he could only think was a cloud, only it was too low, and of a strange colour. 'Wow. How weird.'

Concentrating hard, Vincent took the Cessna off course in an attempt to circumnavigate the thick haze. 'I don't know, Jon, this isn't right. I've seen plenty of strange phenomena in my time, but I've never seen a formation like this one.'

Jon suddenly heard Ellie and Trevor warning him not to fly over the Eleventh House. He stared at the shape ahead. It reminded him of images he'd seen of black holes, strands of silky, golden fibres surrounding a dense dark body like a mass of boiling fog.

'I'd like to take a closer look,' murmured Vincent, 'But when I . . . Oh, this *really* isn't right. There's something . . . Shit! I'm losing power.'

'Get away from it!' cried Jon. 'Whatever it is, it's warning us to back off.'

They pulled away, and immediately the plane began to fly normally again, and Jon's heart stopped hammering in his chest.

'Jon,' Vince said urgently. 'My old aerial camera is down to the left of your seat. Try and get a picture of that thing.'

Vincent circled the plane around while Jon focused the lens on the object. It swam into view, a great mushroom cloud surrounded by a halo of shimmering light like a corona. He took shot after shot until it began to lose definition as the plane moved away.

'Manage to get any, did you?' asked Vincent.

'Yeah, I've got some! But look, it's fading,' Jon said.

Vincent turned the plane around and once again approached the cloud circuitously, but the nearer he went, the darker and more intense the cloud became, until Jon yelled at him to back off.

Finally, Vincent gave up, and set a course for home. Behind them, the cloud dispersed until nothing remained of it but a fine mist. Jon let out a sigh of relief. No point trying again, the cloud would only be waiting to turn them back.

'Don't tell me that weird shit has something to do with the reason why we are up here,' said Vincent, raising an eyebrow. 'Correct me if I'm wrong, but I'm pretty sure that . . . thing was hovering right over the area you wanted to look at. I've never seen a formation like that, and I'm betting none of the pilots I know have either, which makes me wonder just what the fuck you guys are mixed up in.'

'I wish I knew, Vince, but I swear I never expected to meet anything like that.'

'Well, when you do find out what it was, for heaven's sake tell me.'

Jon said he would, if and when he was given permission. 'And, please, when you get those photos developed, can I have copies?'

'Yeah, of course, mate. I'm just sorry I didn't splash out on a digital camera, then I wouldn't have had to send the film to be processed.'

Looking up into the clear sky, it was hard to believe that strange cloud had ever existed. Maybe it hadn't. Maybe it had all been a mirage, a Brocken spectre reflecting their plane and surrounding it with a ghostly halo. No, it had been real all right, what else could have caused the plane to lose power when they got too close? He exhaled, his head feeling a little like a cloud itself, swirling with unanswered questions.

CHAPTER TWENTY-NINE

Trevor and his crew of uniforms had only been out for a couple of hours when he came to the conclusion that they were wasting their time. Every single one of them had been thwarted in some way. Many of the residents were out, some complained about them tramping through their property, one or two houses were closed up, either because they were for sale or because the owners were abroad. Some parts of the more affluent properties had been turned into wildlife gardens, and it was almost impossible to detect where the private land ended and the woodlands began.

He was trekking down to the bottom of a paddock owned by a well-off family whose two daughters both had ponies when he had the oddest sensation that he was being watched. Trevor turned and looked back. All was quiet, the only sound being the birds singing in the surrounding trees. He didn't feel particularly frightened, just uncomfortable, as if he were being scrutinised by someone, or something, just out of sight.

'Tell me what you want,' he whispered.

A breeze blew gently around him, like an inquisitive but wary puppy sniffing at his clothes and hair.

No, not this way.

It wasn't a voice as such, just a thought, but it came from somewhere outside of himself. At first he thought he was being told they were searching in the wrong direction. Then he understood the meaning of the words. They would never find the perimeters of Belcastel by searching for them in this way. Their house-to-house was pointless.

Just as he was about to turn back, he thought he saw a slight movement in a dense stretch of woodland beyond the paddock. Then the strangest thing happened. He was staring at this solid, impenetrable thicket of overgrown trees, ivies, brambles and nettles when his vision blurred. He blinked and rubbed his eyes, and when he looked again, the patch of woodland had changed. No longer dark, it was a glade, bright with dappled sunlight. The trees, in full leaf despite the season, stood in a carpet of bluebells, white wood anemones and butter-yellow celandines, with grassy paths meandering through the flowers.

His immediate impulse was to run forward and step into this magical scene, but he held back. Instead, he stood still, gazing at it in wonder. The vision lasted only moments, and then his vision blurred again, and once more there was just the dark, inaccessible woodland.

'I understand,' he said softly to the shy little puppy still circling around his feet. And he did, but how he was to explain it to the others was another matter.

The breeze intensified, and a voice so faint it seemed nothing but the wind rustling the leaves, said, *'I am Serena. Stay open to me. We are the contacts.'* Then all was still again.

As he hurried back to tell his team to abort the enquiry, he called Wendy.

'Soon as you can, Sarge! Get hold of Ellie and Michael. The Eleventh House have made contact. I'm coming in now.'

* * *

Beth Saunders watched her little girl as she played a memory match game with a neighbour's daughter, and sighed. What could be more natural and ordinary than two little girls giggling as they tried their best to outdo each other?

'Izzie's much better at this than my Phoebe,' said Dana, Beth's next-door neighbour.

'Probably because she's played it a lot. I used to play a similar version with my gran,' said Beth. 'She called it Pelmanism. We laid out a whole deck of playing cards face down, and took it in turns to turn up two cards. If they matched, like five and five, or Jack and Jack, you picked them up. If not, you had to place them back exactly where they were, and the other person had a try. I've played it with Izzie, but she likes this kids' version better.'

Beth felt quite nostalgic. She'd had some wonderful times playing with her gran, and she missed her dreadfully, especially now. Gran was the person she always took her problems to, and she would have been no end of help with Izzie. But she died just before Izzie was born, and never met her granddaughter.

Pushing the memories away, she asked, 'Would you two girls like a drink of milk?'

Izzie looked up at her, smiling. 'Please, Mummy, and could we have a brownie too?'

'I don't know about that, Izzie, it's almost lunchtime.'

'Pleeease, Mummy.' The child looked at her imploringly.

Beth's heart almost broke. Why couldn't she always be like this? She dreaded what Izzie would have to say when Phoebe and Dana went home and they were alone. Instead of asking for chocolate brownies, would she be wishing her dead again, hoping she choked? 'Is it okay if Phoebe has one, Dana?' she asked. 'I made them myself, they've no additives or anything.'

'Of course,' said Dana. 'Especially if they are homemade. I am not the most domestic of mothers, I'm afraid. When it comes to cakes it's Lidl or nothing.'

'Mummy makes the best cakes ever,' said Izzie proudly.

Beth swallowed hard. If only they could find a way to rid her daughter of that foul-mouthed entity, or whatever it was, that reared its ugly head whenever they were alone. At least she now had someone to turn to, even though she didn't quite understand their bizarre explanation of Izzie's condition. She trusted Ellie and Michael. If anyone could get her daughter back, it would be them.

Dana followed her into the kitchen when she went to fetch the drinks and the brownies. 'I hope you don't mind me saying so, Beth, but you've been looking really quite harassed of late, though you look much better today. I was worried about you, but I didn't like to ask what the problem was in case you thought I was being too nosy.'

What to say? Oh, nothing much, Dana, just that my child is possessed. Oh, and she wants to kill me. 'Sorry, Dana, things have been getting a bit on top of me recently. Nothing serious, just one of those periods you go through sometimes with a small child and a husband who works long hours.'

'Tell me about it! My Lance and me are forever up in arms about something or other to do with the kids, especially when he goes swanning off on some work trip and I get left to juggle school runs, after-school activities and the like, and we only have two! What it must be like with a big family I can't imagine! Anyway, thank goodness you are all right,' said her friend with a sigh. 'I was starting to wonder if there was something, er, wrong between you and Lee.'

Beth sincerely hoped that wasn't going to be the case, but if Izzie's behaviour got much worse, she couldn't rule it out. 'No, Dana, it's just kid stuff. It'll blow over. Lee is working up north for two or three days this week, and hopefully things will be back to normal when he's home.'

As they carried the cakes and milk back into the lounge, Beth thought what an accomplished liar she had become over the past month. Though come to think of it, it was hardly surprising. Who would ever believe her if she told them the truth?

Ah, but somebody did. Not only that, but they had witnessed one of Izzie's vitriolic attacks and had been horrified by it. Oh yes, she had seen the look on Ellie's face when she emerged from her office, and the relief had flooded out of her like the air escaping from a giant balloon. Just knowing that Ellie and Michael were supporting her gave her the strength to cope. She'd see this through, and win her daughter back.

When, half an hour later, Dana and Phoebe left, Beth braced herself for her darling daughter's next onslaught. To her surprise, Izzie quietly put the coloured cards back in their box and took it up to her room.

Beth went to do the washing up, making the most of the few moments of precious peace her daughter's absence granted her. Her thoughts drifted back to when Izzie was still a young baby, still the perfect child. It hadn't been an easy birth, far from it, and she had often wondered if what they had both endured might have had something to do with Izzie's current behaviour. She'd read about the effect a traumatic birth can have on the baby, in some instances causing the child to reject its mother, especially if they were separated in the hours following the birth. Beth had suffered primary postpartum haemorrhage and had almost bled to death, which had prevented her from being with her daughter during that important time.

As she put the glasses and plates away and began to think about lunch, Beth wondered if she should have mentioned this to Ellie and Michael. Suddenly, she realised that Izzie was still upstairs in her room. This wasn't like Izzie, who normally took advantage of every moment she was alone with her mother to torment her with spiteful remarks and threats. Reluctant to put an end to this peaceful interlude, she nevertheless grew apprehensive. What was Izzie up to?

On the pretext of going to her own bedroom, she paused at Izzie's open door. The little girl was sitting on the floor with two teddy bears and a fluffy toy dog, happily chatting away to them. Seeing her mother in the doorway, she smiled up at her. 'Phoebe is jealous of me because you make me cakes, and her mummy buys them in the supermarket. I told her not to be silly. Some children don't have cakes at all, so even if they aren't homemade, she's still lucky, isn't she?'

Beth felt tears spring into her eyes. It had been so long since Izzie had behaved normally towards her when the two of them were alone that her heart swelled with emotion. 'Yes, darling, she is lucky, and it was sweet of you to think of children who go hungry.'

Leaning against the door-frame, she watched Izzie play contentedly with her toys. Big Ted, said Izzie, didn't want to be called that anymore, so she and Fred and Fluffy were thinking of a new name for him.

Beth watched her for a few more minutes before turning away to go and prepare lunch. At the top of the stairs, she was suddenly struck, full in the face, by a blast of icy wind, followed by a stench so foul her stomach convulsed with an urge to vomit. She put her hand over her mouth and turned back to get to Izzie before it reached her, but she was frozen to the spot. As if she was in one of those dreams in which you try to move but cannot, she dragged her feet forward, each step felt like she was walking through setting concrete. She was still some way from the door when she heard a deep throaty laugh, and a voice spoke from somewhere behind her. *'It won't work, you know. Your lovely little friends? They are nothing to me. Amateurs, playing a very dangerous game, and by the time it is over, I will have swept them away like dust.'* Another chilling laugh followed, then, *'I will have her.'*

An explosion of rage filled Beth, and she yelled at the top of her voice, 'No! You will not! You will not have my child! Help me! Please, help me!'

She had no idea who she was pleading with in her anguish, but as the last 'help me' escaped from her lips, she found she was free to move again. She lurched forward and threw herself at Izzie, clasping her daughter to her chest, saying, 'You will not have my daughter, you will not! You will not have her.' As she repeated these words, she became aware that the room was suddenly less cold, and the terrible stench was fading, gradually being replaced by the sweet scent of . . . was it flowers? Perfume?

Without loosening her hold on Izzie, Beth opened her eyes and blinked. When she tried to describe it later, she could only say that she and Izzie seemed to be immersed in a soft lavender mist, while beyond it the elements seemed to be locked in combat. The air itself seemed to rush and twist, constantly changing direction like a tornado, while a thick dark fog slowly encroached on her and her child, until she feared it might swallow them up. Then something began pushing against it, forcing it backwards and away from them.

As to what was doing the forcing, it seemed to consist of shafts of vivid blue light that flared and dimmed, and then flared again, each time gaining in strength and brilliance until it was so blinding that Beth had to look away.

Then it stopped. The room was still. All that remained was the lilac perfume, and an atmosphere of utter tranquillity. Beth let out a long, shaky sigh.

'I'm frightened, Mummy!' Izzie whimpered.

'There, there, my love, it's all right,' Beth murmured. 'We'll go somewhere safe the nice ladies who just helped us have told me about. Now, dry your eyes and fetch Big Ted and we'll pack a few things to take with us. We are going on an adventure.'

Beth hadn't the slightest idea why she had said 'nice ladies', it had just come out. And was she imagining the faint mist, sometimes the colour of amethyst and sometimes blue, that seemed to hover about them while she packed and hurried to her car.

The mist stayed with them all the way to the C-M Centre, until the moment she and her daughter burst into the front entrance, when it floated upwards and dispersed.

CHAPTER THIRTY

On being told that Beth and her daughter were in the foyer, Ellie and Michael stared at each other in dismay. 'Are they alone, I wonder,' Ellie said, 'or did the child bring that horrible thing with her?'

'Well, we'll soon find out,' Michael said grimly.

But as soon as Ellie saw the child's aura, she knew they were safe. Apart from that odd absence of the colour pink, it was as normal as that of any six-year-old.

'Beth. Izzie. Welcome!' Just to be safe, she decided to take them to a part of the clinic that hadn't been touched by the dark force that had accompanied the child on her previous visit. You never knew, there might be one tiny particle of evil that had been overlooked, and if the child were to come into contact with it, it could well take over again.

'We'll go to the quiet room,' she said, and beckoned to Michael. 'Find Janie, and . . .' she thought for a moment, 'and if Carson, the Reiki Master is in, fetch him too. He'll be able to direct positive energy into that room and ensure that it remains a sanctuary for our two new guests. Chop, chop, Michael! Hurry along now.'

Seeing his amused expression, she realised what had caused it. The old Ellie would never have spoken like that. Callum had been right, she was now a conduit, used by the woman whose name adorned the front door of the clinic. Carole was issuing her instructions in the only way she knew how — with clout.

Michael hurried off, still chuckling to himself, and Ellie led the way up the wide staircase to the upper floor. Even before they had embarked on their renovations, that room had possessed an air of calmness. It had a high ceiling with an ornate central rose and coving. Tall floor-to-ceiling windows overlooked the gardens, and beyond them, the rolling hills and woods of Surrey. The room was kept for use as somewhere to spend a quiet time, to relax, sit and read, or merely reflect.

She watched carefully as Izzie started to unwind, and accompanied by a large moth-eaten teddy bear of indeterminate vintage, explore the room. Relieved, she took Beth aside. 'You will have someone with you every second of your stay. Don't ask me why, but I know you won't be here long. Soon, you'll be going somewhere safer.' She took hold of Beth's arm and squeezed it reassuringly. 'Trust us. We'll be told where we need to take you, and you won't go alone. We'll go with you.'

'This place — is that where I get my daughter back for good? My Izzie?' asked Beth.

'That's my belief,' Ellie said. 'Although I should warn you it won't be a walk in the park. We might all have to put up a bit of a fight.'

'Bring it on. It's worth a fight if it means I can have her back.'

Ellie could see that Beth meant it. This was a very different woman to the poor frightened creature who first visited the clinic. This was a fighter, a lioness defending her cub.

'Now, you'll have to excuse me,' said Ellie, 'I've got a few things to organise. Make yourselves comfortable, and I'll get some drinks and snacks sent up shortly, you must be hungry by now.' She smiled at Beth. 'Our chef loves nothing better than catering for children, so your Izzie is in for a treat. Janie will be here in a minute, and she'll stay with you until either Michael or I are back. Janie will be conducting some rituals which may seem a bit odd, but just go with it, okay?'

'That's fine,' Beth said. 'I won't ask any questions. This is the first place I've felt really safe in for a very long time.'

The thought of those blackened and dying plants came into Ellie's mind, but she dismissed it at once; she certainly wasn't going to mention those to Beth. The door opened and Janie and Michael walked in. She introduced Janie, and made her way down the stairs.

She hadn't yet reached the bottom when her mobile phone rang.

'Ellie! Get ready to receive visitors,' Wendy said excitedly. 'It looks like you can't keep us away. Things are moving fast. Trev has just called to say the Eleventh House has made contact!'

Despite her excitement, this news came as no surprise to Ellie. She had always known that no matter how many policemen were sent to tramp through the leafy lanes of Surrey, they would never succeed in finding the Eleventh House. The Eleventh House would come to them. She went back up the stairs to tell Michael. She didn't know how long they had, but they needed to make themselves ready for what was to come.

'Now I think about it,' said Michael, biting his lip thoughtfully, 'we have everyone other than Christopher under our roof: Harry, Lucy, Callum, and now Izzie and her mother, Beth. Does this mean the time has come to get them to safety?'

'Almost,' said Ellie, 'but I'm still not sure about Christopher and his part in it all. I honestly believe he's not one of these special children, but is simply a courier, chosen because of his proximity to me and Snug Cottage. I'm worried about that encounter he had with evil on the night he tried to deliver a message to me, though. We can't leave him unprotected. He might not be a target in the same way as Izzie and Harry, but what if our opponents are thwarted and decide to take out their anger on the one child who has been left behind?'

'Hmm. You're right. That cannot be allowed to happen. He must come with us, or at the very least be brought here and kept safe with someone we trust, and who has the power to protect him psychically.' Michael frowned. 'The trouble is, who?'

Ellie had no idea either. 'Then he must come with us, and in that case Daniel and Marie will have to come too.' She began to work out the logistics of this strange exodus to an as-yet-unknown destination. How many cars should they take? What should they carry with them?

She was about to discuss it all with Michael when that same odd feeling of well-being came over her again, and she relaxed. They would be told what to do when the time was right. 'I'm going to phone Marie. I need her to get the Scrubbses to prepare themselves to look after the dogs. They'll need to feed and exercise them, and maybe stay with them for a night. Luckily, I've already sounded them out on the possibility and they're fine with it. Then I want Marie to bring Daniel and her precious grandson here with an overnight bag.'

'And if I might add, maybe you should send a message to Alice, just to keep her happy?' Michael said. 'If she rings you while we're on our way, it could be distracting for you, and worrying for her if you don't answer.'

'Good thinking,' said Ellie. 'I'll do that as soon as I've spoken to Marie. Will you stay here until I get back?'

He smiled reassuringly. 'Of course I will. Now, go and make your calls. Meanwhile, I have one small person's aura to study. I'd like to compare it with what I saw when I last met the child.'

Downstairs in her office, Ellie rang Marie.

'Oh, Ellie, you must be psychic! I was just going to ring you. Christopher has just written another message. It quite derailed me for a moment. It . . . well, suddenly it wasn't Christopher sitting there at all, it was Vera, looking just as I remember her, sitting at my dining room table, writing. She looked up for a moment, straight into my eyes, and smiled at me. Oh, Ellie, there was such a lovely, lovely angelic look on her face. Then it was Christopher again, writing away as if there'd been no interruption.'

'Did Daniel see it too?'

'Only fleetingly, but he recognised her all right. But the letter. We think it's the last one, or that's what it indicates anyway, and we need you to see it as soon as possible. Daniel said we should get in the car and drive over to you with it. Is that okay?'

'More than okay. But listen, Marie, get yourself together, okay? I need you to go over to Snug Cottage and talk to the Scrubbses for me. I could phone, but you know what Mrs S's hearing is like, and I want her to be clear about what she's to do with my precious dogs.'

Ellie then told Marie to get Daniel to pack a few things for himself and Christopher, as they were all going to spend a night at the clinic. She could make up whatever excuse she saw fit to give to the doctor. Then they must all get to the C-M as fast as they could.

'I don't want to scare you, Marie, but don't stop for anyone or anything. Just come straight here. Do not get out of the car. All right? Tell Daniel that if he's asked to open the door or step out of the car, even if it's an official asking, he's to drive on. I could be wrong, but there's a chance that someone will want to prevent that letter getting to me.' She felt bad about being so blunt, but she needed to get the message across. 'I'm going to alert Bob Foreman, and get him to send a couple of patrol vehicles to clear the way for you if they can. Will you be using your car, or Daniel's?'

'Daniel's probably, it's faster and more reliable than my old banger.'

'Give me his registration number and the make of the vehicle, and I'll pass it on to Bob. Pop in to see the Scrubbses and then head here, fast. Okay?'

'His car is a royal blue Ford Focus — I'll have to get him to tell you the number. Hold on, Ellie, he's just coming in.'

Ellie wrote down the registration number and the make on a piece of paper and pushed it into her pocket. Bob would be here any minute and she wanted him to make sure Daniel wasn't stopped for speeding. If there was anything Bob could do to get them here safely, she knew he would do it.

Next, Ellie sent a warm, affectionate message to Alice, asking her not to ring her that evening as there was a fault with their landline, and for some reason the mobile signal was poor. She promised to ring her the following day, meanwhile, perhaps Alice could send her a message in case that got through. Fortunately, this had actually happened on a previous occasion when Alice had been abroad. Ellie hated lying, but it would be much worse if Alice rang and got no answer.

Her head buzzing, she went out into the corridor. As she was closing her door she heard a voice inside her room. The room she had been alone in.

'Wait.'

Carole was sitting on one of the sofas. She was wearing her signature old wax jacket, looking for all the world like the same old Carole.

'Sit, my dear, just for a few minutes. I don't have long.'

Ellie closed the door again and sat down opposite Carole, gazing at her in wonderment. 'I miss you so much,' she whispered.

'I'm not far away, my dear, I'm always nearby. Now, buck up, my girl, this is no time to start getting all emotional. I've brought you something.' She pointed to a velvet drawstring bag lying next to her on the couch.

'That's your tarot cards, isn't it?' said Ellie. The last time she had seen those cards they were in a drawer in the summer house, back in Compton.

'They are yours now, Ellie, and you must use them wisely.'

'Oh, Carole, I never could read them like you. You had the gift, unfortunately I do not.'

'Trust me, you'll be able to read them as well as I ever could. Let's just say that much as Vera helps Christopher to write, so I will help you to read. Every time you lay those cards out, I will guide you to the answers you seek. You are right, I had the gift, and now I'm passing on that gift to you.'

As she spoke, Carole began to melt away. Ellie wanted to cry out, beg her to stay and not leave her, but she knew it was useless. Soon she was staring at an empty couch. Carole had gone, but she had left her tarot cards behind.

'I'll do my best,' she whispered. 'And thank you.'

'Your best is all that can be expected of you, but it is enough.' The voice was like a soft breeze blowing through the room. Then all went silent.

Ellie picked up the cards. Immediately, she felt a quiver of energy travel from her hands to the rest of her body. Carole had passed on her gift. They were her cards now, and she would call upon them for insight and inspiration, and most of all, answers.

Ellie thrust the precious bag deep into her jacket pocket, and again started for the door. *'You are the High Priestess now, Ellie McEwan, and your mission is to save the children.'*

She had her orders, and she knew what she had to do. She went in search of the children.

* * *

Three cars pulled up in front of the Carole Cavendish-Meyer Healing Centre. From the first emerged the bulky form of DCI

Bob Foreman, closely followed by Wendy. Parked as close to the first car as he could get, Jon Leatham anxiously watched Trevor Grant, the last to arrive, ease his old Vauxhall Corsa into a space between two other vehicles.

With a brief exchange of greetings, they hurried across to the entrance, where Ellie was waiting for them. Bob thought she seemed changed. She had an air of authority that he hadn't seen in her before.

'Bob. Before we do anything, I have a request to make.'

Ellie told him the Littlewood family were on their way, but she was afraid something might try and stop them.

Bob said he understood. 'I'll put in a call for an escort. Don't worry, there won't be any blues and twos, they'll keep their distance, but they'll be able to clear the way for them.'

'Thank you so much,' said Ellie, looking relieved. 'Now, we'll just have a quick word, and then I'll take you up to meet our latest special child.'

Once they were seated in her consulting room, Bob asked Jon to tell Ellie about his attempt to get a look at the Eleventh House from the air.

Bob still found it amazing, but Ellie didn't seem surprised in the slightest. Then he recalled how anxious she had looked when Jon first suggested that flight. She had known it would fail, and was worried Jon might be harmed in the attempt.

'It's not really something I know much about, but from what you say it sounds like they have established a very powerful force field to keep intruders at bay. I think that when the aircraft lost power it was a gentle nudge to tell you to back off. You weren't intending any harm, and they recognised that.'

'So, even though we didn't get to trace the boundaries, we now know that we are looking in the right place,' said Wendy.

'Absolutely,' agreed Ellie. 'And although I have no idea how, we will be shown the entrance, we don't have to keep looking for it. You agree, don't you, Trevor?'

'I do. What's more, if we were to find what we thought was an entrance, it would turn out to be an illusion. I was contacted by someone called Serena, and she showed me a glimpse of what they can do. I thought I was looking at a dark patch of almost impenetrable woodland, and she showed me it was really just natural woodland with paths and wildflowers instead of the thickets of brambles I'd seen.'

This was all a bit much for Bob. 'I'm trying hard to keep an open mind, but, honestly, energy fields warning off aircraft and woods that aren't woods?' He glared at the others.

Jon couldn't help laughing. 'Boss, you should see your face!'

'Give me a break,' Bob said. 'I'm struggling here.'

Ellie smiled at him encouragingly. 'Don't mind him, Bob. You're doing fine. It would be difficult for anyone to take in. Believe me, it's not exactly plain sailing for Michael and me either. Sure, we have some special abilities, but some of the things that have been happening have blown us away. Just this morning we've seen a five-year-old child produce a painting that an established artist would have been proud of. As to that protective illusion, I've never heard of anything on that scale before. In fact, now I come to think about it, I reckon no human being could have created it. I suspect that our friends asked for help, and it was given to them. Like that 'cloud' protecting their sanctuary, they prayed for that too. It's a mystery, and I guess it will remain so. What I do know is that those higher powers — who or whatever they are — consider the Eleventh House and those special children worth protecting.'

'All children are worth protecting,' said Bob quietly.

'Which is exactly why you are with us on this extraordinary venture,' murmured Ellie. 'Because of your unconditional love of children, and the fact that you'd do anything to protect them.'

Bob gave a slightly embarrassed shrug. 'Well, no one would deny that I'm a hardened old cynic, and it would be hard to find anyone less spiritual than me, but there's no denying that I'd walk through fire in order to help a child in need.'

'And there you have it,' said Ellie. 'In as much as we seem to be the guardians of three little children, you are *our* guardian. When it comes to it, we will get those children to their place of safety, thanks to you.'

'That sounds like a prophecy,' said Wendy, looking intently at her friend.

'Because it was,' added Trevor. 'Each of us has a part to play, even if it isn't yet clear what that part is. And once that other child, Christopher, brings us his next message, I think we will know.'

Trevor looked to Ellie for confirmation, and Bob saw her nod.

'Then maybe we should go and meet this new young guest of yours,' said Bob, 'before the Littlewood family arrives. Oh, and I'd like to see Harry's picture, if I may?'

'Then prepare yourself for a surprise, on both counts.' Ellie stood up. 'Okay, troops, follow me, and we'll go and meet Izzie.'

CHAPTER THIRTY-ONE

Anyone looking down on the Winter Circle would have seen a gathering that resembled a pagan ceremony, or a Wicca spell circle, and in essence, that's what it was. They were not religious in the accepted sense of the word, but much like a church, this place contained a vibrant spiritual energy far removed from the chaos of the outside world.

Every member of the Eleventh House wore white, and most stood at intervals along the perimeter line of the carefully designed garden. Eight members of the family stood within the next concentric ring, and close to the centre were Rae, Serena, Mark, Roku and Luna.

Alone on the central bench, standing with his head bowed, was Gideon. The perfume from the daphne bushes wafted around him. Everything was still, everything felt right.

'Serena?'

'Yes, Gideon?'

'How long do we have?'

'They will need us in a little over an hour.'

'Luna? Are there good conditions for the journey?'

'Yes, Gideon. We will have two and a half hours before we start to lose the light. The weather will be with us, and God's creatures know of the importance of this journey, and they will be beside us every step of the way. When the corridor opens and our friends depart their own sanctuary en route to ours, the universe will conspire to bring them to us without harm.'

'News from outside, Mark? What of Josh at the lake-house?'

'As we know, they will muster all their forces to prevent this happening. Their main target will be Zillah. I am told that shadows are gathering already, and the news from the lake is that Josh fears there will come a moment when he can no longer keep watch. He will tell me, if that is the case—'

'And I will send help to him,' said Luna emphatically.

'Tell him, Mark,' directed Gideon, 'that he must not try and hold out too long. One man, however good, is no match for a horde of black-hearted demons.'

'He knows that, Gideon,' said Mark. 'But he is stubborn. I fear that so long as he thinks he can hold back their onslaught — even for a minute — he will stand fast.'

Gideon prayed that Josh would not make a martyr of himself. Keeping watch over the lake was a daunting task, one that few would wish to take on, but Josh considered himself its appointed guardian. It was his life, his reason for being.

'Roku?'

'Yes, Gideon?'

'You and your wonderful gift may be sorely needed as the forces of evil draw close. Are you ready, my son?'

'I am. And I've never been more serious about winning a game. I may be a joker, but on this occasion I'll play my cards in deadly earnest.'

'Good boy,' said Gideon. 'Then we are ready. All of you, go and spend some time in contemplation. Fast if you can. Drink only water. Pray to your own particular god or spirit that our friends be granted safe passage to the Eleventh House. Return here in forty minutes, ready for battle. If we win this one, we will have all the children home at last, and then we will win not only the next battle, but the war!'

* * *

With Christopher and his mother in the back of the car, Daniel Littlewood set off for the Cavendish-Meyer. To say he was nervous would be an understatement. Daniel was terrified. Marie, on the other hand, seemed suddenly calm. She had rushed over to Snug Cottage to make sure all was well with the house, and ask Mr and Mrs Scrubbs to look after the dogs. On her return, she gave Daniel's dad a somewhat implausible reason as to why they would be staying the night at the clinic, which he nevertheless accepted. Then she packed an overnight bag and was ready even before him. Once he was behind the wheel and they were on their way, Daniel felt slightly less panicked. That fleeting glimpse of Vera in place of Christopher had shaken him to the core, making him realise they had become embroiled in something utterly beyond his comprehension.

'It's all right, Daniel. Don't worry. Nothing will happen to you or Christopher. Just get everyone to the clinic as fast as you can. Nothing will stop you, and nothing will harm you.'

The voice came from the back seat, but it was not that of his mother. He knew at once who that voice belonged to, the woman who had sat with him in the summer house at Snug Cottage on that terrible night when he had believed his shattered world to be beyond repair.

Daniel took a deep breath, took a firm grip on the wheel and put his foot down.

* * *

Callum glanced through one of the Orangery windows overlooking the main drive. 'Who in heaven's name is that?'

A tall woman was striding towards the front door.

The woman was completely unknown to him, yet for some reason he knew he should go and greet her.

With Lucy and Harry behind him, he reached the doors just as she was pushing them open.

She gave him a warm smile. 'I heard I am needed here, so I have come.'

Callum accepted this without question, again he had no idea why. 'Please, come in. You're right, we do need you. I'm Callum. And this is Lucy and Harry.'

'I am Rebecca, Janie's friend.'

'I'll take you to her,' said Callum. 'We were just on our way there. I think Ellie will be there too, and Michael. They will explain what's been happening.'

Rebecca was striking to look at, with long, straight dark hair interspersed with a few threads of grey that fell to her waist. She held herself very erect. Callum thought she could be any age, from seventeen to seventy, but whether she was young or old was immaterial, her air of calm wisdom was ageless. She wore a long, flowing dress of a rich emerald green, with a loose scarf in a darker green that made Callum think of pine trees. Slung over her shoulders was a thick, warm cape; that too was green. Around her neck she wore a gold chain, suspended from it a stone of Malachite, used for psychic protection.

When they reached the quiet room, Rebecca stopped at the door and rested her hands on the door-frame. She closed her eyes and breathed deeply for a few moments and nodded. 'Good energy,' she said with a smile, and they went inside.

Janie ran up to her friend and hugged her. 'Rebecca! You came!'

'Of course. You needed me.'

'But I never got around to contacting you! I meant to phone,' said Janie, 'but something always stopped me, and—'

'No need. I knew.'

Janie turned to the others. 'This woman is unique, I'm telling you. Oh, but let me introduce you.'

The children, in particular, were evidently enthralled by this tall, enigmatic stranger. Harry couldn't take his eyes off her, and Izzie, peering at her from behind her mother, looked totally awestruck.

Everyone began talking at once. Callum, however, was watching Trevor, who was gazing past Harry, directly at the airman. Philip hadn't actually materialised, but Callum was sure Trevor sensed his presence, even if he couldn't see him.

After watching him for a few more moments, Callum went over to the detective. 'Can you see him?' he whispered. 'He's rarely more than a few feet away from Harry.'

'Not really, I see this indistinct shape, and I know it's benign. I never see spirits as such, but I get pictures in my head, and I receive messages. I can pick things up and transmit them telepathically, but that's as far as it goes.'

'You are looking at Philip Nancarrow,' Callum said. 'Later, when this is all over, I'll tell you what I know about him.'

'Ditto. In fact I probably know more about his life than you,' said Trevor. 'But I'm sure you have more of an insight into the man himself, and the truth about what happened to him — and most importantly, why he is here.'

A knock at the door heralded the arrival of Marie, Daniel and Christopher.

'Well done, Daniel!' Ellie exclaimed. 'You've delivered the precious cargo safely.'

'Thanks to my police escort,' said Daniel. 'I don't think I've ever driven so fast, without even getting done for speeding.'

'Just don't try it too often,' said Bob Foreman, grinning.

Christopher went up to Ellie. In his outstretched hand he held a white envelope. 'This is for you. My friend said to tell you it's the final letter, and that it's the most important one of all.' He handed Ellie a white envelope.

Ellie took the envelope and gave Christopher a hug. 'You've been very brave, young man, and we're all proud of you.' She looked at the others. 'Now we'll know what we must do . . .'

* * *

Ellie took a deep breath and read:

'Walk towards the light. Focus on it, and walk on.'

'My God!' said one of the Guardians. 'Isn't that like dying?'

'No, not death, it's about life and living. Walk towards the light.'

The group moved away from the place they called home and stopped at the gates. The Pathfinder then told them to line up in strict order. Once they were in the right formation, the Pathfinder moved to the front of the column, raised her eyes heavenward and waited.

'Prepare yourselves,' said the Voice in a tone that both encouraged and cautioned. 'Think only of your next step. And whatever you do, you must not lose your hold on the child assigned to you. The children are the reason you are here, your purpose is to take them to safety. Much rests on the courage you show today, for each child in your care has a part to play in the future of humanity.'

A gentle breeze arose and swirled between them, spreading a faint perfume of flowers. The air around them was warm, and filled with gossamer cobwebs in soft blues and amethysts.

'You will succeed, for you are not alone, but nevertheless you must take care, because the path is surrounded by the forces of darkness. Never deviate from that path by a single step. Never believe anything you see, because it will be an illusion, thrown

up by those wishing to prevent you reaching your goal, and they will stop at nothing to achieve their objective. They are masters of deception, they know what you most fear and will confront you with it. Know that it is not real. Know only the light, and that you must walk towards it, you and the precious children in your care.'

Then the Pathfinder gave them the word, and the column set forth on their journey to the Eleventh House.

'The rest lies with you,' said the Voice. 'And God speed.'

A silence of several seconds followed Ellie's reading. Then everyone spoke at once.

'We are going to *walk* there?'

'But it could be miles!'

'What about the little ones? They'll never make it!'

'How on earth . . . ?'

'I can't walk that far! And Izzie certainly can't.'

'Or Harry!'

A single voice broke through the clamour. 'It's all right.'

They all looked at Ellie.

'This is no ordinary journey, it's not governed by distance or time. The path we will follow will be one that none of us has known before. It will require all the strength and courage we possess, but if we have love in our hearts, we will reach our destination.'

Ellie knew this to be true, and that the assurance with which she spoke came directly from a higher power. Amid the shocked faces of those around her, one regarded her serenely.

The gaze of the Shaman, Rebecca Stillman, was filled with admiration and respect.

'I have travelled such a route in the past,' Rebecca now said, 'many years ago and in another country. It seems I am meant to be here with you now.'

'Are you the Pathfinder?' asked Ellie.

'No, the Pathfinder is you. I am simply here to protect you. Only you, Ellie, can lead these children and their guardians to safety, and it is right that you do so. You had the courage to overcome much adversity in the past. You have more love in your heart than many others come to feel in a lifetime. You were born to lead.' She looked around the room until her eyes came to rest on a spot near the back of the room. She gave a small smile of recognition. 'You will not be alone. There is another who will be your navigator. That is why he is here today. Together, you and he will guide us to the Eleventh House.'

Ellie nodded slowly. Rebecca was speaking of Philip Nancarrow. They were going to his former home. Suddenly, she understood what part Harry was playing. Without him, the airman could not help them, for he could only communicate through the child. Yes, he had spoken to Callum, but he quickly weakened, addressing an adult soon depleted his energy. He needed a child in order to take shape and make himself heard in this world.

The room was silent, all waited anxiously for what would come next.

Wendy broke the silence. 'Will we all go?'

'No,' said Ellie thoughtfully. 'Christopher, Daniel and Marie will wait here, in the care of Janie and . . . at least one other good soul, although I'm not sure yet who that will be.' She looked affectionately at the Littlewoods. 'They have played their part, and now they will be cared for.'

Marie gave a loud sigh of relief. 'I am glad, if only for the sake of Christopher and my beloved Daniel. But if you think it would help, I'll walk with you willingly.'

Ellie's heart swelled with love for her loyal friend. 'I can't tell you how much I appreciate your offer, but your place is with your family. Knowing we have your support will make the journey easier.' She turned to Janie. 'I charge you with the care and protection of these three special people. Will you accept that charge?'

'Gladly,' said Janie. 'Now I understand why Rebecca is here. She is to take my place on the journey, and that is as it should be. Her powers are much stronger than mine. What power I have will be better employed here, keeping everyone safe from harm.'

This final problem being resolved, Ellie turned her attention to the journey. Christopher's writing had said she should establish the order in which they were to walk, but how? As she pondered, she felt a piercing heat in her side as if she had been burned. She reached down to touch it and her fingers rested on the bag of tarot cards in her pocket. Of course. She had only to ask and the cards would tell her what she needed to know.

'Forgive me, I need a little time alone before we set off. I'll be back soon.' Her room would be the best place for what she had to do now. It was where Carole had sat with her, and where she could think most clearly. She would make her first attempt at reading the cards there.

Inside, she sat down at her desk, the cards, still in their velvet bag, in front of her. Ellie closed her eyes and asked for protection and guidance. She asked the Great Spirit to send a shield of golden light to protect her as she went about her task. She asked that the angels, her guides, and her spirit helpers would help her find the solution she sought.

She remained for a moment in silence, and then she opened her chakras to balance her energy, as Michael and Carole had taught her, allowing their shimmering colours to travel through her body. And then she gave herself up to spirit.

First, Ellie took some Post-it notes from a drawer, and on each one she wrote the name of one of the travellers.

Michael, Bob, Wendy, Trevor, Jon, Callum, Lucy, Beth, Rebecca, Izzie and Harry.

She laid these out on the desk and opened the bag. Reverently, she removed the cards and laid them out. Instead of a traditional divination spread, she chose a card to represent each individual. This would be the significator card. Taking a deep breath, she then shuffled the remaining pack three times and laid a card from the top of the deck face down beneath each significator card. When that was done, she turned them over to read the divinatory meaning, noting that not one card was upside down, which would have yielded a contrary meaning.

Each card spoke to her when she looked at it. Each told her something about the journey to come, and what it meant to the person signified.

The Eight of Rods told her of a journey to new surroundings: positive movement and a safe arrival.

The Wheel of Fortune called out destiny: a conclusion, light at the end of the tunnel. A happy outcome.

The Six of Swords was particularly auspicious: an imminent move to a calm and peaceful place. A spiritual journey, success following anxiety.

As the King of Pentacles revealed itself beneath Bob's name, Ellie gave a quiet chuckle. Among the card's many positive attributes, such as being an intelligent and worldly-wise chief of industry, the King of Pentacles was fiercely protective of those he loved.

When eleven cards lay beneath the names of her fellow travellers and the two children, she turned over the final card. Hers.

The High Priestess.

She swallowed. For a while she sat quietly, simply paying attention to her breath flowing in and flowing out. She understood how significant this card was, and was humbled by it, praying that she would be able to do it justice. After a few moments' reflection, she decided to hold on to the main thing she understood from it, that she would be a positive guiding force, and a leader by virtue of her psychic abilities. That those abilities were not hers but Carole's was perfectly clear to her, but that wouldn't stop her making full use of them on the journey to the Eleventh House and safety.

She looked again at the cards. Two, in particular, had given her some cause for concern. These she looked at again, more carefully.

The first was the card representing Izzie, which had dark undertones, but she soon realised that this was only to be expected. The child was a magnet for some evil force, but it didn't mean that Izzie herself was evil. Something had occurred in her life that had left her open to being made use of in this way. The Major Arcana card had been the Tower, which on the surface symbolised chaos and destruction. But it also signified change, and Ellie concluded that what was in store for the little girl was a transition to a new freedom. But liberation would only be gained at some cost to the child. They just had to get her safely to the Eleventh House, and then its occupants would take over her care and recovery.

Callum's card, too, had worried her slightly, but she decided to simply trust him and he would in the end emerge triumphant. The card was the Seven of Cauldrons, meaning making the right choices. He would have important decisions to make, difficult ones, but if he learned to trust his intuition, it would guide him to the right one.

What remained was the order in which they were to walk. Gazing at the cards before her, she hesitated. How would the cards tell her something like this? What if she got it wrong?

'For heaven's sake, girl! We don't have all day. Just do it.'

So she did. The names on the Post-it notes seemed to arrange themselves without the slightest input from her. When she checked each person's cards, she could see it made perfect sense. After all who better to flank Harry, than Callum and Lucy?

Recalling the vision she had shared with Trevor, of the three of them holding hands, Ellie no longer had the slightest doubt that this arrangement was the right one.

She looked at the rest of the layout and was satisfied.

She would walk at the head of the group. Immediately behind her would be Harry, with his two guardians. Philip, she knew, would be walking with his hands resting lightly on Harry's shoulders, assisting her through the child.

Following them, Rebecca, who would be walking alone. Hers was the task of keeping the darkness at bay, and when it seeped through their defences, as no doubt it would, she would call upon spirit to drive it away. Rebecca would also be the voice of reason should anyone succumb to illusion. It was a heavy responsibility to bear, requiring her to be a true master. The very fact of her arrival at this very moment was a miracle, and it served as a good omen for the outcome of their journey.

Immediately after Rebecca would be Izzie, the single weak link who must be protected at all costs. It was because of her that their venture was so perilous, and she would form the main target of their enemy.

Izzie would, of course, walk with her mother, Beth, but also Bob Foreman. Bob's fierce love of children made him a formidable adversary, even when what faced him were not earthly beings but the powers of darkness.

Flanking them were Wendy on one side and Jon on the other. They would be acting as lookouts. Keeping the light ahead always in sight, they would also take note of anything that looked like it might break through the protective shield surrounding them.

Last would be Michael and Trevor, the rear guard. Apart from Rebecca, they were the most spiritually connected souls of them all. Hopefully, Michael would also be able to restore damaged auras if they became so depleted that they became a danger to the rest of them.

It was done.

Ellie blessed the cards, thanked her guides and helpers and put the cards back in their velvet bag. With the bag in her pocket, she got to her feet, momentarily dizzy, which was only to be expected after such intense concentration.

Now she must go back to the others, and give them their instructions. They must leave soon, before darkness overtook them.

CHAPTER THIRTY-TWO

'Pull those top windows in for me, would you, Scrubbs. The wind is getting up something awful.' Mrs Scrubbs hurried from room to room checking that the catches on all the windows were fastened.

'I don't know where this weather has come from so sudden-like,' grumbled Scrubbs as he secured one of the locks. 'They said it'd be a chilly one today, but they never mentioned no bloody gales.'

'Well, one thing's for sure, those dogs ain't going down to the orchard after their dinner. Poor little mites,' Mrs Scrubbs said. 'There's a black cloud hanging over them trees, and I reckon we are in for one helluva storm.'

Scrubbs frowned. 'Speaking of the dogs, have you seen them in the last half hour? They're all terrified, tucked up tight in their beds and huddled together like they's either frozen, or frightened stiff.'

'It'll be the storm making them act like that,' said his wife. 'Dogs hate thunder and lightnin'. They can detect it long before we do.'

'Never seen 'em like that before, though.' Scrubbs stared out of the window. 'Goodness, stuff's taking a right battering out there! I've turned off the pump to the water garden as the water was blowing all over the place, and I've locked up the summer house. I just hope my old shed at home lasts out, that's all I can say. It's not exactly in the prime of its life.'

'Well, you ain't going back to check on it, that's for sure. The way that wind is blowing, you'd be off your feet. I'll put the kettle on, and we'll go and sit it out with the dogs. What say you?'

'Well, no good trying to fight weather like this. I'll just have to pick up the pieces afterwards. Yes, love, you go and get that kettle on.'

* * *

Dr Littlewood was driving home from his GP practice in the town when he noticed the sky turn dark. Storm clouds were gathering above his house.

'Funny,' he muttered. 'It's a bit chilly today, but I don't recall rain being forecast.' He glanced in the rear-view mirror. Behind him the sky was perfectly clear. He speeded up a bit, not relishing the thought of getting soaked to the skin on his way into the house.

He didn't make it. Now, with his coat and shoes drying out in front of the hall radiator, he listened to the sound of the wind tearing at the gables and the roof tiles. He didn't like storms, and this was a belter. He turned up the heating, relieved that at least Marie and the family were safe over at the clinic. Like him, Christopher hated stormy weather, and especially lightning. Some kids enjoyed counting the seconds between the lightning flash and the thunderclap, to work out how far away the storm was. Christopher wasn't interested, all he wanted to do was hide. He would hunker down under a table, well away from the windows.

The doctor stood at the window, wondering what had happened to his pride and joy. The garden was a wreck. First there had been that horrible virus, blackening the leaves and even killing some of his favourite shrubs. And now this. A vicious storm they appeared to be at the epicentre of, laying waste to the greenery and sending garden ornaments crashing to the ground.

'Sod this,' he muttered. 'I'm not on call this evening, and I don't care how early it is, I'm having a whisky!'

* * *

From the margin of the lake, Josh gazed across to the forest on the other side. The trees were being wrenched this way and that, and the air was full of the howl of the wind and the crack of breaking branches. Not all the noise was coming from the forest, some was from the lake itself. Josh had never seen the water so turbulent. Waves smashed into the little bays he sometimes fished from, apparently intent on splintering the jetty where he moored the boats to matchwood. He was glad he'd had the foresight to drag all the boats into the boathouse before the storm took hold.

Josh knew well that this was no ordinary storm. It was an expression of rage. Despite the drama unfolding across the lake, this side of the water was perfectly calm, not even the slightest breeze stirred the leafy shrubs where he stood. What troubled him was that for the first time ever, the whole lake had been stirred up by the force of this anger. The jetty was all but gone, and he was beginning to fear for his boathouse home. The rope was key. As long as it held, the devastation would be confined to the lake. If the rope broke, the dam would burst, unleashing the dark forces in the forest, and the whole of the Eleventh House would be vulnerable. The rope was his responsibility. He had tied the knots that held it fast, and sealed them with divine assistance. They had never weakened yet, never given way. It was his responsibility to make sure they never did.

Mark contacted him, telling him to evacuate the lake. He had done his bit, and now it was time to join the others in the circle and ask that the last child be brought home safely. Mark said he was needed just as much there as he was guarding the rope. The time had come to hand the lake and the rope over to spirit. If he stayed, he would be in mortal danger.

Despite Mark's admonitions, Josh stood fast, mustering all the energy in his power, and directing it across the churning water into two vital knots.

* * *

Serena stood in the doorway to Gideon's room. 'They are preparing themselves, Gideon. They'll soon be at the gate. It's time to return to the Winter Circle.'

'Have you made contact?'

'With one called Trevor. I've told him we will do everything we can to guide them in. You should see them, Gideon,' she added, looking somewhat amused. 'With two major exceptions, they are a rather motley crew — until you look beneath the skin.'

'What do you mean?' Gideon asked.

'Walking with them is one of the most powerful shamanic practitioners I have ever come across, and this is not the first time she has traversed the corridor. Her help will be invaluable.'

'And the other?'

'Philip Nancarrow.'

Gideon stared at her. 'Philip? Are you sure?'

'Yes, Gideon, he is coming home,' said Serena. 'He will be their guide should the forces of evil try to force the Pathfinder off course. He is speaking to them through a child. Not one of those we are expecting, but special nevertheless, and though he won't remain with us, he needs us now.'

'Then we will welcome him with open arms. And Philip — this is wonderful news indeed.' The Eleventh House owed its very existence to the generosity of the last of the Nancarrows. 'And the others?'

'Two are the owners of a healing centre, one of whom studied complementary medicine, while the other, would you believe it, kept a flower shop. Both are gifted with auric sight, but no more than that. There is also a young mother, a schoolteacher, a male nurse who has been seeing spirits all his life, and four policemen.'

'A motley crew indeed. I hardly know what to say. Policemen!'

Serena laughed. 'I think they have been chosen for their capacity to love, and love children in particular. Furthermore, they are closely connected to two very powerful spirits. I may be mistaken, but I have an idea they are the very spirits that took Mole's soul to its final resting place.'

'Then let's make haste and join the others at the Circle. Ask Mark to try one last time to persuade Josh to leave the lake, and then we'll prepare to ease the passage for our new, and very diverse, friends.'

* * *

Ellie hugged Marie, Daniel, and finally, Christopher. She told him how brave he had been, and that without him, who knew what might have happened. She assured them she would find a way to let them know when they arrived at the Eleventh House and had delivered the children safely.

Then she turned to the others. 'Time to go. Is everyone ready?'

'As we'll ever be, considering we're heading into the unknown,' said Bob. 'But, yes, Ellie, we are ready.'

'Stay safe,' whispered Marie, tears in her eyes. 'All of you.'

Ellie turned to Janie. 'Look after my friends, won't you?'

'Oh, I will, never fear,' Janie said. 'And I won't be alone. We're going to be joined by some of the others who practise here. They all love this clinic, and they want to help protect it if the need should arise. The C-M is safe with us. Now go. Be strong, be brave, and above all, be successful. The universe needs you to succeed.'

And so they set off, through the grounds and down the drive towards the gates.

A couple of metres in front of the entrance, Ellie came to a halt, and allocated them their positions. Giving each one a hug, she enjoined them to repeat her instructions, and keep repeating them as they walked. They must move forward toward the light, and not be distracted by anything else, including their thoughts. The forces of evil would transmit dark thoughts into their minds, and use them to try and frighten them. These things were not real. They would all be tempted, probably threatened too. They would be shown the things they most dreaded. But all this was an illusion, and none of it would hurt them. They must keep walking on. Above all, they must never loosen their hold on the children in their care.

Satisfied that everything was in place, Ellie moved to the front, took a deep breath and waited.

Harry's voice rang out loud and clear. 'Walk through the gate, Ellie. We are all behind you. It is time to go.'

Ellie stepped forward.

In an instant, the lane leading to the healing centre disappeared, and Ellie almost came to a stop. Ahead of her was a long, wide tunnel of white and gold light. The path glistened, and as she moved forward she felt as if she were walking on water. The ground beneath her feet seemed to have no substance, yet it held her weight like granite. She fixed her gaze on the source of the light at the very end of the bright corridor.

Gradually, she began to realise that she could see through the walls, as if the tunnel were made of glass. While keeping her gaze fixed on the light, she caught glimpses in the corner of her eye of the landscape beyond — trees, fields and forests stretching into the distance on each side of the tunnel of light.

She resisted the urge to turn around and make sure they were all still together. She was the Pathfinder, there were others whose task it was to look out for the followers. After a while, she began to make out snatches of the conversations behind her, and hear the cries of amazement. Amid the chatter, she heard Rebecca uttering soft words of encouragement. The only voice that was absent was that of Izzie, and she became concerned.

'It's all right, Ellie. She's sleeping. Walking on between Bob and her mother, but in an induced sleep state, rather like sleepwalking. Harry, too, even though the airman is using Harry's voice to direct you if you should need his guidance. It is better for the children this way, better that they have no memory of this journey.'

'Who are you?' asked Ellie, wondering if she could trust this soft voice.

'My name is Rae. I've come from the Eleventh House to walk by your side, for you have a difficult task ahead of you. The airman will guide you, while I am here to help you dispel the demons. You, of all of these people, need to know what is real and what is illusion as you tread a path between the worlds.'

'How do I know you're really who you say you are?' asked Ellie.

'Look into your heart. You will find that you already know that I'm here to help you. Your instincts are very good, Ellie. Trust them, and you'll be fine. Should you hesitate, I will be beside you, and when we reach home we'll meet in person.'

'Since this strange corridor is so straight, why do we need a guide?' Ellie asked.

Rae laughed softly. 'It won't always be like this. Think of it as going into the baby pool before you dive into the big pool. It's to accustom you to walking towards the light.'

It was strange talking to a disembodied voice, although come to think of it, people did that all the time when they used a phone. Then Ellie suddenly realised that she hadn't been speaking out loud. 'Telepathy,' said the voice in her head. 'Easy as pie when you get your head around it. Now, listen. Things will soon start to change, but don't worry, Rebecca will calm the others and they'll be fine. You are on your way, and that's what matters. Stay strong, and think of the children.'

Already, the scene outside the tunnel had become clearer, less abstract. She recalled a childhood visit to the aquarium in a sea life adventure park, although in this case it was they who were behind glass, watching the world swimming around outside. And she was looking at a landscape, not fish. Like being in a train, perhaps, watching the countryside speed past the windows.

Were there people out there? She had detected movement and was tempted to look, but dare not take her eyes from the light. A glance wouldn't hurt, would it? She was sure she'd seen someone walking quite close to them, someone she recognised. Yes, there was a track running parallel to the tunnel, and someone on it who was waving to her frantically!

'The light, Ellie! Concentrate. There is no one out there, it's a mirage. They're tricking you.'

Ellie narrowed her eyes and stared ahead. Alice was hammering on the glass, right next to her! 'Ellie! For heaven's sake! What are you doing? My flight was cancelled! I'm back! What the hell are you up to? Please, talk to me!'

Ellie stared harder at the light and gritted her teeth against the temptation to turn to her beloved partner. She knew the plane had left on time, she'd checked. No flights to the States had been cancelled.

'I love you, Ellie! Why are you ignoring me? I know you can hear me!'

The voice became desperate, pleading.

Her cheeks streaked with tears, Ellie strode on, repeating to herself, 'You are not real, you are not real.' Then she heard her mother. 'What was it we used to do, to pass the time on long car journeys?'

Ellie began singing to herself. 'If you're happy and you know it clap your hands, if you're happy and you know it . . .' 'Alice' began scrabbling at the glass, howling in rage and frustration. As Ellie walked on, the figure fell behind, until it was gone.

'Well, well,' said Rae approvingly. 'I've never heard of using a kiddies' song to dispel a demon. Anyway, now you've seen what they can do, it won't be so scary next time.'

'What about the others?' Ellie asked anxiously. Bob, for one, had children of his own, and she was certain the tricksters would use them to derail him.

'They are all facing similar demons, but they are coming through fine, just as you did. Your shaman managed to dispel some of the apparitions before they even reached their target. She's an amazing woman.'

'A true godsend,' added Ellie, 'in every sense of the word.'

'Ellie! If you are given a choice, take the path to the right.'

Harry's voice was as clear as a bell, though Ellie knew he had no idea he was even speaking. The tunnel ahead was changing. No longer a passageway of light, it was more like a shadowy path through woods, and sure enough, ahead it forked. She took the right-hand path, and immediately was back in the tunnel, the distant light still beckoning to her. She should have been relieved, instead she became increasingly anxious. It was getting darker, and the world outside — real or not — was growing more and more menacing. Noises started to drift in, noises that made her flesh creep. Sniggers and chuckles, whimpers and cries. Animal? Human? Whatever they were, they were creatures in pain.

'Don't listen, Ellie. They don't exist.'

'Surely I took the wrong path?' asked Ellie fretfully. 'I must have.'

'Trust the airman, he will not let you down.'

'I will never let you down,' Philip echoed.

Ellie straightened her back and silently berated herself for being such a bloody wimp. 'Okay, Rae, how much further? I'm getting mighty pissed off with these stupid illusions.'

The golden light burst forth with renewed brilliance, and Ellie heard a sigh of relief from somewhere behind her.

'That's the spirit, girl! You hang on to that Cavendish-Meyer attitude, and we'll beat these bastards in no time!'

'Carole!'

'Who else?' Her old friend, still wearing her wellington boots, strode along beside her. 'I can't stay, because I cannot afford to become too drained, my work is outside this corridor. They were beginning to weaken you, and I'm here to make sure that doesn't happen. Consider this a kick up the backside from the other world. You have more strength than anyone I know, so bloody well use it! Take these people out of their hell and give them some peace. Bob is seeing images of his daughter being carried off by demons. Beth has snakes slithering around her. Wendy is fighting off giant spiders, and our dear Callum is back in Rwanda, amid the mire of death and destruction. Each of them has their own nightmare, so act like a true Pathfinder and lead them home.'

Then she was gone, leaving Ellie alone, but with renewed strength and vigour. She quickened her pace. As she strode forward, other paths appeared, more decisions had to be made, but every time, the airman directed her where to go. When the daylight began to fade, she found she could project streams of colour from her own aura down the corridor.

At last, the light they had been following seemed closer, and her heart beat faster. They were almost there.

'This will be your greatest test,' said Rae. 'If you deliver the child of the shadows to Gideon, the darkness will be defeated. Their rage is at its peak, so be warned. If you can break through their onslaught, you will find a door, behind which lies safety. Only you can open this door. Alone, you must deliver the children to safety.'

But Ellie was not alone. She was aware of every one of her friends supporting her, all sending her what little energy they had left. Carole and Vera were there, all she had to do was ask for their help.

'Yes, Rae, I can. I will do what is asked of me.'

Ellie fixed her eyes on the light. While all around her dark clouds roiled, thunder and bolts of lightning crashing with a deafening roar, Ellie held her head high, and plunged forward.

CHAPTER THIRTY-THREE

They knew they were close to their goal, but doubted they would make it. The small group of people were battered, mentally and physically, and while Rebecca continued to urge them to make this one final effort, Michael, for one, knew his strength was failing.

'Come, my friends, one more hurdle, one more task and your work will be done. A new day is about to dawn.'

After all this time, all they had been through, Rebecca's voice remained strong. But how long had it been, really? Michael had no idea. It could have been years. Or minutes.

'Have faith,' Rebecca was saying. 'What you see next will be terrifying, but others are coming to see us through. You no longer need to keep to your assigned positions, just stay close to each other and keep the children between you. And, remember, the evil waging war against us is a master of deception. Above all, have faith. Believe you are still protected, even if it appears you are not.'

The light having gone, they were no longer obliged to look forward. Glancing around at his companions, Michael thought, *Oh dear, what a bedraggled lot we are. Do we really have the strength to withstand one more onslaught?*

'Damn it, man! An attitude like that will hardly get the baby a new bonnet. You silly old duffer. Take a look at Bob, and take a lesson from him.'

Never having dared contradict Carole in life, Michael had no intention of starting now she was dead! He looked at Bob. Determination was etched into every line of his face. He was still clutching hold of Izzie's hand, and he wasn't going to let it go until she had reached the Eleventh House, and safety.

'Okay. Now look at Callum,' Carole said.

He did, and what he saw was truly beautiful. Callum stood with the two people he most loved, Harry and Lucy. They were smiling at one another, while around them floated tiny silvery particles like diamonds.

'So, my dear old friend. Got the message?'

Slowly, a smile began to spread across his face. 'Loud and clear, old girl, and thank you.'

'Not so much of the *old* if you don't mind!'

All at once, Michael caught a glimpse of Carole, not as he had last seen her, but as a young woman — tall, imperious and of a radiant beauty.

'Now, if your Ellie is capable of opening that door, alone, surely you can help these brave souls follow her through it.'

Carole's parting words before disappearing were, 'Above all else, remember, you *are* protected, even if it seems you are not.'

Michael noticed Trevor watching him, smiling broadly. '"You *are* protected . . ." She's something else, isn't she?'

'You'd better believe it!'

At that moment, Rebecca's voice rang out. 'Prepare yourselves, my friends, we are about to embark on the final stage of our journey. Hold firm to those children! Hold firm to each other, and hold firm to the belief that good will triumph over evil!'

As her words died away, the strange translucent protective barrier between them and the outside fell away. Everyone gasped. They were standing on the threshold of an abyss, a swirling vortex of nameless threats. Every one of them felt instantly vulnerable.

They were assaulted from every direction. Michael choked on the acrid stench of burning, the nauseating stink of rotting flesh. His skin crept. He had the impression that some slimy disgusting creature was sliding over his limbs. Misshapen animal forms crept from the trees and stalked through the undergrowth. He was bombarded with unearthly sounds — shrieks, cries and fiendish laughs. It was all too much. Michael felt he couldn't stand it a minute longer.

But a voice rang out.

'If that's the best you can do, you'd better go back to the practice nets! We've faced worse than that in the old people's home!' Bob roared with laughter. 'Hey, Professor! Your turn. Call in our star players!'

Grinning from ear to ear, Michael turned his face to the raging wind and yelled, 'My pleasure! Vera! Carole! We need your help!'

'They're already here!' called Wendy. 'I can smell lilacs, and that awful stench has gone.'

'And look!' Trevor pointed. A mist the colour of amethyst and pale blue was drifting down towards them, while above, the sky was clear and bright.

Trevor heard a voice in his head: *'We are with you too.'*

'Serena is here, and she's brought Luna and her friends!'

A warm wind was blowing away the last of the shadows. A magnificent stag appeared on a nearby rise, and with a mighty toss of its antlers flung the dark creatures away from them.

'Nearly there,' breathed Rebecca. 'Ellie is approaching the door! You must not let her weaken now. They are trying to drain her energies. Send her all the help you can! Send her your love!'

* * *

'Luna!' Mark called across the circle. 'Josh needs help at the lake!'

'I'll send my friends to see what they can do. Go! Help Josh!'

With a howl, a massive wolf sprang out of nowhere and made for the lake. Then a majestic falcon appeared in the sky above them. Descending, it circled once and with a single flap of its wings flew after the wolf.

Luna knew she could afford to leave Serena in charge of Trevor and his friends for a while. She had Rebecca, and two higher spirits to help, while Josh only had her and her beloved creatures.

She closed her eyes, visualised the lake and was horrified to see Josh lying prone on the shoreline, his hands gripped tightly around the rope that separated their domain from the darkness beyond the waters. Every so often, some ill-formed shape would dart from the water and try to drag him back after them, but his grip held firm. She prayed he was still alive.

The wolf, along with the rest of his pack, soon made short work of the creatures from the lake. The falcon, too, bore down on them from above, and soon only Josh remained, the waters gently lapping at his still body.

Luna spoke gently to him, and he stirred slightly. He had bloodstains on his face and limbs, but he was alive. 'Can you stand?' she asked.

He shook his head, too weak to speak. 'Hold on, Josh. We'll come and get you.'

'No,' he said in a hoarse whisper. 'I must hold the rope. If I loosen my grip, even for a moment, we are lost. It is my destiny. Both knots were sealed — the one on the far bank for eternity — but this one can still be undone, in the event that evil is one day overcome. It is the weak link, and they know it, but while I have it in my grasp, it will hold fast. Even when I die, they will not take the knot from my hands. So long as I have it, they cannot win.'

'Josh, no! We can help! Spirit can!'

'Bless you, Luna, but no one knows this lake the way I do. I have lived my whole life with it, I have loved it, and now I'll die with it.'

Josh turned his face to the water.

Luna bowed her head, and the others followed suit. They all knew they had lost their friend.

'We must save our grieving for later,' called out Gideon, though there was a catch in his voice. 'For now we must protect the living. Prepare yourselves, the door is about to open. Make them welcome, but make sure nothing slips in with them.'

A silence descended on the circle, and they waited.

* * *

The door was just five metres further on, but Ellie was beginning to weaken. Her legs felt like lead, and she could barely drag each foot forward. She had struggled through a nightmarish welter of sensations to get this far, but through it all she had never doubted that she would open that crucial door. She had not broken her stride, had not succumbed to the horrible visions that assailed her every step of the way.

Carrying her memories of Carole in her heart, Ellie kept moving. Throughout her life, Carole had never backed down, never given an inch, and Ellie was determined to live up to her example. The fate of a child rested in her hands, and she would not fail her. She would deliver that child from evil.

Just a few more yards . . .

* * *

Callum wasn't sure how it had happened. Maybe he had wavered in sending his love to the struggling Ellie. Maybe he had no energy left to give her.

Whatever the cause, something dark and malign had found its way in. One minute he was concentrating on their Pathfinder, the next he was struggling with some vile shadowy creature that stretched out its claws to Harry and Lucy. It broke free of his grasp, and Callum had a split second in which to decide who to save. It was an impossible decision. His heart breaking, he made a lunge for little Harry and snatched him up, away from danger. Through his tears he saw Jon wrestle the hideous thing away from Lucy.

Taking his eyes from Lucy for a moment, he saw Jon now helping Wendy battle with two disgusting bat-like creatures that had landed on Izzie and Beth. Along with Bob, they hauled the beasts as far away from the children as they could get, and then Rebecca took over. She raised her arms, uttered a loud incantation, and the things were reduced to ashes.

Finally able to draw breath, Callum looked up, and saw a blue and amethyst mist descend over them.

'Each of you, hold out your hands, join together and send one last burst of energy. Nothing will break through the ring of protection around you. Send Ellie every last ounce of your strength!'

They held hands and willed Ellie to go through that door. As they did so, a blaze of light surrounded them. They smelled lilacs, and then every one of them fell to the ground, unconscious.

* * *

Ellie found herself lying in a flower bed, gazing at a pretty little scented shrub. She sat up to take in her surroundings, wondering where she was. She and the others were lying in a circular garden, all looking similarly bewildered.

A tall, smiling man knelt down beside her. 'Oh, I am so pleased to see you! Welcome! Here, let me help you to your feet.'

'The children!' Ellie said at once. 'Where are the children?'

'All safe. Look, there they are.' The man pointed. Harry was lying with Lucy and Callum, and not far from them, Bob was supporting Beth, who cradled a sleeping Izzie in her lap.

Too exhausted to speak, Ellie let out a long sigh of relief. The children were all right. Now all she wanted was to close her eyes and surrender to sleep.

'Come, we must get you all indoors, it's cold out here, and soon it will be dark. It's going to be a beautiful clear night, thanks to you and your friends.'

Ellie was barely conscious of him lifting her up and helping her forward. Around her, people were helping the others, beyond them the house they were being led to.

'Belcastel,' she whispered.

'That's right,' said the man.

'But I thought—'

He held up his free hand. 'Later. We'll explain it all later. Right now we must get you something to drink, and then you can rest for a few hours. We'll eat together later this evening, and you can ask all your questions then. You will stay at the Eleventh House as our guests, safe from all harm, thanks to you and your bravery.'

Ellie vaguely recalled being given a hot drink and taken to a room to rest. She fell asleep immediately, waking up to find Michael sitting on the edge of the bed, smiling at her.

'Is everyone safe, Michael? Any casualties?'

'We're all here, safe and well. We have played our part, Ellie, and delivered the children to the Eleventh House. The rest is up to the good people here.'

She sat up and stretched. 'Goodness, Michael, my head is full of questions. Do you realise we're actually in Belcastel?'

'Yes, I know,' said Michael. 'But slow down, Ellie. The man in charge, whose name is Gideon, says he'll tell you all you want to know, but we need to eat first. We are all starving, including the residents. They've been fasting to help us on our way.' He stood up. 'Come on, Ellie, let's go downstairs and you can meet the others. They are an amazing group of people! Oh, and there's someone called Rae who is itching to make your acquaintance.'

'Ah, Rae! She walked with me. I'm not sure I'd have made it without her support.'

'Oh, yes you would. You were an inspiration to us all. You'd have got us here no matter what. Now. Food!'

Rather than a formal banquet, the residents of the Eleventh House had chosen to welcome their guests with a barbecue on the terrace of Belcastel. Tables placed end to end formed a long trestle table like one you might see in a refectory.

Ellie could hardly believe her eyes. What, outside, at this time of year? They'd freeze. Then she realised that despite the bare trees, the air was pleasantly warm. She looked around but could see no heaters. Maybe she was still asleep and dreaming. After all, they were in a house that didn't exist, so why not a barbecue in the depths of winter!

Ellie sat between Gideon and Rae, whom she felt she already knew well despite having never met her in person. But conversation could wait. First, they all got down to the serious business of food. It was over half an hour before curiosity got the better of her and she looked helplessly from one to the other of her hosts.

'I don't know where to start, but first I've just remembered that I promised to let my friends at the healing centre know that we are all safe. Is there some way we can contact them?'

Rae laughed. 'It's okay — tonight, we're firmly back down to earth.' She pulled a mobile phone from her pocket and handed it to Ellie. 'Or there's a landline in the hall if you want some privacy.'

Ellie laughed with her. It was all so wonderfully . . . normal.

She rang the C-M, and had a few words with Janie, who handed her over to Marie. Through tears of joy, Marie said they were fine, although there had been a dreadful storm earlier, which had caused some peripheral damage to the house. 'Just some slates off the roof, I think. The garden came off worst. You'd have thought a hurricane had blown through. My husband just phoned and he said it was the same at ours, so I rang Snug Cottage, and Scrubbs confirmed that your lovely garden looks like a battlefield.'

Ellie told her not to worry. 'It's easily rectified. The main thing is the children are here, you and the family are all right, and no one was harmed. We must have ruffled a few feathers in the underworld, and they took out their bad temper on us. It's over now, Marie. Tomorrow, Daniel can drive you home again — this time observing the speed limit! Sleep well, dear friend.'

While she was on the phone, Ellie had been watching Gideon. There was something wrong, although he was doing his best to cover it up. She became anxious. Were the children really all right? She hadn't seen them since they all woke up in that garden.

Not wishing to ask him straight out, she mentioned it to Rae.

'We lost one of our own tonight,' she said with a sigh. 'Gideon didn't want to spoil your welcome by telling you, especially after all you've been though, but all the same it's hard not to feel sad.'

'It wasn't our fault, was it?'

'Oh no, the darkness was always there, whether or not you made the journey. And Josh had a choice. He could have lived, but for the good of the whole, he decided to sacrifice his life. And in doing so he has secured a weak spot in our defences and ensured no harm reaches us that way.' Rae reached out and brushed Ellie's cheek with her fingertips. 'Don't allow this to spoil your welcome. You and your friends have done a great thing. Your act of generosity will mean a great deal for the future. With the right guidance, the young people in our care will all go on to do amazing things for the good of humanity. Someday, Ellie, you will hear a name, or see a face you recognise on the news or in the papers, and that person will be engaged in doing something that saves lives or benefits humanity. What's more, they will only be doing that because a group of brave people faced the unknown, and emerged victorious. We will grieve for Josh, but not tonight. He is now in a place he loved, watched over by the angels. Tonight is for you and your friends, and as soon as we've finished eating, we'll be ready to answer your questions.'

Ellie raised an eyebrow. 'How long have you got? I, for one, don't even know where to start. There's so much I don't understand.'

'Relax and enjoy your food. You're with friends. It will be explained to you, all in good time.'

CHAPTER THIRTY-FOUR

It was almost midnight by the time they adjourned to the chapel. Gideon had chosen it as the most fitting place for their meeting. The children had gone to bed. Izzie was fast asleep, watched over by two of the helpers and their spirit guides. Harry was asleep in the same room, and back at the Centre, Christopher also slept soundly.

Rebecca walked to the old chapel with Ellie and Michael. 'I have something to thank you for. For a while now I've known I have a calling, but I didn't know what I was meant to do. Until I met you, that is. I've been talking it over with Gideon, and I've decided I'm going to stay here for a while. I might even make the Eleventh House my home. I know I have a place here, and I can contribute in a way that will benefit everyone. This place is safe for now, but that won't last forever. I can teach the people here my practices, and together we can make it stronger. So, thank you. You have opened more than one door today.'

Inside the chapel they all found seats, while two older boys, one of whom Ellie later found out was the missing Oliver Cruise, passed round mugs of hot drinks.

When everyone was settled, Gideon gave a brief introduction to the Eleventh House and its purpose. One of a number of such places scattered across the globe, the Eleventh House had been established as a secure environment for especially gifted children to grow in and flourish, nurturing their talents so that they might use them for the good of mankind.

He spoke of good and evil, and how people consumed by greed and the lust for personal gain do everything in their power to thwart what is good in humanity. 'There are those who have discovered how to harness malevolent forces in order to bring about chaos, suffering, disease and conflict. When they identify a special child, such as those in our care, they either hold them back, or make sure their gifts are destroyed before they can manifest themselves. Ollie, for example, was called a "weirdo", and made to believe he would never amount to anything. Others are either destroyed outright, or set on a path to self-destruction. We at the Eleventh House believe it is our sacred duty to find these children and bring them home, before it is too late and the world loses its future peacemakers, healers and teachers.'

Michael raised a hand. 'May I ask something about the children we brought with us?'

'Of course,' said Gideon.

'My dear,' Michael said to Beth, 'forgive me for saying this about your daughter, but I suspect it's something you want to know too.' He turned back to Gideon. 'Izzie was possessed by a powerful and malignant entity that took possession of her whenever she was alone with her mother. Ellie witnessed one of these episodes, and it shocked her to the core. Following their visit to our healing centre, every place that entity had passed through had to be cleansed — and not just once, either. It poisoned and tainted everything in its path. What will happen to Izzie now that she is with you? Could that vile entity find her again? And how, if she is a magnet for this evil presence, can she ever go home?'

'I appreciate your concern,' said Gideon, 'but believe me when I say we are extremely well protected. The evil forces ranged against us have lost their power, not for ever, but for the foreseeable future.' He smiled sympathetically at Beth. 'I know what a strong woman you are, and how much you love your daughter, so maybe now is the time to tell you and those who brought you here that there are things about your child that you do not know.'

He turned to Rae, who addressed Beth, speaking gently. 'Am I right in thinking you had trouble both conceiving and giving birth to Izzie?'

Beth nodded. 'It was a nightmare.'

'And after she was born, it was a while before you had any contact with her?'

'Days, I think. The doctors said I was fighting for my life, so I was barely conscious.'

With a nod, Rae called across to a woman who had been standing at the back, listening quietly to what was being said. 'Lori, would you come up here for a moment, please?'

Beth glanced at the woman standing in front of her, then looked again.

'I know you!' she exclaimed. 'You were in the clinic, and then the hospital, at the same time as me! You had a daughter, too, I remember, and we both had really difficult births.'

Lori sat down next to Beth and took her hand. 'That's right, and neither of us saw our child for two days.' She looked down. 'But after we left the hospital, our lives went in very different directions . . .'

Rae took up the story. 'There was a scientist who worked at both the fertility clinic and the hospital where you gave birth. He was a brilliant geneticist, many considered him a genius. Your typical mad scientist, you might say, and nobody thought to contradict his findings.'

Ellie shivered, wondering what Beth must be thinking now. Tuning in to Beth's aura, she seemed oddly unmoved by what she was hearing. Maybe she was relieved to at last hear the truth about her daughter.

'When Lori came to us,' Gideon said, 'we undertook some research into the man who had treated her. We discovered that his work centred on manipulating the human genome to produce children of exceptional talent. However, he wasn't looking at aptitudes like a gift for music or numbers, his focus was the metaphysical, his aim being to enhance people's psychic ability, thereby becoming more powerful than the rest of humanity.'

'He interfered with their genes?' asked Michael.

'We believe so,' said Gideon. 'Unfortunately, he was found dead in his laboratory three days after Izzie and Clover were born, his research notes destroyed.'

'However, before his obsession took hold, he had published dozens of papers on the subject,' added Rae. 'One piece of research followed a number of children, and their development from birth to the age of six. These children all turned out exceptionally gifted, and perhaps because they were the focus of so much interest, they are all, up to now at least, safe and thriving.'

'But what about *our* children?' asked Beth. 'For a start, are they really ours — my husband's and mine?'

Lori gave Beth's hand a reassuring squeeze. 'Yes, they are, there's no doubt about it.'

'Lori's right, Beth,' confirmed Gideon. 'However, we also know that this scientist, who was a fully qualified gynaecologist and obstetrician prior to moving into pure research, was involved in your IVF treatment at the clinic, and subsequently had access to your babies in the two days following their birth.'

Ellie's mind was racing. What had that madman done to those children that had turned them into . . . well, something else?

'Our biggest problem was that having been alerted to the fact that there were two special children out there who needed our protection, we had no idea who or where they were,' said Rae. 'We had no names, and certainly no address. He had always referred to them as X and Z. Our scouts only ever heard about one child — your girl, Lori. But every time we tried to find you, you had moved on, and we lost track of you.'

Lori turned to Beth. 'Very early on in her life, I knew Clover was special in some way, but bad things kept happening around her, and to save her from harm, I started running. We went from one place to another, sometimes with travellers, at others we stayed in communes for a while. All the time I kept hoping I might find someone who could help us.'

Ellie recalled Christopher's book. He had described this almost word for word in his story. She and Michael exchanged a glance.

'And my Izzie?' asked Beth. 'For ages she was the perfect child, I didn't suspect a thing! So what happened to her?'

Gideon looked at her. 'We'll have to spend time with her to make sure, but if we are right about what we suspect happened, we will be able to help, don't worry.'

'So what *do* you suspect?' Beth demanded.

Gideon glanced at Rae, who nodded. 'Beth's love for Izzie is strong enough for her to hear the truth, or as much of the truth as we know.'

'From something our scout discovered, we think that Clover and Izzie were to be his magnum opus, the jewel in the crown of everything he had worked to achieve. While you were both at the clinic, he had full access to your notes, and he would have studied your backgrounds carefully. He must have liked what he saw. His colleagues report that he had become intensely excited about two special children that he said would one day astonish the world.'

Beth stared at him. 'Are you saying that some . . . Frankenstein tampered with my child, even before she was born?'

Lori smiled at her. 'Don't worry, Beth. I really struggled when it was explained to me, but just listen, and try not to be too upset by what you are told. You will get your lovely daughter back, you really will.'

'Our scout,' Gideon continued, 'spoke to some of the scientist's colleagues. They had come to the conclusion that he wanted to dispel the theories that conditioning, or the environment people were raised in, affected the way they turned out. People were just born good or evil, it was all in the genes, and to prove it he aimed to engineer one good child, and one evil one.'

Beth's aura began to scintillate wildly, and Ellie signalled to Michael to watch her carefully.

'Are you honestly telling me that my child, my beautiful child, is *evil*?' Beth cried, struggling to get to her feet. Lori reached out to her, but Beth shrugged her off.

Gideon hurried over to her. 'No, Beth. She is not evil. He had intended to make her so, but he failed. We think a divine power intervened to protect Izzie, and that he killed himself and destroyed his records when that happened.'

Beth sank back in her seat.

'What we think happened,' Gideon said, 'was that Izzie, who in all other respects is a perfectly normal little girl, is highly susceptible to outside influences. She's psychically vulnerable; you might say she's like an open door to a burglar. You might have heard spiritual people and clairvoyants say that they "open up to spirit" when they wish to communicate with another realm — well, we think Izzie is constantly open, and that's how that evil entity was able to take possession of her.'

To her relief, Ellie saw colour creep back into Beth's aura.

'So, she is a normal little girl, except for this one . . . weakness in her make-up? And you can help her?' Beth asked.

'We can, and we will,' said Gideon. 'We will call upon that same divine power to close her down, and then nothing bad can ever enter her again.'

Beth put her hand to her mouth. 'Oh, but if I leave her here with you what will my husband say? How on earth can I explain it to him?'

'You won't have to, Beth,' said Gideon. 'We are going to bring him here, and talk to him.'

'He loves you, Beth,' Rae said, 'he's just in denial. He couldn't face what she'd become. But he will. We'll make him see things as they are.'

Beth looked doubtful. 'I don't know . . . He's such a down-to-earth person, he sees everything in black and white. I'm not sure he'll understand any of this. And how will you bring him here, surely not by the route we took?'

Rae laughed. 'Relax. That route is firmly closed, thank you. We are back to using cars and public transport!'

'And you don't come any more black and white than me,' said Bob. 'But I've come to realise that there's a lot more to life than I could have ever dreamed of!'

'Leave bringing him here to us, Beth,' said Rae. 'And in the not-too-distant future, you will all be back home, a happy family again.'

'What about you, Lori?' asked Beth. 'What will you and Clover do?'

'We'll stay here,' said Lori. 'This is the home we were searching for. Clover has a lot to learn, and a lot of good work to do as she grows, and this blessed place is where it will all happen.'

Beth wished them well. It was clear to Ellie that Beth had no grand ambition to make the world a better place, she just wanted a family, with a happy, ordinary child at the heart of it.

'What of Harry?' Callum asked. 'Can he go home now he's done what the airman wanted of him?'

'Yes, he can,' said Gideon, 'but we'd like you, him and Lucy to stay on with us for a few days — maybe a week, if that's possible. The child has played such a key role in what has happened, we'd like to spoil him a bit. And I have to admit he intrigues us. He could turn out to be very special one day. I have an idea that he'll come back to us when he's older, bringing a particular skill that he will have honed over the years. And you, my friend, will be involved somehow. Don't ask me how, but you will always have a strong connection to that little boy.'

Callum looked at Ellie. 'Is that okay with you? Lucy has already been given time off school, and we have Harry until his mother has got her life organised.'

'Of course it is,' said Ellie. 'Enjoy some time together.'

Thanking her, Callum put his arm around Lucy, and Ellie saw what had so amazed Michael. A shower of frosty, diamond-bright sparkles seemed drift down over them both. *Oh, Michael,* she thought, *really! Don't you recognise love when you see it?*

* * *

In the discussion that followed, Michael learned that Finn, the blind boy, was destined to work with the UN Peacekeeping Organisation in the field of conflict resolution. His wisdom and courage would contribute to the saving of hundreds, maybe thousands of lives. He also discovered that when the Eleventh House embarked on the search for the two girls, they didn't know their names. They found Lori's child first, and that she was called Clover, but they had no idea about Izzie, so they named her Zillah. The two names meant 'love' and 'shadow' respectively.

Gideon told the police how Oliver Cruise's parents and teacher had brainwashed the boy, and had he not left when he did, he would most likely have ended up on the streets, prey to drugs and alcohol. Jon asked about the cloud he and his friend had encountered when they were flying in search of Belcastel. He was told that the Eleventh House had asked for protection for the children, and the universe had granted their request.

By this time Michael was having trouble keeping his eyes open. *I'm getting too old for this much excitement,* he thought. But then a question Callum posed sparked his attention.

'Where is Philip? I haven't seen him since we arrived. Is he all right?'

'You'll see him before you leave,' said Serena. 'He wants to see you, but he's tired right now, and he needs a little time to adjust. He's home now, being cared for by the spirit souls who look after the Eleventh House, and in a while he'll be able to move on from purgatory.'

Home, thought Michael drowsily. *Yes, what is this place they call home? What is Belcastel, and does the dilapidated house with the old man and his nephew really exist? I must ask . . .*

Michael was barely awake when strong arms guided him to his room, laid him on his bed and pulled the duvet over him. He didn't stir until the following morning.

* * *

Ellie, too, was weary after her momentous day. When she finally got to bed, she wondered why she had forgotten to ask about Belcastel, and how it was that they were unable to locate it. So many questions she hadn't asked . . . somehow she couldn't quite recall them . . . And Ellie fell asleep.

EPILOGUE

'The boss asked me to give you this, Callum.' DC Trevor Grant handed him a faded old newspaper cutting. 'He doesn't want it back, and he thought you might like to keep it.'

Callum very carefully unfolded it, afraid it might disintegrate in his hands. He peered at the photograph above the article.

'It's Philip!'

'The old guy who gave it to us said your airman was a hero. And he certainly was,' said Trevor.

Callum felt as if he were reading about someone he knew well, a friend of his whom he liked and respected. It was hard to believe that he had died long before he himself was born.

'The old guy was right,' he said. 'He was a hero.'

After the raid on Dresden, Philip had made it back across the Netherlands and the North Sea, and wasn't far from his Lincolnshire base when he was spotted by two Junker Ju 88 twin-engine fighters. Despite suffering critical damage from the German plane's upward-firing autocannons, he fought to keep the plane flying long enough for the rest of the crew to parachute to safety. One of the survivors, a close friend of Philip's, said he could have bailed too, but he chose to stay, in order to steer the stricken Lancaster back out over the sea, thus ensuring that no innocent civilians would be killed when it crashed. As his friend was about to jump Philip had said to him that he'd killed enough people, too many to ever atone for, and he would not take another life. Philip and his plane were never recovered.

Now Callum understood the grief in the eyes of Philip's earth-bound spirit. *If only I could go back to the Eleventh House and talk to him*, he thought. But you didn't go back to the Eleventh House. You didn't go back because you couldn't. If he were ever to see that wonderful place again, it would be because they had come to fetch him. He could search for a way in until Doomsday, but he'd never find it.

Trevor and he had met in the café at the centre, and now they sat in silence, probably both thinking about the same thing — a beautiful house in a forest, populated by special people, beings that to all intents and purposes didn't exist.

'In some ways I wish I'd never seen it,' said Trevor wistfully, 'because nothing that happens to me in the rest of my life will ever match up to it. It was the most exciting experience I've ever had. And to think, you got to stay a week longer than me!' He laughed. 'I'm green with envy, Callum.'

'Well, I only got to stay because of Harry, although we did learn a lot.' Callum sighed. 'And now he's home again with his mother. Someone must have pulled a lot of strings somewhere. Suddenly, out of the blue, there is help available for little Jordan, including two days a week in a special unit for children with serious long-term medical conditions, as well as benefits and allowances for Dawn as a single parent.'

'Do you and Lucy get to see him at all?' asked Trevor.

Callum nodded. 'Yes, we do, thanks partly to Lucy's deputy head. We get to take him out every weekend, ostensibly to ease the strain on his mother. Somehow Nicole, this deputy head, has managed to convince the school governors that it's a Good Thing. I have no idea how she pulled that one off. And Lucy's beloved job won't be in jeopardy.'

Trevor sat back. 'I'm dying to know if Harry still paints.'

Callum raised an eyebrow. 'Yes, he does, and he is very good at it. But not Lancaster bombers or firestorms. The people at the Eleventh House watched him while he was drawing and painting. He no longer has the airman with him, but they are pretty sure he still channels his pictures from, how shall I put it . . . other sources. They are quite excited about Harry, they are convinced he has a talent that hasn't manifested itself yet. They believe he will return to them one day, and they will help him realise his purpose in life.'

Callum went to get them more coffee. When he returned, he said, 'Trev, do you ever get any more messages from Serena? Can you contact her, or any of the others, for that matter?'

'I know she's around sometimes,' said Trevor thoughtfully. 'And I also get the feeling they are watching over me. I think they want to make sure we are all okay after what we went through, and I just happen to pick up the vibes, whereas someone like our Wendy wouldn't have a clue!'

'How is Wendy? I haven't seen her for a while.'

Trevor grinned, 'Still beating up her keyboard and desperately trying to see her first spirit.'

They both laughed. 'I'd have thought it would be the last thing she'd want to see after she tackled that God-awful creature that went after Izzie,' Callum said. 'That thing that tried to get Harry, yuk. It felt like a cold, slimy piece of liver! I can smell it now. What a stink!'

'Until Rebecca nuked them,' said Trevor. 'What a woman! Thank God we had such amazing people on our side.'

They finished their coffee, and Trevor said he had to get back. 'The boss has called a meeting. I'm guessing it's to tell us that this case never happened — which is a rather interesting concept when you think about it — and that it'll be registered "No Crime Detected".'

'I can't say I'm surprised,' said Callum. 'Imagine being the officer lumbered with writing up the report on that case!'

'Too true.' Trevor stood up. 'Thanks for the coffee, Callum, love to Lucy — oh, and Harry when you see him next.'

'And thank *you* for bringing me this.' Callum held up the press cutting. 'Tell Bob Foreman I appreciate it.'

After seeing Trevor to the door, Callum went along to the Orangery and sat on a stone bench just outside its glass walls. He had a phone call to make, and he didn't want anyone overhearing.

'Are you psychic, Callum Church?' Lucy asked. 'My morning break has just started.'

'Ah, then it was written in the stars that I should catch you,' said Callum in a sing-song voice. 'Cross my palm with silver, beautiful lady, and I'll tell you your fortune.'

Lucy laughed. 'Shut up, Callum, and just tell me what you want.'

'Charming!' said Callum. 'Actually, I'm calling to ask you out to dinner tonight. And don't tell me you have a mountain of paperwork to deal with, because I'm not taking no for an answer.'

'In which case, I accept. Just be prepared, though, I might eat my way through the entire menu. I missed lunch! Where are we going? The C-M café?'

'Nope! Best bib and tucker tonight. I'll pick you up at seven.'

'Oh, I say! Are we celebrating something?'

'Well, that remains to be seen,' he replied cryptically. 'See you at seven.'

He walked back to the foyer, with a broad smile on his face, and if he could have seen himself as Michael and Ellie did, he would have been amazed at the diamond-bright glow of his aura!

* * *

Bob decided to gather his small team together in his office rather than use the CID room. It was an informal meeting, and there would be no official report.

He closed the door behind them, looking around for a moment at the faces alight with curiosity. He was proud of the way these very different people had pulled together and acted as one when the chips were down.

'Okay, folks, this meeting has a twofold purpose. Now, as you've probably already guessed, a line has been drawn under our, er, unorthodox investigation, and it has been marked "No Crime Detected". Having managed to cobble together the most vague and negative report ever, I've explained to the superintendent that the whole episode was the result of a mixture of misunderstandings and misinformation. He seems happy with that, so we can tiptoe quietly away from it, and get back to some proper police work.'

'But what about the guy who found that boy's body, sir?' asked Wendy. 'He was adamant that he saw the lad and that he was dead.'

'Well, now, here's a funny thing. Mr Harrison rang in while you were off duty yesterday, Wendy. He wanted to thank you for believing him, but said that he was grateful to you for sending the boy's father to see him.'

Wendy stared at him. 'What? But I never sent—'

Bob held up his hand. 'I know, I know. But someone called on your Mr Harrison and thanked him for trying to get help for his boy. He said he'd been searching all over for him when he didn't come home. According to him, the boy suffered from seizures. He said he came upon him at the side of the road and rushed him to hospital, but he was too late. He said that some time later, he contacted the police and was told that you were going to call on Mr Harrison and explain, but that he felt he should do it himself.' With a smile, Bob gave them Will Harrison's description of the 'bereaved father'.

'Ah, Gideon,' breathed Wendy. 'I see. And the blanket that was sent to Forensics? Don't tell me—'

'Would you believe it, there seems to have been some kind of mix-up, and it's been, well, mislaid.'

'What a surprise!' said Wendy, shaking her head. 'A very tidy clean-up job, I must say.'

'Indeed,' Bob said. 'Now I must ask you all to step away from that case and everything to do with it. No more hunting for a house and grounds supposedly located behind Knightswood House, and no more enquiries into the Nancarrow family. On that score, I can tell you that there is no frail old man with dementia living in that wreck of a house. No one lives there, and the Lodge House is empty. The lodge keeper, Howard Fenton, has moved on, and the gates are padlocked. The area around that old house is completely surrounded by an old stone wall. Trevor? Wendy? Are you prepared to accept that, despite having seen evidence to the contrary?'

'How can we not?' murmured Trevor, and gave an exasperated chuckle. 'We have no choice, do we? We'll only see what they want us to see.'

Wendy merely shrugged. 'Don't worry about me, sir, I lost the plot ages ago, and by now I'm beginning to wonder what we did see.'

'Then all that remains for me to say is that I'm proud of the lot of you. It's been an honour to work with officers of your calibre on the strangest case of my career. There'll be no awards handed out, I'm afraid, but if it was up to me I'd have you up on the roll-of-honour board at Headquarters.'

When they all began to speak at once, Bob held up his hand again. 'Now, if you remember, I said there were two reasons why I called this meeting. 'I'm telling you this before I let everyone know officially, because as my dear friends, I think you deserve to hear it first. I'm retiring as of the beginning of next month. It's not been an easy decision, but as you know, I'm a lot older than my lovely Rosie. Frances, my oldest, has gone off to uni, but Max and Liam are still at home. The fact is, the job has made me miss my kids growing up, and Rosie has been left to shoulder it all alone. So I think it's time I pulled my weight at home. Plus, Rosie and I plan to do all the things we weren't able to while I was working.' Seeing the lack of surprise on the faces of his friends, Bob smiled inwardly. So much for the big reveal. Clearly the mess room grapevine was still alive and well. 'However,' he added, 'there's a possibility you haven't seen the last of me yet. Rosie insisted I make my retirement conditional, meaning I step away for a year, and see how retirement suits me. If I find myself missing the job too much, I have the option of coming back as a civilian. Police staff investigators with my years of experience can be pretty useful, or so I'm told.'

'Somehow I can't see you pottering around in the garden, sir,' said Jon, with a grin and a raised eyebrow.

'Oh, you never know,' Bob said. 'I'm starting to believe a lot more in fate. If our lives are in the hands of forces way beyond our control, I might as well give "going with the flow" a chance.'

'Good for you, sir, though we'll miss you, that's for sure,' Jon said.

After the other two left, Trevor stayed behind for a moment. 'Sir, I don't suppose you had anything to do with what's just happened with my mother, did you?'

Bob looked blankly at him. 'No, son. What *has* happened?'

'She rang me this morning, sir. Apparently, she's received an official apology for the way the police treated her after she reported that man she saw. She was told he committed another serious crime elsewhere in the country, and this time he was caught and charged. She is to receive compensation. A lot. I could hardly believe it when she told me the sum. Plus a public apology — if she accepts it. Knowing my mum she'll most likely tell them where to stick it. Nevertheless, the truth is finally out there, and she could even go home to her beloved Northumberland if she chose.'

'Well, it wasn't me, son, though I wish it had been.' He clapped Trevor on the shoulder. 'I think divine providence just gave you a little thank you gift. But now, call the other two back, because you and the rest of my motley crew are coming to the pub with me. The drinks are on me, and the only spirits you'll find will be in bottles!'

* * *

It was a surprisingly pleasant day considering the time of year, there was even some warmth in the sun. Lennie sat on his usual bench on the tow-path, with Dozer snoring at his feet. All at once the old dog sat up, and gave a little bark of recognition.

'Who've you seen, lad?' asked Lennie, squinting into the low winter sun.

Then he saw what his old friend was barking at, a couple strolling along the tow-path, a little girl running back and forth in front of them.

'Look at the ducks! Look, Mummy! Look, Daddy!'

'Lovely, sweetheart! But not too close to the water, Izzie,' called out the little girl's mother. 'We don't want you in there with them, do we?'

A smile of recognition spread across Lennie's face. 'Good for you, Beth,' he whispered to himself. 'Didn't I tell you help would come?'

They passed by without seeing him or the old dog. That, too, was how it was meant to be.

With a contented sigh, Lennie watched the happy little trio walk on, the man's arm around his wife's waist, until they disappeared from view. Sometimes being an earth angel could be really quite rewarding.

He stood up and stretched his aching back. 'Come on, lad, it's time we went home.'

* * *

However, Lennie hadn't been completely disregarded. The woman stopped in her tracks and turned around, but the tow-path was empty.

Looking back in the direction of the wooden bench, she mouthed a silent *thank you*. And for a brief moment the scent of lilacs wafted back to her on the breeze.

'What's the matter, babe?' asked her husband.

'Nothing, my darling. Nothing.'

* * *

'What did Alice say when she got home and saw all the damage from the storm?' asked Michael.

They were sitting in the Orangery, taking a quiet break between patients.

Ellie laughed. 'She was so hyped up after her success in the States, she didn't even see it! And when she did notice it, she was just thankful that her office in the old cricket pavilion had held up.' Ellie took an appreciative mouthful of the slice of coffee and walnut cake Si had baked that morning. 'My, but this is good! Anyway, good old Scrubbs had talked a couple of friends of his into helping him clear up the garden at Snug Cottage, so by the time Alice saw it, it looked like it had just had a heavy winter prune. What was weird was that the orchard hadn't been touched. Even Vera's windchimes were still hanging from their branch.'

'Methinks our two old friends drew the line at having their precious orchard decimated,' said Michael.

'Absolutely. It looked like poor old Marie's garden took the brunt of it. Thank God we got her and Daniel and Christopher away, or I dread to think what might have happened. It certainly scared the life out of the doctor. The house was okay, but the garden was a shambles! I paid Scrubbs and his small workforce to spend a few days on it.' She made a face. 'I felt kind of responsible.'

'It even made the papers. And it prompted the Environment Agency to propose launching an enquiry into the effects of climate change,' said Michael. 'Not that I think it'll ever happen, but it does seem that it was the most ferocious storm in that part of the country ever recorded.'

'Mmm, and it travelled along a corridor that went from here, through the forest, directly to Snug Cottage. I reckon the forces of evil were somewhat miffed with us and our friends at the Eleventh House.' Ellie rolled her eyes, 'Oh, talking about evil forces, have you seen Beth and Izzie in the last few days? I was wondering what the child's aura is like now she's home.'

'It's quite lovely, Ellie. And there is pink in it too, so it's as normal as I could ever wish it to be. Somehow, I believe the entity that took hold of her stripped it away. Pink, as you know, represents love, and it didn't want her feeling even a slight vestige of love for her mother while she was in its power. Now she's no longer open to the forces of evil, she can love again. And just to make sure, she and her mother and father are taken to the Eleventh House every so often so she can be monitored . . .' Michael trailed off, apparently lost in thought. 'Erm, Ellie? Can I ask you something?'

'Of course. Anything you like, Michael.'

'Are you starting to forget things — you know, about what happened? Is it all becoming sort of blurred in your memory?'

'Funny you should ask, Michael. I was going to ask you the same thing. Great parts of it are fading, and I fear that in time, it will be like a half-forgotten dream. Even Christopher has no memory of writing his famous book. All he's interested in now is working with animals. He wants to become a vet. He doesn't even mention his 'friend' anymore. What upsets me most is that everything Gideon explained about the Eleventh House, all the questions he answered, were the first to go. Especially Belcastel. Why can I not remember all he said about that lovely house and how it came to be there?' She stared at him. 'What?'

Michael was regarding her with a mischievous twinkle in his eye. 'Ah, well, that's why I kept this.'

He took a small notebook from his pocket and handed it to her. 'I'd read it very soon, if I were you. I might be wrong, but I suspect this little diary of events will somehow disappear, or meet with an accident. Whatever, we are not meant to remember the details, especially the location of the Eleventh House. The spirits are protecting it and its inhabitants, and in a way, they are protecting us too. It's time we moved on and answered our own calling in life. If they need us again, they will contact us, but we have our own paths to follow now.' He beamed at her. 'However, one thing I do know is that you will never lose those abilities Carole bestowed on you. You are going to take her healing centre to great heights, my young friend, and you'll have a very strong ally in everything you do. I told you your aura had changed, didn't I? Every day it radiates more Aegean blue.'

'Aegean blue, eh?' Ellie said thoughtfully. 'Then maybe it's for a reason that Alice and I are going to Naxos, and a couple of other unspoilt Greek islands in the Cyclades.'

'Could be,' Michael said. 'I bet you didn't know that Carole and Vera went to Naxos just after they first met. Back then it wasn't a tourist attraction, but Vera knew a Greek family there, and they stayed with them. Carole once told me it was the most peaceful and idyllic place she'd ever been, and she always regretted never having gone back.' His smile broadened. 'And I bet you thought you'd chosen that particular island all on your own!'

Ellie laughed. 'I might have known! Looks like there'll be three of us watching the sunset from the peak of Mount Zas.'

Ellie picked up Michael's journal and hesitated for a moment with it in her hands. 'Thinking about it . . . In my heart, I know Belcastel exists, and that it's there so that a future generation of peacemakers and healers will thrive and bring some good into this world.' She handed the book back to Michael. 'I don't need to read this. If I'm meant to remember it, I'm sure I will, and if not . . .' She spread wide her hands.

Michael looked at her lovingly. 'You really are becoming wise, Ellie. You're right not to want to read it.' Looking down at the journal that had taken him so many hours to compile, he opened it. And let out a little snort of surprise.

It was empty. Every page was blank.

'Well, that's that then. Like I said, Ellie. It's time we moved on!'

THE END

ALSO BY JOY ELLIS

JACKMAN & EVANS SERIES
Book 1: The Murderer's Son
Book 2: Their Lost Daughter
Book 3: The Fourth Friend
Book 4: The Guilty Ones
Book 5: The Stolen Boys
Book 6: The Patient Man
Book 7: They Disappeared
Book 8: The Night Thief
Book 9: Solace House
Book 10: The River's Edge
Book 11: Black Notice

THE NIKKI GALENA SERIES
Book 1: Crime on the Fens
Book 2: Shadow over the Fens
Book 3: Hunted on the Fens
Book 4: Killer on the Fens
Book 5: Stalker on the Fens
Book 6: Captive on the Fens
Book 7: Buried on the Fens
Book 8: Thieves on the Fens
Book 9: Fire on the Fens
Book 10: Darkness on the Fens
Book 11: Hidden on the Fens
Book 12: Secrets on the Fens
Book 13: Fear on the Fens
Book 14: Graves on the Fens
Book 15: Echoes on the Fens

DETECTIVE MATT BALLARD
Book 1: Beware the Past
Book 2: Five Bloody Hearts
Book 3: The Dying Light
Book 4: Marshlight
Book 5: Trick of the Night
Book 6: The Bag of Secrets

NOVELLAS
Guard Her With Your Life
One More To Die

THE JOFFE BOOKS STORY

We began in 2014 when Jasper agreed to publish his mum's much-rejected romance novel and it became a bestseller.

Since then we've grown into the largest independent publisher in the UK. We're extremely proud to publish some of the very best writers in the world, including Joy Ellis, Faith Martin, Caro Ramsay, Helen Forrester, Simon Brett and Robert Goddard. Everyone at Joffe Books loves reading and we never forget that it all begins with the magic of an author telling a story.

We are proud to publish talented first-time authors, as well as established writers whose books we love introducing to a new generation of readers.

We won Trade Publisher of the Year at the Independent Publishing Awards in 2023 and Best Publisher Award in 2024 at the People's Book Prize. We have been shortlisted for Independent Publisher of the Year at the British Book Awards for the last five years, and were shortlisted for the Diversity and Inclusivity Award at the 2022 Independent Publishing Awards. In 2023 we were shortlisted for Publisher of the Year at the RNA Industry Awards, and in 2024 we were shortlisted at the CWA Daggers for the Best Crime and Mystery Publisher.

We built this company with your help, and we love to hear from you, so please email us about absolutely anything bookish at feedback@joffebooks.com.

If you want to receive free books every Friday and hear about all our new releases, join our mailing list here: www.joffebooks.com/freebooks.

And when you tell your friends about us, just remember: it's pronounced Joffe as in coffee or toffee!

Made in the USA
Monee, IL
16 May 2026

49930770R00246